Praise for the Nov
Her Majesty's

Most Ea

"This romance has an intellig
against the queen, intriguing t
makes Chase's first Her Majesty's Secret Servants novel a page-
turner."   —*Romantic Times*

"A perfect balance of history, mystery, and romance that promises further adventures in this series."   —*Fresh Fiction*

"A wonderful beginning, leaving me eager to know how the other sisters may act as the queen's 'secret servants.'"
                —Romance Reader at Heart (a Top-Pick Rose)

"Fast-paced.... Fans will enjoy the opening act of Her Majesty's Secret Servants as dueling investigations lead to a traitor
and love."   —*Genre Go Round Reviews*

"Chase creates each scene of this historical novel with vivid
and precise words that fill each page by painting the intricacies so well that the reader feels as if they are revisiting an old
friend."   —Romance Junkies (4 ¾ Blue Ribbon rating)

"I'm going to be eagerly awaiting her next book."
                —Teresa Medeiros, *New York Times* bestselling
                                author of *Some Like It Wild*

"I thoroughly enjoyed *Most Eagerly Yours*. Allison Chase is a
masterful storyteller. Her plots are intriguing, her talent for
crafting a mystery unparalleled, and her love stories are touching as well as sensual. I am now a fan! She is a writer who
delivers a book that delights me in every way, interlacing sensuality and romance with stunning detail, gripping mystery,
and intrigue, plus fabulous characters who steal into my heart
and keep me turning the pages. If you yearn for a story that
engages all your senses and makes you sigh with satisfaction at
the end, I highly recommend an Allison Chase book."
        —*New York Times* bestselling author Catherine Anderson

continued ...

"Vivid and evocative, the voice of Allison Chase will whisk you away to a thrilling and sensual world of historical passion and intrigue."

—Julianne MacLean, *USA Today* bestselling author of *Captured by the Highlander*

"This book was a delight from cover to cover! I can't wait to see what happens with the rest of the Sutherland sisters and the adventures they will have as this series continues."

—Historical Romance Writers

The Blackheath Moor Novels

Dark Temptation
Winner of the *Romantic Times* Award for Best Historical Romantic Gothic

"An enthralling adventure. Sophie is a spirited, witty heroine and Chad is a tortured hero who truly has some heavy crimes on his conscience. . . . Allison Chase takes the classic gothic romance style of Victoria Holt or Daphne du Maurier and brings it into the twenty-first century with her addition of some spicy love scenes . . . makes an enthralling read."

—Romance Junkies

"In *Dark Temptation*, the reader will want to go all the way to the end . . . an interesting read for both mystery and romance fans. Get cozy and prepare to have an adventure."

—Romance Reviews Today

"Contains a strong amateur-sleuth suspense subplot that enhances the lead couple's romantic relationship. The story line is filled with warm passion and terrifying events that will keep readers on the edge wondering who is chasing whom in this dangerous search for the truth."   —*Midwest Book Review*

"The windswept, forbidding coastline is the ideal location for Chase's second Blackheath Moor gothic, where fear, deception, and passion dwell together. She sends chills down your spine as she heats up the pages with passionate love scenes and frightening incidents. Chase's name is fast becoming synonymous with delicious, heart-stopping thrillers."

—*Romantic Times* (Top Pick)

Dark Obsession

"Dishes up a wonderful story in a charming, romantic tradition, complete with a handsome and tortured hero, real conflict, and a touch of mystery! Anyone who loves . . . a well-written historical romance will relish this tale."
—*New York Times* bestselling author Heather Graham

"This wonderfully moody and atmospheric tale, with its brooding hero, troubled young child, unquiet spirits, and unfriendly housekeeper, has many of the accoutrements of the classic gothic of the sixties. In fact, except for the ramped up sensuality . . . it is reminiscent of Victoria Holt. . . . The solid writing, riveting opening, and clever plot twists recommend this worthy debut." —*Library Journal* (starred review)

"A compelling and exquisitely written love story that raises such dark questions along the way, you've no choice but to keep turning the pages to its stunning conclusion. Allison Chase is a master at touching your heart."
—Jennifer St. Giles, author of *Silken Shadows*

"A dark tale of danger and desire."
—Eve Silver, author of *Dark Prince*

"Set in 1830, the book moves at a spanking good pace. Readers who relish the passionate interludes will enjoy it all the more."
—*The Historical Novels Review*

"In this first book in the Blackheath Moor series, Allison Chase delivers a gothic tale complete with a house filled with secret passages and a ghostly presence. Impending danger permeates the tale, capturing readers' attention as the dramatic struggles between Nora and Grayson escalate. The tale ends in a dramatic and thrilling conclusion on the cliffs where it all began." —Fresh Fiction

OTHER BOOKS BY ALLISON CHASE

Her Majesty's Secret Servants Series
Most Eagerly Yours

The Blackheath Moor Series
Dark Temptation
Dark Obsession

Outrageously Yours

HER MAJESTY'S SECRET SERVANTS

ALLISON CHASE

A SIGNET ECLIPSE BOOK

SIGNET ECLIPSE
Published by New American Library, a division of
Penguin Group (USA) Inc., 375 Hudson Street,
New York, New York 10014, USA
Penguin Group (Canada), 90 Eglinton Avenue East, Suite 700, Toronto,
Ontario M4P 2Y3, Canada (a division of Pearson Penguin Canada Inc.)
Penguin Books Ltd., 80 Strand, London WC2R 0RL, England
Penguin Ireland, 25 St. Stephen's Green, Dublin 2,
Ireland (a division of Penguin Books Ltd.)
Penguin Group (Australia), 250 Camberwell Road, Camberwell, Victoria 3124,
Australia (a division of Pearson Australia Group Pty. Ltd.)
Penguin Books India Pvt. Ltd., 11 Community Centre, Panchsheel Park,
New Delhi - 110 017, India
Penguin Group (NZ), 67 Apollo Drive, Rosedale, North Shore 0632,
New Zealand (a division of Pearson New Zealand Ltd.)
Penguin Books (South Africa) (Pty.) Ltd., 24 Sturdee Avenue,
Rosebank, Johannesburg 2196, South Africa

Penguin Books Ltd., Registered Offices:
80 Strand, London WC2R 0RL, England

First published by Signet Eclipse, an imprint of New American Library,
a division of Penguin Group (USA) Inc.

First Printing, December 2010
10 9 8 7 6 5 4 3 2 1

PUBLISHER'S NOTE
This is a work of fiction. Names, characters, places, and incidents either are the
product of the author's imagination or are used fictitiously, and any resemblance
to actual persons, living or dead, business establishments, events, or locales is
entirely coincidental.

The publisher does not have any control over and does not assume any responsibility for author or third-party Web sites or their content.

To Dr. Yakira Frank, who recognized the romance writer in me years before I did, and whose parting words to me as I graduated from the University of Connecticut have proved prophetic. Thank you, Dr. Frank, for your wisdom, your encouragement, and your uncanny insight into what the future held in store for me.

ACKNOWLEDGMENTS

I would be remiss if I didn't acknowledge the exquisite job NAL's art department did on this cover . . . and for that matter, on all my covers so far. You have consistently gotten each one perfectly, beautifully right.

My gratitude also goes out to the unsung heroes in copyediting. Your skills and remarkable eye for detail have more than once saved me from some rather embarrassing errors.

To my editor, Ellen Edwards; her assistant, Elizabeth Bistrow; the marketing and publicity departments; and all the others at NAL who believe in this series and have lent their invaluable support, my sincerest thanks.

Finally, this book could not have been written without the support of my husband, my family, and my intrepid critique group. I'm grateful to have all of you in my life.

Chapter 1

London, 1838

Ivy Sutherland slapped the morning edition of the *Times* onto the counter in front of her. Her shocked gaze darted over the books lining the walls of her family's tiny shop. Had she read correctly? She snatched up the paper again and reread the headline:

PRICELESS JEWEL STOLEN FROM BUCKINGHAM PALACE

Her eyes skimmed over such phrases as "without a trace," "no clues," and "queen distraught."

The rap of knuckles against the shop door made her flinch. She had locked up not ten minutes ago, shortly after her two sisters, who helped her run the Knightsbridge Readers' Emporium, left for the opening of a new play across town. Ivy hesitated. Ever since her eldest sister, Laurel, had returned from Bath last spring, there had been changes in the Sutherlands' lives. Laurel's new husband, the Earl of Barensforth, saw to it that his three sisters-in-law enjoyed heretofore unattainable luxuries like plays and new frocks and more books than Ivy could ever hope to read.

There had been other changes, too ... such as a pair of servants, the Eddelsons, who lived in the third-floor garret. With his previously broken nose and tree trunk of a neck,

Mr. Eddelson seemed, in Ivy's estimate, more suitable for prowling London's back alleys than carrying in deliveries and driving the sisters about town in their shiny new phaeton.

Then there was that morning not long ago when Ivy had spied Mrs. Eddelson sharpening the kitchen knives in their tiny rear garden. As Ivy had watched, the woman had cast a circumspect glance over her shoulder before grinning and sending the meat cleaver sailing end over end to sink some two inches into the trunk of the stunted birch tree growing in the corner.

It hadn't taken Ivy long to conclude that their brother-in-law's precautionary measures stemmed from more than mere prudence. Something had happened during Laurel's adventures in Bath to warrant stringent safety measures . . . such as never opening the door to strangers at night.

Another knock resounded, louder and more insistent than the first. Slipping off her stool, Ivy went to the window and peeked through the gap in the curtains. A coach-and-four of the finest quality stood at the curbside. No identifiable crest adorned its sleek panels. The plain livery of the three attending footmen gave no clue as to the individual they served.

No clue, that was, to anyone but the Sutherland sisters, who had seen this coach before. Recognition rushed through Ivy; with a gasp, she hurried to the door and turned the key.

A figure draped from head to toe in black wool stepped over the threshold. "Quickly, shut the door!"

Once Ivy had complied, a pair of softly plump hands flipped back the cloak's hood and then reached for Ivy's own hands. "Something dreadful has happened."

"I know." Ivy pointed to the newspaper angled across the countertop. "I just read about it."

"Yes, well, there is more to the story than the papers, or anyone for that matter, knows. Please, Ivy, I need your help. May I count on you?"

Ivy gazed down into the solemn eyes and sweet features

of England's nineteen-year-old queen and smiled. "I am your servant, Your Majesty. Now, please, dearest, come up to the parlor and tell me everything."

The hired caléche jostled laboriously along the weather-pitted highway north of Cambridge. Inside, the single passenger, dusty, hungry, and exhausted from the three-day journey from London, entertained grave doubts about the rash decision that had brought her here.

Lady Gwendolyn de Burgh had done a very, *very* bad thing, and now she didn't know how to set about making it right. Borrowing the queen's mysterious stone hadn't seemed so terrible when the idea had first occurred to her. It was really nothing but a rock, after all, not shiny and faceted and richly hued, but a jagged, granitelike hunk speckled with bits of silver. Other than the odd, tingling energy that emanated from its surface, there was hardly anything remarkable to be said for Her Majesty's stone.

Except that it had been a gift from that German gentleman, the one the queen strictly forbade her ladies-in-waiting from discussing outside the private royal chambers. That man, Albert, believed the stone held special properties—electromagnetism, the queen had said—which was what had prompted Gwendolyn to steal . . . borrow . . . the stone in the first place.

Gwendolyn's gaze fell to the ornate box on her lap. Even through the carved wood with its inlaid design of jade and ivory, she thought she perceived a faint vibration beneath her fingertips. Or did the sensation originate from her jangling nerves? She couldn't refrain from noting that the dimensions of this particular box could neatly accommodate a human head—*her* head. A century or two ago, that very well might have been the unhappy outcome for anyone foolish enough to steal . . . borrow . . . from his or her monarch without permission.

Oh, *dear*.

In the distance, beyond the flat, boggy fens streaming past the carriage window, a lingering splash of sunlight turned Cambridge University's loftiest towers to amber. As the vehicle rambled farther away from the city, a box hedge sprang up along the roadside, replaced all too soon by familiar high stone walls topped by a wrought iron railing with lethal-looking spikes.

Gwendolyn was almost home. With a rap on the coach ceiling, she called out, "Stop here."

Here was the base of the curving drive that snaked through a heavy growth of oak and pine planted nearly a hundred years ago by the first Marquess of Harrow. That the iron gates stood open did not make the shadowed entrance of Harrowood any more welcoming. Clinging to the safety of the open road, Gwendolyn hesitated in ordering the coachman to turn in. Would the present marquess, her brother, welcome her back after all these months?

A chill of doubt crept across her shoulders as the last of the sunlight seeped away, plunging the road into sudden darkness. The box on her lap seemed to give off a cautionary tremor.

Above the trees, a fiery burst of light illuminated the house's sloping rooftops. Gwendolyn gasped. From Harrowood's central turret, an angry conflagration of sparks shot upward. The caléche jolted as the pair of grays whickered and tugged at their traces. In the stillness that followed, a crack like thunder echoed down the drive, rousting a flock of blackbirds from their nests to scatter in a panicked flurry across the twilit sky.

Both sights fueled Gwendolyn's growing misgivings. The sparks served to remind her of her brother's rage and the blistering words they'd exchanged the last time they had seen each other. Like those scattering birds, her courage flitted away.

"Ma'am?" The coachman's voice rose an octave and caught.

This was a mistake, Gwendolyn concluded, a foolish, dreadful, ill-advised mistake. She should not have come here alone. How silly of her not to seek help from someone who was capable of talking sense into that brother of hers.

A new idea occurred to her, one that, with luck, just might work.

"Drive on," she cried as another flash lit the night sky.

Simon de Burgh, Marquess of Harrow, cursed the cinders that showered back down into his laboratory through the turret's open skylight. With an exasperated sigh, he seized the woolen blanket from the table behind him and smothered the tiny flames dancing amid his equipment. Then he stamped out each glowing ember to prevent the oaken floor from catching fire.

Only when he was satisfied that flames no longer threatened his ancestral home did he pause to survey the damage to himself. His singed cuffs indicated the ruination of yet another shirt. His palm and fingertips stung, and the muscles across his shoulders and down his back quivered as if he'd just carried a sack of bricks a mile uphill. At least this time he smelled no burning hair, though his ears would ring for the next day or two, undoubtedly.

Taking up the blanket again, he waved it up and down to clear the smoke from the circular room set high above Harrowood's sprawling wings. Damn and double damn. He had been so certain that *this* time his calculations had been correct, that the current flowing from his electrical generator was at the proper level. He'd believed he had made all the necessary adjustments to the negative and positive charges. He had recalibrated the force of the steam passing through the conducting coils, and positioned the electromagnets with meticulous care.

But flipping the lever and releasing the energy accumulated in the steam duct had brought only flames, sparks, and dashed expectations. Cursing again, he crossed the room to the brandy he kept on the bookcase beside the south window. The wide stone sill offered a convenient perch. He loosened his neckcloth, propped up a booted foot, sipped the burning liquid, and considered.

Perhaps it was time he admitted defeat. Perhaps, as people continually said behind his back and occasionally to his face, he *had* been tilting at windmills in this laboratory of his.

But as the pungent spirits spread warmth through his veins and eased his smarting fingertips, the old tenacity surged back. Simon was far from ready to surrender, and he couldn't deny a certain fondness for windmills, with their wide-open arms and their ability to harness one of nature's greatest powers and tame it for practical use.

That was all he wished, really, to tame a natural force and put it to good use. But perhaps he couldn't do it alone.

Alone. How he had come to hate that word and the way it had redefined his life. How he detested the sidelong glances of his acquaintants, their gentle queries into his welfare, and, worst of all, the pitying whispers they thought he couldn't hear. How he dreaded waking to the deafening roar of those midnight silences that could not be filled because . . .

Because he was *alone*, and there was no longer anyone to talk to or reach for or hold.

With another generous draft, he banished those and other pointless broodings. Life was what it was. His gaze drifted out the open window. From this vantage point, he could see across the open fenland to the twinkling cluster of lights that was Cambridge. Something closer caught his attention. Was that a coach speeding away down the road? Had someone passed his gates as the flames and sparks shot up, or had the passerby simply remembered that the Mad Marquess lived here, and urged his team to a gallop?

It didn't matter; it was no concern of his. No, Simon knew what he needed to attain his goal. But he also knew that what he needed would not come easily, if indeed it came at all.

Ivy poured tea, added cream and the heaping teaspoons of sugar Queen Victoria favored, and passed the cup and saucer into her royal guest's hands. "Drink this, dear. It will help calm you."

Victoria obeyed with a small sip. "You don't understand," she said with a shake of her head. "I cannot be calm until the stone is back safe with me. Oh, I'll be a laughing-stock, and Albert will never wish to speak to me again. . . ."

Wondering about the identity of this Albert, Ivy held up a hand. "Please slow down and tell me why this stone is so special. You say it is not a priceless gem as reported in the newspapers?"

"Indeed it is not, at least not in the typical sense. But I dared not let the real truth be known. You see . . ." Victoria's bosom rose on a sigh. "It is infinitely more precious than a jewel. It was a gift from . . ."

"Yes?" Ivy gave Victoria's shoulder a reassuring pat. "You may speak freely. You know my sisters and I would die before we betrayed your confidence."

A fleeting smile of gratitude softened Victoria's expression. "The gift came from Albert, my Saxe-Coburg cousin. He is a dabbler in the sciences, you see, and this stone . . . It is believed to have fallen from the sky . . . a meteorite. And, oh, Ivy, it is extraordinary indeed."

"How so?"

"There is a certain energy about it." The queen's voice dropped as if someone might overhear. "A kind of warm field that at once pushes some objects away from it and draws others to it."

"It is magnetic," Ivy ventured.

"Oh, more than that. It is *electro*magnetic, and Albert believes it might even be a key to providing scientists with the means of generating . . . someday . . . useful and effi-cient electricity."

A ripple of excitement traveled Ivy's length. "To replace fire and steam in the powering of our industries, yes?"

Victoria gave a little shrug. "To be quite honest, I'm not certain what all this hocus-pocus is about." With a faint frown, she raised her cup for another sip.

Then her features crumpled in dismay. "Oh, but what does it matter? Albert entrusted this stone to me as a sym-bol of our commitment to each other." In a whisper, she said, "Ivy, he has asked me to *marry* him."

In a burst of elation, Ivy threw an arm around her younger friend, careful not to upset her tea. "That is wonderful news. My dearest, I am so happy for you. When will the joyous occasion take place?"

She didn't ask if she would be invited, for she knew the answer to that. The Sutherland sisters had stopped being suitable companions for the then princess Victoria some seven years ago, when she had become heir apparent to the throne. Soon after, they had lost touch with her, only to reestablish ties—secret ones—last spring when Victoria had appealed to them for help in a matter requiring the utmost discretion.

"I don't yet know," Victoria replied to Ivy's question. "These things must be handled through the proper channels. But once we *are* married and Albert is here in England, he intends to put the stone in the hands of the right man, a scientist of singular brilliance. But now I have lost it and . . . Oh, Ivy! Albert will be so angry with me! And so will my dear Lord Melbourne."

"Your prime minister?"

"Indeed, yes." Placing her cup and saucer on the sofa table, Victoria leaped up from the settee and began pacing the small area of faded carpet in front of the fireplace. Ivy noted that her petite figure had grown plumper in the months since her coronation, her youthful features more careworn. Or was the latter due to her present predicament?

"I don't understand why Lord Melbourne should care one way or another about such a private matter," Ivy said.

Victoria came to an abrupt halt, her eyes as round as an owl's. "That is exactly the point."

When Ivy stared back blankly, the queen continued impatiently, "My dealings with Albert should never have *been* a private matter. I am a monarch, and for me there can be no affairs of the heart, not in the truest sense. Such matters must be conducted through proper diplomatic procedures, but Albert and I have been skirting those procedures on the sly. Nothing has been officially approved, not yet. Should anyone find out that I have already pledged my hand . . . Why, think of the scandal!"

Ivy could indeed imagine the tittle-tattle certain to fill England's drawing rooms should it become known that the queen had behaved in a manner deemed inappropriate. "It isn't fair. Your uncles—"

"Were men. It is one thing for a king to carry on with his mistresses, but let a queen set her big toe beyond the dictates of proper decorum, and oh!" She made a noise and tossed her hands in the air to simulate an explosion. "Royal or no, I am foremost a woman in the eyes of my subjects, and an impropriety like this . . ."

"I understand." Ivy pushed to her feet and went to stand before her queen. "What can I do?"

"Find the stone, Ivy. I don't know how soon Albert might visit again, but I must have the stone back before he discovers the theft. What if he should speak of the stone in his letters? What will I do then?" Her eyes widened with alarm. "I couldn't possibly lie to him."

"Good heavens, no." Ivy clasped her hands together and considered. "Do you have any idea who might have taken the stone?"

"Indeed, I do. One of my ladies-in-waiting, Gwendolyn de Burgh."

"Are you certain?"

"Yesterday morning the stone was gone, and so was Lady Gwendolyn—quite without my permission. Why, she'd been asking so many questions, I should have realized her interest in the stone was more than cursory. But I trusted her as I trust all my ladies, or most of them. Never could I have imagined such treachery from within my own private chambers."

Ivy's heart fluttered. If only Laurel and Aidan were home. If anyone could recover the queen's stolen property, they could. Last spring, Victoria had sent Laurel to Bath disguised as a widow in order to spy on George Fitzclarence, a royal cousin whom Victoria had suspected of treason. Together, Laurel and Aidan had followed a dizzying maze of clues to solve a murder, stop a financial fraud, and put a very nasty individual behind bars where he belonged.

But Laurel and Aidan were away in France on some mysterious business neither seemed inclined to discuss.

"If only Laurel were due back soon . . ."

"No, Ivy, it is you I need."

"But I'm not the adventurous one. Everything I know I've learned in books—"

"Precisely. I need someone bookish, someone who would fit in with scholars and men of science. I am all but certain Lady Gwendolyn has headed to her home outside of Cambridge. Her brother disowned her some months back, and I believe she intends giving him the stone as a peace offering. You see, he's something of an amateur scientist, if a rather mad one, and the stone would be of particular interest to him."

At mention of Cambridge, home of one of Europe's most prestigious institutions of higher learning, all of Ivy's senses came alive with interest. What she wouldn't give to be allowed to attend lectures in those celebrated halls. The word *scientist*, too, had seized her attention. But she hadn't at all liked Victoria's one quick reference to the disposition of the man in question.

"Mad?"

After a brief hesitation, Victoria admitted, "Some call him the Mad Marquess of Harrow, but I'm sure it is merely collegiate fraternity nonsense. He maintains close ties with the university. That is where you will find him, Ivy, and perhaps the stone as well."

"I see." Ivy tapped her foot nervously on the carpet. "Then I am to appeal to him for the return of the stone."

"Goodness, no!" Alarm pinched Victoria's features. "He may not be mad, but neither is he known for being a reasonable man. He disowned his sister, didn't he?"

"Then . . . ?"

"You must earn his trust. It so happens he is presently searching for an assistant for his experiments. If you could win the position, you would gain access to his private laboratory, and you could steal back what is rightfully mine."

The outrageous proposal sent a chuckle bubbling in Ivy's throat, one quickly coughed away when Her Majesty's expression failed to convey even the faintest trace of humor.

This, apparently, was no jest but a true call to Her Majesty's service, one that left Ivy more than a little perplexed. "How on earth shall I, a woman, track down a man in an academic setting? I wouldn't gain admittance through the front gates, much less the lecture halls."

Victoria smacked her lips together. "I have a plan for that, though admittedly a shocking one. More shocking, even, than when I asked Laurel to pose as a widow last spring and work her charms on my inebriate, adulterous cousin."

More shocking than *that*? Ivy dreaded to ask, but ask she did. And the answer she received stunned her more than anything she had ever heard before in all her twenty-two years on this earth.

Chapter 2

"Oh, Ivy, surely not all of it?"

In the Sutherlands' small kitchen to the rear of the bookshop, Ivy sat perched on a high stool. A linen towel was draped over her shoulders, while another covered her lap. Holly, her twin sister, stood directly behind her, a pair of freshly honed clipping shears clutched in her trembling hand.

"Yes, Holly," Ivy replied. "Every bit of it. But do stop shaking or you'll nip my ears clear off."

Sitting at the head of the oblong kitchen table, their younger sister, Willow, hugged her arms around her middle and attempted, unsuccessfully, to stifle a sob. "Couldn't you simply tuck it up under a cap?"

"No, Willow," Ivy responded with stoic calm that surprised even her. "Caps come off, and then what?"

"Oh, but *why*, Ivy?" Holly gathered a handful of Ivy's nearly waist-length tresses, letting them glide through her fingers to swish down her back in a torturous reminder of what she would shortly no longer have. "Why must you cut it *all* off?"

"Because Victoria asked it of me," Ivy said. "Because she needs me, and, as you'll remember, we have more than once pledged to be her secret servants. Are we to go back on our word simply because of a minor inconvenience?"

"But ... it's so beautiful." Willow's last word emerged as a wail.

Ivy shook her head. "It is not so *very* beautiful."

No, while shiny and thick, her hair had always lacked the natural curl society deemed fashionable. Being neither golden like Laurel's nor auburn like Holly's, nor boasting Willow's wondrous combination of both, Ivy's dark chestnut mane, forever slipping from its pins, possessed little to recommend it and would therefore hardly be missed, not by her or anyone else.

Yet, as Holly obediently raised the shears and began snipping, a part of Ivy cringed at each snaking shank that littered the floor at her feet. But then, her misgivings amassed around far more than hair, or the loss of it. Victoria had led such a sheltered life that she could have little grasp of the sundry ways in which this plan could go awry. A woman in trousers was bad enough, but a woman pretending to be a man and entering a university's precincts on her own, without a proper chaperone ... She would be ruined—ruined for all time—and the queen herself would not have the power to save her.

For several minutes the only sound in the cramped kitchen was the ticking of the wall clock and the metallic scrape of the clippers ... and Ivy's labored breathing, which she hoped her sisters couldn't hear. She would simply have to make certain that no one at Cambridge ever learned the truth, or ever traced the young male student back to the Sutherland sisters. It wasn't so much her own reputation for which she feared, for to her, marriage seemed little more than a silk-lined trap.

She'd take her books over a husband any day. If the truth be told, she wished she *could* be a university student, and spend her days reading and learning and being among the intellectuals fast shaping a modern world. As far as marriage went, she doubted she would ever be as fortunate as Laurel in finding a husband who respected her intellect and treated her as a partner rather than a subordinate.

But what of Willow and Holly? With their parents and now Uncle Edward gone to their graves, it remained up to them to make their own decisions in life, yet in a world where breeding and background played such vital roles in the marriage mart, Ivy feared her manly masquerade could utterly obliterate her sisters' chances of future happiness.

She had not explained any of that to Victoria. She had taken a vow; they all had. Surely their queen's needs superseded their own. . . .

"You know, of course, that I am going with you." Holly's assertion broke the silence and made Ivy wince.

"Me, too," Willow said eagerly, but with a conspicuous sniffle. "We'll simply have to close up shop for however long it takes."

"To what purpose?" Ivy shook her head. "How many university men do you know that have female chaperones?"

Willow pulled a lace-edged handkerchief from her sleeve and dabbed at her eyes. "You know very well that there are no university men in our acquaintance."

"No, nor will there be," Ivy said. Then, "Ouch! Holly, that was my earlobe!"

"Sorry! Hold still."

"That's enough. Holly, don't cut it any shorter than that." Willow came to her feet. Mopping her cheeks with her hankie, she cast Ivy a look of sober assessment and drew a shaky breath. "You know, it really isn't *so* very bad."

"How reassuring," Ivy said drily. She gathered her courage and ran a hand through it, only to experience a burst of frustration when far too much length glided through her fingers. "That can't be short enough. Holly, please continue and this time do the job properly."

But Holly held the shears to her bosom and stepped back. "It is plenty short. Many a university student has unkempt hair. They either don't have time to visit their barber or consider such details beneath their notice."

"Holly's right, Ivy," Willow concurred. "And since it has suddenly taken on a propensity to curl, it feels much longer to you than it looks."

"Truly?" From under the towel, Ivy stretched out an arm. "Holly, hand me the glass."

"Perhaps the ends do want a bit of neatening first. . . ."

"The looking glass, Holly, if you please."

Ivy resolutely clamped her fingers, gone cold these many minutes, around the gilt handle. Upon discovering, however, that she was not quite as brave as she would like to pretend, she pressed the mirror facedown in her lap.

Then she looked—*really* looked—at each of her sisters in turn. Were they horrified by her new appearance? Dismayed? Their countenances revealed no trace of either sentiment. Quite the contrary. But then, Ivy had long considered herself the least attractive of the four Sutherland sisters. That she might now be *less* attractive was perhaps a matter of marginal significance.

With a sigh, she raised the mirror . . . and gasped. "Is that *me*?"

Coming closer, Willow touched her fingertips to Ivy's cheek and whispered, "Indeed. Goodness, Ivy, I never realized what high cheekbones you have."

Holly came around to stand at Willow's side. "Nor did I ever notice how large your eyes are, and how delicate your nose and mouth are in comparison." Holly's own eyes misted. "To think, Ivy-divy," she said, using the childhood nickname she had once made up for her, "all this time, you have been this family's undiscovered beauty."

Even Ivy couldn't deny it, though neither could she quite believe the evidence gazing back at her in the mirror. Though her neck was bare and her ears stood out a bit awkwardly, Holly had left enough length for a miracle to have occurred. Her hair now covered her head in soft, thick waves that framed her face and emphasized her best features in ways her long, heavy, woefully straight locks never had.

"Why," she whispered, "the effect is . . ."

"Charming," Holly supplied.

"And lovely," Willow added.

"And thoroughly contrary to Victoria's aims," Ivy concluded with a groan of frustration. "What am I to do now? They'll never let me into Cambridge looking like *this*. I'm more feminine than ever!"

Their eyebrows gathering tight, her sisters drew closer and considered.

"You'll be wearing a man's suit of clothes. Surely that will help create the desired illusion." Willow's doubts rang through her attempted optimism.

"And you'll . . . well . . . bind your breasts, of course. Not that . . ." Holly didn't finish the sentiment, but Ivy guessed that her twin had been about to comment on the size of her bosom, just as Victoria had done when she'd attempted to dispel Ivy's qualms.

"Of all of the Sutherland sisters, you alone have the technical knowledge needed for this scheme," the queen had said. "The study of mathematics and natural sciences comes easily to you. And with your slim figure, narrow hips, and—forgive me, dearest—but decidedly small bosom, you are the most likely to fool people into believing you are a young university student. Trust me, Ivy. This plan will succeed. It must."

It must.

And if it didn't?

"I have an idea." Grabbing a ladle off the work counter, Willow disappeared down to the cellar, returning out of breath a few minutes later. She held out the ladle, its shine obscured by a coating of black powder.

"Coal dust," she announced, and dipped in two fingers. "Now, Ivy, hold still."

The next time Ivy gazed into her glass, she was taken aback to behold a fine-boned youth of about seventeen, just beginning to sprout a beard—too sparce to require shaving, but enough to be noticeable.

"What do you think?" she asked in a hushed voice.

"I think I am no longer the baby of the family," Willow said with a laugh, "for it would seem I have acquired a younger brother."

"I think," Holly said slowly, tapping a finger against her

bottom lip, "that once Victoria's tailor makes you a proper suit, Ivy Edwina Sutherland will vanish and the doors of Cambridge University will swing wide to welcome young Mr. Edwin Ivers."

With his fiercest scowl fixed in place, Simon marched to the front of the lecture hall, allowing the flapping edges of his cloak to whip at the shoulders of those sitting in the aisle seats. The thirty-odd natural philosophy students assembled to take part in his challenge watched him intently, their expressions ranging from baffled to anxious to downright intimidated.

Their trepidation pleased him, even made him smile a little beneath his show of animosity. He fully intended to intimidate them all—or, more precisely, all but one. Perhaps today would be the day he discovered that singular student with the knowledge, ingenuity, and courage necessary to become his laboratory assistant.

An assortment of mostly first years filled the room, fledglings fresh out of schools like Eton, Merchant Taylors', and Charterhouse. He might have found an assistant without resorting to such dramatic tactics had he looked to the more experienced ranks of the upperclassmen; certainly he would have found a qualified scholar among the university dons or fellows. But he wanted neither, for both tended to come burdened with too much ego and ambition, not to mention preconceived notions that could prove difficult to contend with.

What he wanted, *needed*, was someone learned enough to understand the latest in scientific theory and technique, but young enough to have retained his idealism. Too much to ask? Perhaps. He wouldn't get his hopes up.

Upon reaching the laboratory table at the front of the hall, he pivoted, once more making theatrical use of the cloak that swirled around his booted ankles. He leveled his timorous audience with a glare, and for good reason.

There was no place at his side for the faint of heart. Discovery and innovation depended upon a sound theoretical process, sharp intuitiveness, and nerves of steel. In the field of electromagnetism, apprehension and indecisiveness led to experimental failure at best and dead scientists at worst. Not a risk he was willing to take for either himself or any of these wet-behind-the-ear hopefuls.

Shrugging the outer garment from his arms, he tossed it to an occupant of the first row. The surprised student nearly fell out of his seat in his effort to catch it before it hit the floor. Simon thanked him with a brusque nod and gestured to the apparatus arranged on the table before him.

He curled his lip in disdain. "I trust you have all had an opportunity to view the equipment." After an instant's hesitation, a head nodded, initiating a domino effect throughout the hall, though more than a few students remained frozen in their seats.

"Good." As part of the challenge, he allowed them no questions and set them precious few guidelines. "Can you all see?"

Nods again rippled through the hall.

"Then let us begin."

He raised the lid of the three-foot-long, coffinlike casing of a voltaic cell, exposing the internal spine of alternating copper and steel squares. Selecting a jug, he poured in the powerful acid solution he had mixed that morning. Pungent fingers of heat rose from the contraption, forcing Simon to avert his face from the chemical reaction of the liquid against the metals. Blinking and holding his breath against the fumes, he replaced the lid.

Taking up a glass cylinder about six inches long and three wide, he filled it with potash, a mixture of soaked wood and plant ash. After corking either end of the cylinder and setting it onto a pair of brackets, he threaded a length of copper wire into each end. One of these wires he wound around the brass contact terminal at the end of the battery that emitted a positive charge.

He pulled on a pair of leather gloves lined with a thin, flexible layer of cork. "Observe."

With a pair of foot-long tongs insulated with a coating

of India rubber, he plucked up the remaining wire attached to the cylinder and, holding it at arm's length, touched it to the negative terminal of the battery.

A burst of light inside the cylinder set off several cries of alarm. Brighter and brighter the illumination grew, a small, enclosed nova of lustrous globules that erupted around the wire at the negative contact. From the positive end of the cylinder, wisps of gas spiraled into the air. As though he were part of the circuit, energy vibrated up Simon's arm and spread through his chest. His heart raced, though mainly from excitement and not electrical shock. The combination of cork and rubber insulation protected him from the full, potentially dangerous effects of the charge.

Peering through half-closed eyelids, he kept the tiny conflagration in his sights until experience alerted him that the process had nearly reached completion. He released the tongs and stepped back. Immediately the glass shuddered, splintered, and exploded in a shower of flame and sparks.

As one, his audience pulled back in their seats. Some leaped to their feet, poised to run. Others turned away, shielding their eyes with their forearms.

Fools, they should be watching closely, not ducking for cover. Didn't they understand the small miracle of science taking place before their very eyes?

Simon stepped back to the table's edge. The copper wires now hung free. Glass shards and bits of incinerated potash littered the tabletop. Scattered among them, molten lumps of a silvery metal writhed and glowed, though they were fast cooling. He pointed at these lumps and raked a severe glance across the startled faces before him.

"Your task is this. . . ." He paused as a sudden flurry produced writing tablets, quills, and pots of ink. "Tell me what this mercurial metal is, and no, it is not mercury. Tell me how I produced it: the exact process from start to finish. Most importantly, tell me *why*."

The mosaic of blank stares almost made him laugh. That last bit of instruction he had added as another means to weed out the mediocre, to separate the wheat from the chaff. Instead of expressing his amusement at their reaction, he drew his brows in tighter. "Yes, gentlemen, you heard me correctly. It is not a mere list of instructions I am seeking, but a full and clear understanding of the properties demonstrated here today.

"There is to be no discussion," he reminded them sternly, "not a word exchanged between you. The slightest sidelong glance toward your neighbor's work is grounds for immediate disqualification from this challenge. You may leave at any time, but once you have done so, you may not reenter the hall. Upon taking your exit, you will submit your thesis to Mr. Hendslew." He gestured to the middle-aged man just then entering through the arched door at the rear of the hall. "Good day and good luck."

Retrieving his cloak from the student in the first row, he started down the aisle. He'd retreated about halfway when, from within the rows of seats to his right, a hand slid tentatively in the air. Simon ground to a halt, his glance landing on a wisp of a youth with a mop of dark, curly hair.

As a silence as thick as the bogs beyond the city settled over the hall, Simon's gaze met a pair of dark eyes that glittered like onyx within pale, almost feminine features, so delicate that for an instant he was taken aback. He shifted his scrutiny lower, to a high starched collar held by a silk neckcloth tied with an uncommonly fussy knot, and then to slim shoulders encased in the artful cut of a frock coat the cost of which would have fed a working family for a month.

Too neat, too clean, too oblivious to what he was just told. A dandy in the making, Simon concluded, one who exemplified all the spoiled arrogance one would expect from the scion of an upper-crust family. There were generally two types of students at Cambridge: those like this impertinent young bounder who hailed from pedigreed, landed wealth and who believed rules were not for him, and those whose families made great sacrifices to send their exceptional if penniless sons here in hopes of providing them with better futures.

Despite the fact that he himself hailed from the former

category, or perhaps because of it, Simon's annoyance at that hovering hand turned his mood as black as the scowls he had been feigning.

"Have you a problem with your ears, sir?" he growled. "No questions."

The hand wilted out of sight, and Simon exited the hall with a bafflement he could not dismiss. The words he had intended to speak were far different from the ones his lips had formed. He had meant to summarily disqualify the youth and send him packing in disgrace as reward for his galling audacity. But in the instant before Simon had opened his mouth, he had seen some intriguing quality glimmering in those sharp, dark eyes, a quality that had momentarily made him regret his rule against questions.

What would this bold young man have asked?

Ivy's quill hovered above the page in her tablet. Lifting her other arm, she dabbed with her coat sleeve at the moisture beading across her brow. The air trapped within the paneled walls of Burgh Hall, endowed to the university by the grandfather of the very man who had just stormed in, barked orders, and stormed out, smelled of concentration, desperation, and a smidgen of fear.

Touching the back of her hand to her chin, she looked to see if traces of her coal dust "beard" came away. Beneath the unfamiliar sensations of woolen coat, waistcoat, and linen shirt, her back itched and her sides trickled with perspiration. Ivy had always assumed men's clothing would be liberating, but quite the contrary; what they lacked in corsetry and petticoats they more than made up for in tailoring that constricted and stifled. In her trousers and boots, her legs felt as hotly encased as sizzling sausages; her arms felt trapped by her cumbersome sleeves.

She tugged on her cravat to relieve the pressure against her neck, but she could do nothing to ease the strain of the silk strips binding her breasts beneath her shirt. Neither could she ease her mind of the discomfiting images of the Marquess of Harrow—an impression that left her flabbergasted and breathless, until she could barely concentrate on the formulas and equations scrawled across her pages.

He was not at *all* as she had imagined. Then again, Victoria hadn't bothered to describe him, other than to allude to the startling contrast between his nearly black hair and his pale silvery blue eyes, remarkable eyes indeed, Ivy must admit. As for the rest of him . . . her insides fluttered.

In picturing the Marquess of Harrow, she had drawn upon the engraved prints of the famous scientists she had seen in books. They had been middle-aged or older, balding or grizzle haired, bespectacled, paunchy, and stoop shouldered—she supposed from constantly leaning over their laboratory tables. And judging by the mild expressions and intelligent eyes captured in the portraits, those men had possessed another trait Simon de Burgh apparently lacked: patience.

With all the ferocity of a winter squall, he had barreled through the hall, his ill humor evident in every echoing footfall, every terse motion. In his presence, a collective apprehension had descended over the students, but nowhere near as quelling as the apprehension that had swooped down upon Ivy when she had raised her hand.

How could she have been so reckless! Lord Harrow's disdain had struck her like a physical blow, forceful enough to rattle her bones. Yet she had not been about to break one of his hard-and-fast rules. She had only wished to inquire whether he wanted them to footnote their references.

Blinking, she once again attempted to banish him from her thoughts and focus her attention on the sums, diagrams, and lines of neat script filling several pages of her tablet. She had drawn upon the work of men like Alessandro Volta, who had invented the electric pile similar to the one Lord Harrow used in his demonstration, and Humphry Davy, who had patented the process of separating compounds into their unique elements as Lord Harrow had done; and she mentioned André Ampère, who had developed the theory of electrodynamic molecules that explained how the separation occurred.

Glancing through her calculations, she double-checked her citing of Georg Ohm's equation for measuring the voltage of a current. As a chorus of scratching quills continued to resonate through the hall, she sat back and wondered what she had missed. Surely there was something.

The challenge he had set them seemed too easy, ridiculously so. Lord Harrow had chosen a procedure that had revolutionized the electrochemical sciences some twenty years ago. With so much having been written on the subject, anyone with even a mild interest in the natural philosophies should have been sufficiently well-read to adequately explain the process they had seen here today.

Unlike the men around her, Ivy hadn't enjoyed the privilege of a formal education. What she *had* benefited from was time—lots and lots of time during her childhood to explore Uncle Edward's extensive library in his country estate of Thorn Grove. Since his death a year ago, she had commandeered every science and natural philosophy tome that had found its way into the Knightsbridge Readers' Emporium.

If *she* found this challenge elementary, then surely Lord Harrow could have found an assistant several times over by now. That he had not done so gave her pause and made her reconsider the very last, and in his words most important, of his instructions. *Tell me why.*

How cryptic of him. Why what? Why break down a compound to its elements? Why bother to generate electricity at all, and make it run along wires from one place to another? However fascinating Ivy found the phenomenon of electromagnetism, she had always wondered how such raw power might be harnessed in the context of everyday life.

Letting her quill come to rest against her tablet, she closed her eyes and, for the first time in her life, considered *why* she had always spent so much time exploring the laws of such sciences as gravity and magnetism, rather than perusing the latest fashion plates or losing herself in romantic novels. *Why* would she rather see her sisters off to the plays and concerts they enjoyed so much, and prefer to spend her time among her books instead?

Laurel, Willow, and Holly loved poetry, but to Ivy, science *was* poetry. They found beauty in the rhyme and meter that transformed words into music. For Ivy, beauty lay in the symmetrical relationships between numbers, in the balance of the equations, and in the magic of cause and effect.

Suddenly the answer seemed clear as glass—a substance formed from yet another scientific process, thermodynamics, where silica, soda, and lime were fused together at great temperatures. Glass, like the potassium formed from Lord Harrow's demonstration, involved the interplay of molecules and the rearranging of matter . . . even as the cook, the baker, and the tailor manipulated their raw materials into wholly new shapes and forms. How much more extraordinary, then, were the machinations of the chemist and the physicist, who employed earth's greatest complexities to make the impossible possible.

Ivy opened her eyes and raised her quill. If Lord Harrow wanted to know *why*, she would tell him. She began writing, so intent on her task that she failed to realize, until Mr. Hendslew's throat clearing signaled the end of the session, that the hall around her had emptied.

"Thank you, sir," she said to the man as she handed him her papers. She flashed him a grateful smile, then turned quickly away and hurried out the door when his perplexed frown reminded her that men didn't smile like that, with their faces tilted and their eyelashes fluttering.

That she could so readily make such a glaring mistake yanked her confidence out from under her, and she began second-guessing every word she had scrawled across her tablet. Surely her amateur ramblings fell a good mile short of the expertise Lord Harrow sought. Then again, the Mad Marquess had probably ruled her out the moment she had raised her hand in violation of his blasted rules.

Ivy's panicked thoughts swerved to Victoria, alone in Buckingham Palace with her dismal secret. An utter wretchedness washed over her. She had tried her best, but in all likelihood her best would not be good enough.

Chapter 3

"I tell you truly, Ben," Simon said with a shake of his head, "despite his effeminate looks and how timidly that boy's hand disappeared from my sight, I encountered an underlying spark that I have not seen in a long time."

His back to Simon, Benjamin Rivers stood gazing out his office window at the elaborate gateway into Old Schools, one of the university's oldest sections. The view of Trinity Hall, framed by glimpses of the River Cam and the spacious, sunlit lawns of the Backs on its western bank, was in large part why Ben had been so keen to move into this office after the former dean of the School of Natural Philosophies had retired a year ago. To Ben, Old Schools symbolized the best and most steadfast of Cambridge's traditions, which had defined the better part of his life, and Simon's, too.

With an indulgent smile, Ben turned and folded his lean length into the chair behind the desk. A modest porcelain tea service occupied a corner of the leather desktop. Ben poured them each a second cup of tea, then suspended his hand above the plate of biscuits; he carefully studied the assortment before selecting a petit four sprinkled with shaved coconut.

"You have not encountered such a spark," he said between bites, "since you were a student here yourself and happened to glance in a mirror."

With a nod, Simon laughed. It had been ten years ago

this month that he'd strutted, with just the sort of arrogant confidence he found so irksome in younger men nowadays, into a much smaller office in this same building and thrust out a hand to introduce himself to his new physics don. He had sought out Benjamin Rivers after attending the man's lecture on John Dalton's atomic theory, and had been eager to discuss with him the particulars of electromagnetic polarization.

Ben had greeted Simon's initial enthusiasm with a disregard similar to that which Simon himself had exhibited earlier. Straightening his habitual stooping posture, Ben had peered down the length of his hawkish nose and, disdain dripping from his Welsh pronunciations, had demanded, "Tell me, young man, what need might there be for a marquess's heir to dirty his hands in the mire of atomic theory? Shouldn't you be studying law or finance or the proper way to lead a lady onto the dance floor?"

After stumbling through a moment of galling chagrin, Simon had emerged more determined than ever to win the man's esteem. With a mulish heft of his youthful chin he'd declared, "Beg your pardon, sir, but such trifles are lodged in precedent and tradition. Science is the vehicle of our future, and I intend to be among those manning the helm."

"I wasn't sure at the time whether to embrace you or box your ears, but I discovered one of my brightest students and most apt assistants that morning." Ben flicked a strand of charcoal gray hair off his brow. "Perhaps today you've found *your* Simon de Burgh."

Even after ten years during which Simon had more than proved his prowess in the laboratory, the other man's approbation kindled a surge of pride. Simon's response, however, was to smirk, lean back in his chair, and prop a foot on the edge of Ben's desk. "I shan't hold my breath."

"Good God, did I hear some fool attempted to ask a question over at Burgh Hall earlier?"

Simon's gut clenched, an instinctive reaction. He didn't need to turn around to know that Colin Ashworth, Earl of Drayton, had just joined them. But he peered over his shoulder to see the other man leaning in the doorway and grinning with apparent delight. Like Simon but unlike Ben, who had grown up in a Glamorganshire mining town, Colin hailed from privilege. He and Simon had attended university together, had shared rooms, their studies, many a bottle of brandy, and occasionally the same demimondaine. And like Simon, Colin was now a fellow of the university's School of Natural Philosophies.

"One can only speculate," the earl said with a laugh, "as to whether the poor lad is still in possession of his head."

Simon pressed his right fist into his left, gave the knuckles a crack, and struggled to keep his expression neutral. "He is, but only just."

"Ah, we've been wondering when we'd see you again." Pressing to his feet, Benjamin came around the desk to shake Colin's hand. "What has kept you so long at that chilly manor of yours?"

Colin's family's ancestral seat lay far to the west, on the rolling moors of northern Devon. For the most part, the Ashworth family had abandoned their rambling, medieval estate in favor of the comforts of their London and Ascot homes, and they left it to Colin to periodically oversee the accounts, repairs, and welfare of their tenant farmers.

Yet it was to none of those that Colin referred.

"The herds," he said succinctly.

His dedication to the sciences came in close second to his true passion: horses, and the prized stock of Thoroughbred racehorses his family owned. But to his credit, a good portion of his work at Cambridge and for the Royal Society had been in the interest of developing, through chemistry, higher grades of feed and fertilizers to boost livestock viability.

His enthusiasm for riding and the outdoors showed in his athletic build and bronzed complexion. The sunlight pouring through the office window brightened the underlying streaks of red in Colin's blond hair as he sauntered through the doorway.

Dragging a chair away from the wall, he straddled it

backward and regarded Simon like a chemist inventory-
ing his store of solutions and compounds. He also extended
his right hand, and after a brief hesitation, Simon shook it.
"Well?" Colin said. "Any results from today's little experiment?"

The question, as well as Colin's crooked grin, held skepticism and a faint trace of mockery. Simon decided to ignore the latter. The former he couldn't deny feeling himself.

"I wouldn't know yet. The challenge is ending right
about now. But based on my previous two attempts, I'm
beginning to doubt I'll ever find a proper assistant."

Colin's smile lost some of its warmth. "Perhaps you're
too exacting. They're only students, with much yet to learn.
If it's a professional you need, choose one of us. Or don't
you trust your fellow Galileans?"

He referred to the Galileo Club, an association dedicated
to scientific advancement and the practical application of
scientific principles. Named for one of history's bravest and
boldest scientists, the club operated under the assumption
that nothing added more fuel to the fire of progress than a
good dose of fierce if friendly competition—and at times
the inherent rivalries did become fierce. Three of the club's
members presently sat together here in Ben Rivers's office.
The fourth, Errol Quincy, had gone up to London yesterday to head a symposium at the Royal Society.

Ben guffawed in response to Colin's question. "You
know good and well why not. Too many cooks, as they say.
A student is capable of following the recipe without dashing in an ingredient or two himself." After seizing a tiny
lemon tart, he held up the plate of confections and added,
"Biscuit?"

Colin waved a dismissive hand, both at Ben's allusion
and the offered treat. "Perhaps it's time the Galileo Club
pooled its resources rather than behaved like a pack of jeal-
ous debutantes all coveting the same marriage prospect."

"I'm coveting nothing but the results of my theories."
Leaning forward, Simon plucked an almond puff from
the plate, his hand nearly colliding with Ben's as the man

trawled for yet another treat. "Each of us has a very separate, very distinct goal." He popped the confection into his mouth.

"Based on the same principles of electromagnetism," Colin reminded him.

Simon agreed readily enough. He swallowed the nutty pastry. "The pertinent issue is how we put those principles into practice. Generally speaking, I am always ready to share my findings on sustainable electrical currents."

"But no more than that." Colin's statement issued a challenge.

"Not yet." Simon emphasized the last word.

Of the four members of the Galileo Club, contention ran highest between Colin and him; it always had, so much so they'd occasionally nearly come to blows in the laboratory. But while theirs had also been the strongest friendship of the group, circumstances had changed one day last winter, irrevocably as far as Simon was concerned.

Yet it was for a very different reason that he wished to end the discussion. His latest project was still too experimental to be shared, especially with anyone astute enough to grasp the ramifications. His theories were too radical, too . . . dangerous.

"Your reticence has nothing to do with a desire to win yourself a Copley Medal?" Colin accused more than asked.

"Ah, the carrot the Royal Society yearly dangles before our noses." Simon produced a half smile and shook his head. "Sorry, but the Copley Medal doesn't interest me."

Colin scrutinized Simon through half-closed lids. "As always, you remain a mystery wrapped in an enigma. What *does* the Mad Marquess of Harrow have up his sleeve?"

"You'll see soon enough." Simon worked at not clenching his teeth, though his muscles had tensed at the moniker that had dogged him since his wife's death a year and a half ago. Perhaps he had deserved it then, when the slightest provocation had prompted storms of ranting and days of sequestering himself in his laboratory. Grief had driven him nearly beyond the brink, until the people of Cambridge and even his own servants had begun to whisper and to fear him, just a little. And sometimes a lot.

There were men who would not have made it out of that office without blood flowing from one appendage or another, but Simon extended privileges to his fellow Galileans that he would never have tolerated from outsiders. "The Mad Marquess" had become a kind of dark joke between them, a perverse term of affection from the men who knew and understood him best.

Only . . . he had privately revoked such privileges from Colin, but damn the insolent bastard for being too thick-headed to perceive the obvious.

"Gentlemen." Ben held out his hands and said evenly, "A breakthrough for one of us will be a breakthrough for all. As you very well know, Simon, the Copley Medal is more than a carrot. Ah, but I suppose for an aristocrat with a sizable fortune, the grant that accompanies the honor seems a mere pittance."

It was true, he didn't need the funding that came along with the Copley Medal, not in the way Ben or Errol did. Once, the true prize for him would have been winning the instant respect of the scientific community, and bringing his innovations to the forefront. Lately, however, awards and fame no longer held much appeal. Results were now his carrot, breakthroughs the only form of accolade he desired.

"Let's strike a bargain." Ben's dark eyes twinkled, yet behind their humor lay an admonishment, that of a miner's son who'd first entered Cambridge as a subsizar, performing menial tasks in exchange for his education. "Should either of you win, feel free to donate your grant directly to the university, preferably to the School of Natural Philosophies."

Simon chuckled. "That's a promise."

"To be sure." Colin delivered an enthusiastic slap to the back of the chair he straddled. "But perhaps a moot point for me this year, and Errol, too. Our present work in electrochemical conversions isn't typically the stuff of Copley Medals. Not flashy enough."

"It will be once you employ it to ensure this country's yearly harvests." Ben drained his teacup. "Ah, but the consortia will commence soon enough, and it will be up to the Royal Society to decide who wins this year's medal."

He spoke of the process whereby scientists gathered in appointed places throughout the country each year to discuss and demonstrate their recent discoveries. Representatives from England's Royal Society would attend, take detailed notes, and report back to their peers on the most innovative breakthroughs.

Ben's mouth filled with one last biscuit, he rolled his shoulders as he often did in an attempt to loosen the muscles damaged in a cave-in when he was a boy. That accident had marked his final stint in the mines, for immediately afterward his parents had apprenticed him to a relative, an apothecary in Cardiff.

After consulting his watch, Ben came to his feet and tugged his coat into place. "If you'll both excuse me, I've a lecture to deliver."

Outside, Simon set off down a walkway beneath the golden canopy of a double row of oaks. His destination lay several minutes away on Market Street, at a tiny dark-paneled pub that served some of the finest home-brewed ale in all of East Anglia.

"Simon, wait."

His instincts urged him to keep walking, but with a resigned sigh he halted and turned.

Colin slowed down from a sprint and stopped a few feet away. "Look, I know you don't give a tinker's damn about the Copley Medal. But what I said about working together—"

"You're quite correct," Simon interrupted. "I don't give a damn about the Copley Medal or any other pointless honor, which would only bring unwanted scrutiny down on my work. I wish only to be left alone and get on with my research."

"I understand that. Which is why we need to—"

His patience snapped, and he cut the other man off again. "Need to what? Work together? Share our results? What else would you have us share, Colin? What else of mine do you believe you have a right to claim?"

"Simon, please." The whispered entreaty touched a cord inside Simon that hummed with an emotion he'd rather not feel—had not *allowed* himself to feel in many months.

They were once trusted colleagues, the best of friends.

He turned away, started walking.

Colin dogged him, close at his elbow. "You've been avoiding me for months now. Hasn't enough time gone by?"

Simon stopped again, intending to issue a warning for Colin to back away immediately. But the regret in his erstwhile friend's eyes stopped him cold and yanked his disdain right out from under him. Was he being too hard on Colin? Was it time to forgive?

The answer came in an onslaught of images from that despicable day last winter: a drab room in a roadside inn, a hastily packed valise, Gwendolyn's tearstained face, and her steady progression from fear to fury—aimed at Simon. And Colin, leaning in a corner of that room, his arms folded, his head down, his face an unreadable mask.

No, not unreadable. One glance had told Simon all he'd needed to know, and Colin's silence had only confirmed his conclusions. Even now, the pain of the betrayal pierced his gut with a force that threatened to double him over.

He resumed walking, fast, nearly breaking into a run. "You already helped yourself to my sister. I've nothing left of value for you."

Colin's footsteps echoed hard on his own. "There's something I never explained to you about that day. I thought it best I keep silent, but now I'm not so certain. Simon . . . Wait."

Simon's blood scorched his veins. He had awakened that morning last winter expecting a day like any other, until his housekeeper discovered Gwendolyn missing, some of her clothes gone as well. Thank God she hadn't been clever in covering her tracks, for it had taken only a few inquiries in town for Simon to learn in which direction she had gone.

He rounded on the other man, bearing down on him so forcefully that Colin retreated a step. "The only reason I tolerate your existence is because Errol and Ben value your association and because I arrived at that wretched inn before anything irreversible happened to Gwendolyn. If I were you, I would thank the Almighty for that each and every day. Now, good day."

He continued at a brisk clip through the trees, taking a sharp left where the footpath merged onto Trinity Street. His temples throbbed; his clenched jaw ached. He needed that pub more than ever.

"Lord Harrow! My lord?"

"Galileo's teeth. What now?" He stopped and reluctantly turned.

Colin stood where Simon had left him, his features iced over with wounded astonishment. Simon looked beyond him. Across the common, Bartram Hendslew's running feet sent up a flurry of russet and gold leaves. His hair, usually lying flat in an arrangement that began at one ear and trailed across his balding pate to the other ear, flapped like loose vines in the breeze. In his raised hand he brandished a bundle of papers.

"Your dissertations, my lord." Upon reaching him, Hendslew passed the bundle to Simon, then attempted to comb his hair into place with his fingers. "You said you wanted them the very moment the session ended."

"Oh, yes, thank you. I'd nearly forgotten." And almost no longer cared. Any enthusiasm or hope with which he'd awakened that morning had withered, in these past several moments, like the dead leaves rustling across the lawn.

Still, a kind of vague curiosity drew his glance to the top of the pile. Finding nothing extraordinary in the cramped handwriting or meticulously rendered diagrams, he shuffled and perused another, then another and another.

Then, at the very bottom of the stack, his eyes lit on something quite different . . . unusual . . . innovative. . . . He whipped his reading spectacles from his coat pocket.

"Could it be?" Separating the several pages of the essay from the others, Simon shoved the remaining papers back into Bartram Hendslew's hands. He took a step, then several more, unaware of his direction as he first skimmed the drier details and then became absorbed in the first attempt he had yet seen to answer his question: *Why?*

The words *poetry*, *symmetry*, and *balance* filled his vision and ran like music through his mind. He read on, captured by a passion scarcely contained within the neat lines. His hands began to tremble. No one had explained the spirit of investigation and experimentation in these terms before. The author had gotten the basic details of the procedure right enough, but then so had the majority of the others. Not one of them, however, had taken the risk of baring his soul when it came to answering that unassuming yet powerful question.

He flipped back to the first page, and his breath caught in horror. "His name. Galileo's teeth, sir, this student neglected to write his name on the paper!"

He practically pounced on Bartram Hendslew, who stood hugging the rejected dissertations to his chest. As Colin had done, he pulled back in self-defense. "Did he? Well, never fear, my lord. The student who wrote that essay was the last to leave the hall. A very green young lad, new to Cambridge. Has some roundabout connection to Buckingham Palace, I'm told. The son of a high-level secretary to one of Her Majesty's ministers, though which one I do not recall—"

Simon resisted the urge to seize the man's lapels. "Hendslew, his *name*, if you will."

"Ah, that would be Ivers, my lord. Mr. Edwin Ivers. Odd little chap, I must say. In fact he—"

"Do you know where he's gone?"

Hendslew's eyebrows went up. "As a matter of fact, there was a small group waiting for Mr. Ivers when he exited the hall. I heard their intentions of gathering in the rooms of one Jasper Lowbry, at St. John's College."

At a trot, Simon doubled back across the common.

"Ol' Ivers here drinks like my grandmamma. Down that claret, old boy, and then try a real man's drink."

A slap between her shoulder blades nearly sent the glass flying from Ivy's hand and the wine she had just sipped spurting from her mouth. Somehow she managed to prevent both small disasters, but upon swallowing, she received another whack from her neighbor that threw her into a fit of coughing.

The backslapping continued in earnest, a joint effort now from the two young men sitting on either side of her at the small dining table. Their laughter filled her ears. Cheroot smoke curled before her face and made her eyes water until the grinning faces across the table blurred. Despite the cool autumn breeze flowing through the open windows, Ivy sweltered beneath her woolen coat. Her stomach began to roil.

"Ah, leave the poor bloke alone," someone yelled, but to little effect, except to bring on louder peals of laughter.

Setting down her wine, Ivy thrust out her arms and shoved her well-meaning neighbors away. Still coughing, she pushed to her feet and stumbled to the nearest window. She found the frame and gripped it, and leaned out over the sill to suck in drafts of refreshing air. Dazzling sunlight lit the courtyard two stories below. A pedestrian turned his face up to hers, saluted, and kept walking.

With her throat already strained from her efforts to speak in a lower voice, the smoke and liquor only made matters much worse. Gradually, the coughing subsided. The laughter behind her did not. Turning, she perched on the wide stone sill, caught her breath, straightened her coat, and attempted to regain her dignity.

"Here, sip this." The host of the party, Jasper Lowbry, a handsome young man with intelligent eyes and a ready smile, pressed a snifter into her hand.

Bitter fumes spiraled upward to burn her nose. She would have much preferred water, but something told her such an option would never have crossed the minds of these raucous students.

"Go on," Jasper urged. "It'll help. And don't mind them. Making you the butt of their jokes merely means they like you."

Ivy nodded her gratitude and took the tiniest sip. Jasper returned to his half dozen other guests, who continued to gulp down spirits and shovel an assortment of hors d'oeuvres into their mouths. Their boorish table manners made Ivy cringe. Their uproarious conversation increased in volume while steadily decreasing in coherence, but thank goodness for that. A good portion of their language tended to scorch her ears.

Just as with the Marquess of Harrow, these Cambridge men had met none of her expectations. She had supposed university students to be well mannered and scholarly, making use of every spare moment to study, contemplate, and debate. Ha! But for their costly attire, their apparent heedlessness when it came to their coin, and the opulence of Jasper Lowbry's rooms—which put Ivy's modest London town house to shame—they might have been brigands at any dockside tavern.

Still and all, these particular brigands, all fellow residents of St. John's College, had eagerly opened their doors to young "Ned Ivers," along with their liquor bottles, humidors, and snuffboxes. Ivy was finding that being a man taxed the body in ways she had never before considered. Blinking, she attempted to clear her throat but only ended up coughing again.

"I can tell you what's wrong with him," slurred Preston Ascot, the pock-faced son of a Foreign Office diplomat. Mr. Ascot had bulldog features and the heavyset bulk to match, offset by an affable sense of humor. With a slovenly grin he thrust an unsteady finger in Ivy's direction. "Poor sot's been poisoned. The Mad Marquess no doubt slipped him something lethal."

A gangly, bespectacled chap named Spencer Yates drew on his cheroot until the burning end crackled softly. In a billow of smoke he called out, "Wouldn't be the first time, from what I hear."

Another among the group murmured, "You're speaking of his wife, aren't you?"

"No, no," Jasper Lowbry interceded with a roll of his hazel eyes. "Pure rubbish, that. Harrow didn't do her in. But . . ." Still standing by the head of the table, he leaned in closer. The others went quiet and craned their necks to hear what he would say. Curious herself, Ivy hopped off the windowsill and rejoined the group.

"They say he's keeping her body somewhere in that manor of his."

The diplomat's son frowned at Lowbry's words. "What the devil do you mean, keeping her? Keeping her *how*?"

"Not sure, quite. *Preserved* somehow."

Revulsion rippled across Ivy's back and raised the shorn hairs on her nape. The others around her reacted with similar repugnance, swearing, quaffing mouthfuls of brandy or whiskey, and shaking their heads in disbelief.

"You needn't take my word for it," said Lowbry with a casual shrug. "It's common knowledge among the upperclassmen." Hunching, he propped his hands on the table and leaned low. "Generations of de Burghs are buried in Holy Trinity churchyard, but you won't find *her* there."

"Oh, but that's ridiculous," Ivy blurted. "She must have been buried with her own family, then."

Lowbry shook his head. "The Quincys are all buried at Holy Trinity as well. Her father is a don of physics here."

"What on earth would the marquess want with his wife's remains?" Ivy shuddered.

Lowbry cast a grave, and in Ivy's opinion dramatic, glance around the table. "They say he hopes one day to . . . resurrect her. Like in that book. You all know the one I mean."

"You know, it's not that far-fetched," said Spencer Yates. He blew a smoke ring into the air. "Luigi Galvani's experiments on the nervous systems of frogs proved that movement is achieved by the flow of electrical charges between the nerves and the muscles."

"Meaning what?" Ivy demanded. "Surely you're not suggesting that the stuff of fiction can be intertwined with legitimate scientific—"

"Meaning," the youth interrupted with an exaggerated pull of his mouth, "the heart is a muscle, and the Mad Marquess could very well be pumping electricity into his wife's heart in an attempt to make it beat again."

A chill slithered up Ivy's spine.

Mr. Ascot broke the heavy fall of silence. "Bloody hell."

"This *would* explain the flames and sparks people have seen shooting out over the house at night," another of them said.

Nods circulated around the table.

Ivy brought her glass to her lips and drank deeply, remembering too late that the vessel contained foul-tasting brandy instead of a more reviving brew. Another fit of coughing erupted, but this time with the odd result of clearing her head and restoring her to rational thought.

"What you're suggesting is pure insanity," she said. She snapped a hand to her hip. "Surely so many students wouldn't be vying for the opportunity to work with the man if they truly believed him mad."

"Mad does not necessarily a murderer make," Lowbry pointed out mildly. "As I said, he didn't kill his wife. She died as a result of an accident, some sort of fall. Lord Harrow was away from home at the time."

"How awful . . ." A fist closed around Ivy's heart.

She herself was no stranger to the sudden loss of loved ones. Her parents had died in the fire that claimed her childhood home many years ago. She had no precise memories of that day, only vague images of running, shouting, escaping the house with the flames at her heels. She and her sisters had been saved by the servants . . . but her parents . . . no one had ever been able to explain why only her parents had been trapped by the conflagration. . . .

"As to why so many are vying for the position," Lowbry went on, "the man is a genius. His contributions to the field of electromagnetism are said to be inestimable. Besides, who wouldn't seize the chance to work with a bona fide mad scientist?" Grinning broadly, he splashed more whiskey into his glass and raised it in a toast. "To the Mad Marquess of Harrow."

"The Mad Marquess," the others chimed in, all except Ivy. She felt ill again, and as though the walls were closing in on her.

University nonsense indeed. Had Victoria sent her to deal with a lunatic?

A pounding at the door made them all jump. With a quizzical look, Lowbry went to answer it.

"Lord Harrow!" he exclaimed, then quickly recovered his composure and stood aside. "Welcome, sir. To what do we owe the—"

"Sorry to barge in on you like this." In a bound, the marquess crossed the threshold. Ivy's pulse thudded at the sight of him, speeding to a frantic pace when he scanned their stunned faces and demanded, "Which one of you is Ivers?"

Chapter 4

For several resounding ticks of the mantel clock, no one moved, no one spoke, no one dared to breathe. Then, one by one, the gazes of the others settled on Ivy as though she had just been accused of some shocking crime.

She glared an appeal to each of them. Hadn't they taken her under their wing, made her part of their tight little group? Hadn't she accepted their ribald jesting and vile-tasting spirits with good grace? Yet with hardly a blink they abandoned her, or so it seemed to Ivy, who now felt as conspicuous as a peacock in a snowdrift.

Her mind raced with questions. Could she possibly have won the challenge? There had been that brief, glorious moment when she had believed she had answered Lord Harrow's questions with singular brilliance. But no sooner had she handed her papers to Mr. Hendslew than she had realized how parochial and downright idiotic she must have sounded in comparing science to poetry.

She had approached this challenge not like a scholarly gentleman, nor even like a woman, but like a silly, sentimental girl. Her skin ran hot with shame at the memory of the drivel she had composed.

And yet . . . Lord Harrow was here, and he was staring at her.

"Are you Ivers?" His cape flaring out behind him, he bore down on her, prompting her to back away until her heels struck the wall beneath the window. She might have tumbled out had Lord Harrow's hand not shot out and snared her wrist. "Careful, lad. Now that I've found you, I can't have you plummeting to your death. You *are* Ivers, are you not?"

Her head trembled as she nodded.

"Good." Lord Harrow released her, stepped back, and gave her a terse looking over. "You're the hand-raiser," he accused.

Ivy nodded again in short, jerky motions that made the   •
Mad Marquess dance in her vision.

His lips drew tight, and Ivy felt sure he had come to disqualify her from the challenge. A frantic apology ran through her mind, but then he gave a nod of his own. "Come with me."

With that, he turned and strode from the room, tossing out a brisk "Gentlemen" as he went. After an instant's hesitation, Ivy took off after him.

Simon made his way out to St. John's Second Court. The chapel bells rang out the noon hour, a familiar, comforting sound. He had been a St. John's man himself, although his rooms had been in the residence halls of the First Court.

The boy's rapid footfalls echoed from inside the stairwell. A moment later the lad stumbled outside—literally. As if his feet had tangled in an invisible web, young Ivers barreled through the doorway and sprawled headlong, breaking his fall with his hands and narrowly saving his chin from the ravages of the paving stones.

Then he simply lay there, stunned and out of breath. A torrent of laughter spilled from above. When Simon shot a glance upward, a circle of flushed faces in the window scattered out of sight.

He walked to the youth and leaned over him. "I say, Ivers, you seem remarkably intent on killing yourself today. Any particular reason why?"

"No, sir," came a slightly muffled reply. Ivers sniffed

and slowly levered himself off the ground. Once he had achieved a sitting position, Simon offered him a hand up. "Oh, er . . . thank you, sir."

The contact of the youth's slender fingers against his own sent a peculiar sensation through Simon, not entirely unpleasant but nonetheless disconcerting. He pulled his hand away. "Are you injured?"

Ivers brushed dirt and small bits of leaves from his coat. The fine-boned face turned upward, and in the bright daylight Simon saw that his eyes were not as black as he'd previously thought, but the shape and color of almonds. That he should notice the boy's eyes at all was disquieting, all the more so when he glimpsed the sheen of a tear.

The youth averted his face. "No, sir. I'm not injured."

Some unnamed instinct sent Simon a foot or two away, a distance that strangely felt more comfortable. "Tell me, are you typically this clumsy?"

"Sir?" Flustered or perhaps insulted, the youth hitched his small nose defiantly into the air.

"It is a necessary question, Ivers. Surely you can grasp the dangers of having an accident-prone assistant in a laboratory filled with electromagnetic equipment."

"Oh . . . quite right, sir. And no, sir . . . not typically. It's . . ." He glanced down his length, perplexity blossoming across his milky-smooth brow. "It's the boots, sir. They're new, not yet broken in."

Simon's gaze followed Ivers's tapering trousers to where the stirrups circled the soles of a pair of black and tan half Wellingtons with squared-off toes—the very height of fashion. "Only the best, eh, Ned?"

"Sir?"

"Never mind. How soon can you have your things packed?"

"Sir?"

Simon studied those dark eyes and again saw, behind the lad's confusion, the simmering energy that had caught his attention that morning. Puzzlement gripped him, a sense that the spirit embodied by that spark simply didn't fit the outer image of the ungainly Mr. Ivers, as if he'd been encased in a foreign, utterly mismatched shell.

"You know, Ivers," he said, "for someone who is able to pour his heart out through his pen, you have surprisingly scant verbal skills. This could prove problematic."

Alarm filled the boy's eyes. "I promise it won't, sir. I can be as verbose as you please when the occasion warrants it. It's merely that . . ."

"The boots?" Simon joked. "Cutting off the oxygen to your brain?"

Ivers's oddly elegant eyebrows knotted and white lines of tension formed on either side of his nose. Then . . . his generous lips twitched and broke into a grin. "Indeed, sir, that must be it, surely. I must find a way to loosen them posthaste."

Simon joined in the youth's chuckles, until something about their shared mirth felt too familiar, too . . . intimate. He stepped another stride backward. What was it about this fellow that left him so flustered, and would it be a hindrance to their working together?

The thought of screening more applicants overcame his doubts. The lad was awkward and shy, but that would change once they established a rapport. Simon would make this work; either that or he must reconcile himself to working alone.

Simon regarded the boy, waiting respectfully if nervously silent. "*Mr. Ivers* seems too formidable for such a wisp of a youth. What do they call you at home?"

The lad considered a moment before he smiled and lifted his chin. "Actually, sir, my sisters call me Ivy."

"Ivy?" The sound of it made Simon feel like smiling, too, but he didn't. No, like the fellow's laughter, the nickname produced a too cozy, too damnably intimate sensation inside him. "That won't do, either. What did you say your Christian name was?"

"Edwin, sir."

"A bit formal, that. I shall call you Ned. You may call me Lord Harrow."

"Yes, sir. Then . . . I *have* won the . . . the challenge, sir?"

Simon blinked and dropped his gaze in concern. "Those boots really are too tight, aren't they? What the blazes do you think we're doing here? Of course you won the challenge."

"Thank you, sir . . . Oh, thank you!"

"Mind you, we shall proceed on a strictly trial basis. Upon the first indication that you might prove unsuited to the position—"

"There shan't be, Lord Harrow. I promise. I swear, oh—"

"That will be sufficient, Ned." Simon scanned the rows of Gothic, stone-cased windows of the building before them. "Are you presently living here?"

"I am, sir."

"How soon can you have your things packed and ready to be moved?"

Ned's eyes narrowed within their uncommonly thick lashes. "Moved . . . to where, sir?"

"Harrowood, of course."

"But . . ."

"You can't very well assist me from here, can you?"

"But I thought . . ." Ned's hands snapped to his hips. "I assumed the laboratory in question would be located on the university grounds."

Simon emitted a laugh. "My dear boy, I am not *employed* by the university. I have one laboratory, and it is located at Harrowood."

"And it is necessary for me to . . . move in?"

"Sorry, but yes. My research is of a sensitive nature and I won't risk word of it leaking out prematurely. Does this pose some sort of predicament for you?"

Ned emitted a high, squeaky little note, but he shook his head. "No predicament, sir."

"You needn't worry, lad. This has been cleared with the dean of natural philosophies. You'll receive full credit for the semester. Extra, no doubt."

"Then I'll . . . er . . . just go and pack my belongings."

"Good. I'll send my carriage round first thing tomorrow

to collect you. Oh, and one other thing." Simon extended his forefinger, circling it in a gesture meant to encompass Ned's chin and upper lip. "Attempting to grow a bit of whiskers, are we?"

Ned's expression turned pained. "Yes, sir."

"You might wish to consider shaving instead."

The boy nodded glumly. "Thank you, sir."

"I am Lillian Walsh, Lord Harrow's housekeeper. Mind you call me *Mrs.* Walsh when you call me at all, which shan't be often if you know what's good for you."

Well. Dear Mrs. Eddelson at home in London would never have taken such a tone with a guest, Ivy thought. But given the earliness of the hour, perhaps *this* woman suffered from excessive weariness; the church bells in the nearby city had barely finished striking seven in the morning.

When Lord Harrow had said his carriage would collect her "first thing in the morning," he had apparently meant to precede the rising of the sun. She had had to jump into her clothes and race to toss the last of her belongings into her trunks.

Her first view of Harrowood, as she'd been driven through the gates and down the winding, treelined drive, had been shrouded by the dawn shadows. Her initial impression had been one of a drab, brick and stone relic of the pre-Georgian age, nestled at the edge of a gloomy forest and blanketed by an unnatural silence—as if the birds and even the breeze feared to disturb the Mad Marquess of Harrow.

Or perhaps it was Mrs. Walsh they feared.

"Best you know straightaway that I was not put on this earth for the purpose of catering to the whims of university ruffians. Now, follow me, and mind you don't touch anything." Her heels clicking briskly, the housekeeper led Ivy across the marbled entry hall that boasted lofty ceilings presided over by a massive chandelier dripping with equal amounts of crystals and cobwebs. Expansive archways on either side of the hall disappeared into darkness. A wide set of carpeted steps curved away to a likewise dusky first-floor gallery.

"Mealtimes are set by his lordship and strictly adhered to. There'll be no trays carried up to your room, not unless you're half dead of a fever, and perhaps not even then." At the base of the steps, the housekeeper stopped and turned.

Mrs. Walsh was a large woman, though not so much corpulent as broad and big-boned. Even abundant layers of clothing could not dispel Ivy's impression of brawny arms and tree-trunk legs. She had the bulky shoulders and stocky neck of a laborer, a round, pale moon of a face, and strawlike hair that straggled from the edges of her starched white cap.

Her beady gaze raked over Ivy once, twice, and locked.

Ivy pulled up straighter and asked, "Is there something amiss?"

"Let us hope not." The woman quirked her lips and started up the stairs.

Ivy hastened to match her pace, taking extra care not to trip and fall as she had done yesterday, utterly humiliating herself in front of Lord Harrow, not to mention Jasper Lowbry and the rest of her new "mates" who had been watching and laughing from two stories above.

It was the trousers. The weight of the fabric kept informing her brain, wrongly of course, that her legs had become tangled in her petticoats, thus setting off an instinct to kick them free, which threw off her stride and sent her tripping over her own feet. So much for a lifelong belief that trousers would be less confining than skirts.

Below in the hall came the sounds of servants going about their daily tasks. A peek over her shoulder brought two maids, one with a mop and one with a duster, into view. A footman hauled a ladder across the hall while a second liveried manservant trailed him with an armful of fresh tapers. She resisted suggesting that they attend to the chandelier. Instead she asked Mrs. Walsh, "Er, is Lord Harrow up and about yet this morning?"

"His lordship is in his laboratory."

Ivy felt a burst of excitement at the prospect of finding Victoria's stone this very day and making a hasty departure back to London. "Shall I report to him there?"

Mrs. Walsh came to a dead stop. "Certainly not. No one goes near the master's laboratory without his express permission."

Their ascent continued.

"But I am here to assist him."

"And you'll wait until his lordship sends for you."

"How rude," Ivy murmured.

"Excuse me?"

"Nothing."

At the top of the stairs, they crossed the gallery and turned down a corridor, passing many doorways along the way. Larger by far than Thorn Grove, Harrowood made Ivy feel dwarfed and lost, as though she might never find her way out. Nonsense, of course; she could leave any time she pleased.

It was just that she had decided against writing home and alerting her sisters to this sudden change in plan. She hadn't seen the point in alarming them, which they most certainly would be if they were to discover her living beneath a man's roof without a proper chaperone. Especially a *mad*man's roof. Good gracious, could Lord Harrow truly be attempting to resurrect his wife? And . . . would he expect Ivy to assist?

Mrs. Walsh interrupted her thoughts by pausing and drawing a heavy ring of keys from her apron pocket. Their clattering jarred Ivy's already unsettled nerves. The woman unlocked the door before which they had stopped.

"This is your room," she said unnecessarily. "Though why his lordship chose to house a fledgling apprentice—a servant, really—in the main portion of the house is beyond me. Perhaps to better keep an eye on you."

"Perhaps." Ivy bit her tongue to rein her true thoughts in. If only this crotchety woman knew *whose* servant she was—oh, what she wouldn't give to see Mrs. Walsh's face then!

"You'll find bed linens in the bottom drawer of the clothespress. Hot water will be brought in morning and night, and soiled laundry carried out each afternoon. Luncheon is at eleven thirty. Not noon, so mind you don't be late." The woman turned to leave.

"Is there to be no breakfast served?" Ivy's stomach had been giving off ominous rumblings since before she had left her residence hall.

The housekeeper's lips twitched into something resembling a smile, the first Ivy had seen so far. "Breakfast has already been served. Seven o'clock sharp each morning. Why else would Lord Harrow want luncheon so early?"

"Wonderful." As the woman strutted off down the passage, Ivy shut the chamber door with a thud loud enough to convey her frustration, not caring a whit if Mrs. Walsh heard or not.

She found herself in a room of generous proportions, with tall windows and darkly masculine furnishings. And why not? Surely Ned Ivers should not have been accommodated with flowers and chintz. But ... Lady Gwendolyn's room would certainly meet such a description. Ivy wondered which room it was, and whether the runaway lady-in-waiting might at that moment be awakening in her bed and preparing to start her day.

Had she given her brother Victoria's stone? Did he know of its existence?

Ivy crossed to a set of curtained French doors and peeked out to discover a half-round balcony overlooking the rear of the house. As she stepped outside, her breath caught. Formal gardens, far grander than any Thorn Grove boasted, spread out below her. Laid in a sprawling pattern, the flower beds and walkways flanked a magnificent fountain that boasted four marble cherubs playing tiny trumpets around an angel from whose wings and outstretched hands the water flowed.

Blazing autumn colors had already claimed the trees, sharp and bright enough to make Ivy's eyes water. Despite the fall chill, flowers blossomed in abundance: delicate purple asters and drooping hydrangea, fiery chrysanthemums and marigolds, bold red cockscomb and camellias, and roses of every color, dotting every twist and turn along the graveled paths.

Though on a far more modest scale, there had been a rose garden at Thorn Grove, lovingly tended by Uncle Edward himself. It had been there, eight years ago, that Ivy and her sisters had first learned their dear little friend Victoria would one day be their queen; it was there they had pledged to be her secret friends and servants.

The vista before Ivy blurred beneath a bout of homesickness unlike any she had experienced so far. Until now, she had been too intent on fitting in at the university and ensuring that no one guessed her secret. And there had been Lord Harrow's challenge, and the discouraging prospect of letting Victoria down.

But Ivy had played her hand and won the gamble—so far. Now here she was, all alone in this secluded old house where a woman who had died might be here still, her preserved body hidden away by a mad scientist and his beastly housekeeper. . . .

Trousers or no, Ivy's legs brought her downstairs quicker than she could say *Frankenstein's Monster*. A startled footman ran to open the front door for her. Once outside, she gulped cool air, still damp with morning mist, and circled the house at a run. Into the gardens she hurried, desperate to surround herself with the beauty and freshness of— thank heavens—*living* things.

From a window high up in his circular laboratory, Simon gazed down in puzzlement at his new assistant. Where was the lad running? Had Mrs. Walsh frightened him off already?

Perhaps he should have warned the boy, but then again anyone so readily put off by the housekeeper's moods would be equally ill suited to the regimen of Simon's experimentation. With a grin he acknowledged that, like his challenge, the dear woman presented yet another obstacle that must be breached. It disappointed him to think that Ned Ivers had broken and run so soon.

Then again, perhaps not, for the lad gradually slowed and came to a halt in front of the Chorus of Angels fountain. Hands on his hips, Ned leaned back and opened his mouth wide, apparently sucking in drafts of air. When he had caught his breath, he straightened and looked around, taking in the singular beauty of the garden—Aurelia's garden, designed by her and meticulously maintained down to the smallest leaf and blossom, ever since her death.

Simon's heart contracted around the ache that had become a familiar companion this past year and a half. If spirits indeed walked the earth, as some people claimed and he often hoped, he liked to believe that Aurelia continued to inhabit the garden she had loved so much and taken such pride in.

His smile was both bitter and sweet. At times he'd wondered if she had been prouder of her creation than of him, but she had never given him cause to doubt that she had loved him more. In almost the same spot Ned now stood, only without the fountain and magnificent surroundings, Simon had asked for Aurelia's hand and she had bestowed it. . . .

Gripping the stone lintel, he shut his eyes and shook away the memories, but not the pain. Never the pain. It was a grip he couldn't break, no matter how hard he tried, no matter how deeply he immersed himself in work.

He opened his eyes. Ned was now ambling along a winding path that led down the tiered levels to the base of the gardens. Stopping along the way, he stepped over a border of scarlet and white gladiolus to cup a rose in his palm and lean his nose close to the crimson petals.

A vague uneasiness prompted Simon to prop his arms on the sill and lean out. He studied the odd sway of Ned's hips and how when the lad paused again for a deep breath, he propped one hand at his waist and arched his back. When he straightened, he raised both hands and patted his hair into place. . . .

The fussy nature of that gesture held Simon immobile while a fantastical notion formed and bubbled, only to burst with a conviction that balled his hands into fists.

Could it be? Pushing away from the window, he hurried over to a cabinet and found the spyglass he kept there. He returned with it to his vantage point and brought Mr. Edwin Ivers into focus.

Mr. Ivers, indeed. Galileo's teeth!

Chapter 5

"Your young rapscallion from the university has arrived, my lord."

"Yes, thank you, Mrs. Walsh. I know." Simon threaded his way past busy servants, returning their morning greetings with curt nods and attempting to keep his temper in check until he stepped outside the terrace doors. He barely resisted slamming them shut behind him, but what good would come of shattering his own property when what he wished to snap was a certain young man's slender neck?

Except that the young *man* didn't exist.

Damn. Simon didn't enjoy being made a fool of, not in his own home, and most especially not within the context of his own challenge, designed to discover a brilliant young scientist, not a clever little charlatan. Down the terrace steps he stomped, hoping Mr. Ivers hadn't yet gone to the trouble of unpacking *his* bags.

His quarry's burgundy frock coat stood out against the foliage near the bronze sundial, and Simon hurried through the Grecian colonnade in fast pursuit. Ned Ivers had seen his last of Harrowood's gardens, and any other part of Harrowood for that matter. Ah, Simon was going to enjoy this, was going to relish every moment of tossing his soon-to-be former assistant out on that shapely arse of *his*.

"Mr. Ivers," he shouted. The figure clothed in that artfully tailored frock coat jolted to a startled halt.

Quite against his intentions, Simon halted, too, arrested by the sight of her soft mouth and cream-fresh skin and most of all her eyes, velvety soft yet filled with a boundless spirit that captivated him.

Ah, this explained so much. No wonder Simon had felt so discomfited yesterday, so oddly enthralled by the *boy*.

How could he have missed the glaring truth? Yes, the clothes had been subtly altered to hide her womanly curves. Her hair had been cropped short and she had used something to shadow her chin and upper lip. He supposed that at the university people, himself included, had seen what they had expected to see.

But here in the vibrant garden her femininity sang out, a full chorus of ripe womanhood and tempting sensuality. And something else . . . something that made his righteous anger falter . . . and then slip away entirely.

With a frown of uncertainty she started toward him. "Lord Harrow, good morning. I hope I am not breaking any rules by being out here. Mrs. Walsh was explicit about my staying away from the laboratory without your permission, but she mentioned nothing about the gardens."

She came toward him, and through her open coat he again observed the graceful swing of her hips. She wore thigh-hugging breeches tucked into those same black and tan half Wellingtons that had proved so burdensome yesterday. Funny, but they didn't seem to hinder her stride at all now, and for the first time in his life Simon found himself savoring the tantalizing play of muscle and flesh on a woman's thighs beneath formfitting fabric.

"Sir? *Are* there other rules I must know about?"

Simon blinked and gave his head a shake. His pulse raced; his breathing became labored. He grasped his hands behind his back and came to a sudden decision that shocked him. "There are plenty of rules you must learn, Ned, but all of them pertain to the laboratory. As for the rest of the property, when you are on your own time, you may come and go as you please."

Her almond eyes narrowed. "But I may not leave."

Her simple statement held a world of dangerous, sobering implications, ones Simon took into account before he replied. Knowingly taking a young woman into his house posed serious hazards for both of them. He had encountered enough loose women in his lifetime to know of a certainty that *this* woman, with her wide-eyed, hand-raising, eager naïveté, was not one of them.

Was she even aware, then, what this charade of hers could mean for her future? Discovery would result in instant ruination. She would never again be respectable in society, never make any decent man a proper wife. It would not matter whether Simon took her into his bed or not—

A heated tremor traveled his length and pooled in his loins. Why *wouldn't* he wish to have this bold woman, with her perceptive mind and her sleek legs, in his bed? The tremor became a throb, the impulse to gather her into his arms a mounting temptation.

One he tamped down with a reminder of the price they would both pay. For her, a stained reputation. For him, a blot on his credibility. Whores were permissible, as were widows and married women who had reached "understandings" with their often elderly and impotent husbands. Such affairs were to be winked at, dismissed as a man's predilection.

Besmirching an innocent virgin was not excusable. He was a man of science, a scholar to whom integrity meant everything. Without it, any benefits his work might one day yield to society would be lost, scorned and ignored, because he would be a man without honor, not to be trusted.

Then why the devil had she donned a man's breeches and feigned her way into his home? And why had he yet to expose her reckless charade?

"Tell me." He fought the urge to reach out and trace the sensual curve of her mouth with his fingertips. "How is it that you alone understood my challenge?"

The breeze sifted through her short curls, tossing a few strands into her face. She brushed them back and said,

"Your procedure exhibited nothing new. Humphry Davy created potassium by separating the elements of potash more than twenty years ago. Oh, your voltaic pile was far more powerful than the one he used, but otherwise the science involved was rather elementary."

Simon couldn't help grinning at her arrogant show of confidence. To hide it, he started walking, beckoning for her to accompany him. "Go on."

"Knowing you had conducted two previous challenges, I could not believe that everyone before me had failed to grasp the principles of the process. I suspected they had all gone hobbling down the wrong avenue." She tipped her chin and smiled. "You designed that challenge to trick the candidates, didn't you?"

Her impudence knocked him momentarily breathless. Only Aurelia had ever dared confront him in such a manner, always with a saucy grin and a glitter in her eye that was both contentious and conspiratorial, as though she had every assurance in the world that he would come round to seeing things her way.

He always had.

"Lord Harrow?"

He blinked and brought the woman beside him back into focus. Her confidence had slipped, and a particle of doubt flitted across her features. She must believe she had offended him. She could not know what agonizing memories her innocent query had stirred.

"I cannot deny it, Ned," he said evenly. "You see, anyone can be taught the basic principles of electromagnetism. I desired someone for whom science was a passion and an art."

His own choice of words brought him up short. *Desire . . . passion . . .* the terms had suddenly taken on meanings that had nothing whatsoever to do with science. He quickly explained, "I need someone who can grasp the nature of a breakthrough if and when it occurs, and who will not be put off by risk or controversy."

She stumbled over a rock and might have gone down if

he hadn't caught her elbow and steadied her. "I see those boots are still posing a problem."

His jest went ignored. "Controversy, sir?"

He released his hold, but the imprint of her arm seemed branded into his palm. He mashed his other fist against it. "You look alarmed, Ned. Does going against society's grain frighten you? For that is what science often does. It quashes preconceived notions and replaces them with radical new innovations. The public is not always quick to embrace such change."

Much would depend on her answer, he decided. How committed was she to this scheme of hers? And *why*? Just as he had demanded this of his applicants, he wished to demand it of her now but in an entirely different sense. Did she love science and learning enough to risk her future as a wife and mother?

She brought them to a halt. Some vital matter seemed to hang between them as she studied him feature by feature, as he might have studied a particle beneath a microscope. "No, sir, I am not frightened of any judgment society might level upon the work we perform here. I am subject only to the edicts of my own conscience, and those I will never compromise."

Like her impertinence a moment ago, her earnestness echoed Aurelia's spirit and pierced his heart through. The differences between them were marked. Physically they were polar opposites, this woman being dark in coloring, tall, and willowy, with sweet elfin features, and Aurelia having been blond, petite but voluptuous, and classically beautiful.

Having loved the latter, he should not have found himself attracted to the former. Except that wrapped within their dissimilar outward traits, he perceived the same inner core . . . the same uncommon courage. Down to the letter, he truly *had* found the assistant and partner he'd sought. He could not have guessed at the outset how disquieting a prospect this would be.

He set off walking again, trying in vain to escape the

snare he had unwittingly set upon his own heart. "You like gardens, Ned?"

She trotted to match his pace. "Sir?"

"Gardens. Most people take them for granted, sparing them little thought other than to acknowledge the pleasing geometrical aspect of the design. It's a rare individual who understands that every garden has a soul of its own, and is as unique in its needs and potential as a human being."

"To be honest, sir, I've seen precious few gardens of this scale. But my uncle was especially fond of roses, and I *can* say that the present course of my life began, in large part, within the confines of his rose garden."

"Mine, too, Ned." Simon drew the diverse mingling of scents deep into his lungs, absorbing inside him the most tangible essence of the wife he had lost. "I walk here every evening before dusk. The light is extraordinary at that time. It helps me sort out the day's results and plan for the next. Will you join me?"

"Certainly, sir."

He leaned closer to her, so close the clean fragrance of her skin prevailed over the garden's florals to claim his senses. Her pupils dilated, darkening the irises to gleaming, hypnotic obsidian. "I promise you, young Ned, that your conscience shall not be compromised here, not by me."

"Thank you, sir." Her chest rose and fell heavily, and he thought he detected, beneath her coat and waistcoat and shirt, the faint outlines of her woman's anatomy. Or had his mind merely conjured what he now knew to be true, just as yesterday it had conjured what he had *believed* to be true?

A powerful longing tempted him to draw her into his arms and sample those womanly curves, to undo whatever bindings held her in check, to kiss away the confounded shadows across her chin and upper lip and expose her femininity in the ripening fullness of the climbing sun.

The moment stretched as they stood like two deer dazzled by the flare of a hunter's torch, he horrified by the rebellion of his own impulses, and she . . . by the risk of discovery, he supposed. A long, low growl broke the spell.

With a rueful look, she stepped back and pressed a hand to her stomach. "Sorry, sir."

"I say, Ned, have you not eaten today?"

"No, sir. Hadn't time before I vacated my rooms, and Mrs. Walsh said . . ."

"Mrs. Walsh strikes again." Simon made a mental note to have a stern talk with his housekeeper. "Come, lad, let's get something substantial into you. You're going to need it."

A few steps behind Lord Harrow, Ivy made her way up the spiraling staircase that led up the tower to his laboratory. The climb seemed interminable, the narrow windows they passed at intervals providing dizzying glimpses of the treetops. The endlessly curving stairs were beginning to render her light-headed.

Her sister Laurel had once told her that to fight off a bout of dizziness, it helped to focus one's gaze on a stationary object. She did find that centering her gaze on Lord Harrow, a few steps above her, produced a steadying effect, at least on her equilibrium. Her pulse was another matter, launched to a wild canter by the close proximity of his sturdy legs and the ripple of muscle across his back as he alternately gripped and released the rail. The sway of his coattails didn't help, not considering how, from this angle, she was afforded intermittent glimpses of his buttocks, tight and sleek inside his snug breeches.

Risking giddiness, she tore her gaze away. She had no business admiring the Mad Marquess's—

"Feeling better, Ned?"

Snapping out of her musings, she almost replied to the contrary until she realized he referred to the breakfast of eggs and toast that had been served to her beneath the disapproving eye of Mrs. Walsh. Lord Harrow himself had descended to the kitchen to give the order, and the housekeeper had merely sulked as Cook prepared the meal. Though Ivy had wisely kept a neutral expression at the time, she had secretly rejoiced in her small victory over the surly woman.

The memory of it helped take her mind off the climb. "Much better, sir."

"Good. There can be no fainting allowed in my laboratory."

The very suggestion rankled. "Sir, I am no fainter."

There was little Ivy abhorred more than women who swooned at the slightest discomfort. She'd always suspected that the vast majority of them didn't swoon at all, but rather enjoyed the swarm of attention following such an incident.

"No need to be indignant." At long last reaching the landing, Lord Harrow stopped and dug a key out of his coat pocket. "It was a joke."

"Oh." Good heavens, she had reacted as Ivy the woman would have, not as Ned the man, who would have grasped the humor. A careless slip, one she must take heed not to repeat. "Yes, sir. Sorry, sir."

He dangled the key as she joined him on the landing. "Ready?"

"Oh, indeed yes, sir." Her stomach fluttered, partly with the exhilaration of stepping into her first laboratory, and partly with apprehension of what she would witness on the other side of that door.

"Need I remind you that precious few people are permitted to cross this threshold, Ned? Only those I hold in the highest esteem and whose trust I have never had cause to doubt." His levity vanishing, he turned the key in the lock. His pale eyes issued a steely warning. "Do not disappoint me, young man."

His features hardened, and Ivy understood that his words must never be taken lightly. On the contrary, they demanded an oath of honor and loyalty. Her insides fluttered more riotously, and amid her determination to fulfill her duty to Victoria, a new resolve rose up: to prove herself the worthiest of assistants, with the qualities and skills to make him proud.

Thus she could not be certain if her next utterance constituted a lie for Victoria's sake, or the truth for his. "I won't disappoint you, sir. I swear."

With a solemn nod he opened the door and gestured her to precede him inside. Several steps in, she stopped, overwhelmed, overawed . . . overjoyed.

At first the snaking confusion of equipment crowded beneath the domed ceiling swam indistinctly in her vision. She didn't know where to go first, what to examine. She might as well as have been a fairy-tale princess waking up in a magical castle, except that instead of enchanted objects and glittering jewels, wires, cables, levers, and gears formed the ramparts and crenellations of this stronghold that reached as high as the skylight in the ceiling.

If only she knew whether Lord Harrow would turn out to be the prince of the story, or the villain.

Her mouth hanging open, she began a circuit of the room and was immediately relieved to detect nothing that lent credence to Jasper Lowbry's outlandish story. No coffin-sized vat contained fluid and a corpse; there were no organs stuffed into jars, no operating table affixed with wires extending upward to a lightning rod attached to the roof.

Of course, the large armoire across the way could very possibly accommodate an individual, or even several, judging by its formidable size, some six feet wide and at least eight high. She pondered venturing over to peek inside. . . .

"Well, what do you think?"

She jumped at the boom of Lord Harrow's voice, echoing against the domed ceiling. The macabre images faded, and gradually the equipment around her began to take on characteristics her astounded mind could identify.

She saw no sign of Victoria's stone, but it could be hidden anywhere, including inside the armoire. Somehow, she would have to find a way to escape Lord Harrow's watchful eye and search the room.

For now, she surveyed what she could see. A table held a half dozen voltaic cells of various sizes, including the one Lord Harrow had used in his challenge. Beside them was a galvanometer, a compasslike instrument used for measuring the strength of electrical currents.

Along the curving wall a vat was connected to a coal furnace, with copper ductwork extending halfway across the room to a hulking form draped in a shroudlike cloth. Could a body lie beneath? Ivy shook the ridiculous thought away as Lord Harrow crossed the room and with a dramatic flourish whisked the canvas sheeting away.

Ivy gasped at the odd contraption that gleamed and glistened in the sunlight. The apparatus comprised many components, including four tall, upright shafts wrapped in copper wiring. She identified what she believed must be pistons, poised to power a system of gears, a wheel some three feet in diameter, and a center beam that spanned the equipment like the arm of a scale. One end of that beam met a bellowslike instrument that appeared as though it would expand and compress as the beam dipped and rose.

Curiosity sent her to the device, as tall as she was and more than double that across. She reached out a hand.

"Eh, eh." Lord Harrow's admonishment stopped her. "We're looking today, not touching."

She dropped her arm to her side. "It's some sort of motor, isn't it? Like Faraday's, only . . ."

"Much larger. Much more powerful."

She spun about, startled to discover Lord Harrow standing right behind her. She caught a waft of the shaving soap he had used that morning, a scent that stirred her insides to quivery attention. This close she perceived the faint lines at the corners of his eyes, not quite laugh lines, nor worry lines, either, she decided, but the etchings of many hours spent concentrating on his experiments.

"I've never heard of one so large," she said.

Pride illuminated his pale eyes. "That's because there isn't another like it."

"What does it power?"

He shook his head. "That is not for today, either." His faint smile smoothed away her disappointment and eased her frown. "Today is merely for familiarizing yourself with the equipment."

Turning back to the motor, she visually traced the ductwork back to the vat. "It runs on steam power?"

"The *charge* from the steam is what starts it generating its own electricity."

"An electrical charge from steam? Good heavens. I've heard of such a thing in theory, but I didn't know anyone had yet managed it."

He circled the machinery and ran his hand along the duct. "The friction of the water vapor against the copper piping produces a charge. The force of the steam sends the charge to circulate around these magnetic coils to produce a pulsing current."

He pointed to the various components as he explained. "This turns the shafts, which propels the charge through the pistons, along the center beam, and so forth, thus generating a continuous current. The exciting thing is that once my motor is started, it becomes self-maintaining. I can cut the steam and the motor continues running on its own current."

"Electrodynamic force." She reached out again, almost but not quite touching the closest coil. "A generator."

"Yes. Much more efficient than the currents generated by the voltaic cells."

"In theory, this could be used to power all manner of machinery." Tapping a finger to her chin, she considered the workings of the device. "You would simply need to attach the machine's moving parts to your rotating wheel."

"Of course."

"Or . . . you could use wiring to direct the current to a completely separate apparatus, perhaps even powering more than one process at once."

"Even better, Ned. Go on."

She circled the machine, again examining each of its components and longing to see them in motion. "The use of magnetic electrodes would force the movable parts of any separate machinery into motion in response to the current."

"Very good." The admiration in his voice brought her head up. His smile broadened as he approached her. "You've done your reading."

"Yes, lots of it." As he drew near, her heartbeat accelerated.

She caught herself staring, arrested by the firm lines of his face, the power of his silhouette. Then she blinked and shifted her gaze back to the generator, remembering that men didn't look at each other like that; most tended to make eye contact only rarely. "I . . . er . . . had access to a first-rate library for most of my life. My uncle's. It made country life so much more interesting."

She was babbling, and bit the insides of her cheeks to stop herself.

Lord Harrow smiled indulgently. "That should prove enormously to my advantage. Come." With the easy familiarity of a master to his student, he set his hand at her nape. "I wish to acquaint you with the components I work with. The conducting metals, the gauges of the wires, that sort of thing. It's important that you become well versed with the strength of the current produced by the various elements. Have you used a galvanometer before?"

"Uh . . . no, sir." With his palm and splayed fingers producing warmth on her neck, it was all she could do to concentrate on the question he had asked her.

His hold, though gentle, communicated a sense of strength, of authority. His fingertips produced a different sort of current that left her tingling, and scattered her thoughts even as his demonstration yesterday had scattered broken glass and burning potassium across the tabletop.

She swallowed, cleared her throat, and attempted to gather the shards of her common sense. "I have not used one, but I have studied the basic principles."

"Good. Then we'll assemble an improvised current meter together. Come."

She hesitated. "Another test, sir?"

"No, this activity isn't designed to trip you up, Ned." He led her to a second laboratory table and released her with what seemed to her a manly shake of encouragement, even affection.

He took a box off the shelf behind them, set it on the table, and lifted the lid. The interior was filled with what on first glance appeared to be clock parts—dials and gears, rods and shafts. Then he pulled a book from the same shelf, flipped it open, and set it beside the box. "You are quite possibly the most erudite first year I've ever encountered, and I've grown curious as to how far your knowledge will take you. Let's see what you're capable of."

Ivy stepped up to the table's edge and peered down at the labeled diagram that filled a page in the book. Lord Harrow no longer touched her, but the memory of the contact continued to smolder along her nape, a sensation that proved as distracting as it was compelling. With him beside her, it wasn't easy to remember the descriptions of galvanometers she had read in Uncle Edward's library.

"I'm not exactly sure how to begin, sir. . . ."

"I'll guide you, but you do the assembling." He reached one formidable arm around her shoulder and chose a demarcated copper ring from the gadgets in the box. "This was once part of a clock dial, but it will serve nicely in measuring current output. Now, what do you suppose comes next?"

He continued to stand uncommonly close as she consulted the diagram, and then selected a magnetized compass needle, which she attached to a length of fine silk thread. "Like this, sir?"

"Very good. Now you'll need a conductor to catch the current. An improvised coil, perhaps?"

As she took up a thin copper wire and began wrapping it around a slender dowel to form a clumsy coil, he leaned over her shoulder, his warm breath grazing her cheek.

"I'm impressed with your workmanship, Ned. Yes, that's correct. You need to suspend the needle from the coil, and position both over the dial. Are you quite certain you've never done this before?"

"First time, sir." Concentrating on configuring the coil and needle as he instructed, she turned her head only slightly as she replied, but even that small shift brought her mouth perilously close to his. As though generating a thermodynamic attraction, the heat of his lips pulled her closer still. At the last moment Ivy gasped and froze, and Lord Harrow pulled back with a start.

Chapter 6

"Sorry, sir!"

"No, Ned, my fault." Retreating to the other side of the laboratory table, Simon seized the first voltaic cell with which his hands came in contact, while the near collision of his lips against hers continued to heat his loins and propel his heart against his chest wall.

He hadn't been that close to a woman since . . . since Aurelia. And the pleasurable sensations that traveled through him felt like a betrayal of her memory. Not enough time had passed, perhaps never would. She had been infinitely more than just his wife, at least in the sense that most men thought of their wives. She had been his partner, his equal, his lover. When she died, he lost everything . . . *everything*.

Except his work, continued in her memory.

After adding the necessary acid to the cell, he lingered long enough to harness his pulse before returning to his equally unsettled assistant, if her crimson cheeks were any indication. Even without the loss he had suffered at Aurelia's death, how could he have forgotten himself so entirely that he'd come within a fiery hairsbreadth of kissing someone he was pretending to believe was a boy?

"I, ah, had merely been about to point out that your thread had slipped off center of the needle. See there." He pointed, relieved to discover that the thread had indeed slipped a fraction; not enough to skew the measurement, but enough to convince young Ned that he had entered into the employ of an exacting taskmaster.

"Oh, yes, I see. Thank you, sir."

Keeping a good yard or so of space and cool air between them, Simon placed the cell beside the galvanometer she had constructed. "Now we'll measure the current and see how accurate your indicator is."

As she hooked up the wires to connect the cell to the meter, he watched, not her progress, but *her*. The deft movements of her small hands, the adorable crease of concentration above her nose, the secret softness of a body hidden beneath men's clothing, all captured his gaze and his approval. Ah, yes, he approved.

"This way, sir?" She threaded the connecting wire through the coil.

He briefly shifted his focus. "That's correct, Ned. You're almost done."

Galileo's teeth, but he had never encountered a woman like her. Bluestockings and academic-minded suffragists, yes, those he had experienced aplenty. They were usually bespectacled, prudish spinsters who hung about the university gates engaging anyone who would listen in a debate about the importance of women gaining access to formal education and higher learning.

Over the years, a few had even forced their way into the lecture halls, and it was not unheard of for the more insistent of their set to don britches and a coat in the attempt to fool the registrar's office—just as this woman had done.

Some of their antics bordered on the absurd, but Simon sympathized with their plight; theirs was not an unreasonable argument. His mother had been well educated. Aurelia, too. Even Gwendolyn, before her descent into impulsive, self-destructive behavior, had shown aptitude for her studies.

"Ready to make the final connection, my lord."

"Go ahead." He found himself drawing closer to her again, not to assist in the procedure, but to inhale the scent of her cropped curls, to visually caress the creamy curve of her nape exposed above her collar.

This would never do. He had tried telling himself he tolerated her charade only because he championed her desire to explore the field they both loved so well. No one could fake the kind of knowledge she possessed, and no one but the truly passionate could wade through the often dry exposition covering the past several centuries of research.

There were those words again: desire and passion. When it came to "Ned," he seemed unable to govern his impulses or depend upon his common sense.

"It's working!" A vivid flush suffused her cheeks. "Look, sir, the needle is moving in a perfect perpendicular pattern to the current."

Her joy was infectious, so much so that Simon very nearly caught her up in his arms and spun her about. He stopped himself just in time, answering her enthusiasm with an approving if sedate, "So it is, Ned. Well-done."

"Thank you, sir." She jotted down the numbers on the dial indicated by the needle. Her excitement might have been measured on that galvanometer as well; elation lit up in her features and added a tremor to her voice. "What next?"

"I have a store of chemicals and compounds I'd like you to catalogue."

Her enthusiasm dimmed, and he fought back a grin. Who wouldn't rather engage in hands-on experimentation than take up pen and notepaper and sort through a musty storage cupboard? He'd certainly endured his share of tedium as a younger man, but he had learned from it as well, as this student would do.

"Tell me, Ned. How old are you?"

After pausing a beat, she said, "Eighteen, sir."

He wondered how close to her true age that was. If he were to judge her features by male standards, she looked about the age she claimed, if not younger. But in comparing her with other females he knew, his sister included, he guessed her age to be closer to twenty, perhaps even a year or two older than that. For no reason he cared to acknowledge, he hoped she *was* above twenty, making her more his contemporary and so much less a child.

"You've your whole life ahead of you," he mused aloud. "What would you most like to do with it?"

Her answer came without an instant's delay. "*This*. I don't believe I realized how much before today . . . before I stepped through that doorway. I feel at home surrounded by this equipment, in a way I've never done elsewhere."

Her zeal raised an ache in his chest. He empathized with her dream, yet he also grieved that such a dream could never be, not for her. Her pretense could not continue indefinitely. At some point, probably not long hence, someone not as understanding as he would discover her deception, and there could be a lofty price to pay. The thought of the humiliation she would have to endure made him inwardly cringe.

Was he wrong to encourage her? Perhaps she'd be better off if he called her out now and sent her home where she belonged, where she'd come to no harm.

But now that he thought of it . . .

"Where are you from, Ned?"

"London, most recently, sir. I reside in a house my sisters and I inherited from our uncle."

"I see." He frowned as a vague memory prodded. Then he remembered what Bartram Hendslew had revealed about the "odd little chap," information that contradicted the impression Ned had given so far of having been raised by an uncle. "What of your parents? Does not your father serve in Her Majesty's government in some capacity?"

The quick lowering of her lashes failed to conceal a flicker of alarm. "That's true, sir. He is an undersecretary to the chancellor of the exchequer."

She had spoken those last words as if by rote, prompting Simon to entertain serious doubts about their truth. "Then this uncle of yours . . . ?"

"My mother's brother. Mother passed away when we were all quite young, and we began spending a good deal of

time with Uncle Edward. He was retired, you see, had time
to devote to us while business kept Father from home."

"That would explain your having such extensive access
to your uncle's library."

"Yes, sir." She compressed her lips and darted a glance
around the laboratory. "The cataloguing, sir. I suppose I
should be getting on with it. I assume the substances in
question are kept in the armoire?"

He followed her gaze across to the oaken wardrobe
whose doors he always kept tightly locked. "No, not in
there. Follow me."

He brought her to a bank of cupboards stacked two
high. Upon his opening the first of the doors, a package of
powdered resin tumbled out. She moved quickly, catching
the bundle before it hit the floor.

"Rather untidy," she commented brightly, without a hint
of complaint. "Shall I restore order as I catalogue?"

"I would appreciate that, Ned. It's something my wife
used to do for me. . . ."

He left the remainder of the thought unfinished, astonished that he had mentioned Aurelia at all. He rarely
ever did, and then only in the company of friends who had
known her, those whom he most trusted. The topic was still
too raw, too painful for casual conversation.

With a nod, "Ned" went to work, leaving Simon with a
keen sense of gratitude that she had neither probed him
with questions nor bestowed upon him the pitying look he
often encountered and so heartily loathed.

Across the room, he put on his spectacles and settled
in to make some calculations, but his attention repeatedly
wandered to the trim form of his assistant. He wished he
knew her real name. Even if he couldn't address her properly, he would have preferred to *think* of her in feminine
terms, in honest terms.

He again considered whether it would be kinder and
wiser to end her deception now. But he lacked the heart to
crush her aspirations, especially before she had the chance

to accomplish something extraordinary, something she could always look back upon with pride.

In a way, their alliance made perfect sense. Besides her remarkable abilities making her a top-rate assistant, there was also the matter of secrecy, a thing they had in common. Her own need for discretion guaranteed that she would safeguard any revelations he shared with her.

For the foreseeable future, then, he would allow her the benefit of her lie. He would call her Ned, think of her as Ned . . . and maintain a proper physical distance, just as he would if she truly had been Ned.

Coming upon an unlabeled bottle about the size of her smallest finger, Ivy plucked it from the shelf only to have it slip from her fingers. In a sudden panic she snatched at it with her other hand, but it bounced off her palm before her fingers closed around it. The vessel flipped upward, striking her shoulder and then plummeting. She dropped to her knees and somehow managed to capture the tiny bottle with both hands against her waistcoat.

A close call! The very last thing she needed was to be breaking things on her first day in the laboratory. Her fingers quivering, she set the container aside to be identified later, when Lord Harrow was no longer hunched so intently over his work.

Of course, her bout of clumsiness could be blamed directly on him, and on the heat of an almost kiss that had left her senses reeling, her lips tingling. Though she replayed the incident over and over in her mind, she could not quite fathom what had brought Lord Harrow leaning so close that their lips had all but touched.

Did he trust her so little with his precious equipment? She didn't believe that was the case, for then why would he have her here at all? An unsettling thought sent her fingertips to her chin. Perhaps he had noticed the lack of coal dust? His suggestion yesterday that she should shave rather than attempt to grow whiskers had been all the encouragement she needed to discontinue smearing the grimy powder across her face. A mistake?

But no, if Lord Harrow suspected the truth of her gender, he would toss her out on her coattails, not kiss her.

Such a silly notion. Of course he had not meant to kiss her. He thought of her as a university student named Ned, and not as a young woman who . . .

Who could not stop wishing he *had* kissed her, whose lips burned with unquenchable curiosity at what his mouth would have felt like, tasted like. . . .

"Have you encountered a problem?"

With a startled glance over her shoulder she discovered Lord Harrow staring across the way at her from over a pair of gold-rimmed spectacles perched halfway down the strong line of his nose. She hadn't seen him wear spectacles before, and found herself fascinated by the myriad contradictions they produced. He was at once scholarly and dashing, rakish and brilliant, a professor with the vigor and physique of a sportsman. . . .

She held up the rescued bottle. "An unidentified compound, sir."

"No matter. Set it aside with any others you find and I'll look at them later."

She didn't mention that she had already thought of that. Turning back to her task, she felt his gaze lingering upon her. She dipped her quill in preparation of jotting down the next item, pressed too hard on the paper, and broke the nib.

An hour later, her nerves settled thanks to the deadly dullness of her occupation, she stifled a sigh. She might as well have been home again, helping Mrs. Eddelson rearrange the pantry. The marquess's endless supplies of minerals, oils, and resins could just as easily have been spices, sauces, and jellies, all strewn in together without rhyme or reason.

Surely these cupboards could not have been sorted in months, not since . . . Oh, yes, since his poor wife had passed away.

The more time she spent with Lord Harrow, the more

absurd the rumors became. She perceived nothing at all
"mad" about him. In fact, thus far she had detected none of
the brusque ill humor he had exhibited during yesterday's
challenge. His seemed a generous if cautious nature, hardly
the characteristic of someone conducting gruesome experiments on the sly.

If Ivy was to venture a guess, she'd suppose his behavior yesterday morning had been another bit of trickery
designed to encourage those rumors and deter the more
fainthearted of the applicants. He was good at disguises,
good enough to give her pause. How much longer before
he discovered hers?

A container at the back corner of the bottom shelf
caught her attention, and Ivy bent over to retrieve it.

"It's growing late," Lord Harrow said suddenly and with
an oddly husky rasp to his voice. Holding a vial, she turned
in puzzlement. He removed his spectacles and rubbed at
his eyes. "Finish with whatever you've got in your hand and
then you may go."

"Late, sir?" A glance out the window confirmed that
the hour could hardly be approaching teatime. "And go
where?"

Focusing on the papers fanned across his desk as if they
required his utmost attention, he gave a shrug. "I suppose
you could unpack. Do you care for riding? My groom could
saddle a horse for you."

Her eyebrows rose at a possibility she hadn't considered. Victoria had supplied suitable riding clothes, but
Ivy had assumed them to be standard attire for romping
in the countryside with her fellow university students. A
good number of years had passed since she had last ridden astride, and she had never quite taken to the saddle
anyway, not like her much more athletic sister Holly. The
prospect of negotiating woodland paths by herself was not
a welcome one.

"Whatever you prefer," Lord Harrow said, apparently
perceiving her hesitation. "Though I thought perhaps we'd
ride together in the evenings before supper."

Together? That shed an entirely different light on the matter. Ivy delighted in the image forming in her mind, that of riding through the forest at Lord Harrow's side, discussing the elements and fauna, gauging wind velocities—subjects that made her sisters roll their eyes. "I'd like that very much, sir. Though I must admit I'm not the most proficient of riders."

He chuckled faintly. "Too much time spent at your books, Ned?"

"That's it exactly, sir."

"Did the other boys tease you for it, when you were younger?"

A taut silence grew as Ivy regretted the necessity of lying, and as a conviction came over her that Victoria must surely be wrong about him. His sister may have stolen the stone, but Ivy would all but stake her life that Lord Harrow knew nothing about it, and that if he did, he would insist Lady Gwendolyn return the queen's property before another day dawned.

She offered him a sad little smile. "I suppose they did, sir."

His nod conveyed the understanding of someone who had shared a similar experience. "Off with you, then. That's enough for today."

That night, Ivy stood with her ear to her door, waiting for silence to descend over Harrowood. But no matter the hour, there would always be someone awake somewhere in the house—a footman or two, perhaps even a maid working late or getting an early start on the morrow's chores. She must keep to the shadows, make nary a sound, and turn corners with the utmost care to avoid detection.

Noiselessly she slipped out of her room, careful to step over the bare floorboards and keep to the muffling hall runner. With only intermittent shafts of moonlight to guide her, she made her way through the darkened corridors to Lord Harrow's library with its adjoining office. Outside, the wind wailed through the trees and battered a warning against the house. Goose bumps showered Ivy's arms, but she ignored the discomfort, the wind, the little voice inside urging her back to the safety of her room.

Spindly shadows, cast through the library's windows by the tangle of branches outside, danced on the walls and groped along the spines of the books lining the shelves. The ghostly sight drew a gasp from Ivy, but she bit it back and issued herself a stern admonishment to get to work. One by one she searched the desk, the long, low bank of cabinets, and then the tall cupboard with the gilded edges. Next she considered the bookcases. No single volume appeared thick enough to conceal Victoria's stone, but before passing through to the office, she checked that the books sat well back on their shelves, and that nothing could have been hidden behind them.

A cautionary instinct prompted her to slide the nearest book off its shelf before she passed through to the office. A bout of conscience gripped her as she set the small book on the leather desktop, closed the door to the corridor, and once again rummaged through drawers and cabinets. With every pull of a knob, she expected to encounter resistance, but it seemed Lord Harrow saw no reason to lock away estate ledgers and files. No, it became apparent that any secrets he might possess were guarded in his laboratory . . . where she could not tread without his permission.

Just as she retrieved the clothbound tome she'd taken from the library, the office door swung open.

"Who's there?" a male voice demanded. A blinding burst of lantern light filled the room.

Ivy froze. Heart pounding in her throat, she blinked to make out the identity of the tall figure filling the doorway, though she knew from the owner's light tenor that it could not be Lord Harrow. Her shaking fingers held the book up like a shield against her breast. In another defensive gesture, she folded her shoulders inward, for though she wore her gentlemen's clothes and the bindings beneath, she had shed her coat to maneuver more freely during her search.

The lack of that protective layer of wool left her feeling vulnerable.

The lantern picked out glints of gold on a tailored sleeve, and she recognized the footman who had carried her trunk into the house that morning.

"Oh, Daniel, it's you," she said on a sigh of relief.

"Mr. Ivers, is it?" When Ivy nodded, the servant stepped into the room and lowered the lantern. He eyed her up and down, not in the way she was used to, as male customers sometimes assessed her from over the counter at the Readers' Emporium, but in that competitive, mildly hostile manner young men reserved for one another, and which she had encountered once or twice during her brief stay at the university. "What are you doing in his lordship's office?" he accused more than asked.

Ivy raised her eyebrows. "Is this Lord Harrow's office? I fear I'll never learn the lay of the house." She held out her book and silently thanked the foresight that had prompted her to bring it with her from the other room. "Couldn't sleep. Thought a bit of reading might help. Would you be a good fellow and point me toward the stairs?"

The suspicion not quite leaving his smooth features, Daniel stepped aside and gestured with his free hand. "This way, sir."

Ivy spent the next several days becoming familiar with Lord Harrow's laboratory and learning to use the equipment. He taught her how to construct the voltaic cells, how to produce a continuous current, how to direct it, and how to strengthen or weaken its voltage. They experimented with chemical compounds, separating elements as he had done during his challenge, though to much less dramatic effect with fewer sparks and no shattering glass.

With each procedure, he allowed her greater independence until, after issuing a few basic instructions, he stepped back and merely observed. One afternoon he spread sheets of calculations across his worktable. Together they pored over the equations, double-checking his original work and making adjustments. The sums and quotients represented vast amounts of energy, leading Ivy to ponder whether she and Lord Harrow were dealing with theoretical possibilities, or if the figures pertained to his mysterious generator.

"Would not this amount of amperes exceed the resistance of a current and cause an overload, thus culminating in an explosion?" she asked of one equation in particular.

Lord Harrow had pushed his spectacles higher on his nose and peered over her shoulder, only to snatch the paper out from under her hand. "Great bloody heavens, Ned, you're right. How *could* I have missed this?"

He had slapped the page back down, whipped off his spectacles, and seized her shoulders. His beaming face pulled close, so close Ivy braced for the press of his lips against hers. As on their first day together, his eyes widened and he stopped short, but his broad smile didn't lessen. "You have more than earned your keep, dear boy."

The praise had filled her with pride and a secret longing to cast off her gentlemen's clothes, however briefly, and bring that almost kiss to fruition.

It might have been easy, during those wondrous days, to forget the mission that had brought her to Harrowood. Oh, but she hadn't forgotten, and she continued her midnight forays through the house, once having to hide behind a potted palm for a quarter hour to avoid an apparently insomniac Mrs. Walsh. Ivy's own dearth of sleep was beginning to show in the smudges beneath her eyes. But so far she had turned up no evidence of Lord Harrow's sister having been to the estate, with or without the stone.

Once she ventured into a bedchamber that could only have been Lady Gwendolyn's, judging by the initials on the bed pillows. A quick look around suggested that no one but the upstairs maid had entered the room in many months. Ivy stole toward the dressing room, but before she could so much as open a wardrobe door or peek inside a drawer, the housekeeper appeared in the doorway.

"Did Lord Harrow send you in here?" the woman demanded.

Was the woman trailing her, night and day? Ivy quickly arranged her startled features into a moue of innocence. "No, ma'am. I fear I am lost again. A confoundedly enormous house, this."

"And apparently you've no sense of direction." The housekeeper's brow wrinkled with distrust. "Your chamber is in quite the opposite direction, young man. In the east wing. Now get along with you."

Ivy decided it was time to try another tack. As casually as she could, she asked Lord Harrow about his family. He spoke of Lady Gwendolyn only briefly.

"I have a sister, presently in London in service to the queen," he said, and to Ivy's offhand query as to whether she would have the privilege of making the young lady's acquaintance, he replied, "I don't expect her home any time soon."

The terse finality in his tone had ended the discussion, leaving Ivy to wonder. She believed him to be a man of honor who would never steal outright or be a willing party to theft. But was he protecting his sister until he discovered a discreet and tactful means of rectifying matters? Or . . . Ivy couldn't discount the possibility that he might be stalling for time to conduct experiments on the stone before returning it to its rightful owner.

Could she blame him? If Victoria were not her friend, and if Ivy had not pledged her service to her queen, she might be tempted to do the same.

In the evenings, she and Lord Harrow walked in the garden and discussed what she had learned, or they climbed into their respective saddles and took off through the forest at a pace Ivy found manageable enough. She rode Lady Gwendolyn's mare, an even-tempered, sure-footed mount that didn't seem the least put off by Ivy's awkward seat or inadvertent tugs on the reins.

Only once did Lord Harrow break into a gallop on a wide, flat expanse of trail, prompting the mare to sprint in pursuit. Nearly smothered by her own pounding heartbeat, Ivy leaned forward and hung on for dear life, but when it was over and she discovered that she had survived, she was exhilarated and proud and willing to do it again . . . well, sometime soon.

Especially bolstering to her courage was when Lord Harrow swept off his hat and laughingly exclaimed, "Take *that*, everyone who ever believed Ned Ivers too studious to be intrepid."

Those were the glorious times, when her duty became almost a joy; when, for the first time in her life, someone saw through her exterior to the person inside, not the woman, but the scholar, an individual guided by the principles of science and discovery.

Those times made Ivy exultant . . . and wretched. Once she discovered the whereabouts of the stone, she would never—*could* never—see Lord Harrow again. For the person Lord Harrow saw each day, whom he had come to know as Ned Ivers, would cease to exist.

Her sister Laurel had faced a similar dilemma when she'd gone to Bath last spring disguised as a wealthy widow. Laurel made friends, fell in love . . . and feared she would never be forgiven for her masquerade. But *this* was a thousand times worse. Ivy would just as soon enter a brothel as ever admit to anyone that she had worn trousers and kept company with men. And while she refused to allow society's opinions to rule her, Lord Harrow's esteem was beginning to matter—more than she had ever imagined it could.

"You're walking a bit stiffly today, Ned," Lord Harrow commented as they entered his laboratory that Friday morning. "Has Butterfly not been providing a smooth enough ride?"

The teasing glint in his eye prompted Ivy to grin. "I'm afraid it's not the mare that's at fault, sir."

"Never mind. You improve daily."

As on the previous few mornings, Lord Harrow shed his coat and tossed it over the back of a chair. After an initial hesitation Ivy did the same, keenly aware of how she stretched propriety's limits. Being in shirtsleeves freed their arms, which made working so much easier. She had grown more accustomed to wearing trousers as well and no longer tripped over her own feet. But the combination of trousers and no coat exposed her rear, her hips, and the shape of her thighs in alarming ways. She felt on display, almost naked.

This state of dishabille exposed astonishing aspects of Lord Harrow's anatomy as well, and made Ivy's task more difficult still. As her initial delight in the laboratory began to subside, more and more her attention was drawn to him: his sleek hips, his broad shoulders and chest, his tight abdomen and powerful thighs ... and the part of him that formed such a mysterious, formidable bulge at the juncture of his breeches, unsettling her to a degree that worsened rather than eased with each passing day.

"I've a surprise for you today, Ned."

She didn't say that each day with him brought surprises, both joyful and disconcerting. Instead she watched him cross the room and shovel coal into a huge furnace, her ungovernable fascination drawn to the wide stance of his brawny legs, the knotting of the muscles in his forearms, the arc of a rear that made her wonder, scandalously, if it would be as hard to the touch as it appeared.

As she pondered this possibility, Lord Harrow abruptly turned and caught her staring. With a start she flicked her gaze upward to a more appropriate vicinity of his person, but too late. His pale eyes flashed with surprise and then darkened with acknowledgment, and all Ivy could do was look away while her cheeks burned and her vision swam in a haze of embarrassment.

Lord Harrow cleared his throat, and Ivy died a small death inside. Had she revealed the truth in that careless moment? Surely he would realize that only a woman, an inexperienced, spinsterish woman at that, would gaze upon him so brazenly and with such longing. Unless he thought her one of those odd young men with irregular predilections. Surely that would be worse. Surely Lord Harrow would never stand for such a thing.

After an interminable pause he said, "Well, Ned, aren't you going to ask me?"

Ivy's breath trembled. "Ask you what, sir?"

"About the surprise. Aren't you burning to know?"

Oh, yes, burning . . . in his presence, she always felt flushed, inwardly ablaze. His smile grew when she didn't answer. He raised the shovel, then half turned to bring the furnace behind him to her attention.

Her eyes gone wide, Ivy sprang forward. "The generator?"

"We're going to turn it on. If you think you're ready, that is."

"I'm ready." Her voice surged an octave. "I'm quite ready, sir."

"Good. Bring me the lucifers from my desk. The long ones."

Ivy brought the friction matches to him. Within a few minutes the coals glowed brightly inside the grate. "It's going to take a little while for the water to heat. Damn, but I wish steam weren't necessary. I've tried electromagnetic and electrochemical induction, but thus far they haven't generated a strong enough charge to activate a motor of this scale. That is what I am hoping you and I together will devise."

"You seem to have a classic paradox." Ivy loved an intricate puzzle, and the challenge Lord Harrow described sent an electrical-like charge through her. "You've developed a device that can potentially replace nonelectrical sources of power, but which is nonetheless dependent on those sources. What you need is something entirely new, something as yet undiscovered."

"Exactly, Ned." His features took on an animation that matched her own excitement as he crossed the room to her. "*That* has been the focus of my experimentation."

"It isn't so much *what* you wish to power, as *how*." Ivy's pulse took off at a near canter. "That is why your challenge centered on the process of electrolysis. That's the meaning of your question, the answer to your elusive *why*. You've been separating compounds in the hopes of discovering a powerful new element."

Her gaze fused with his, and their combined zeal all but sent sparks shooting in the air between them. "You are hoping," she whispered, "to recombine elements in a manner that improves upon nature. You are dabbling in a whole new kind of physics."

"More than dabbling." A slight tremor shook his voice. "And more often than not, practically blowing myself up in the process."

Her hand flew to her lips, but she quickly dropped it upon remembering that men didn't use such gestures. "Hence your caution in allowing me to operate the equipment."

He drew closer, his next words a caress against her ear. "Can't be blowing up my assistant along with me, now can I?"

He raised a hand, and for one exhilarating, startling moment, the warmth of his expression led her to believe he was going to reach for her, take her in his arms. How eagerly she would have gone, her passion for science and her growing passion for him impossibly entwined.

The moment throbbed with anticipation and uncertainty and nervous fear, and ended all too soon. Lord Harrow merely gripped her shoulder and gave her the shake that had become so familiar, so endearing, and so dreadfully insufficient. No man had ever tempted her like this before, because with every other man came the unhappy prospect of setting her interests and aspirations aside.

Ivy had never wished for a husband, but daily now she found herself wishing for Lord Harrow. Wishing for more than these affectionate gestures of his ... wanting everything she could never have.

Across the room, the vat began to hiss. Lord Harrow grinned and his eyes lit up. "We're ready to begin. Sir, let us start our engine."

Chapter 7

A trill of elation banished Ivy's regrets. "What do I do?"
A release valve at the top of the vat whistled. Jets of
steam shot out. From a cabinet against the wall Lord Harrow dug out two bulky pairs of woolen gloves. "Put these on. They'll protect you from both steam burns and electrical shock."

Ivy remembered the pair he had worn to protect his hands during his challenge. The ones she tugged on now reached to her elbows, while a stiff lining restricted the movement of her wrists and fingers. Lord Harrow brought her to where the ductwork met the generator's four upright coils.

"Stand right here, Ned, and hold the lever. At my command, you'll give a single, forceful flip, opening the valve and releasing the charge into the coils."

"Am I responsible for ignition?"

"You are." He couldn't seem to stop grinning now. Moving to the room's curving wall, he gripped a crank that operated a pulley and cables that stretched to the ceiling. Slowly the skylight opened wide to offer a gaping view of the bright morning sky.

"Allowing too great a buildup of energy in the room could possibly result in an explosion," he explained with a wry pull to his lips that led Ivy to conclude he spoke from experience.

A twinge of apprehension tightened her belly. *The Mad Marquess . . .*

"Now, then." He strode to the furnace and climbed onto a stepladder. At the top of the vat was a spoked wheel like that of a ship's helm. As if navigating treacherous waters, he gripped the wheel in both hands. His shoulders bunched and the muscles of his back strained his linen shirt. He cast a glance at her from over his shoulder, his brow pulled in concentration. "In a moment I'll open the preliminary valve and send the steam through. Be ready, Ned."

She almost said, "Aye, aye, sir." Instead she flexed her fingers inside the rigid glove and tightened her hold on the lever.

"Ned!"

His shout seized her attention. The vat emitted a piercing screech. Spurts of steam erupted into the high, domed ceiling and snaked out through the open skylight. Goose bumps rippled down Ivy's back.

"I nearly forgot. Once you flip the lever, move back several paces. Since we are not powering a mechanical device, the current will not be directed into a controlled outlet. The result is that the charge will simply flow into the room, the excess wafting out through the skylight. You'll feel a strange tingling, but don't be alarmed. It's quite safe."

"Oh," she said somewhat weakly as she briefly questioned the validity of his claim. Excitement won out and she said more firmly, "Yes, sir."

"On my command, then." His forearms thick and corded, his biceps bulging beneath his pushed-up sleeves, he heaved on the wheel, once, twice, again. It gave an inch or so. He tightened his grip, and another determined yank brought it half around. A gushing sound echoed inside the copper duct. A frenzied buzz raced closer and closer to Ivy. Beneath her hand, the lever vibrated furiously.

"Now, Ned!"

Her teeth clamped on her lower lip, she flipped the lever. The moment her hand came away, an invisible force propelled her backward. She stumbled, landed on her bottom, and slid several inches.

A column of steam burst from the duct and into the generator's four coils, creating tiny bolts of lightning that crackled as they spiraled around each coil and zigzagged between them. The gears began to turn, the pistons to pump. The voltage ran along the center beam until it began a steady rocking motion that forced the wheel to turn and the bellows to expand and compress.

Pulsating energy fanned out in all directions. A few sparks flew, like shooting stars. Lord Harrow's box of gadgets slid off the table and spilled its contents across the floor. The galvanometer needles spun. Cupboards rattled, and the doors of the locked wardrobe shuddered as if about to burst open.

Ivy's skin became charged with sensation while the hair at her nape prickled and rose. At the furnace, Lord Harrow tugged again at the wheel. Ivy bit her tongue to keep from calling out to him in fear, to beg him to cut off the power.

Could he? He'd told her that once his generator started, it continued even without the steam-generated charge. The room began to spin in Ivy's vision. A numbing tingle spread through her limbs. Overwhelming and frightening, the current now controlled the rhythm of her breathing and even the beat of her heart, speeding it to match the rocking of the beam and each whir of the wheel.

She shut her eyes. An instant later snapping sparks on both upper arms forced her eyes back open. Having removed his gloves, Lord Harrow closed his hands around her and gently raised her to her feet. With an arm slung around her shoulders, he pressed her to his side. The contact produced a grounding effect, and the awful tingling subsided until only the bottoms of her feet and scalp itched.

She glanced up at the man beside her. His head was thrown back, exposing his corded neck, the strong lines of his jaw and nose. His chest swelled as he drew air deep into his lungs.

His obvious lack of alarm banished Ivy's remaining fears. The air crackled and buzzed like a swarm of bees, surrounding them within the electrical charge they had created. Together they stood as one—one mind, one passion—bound like two separate elements into a single entity by the pulsing electricity and by their shared pursuit.

Thus, when Lord Harrow raised his voice to ask if she had had enough, Ivy shook her head and yelled back, "Never!"

Yet his arm snaked away, leaving her disconnected and solitary, once more vulnerable to the current's effects. Lord Harrow strode to one of the tables, where he had stacked the folded squares of black canvas. With a flick he unfolded the first, brought it to the motor, and tossed it over the coils. The energy in the room palpably lessened, releasing its grip on Ivy. The sparks ceased; the motor decelerated and came to a standstill.

Still hovering where Lord Harrow had left her, Ivy struggled to catch her breath, to blink away the haze that continued to cloud her vision. Holding a fist to her bosom, she ventured a step, then another, surprised when her trembling legs didn't fail her. She pulled the gloves from her hands.

Gradually her heartbeat slowed, but the force of Lord Harrow's gaze had her tingling all over again. "Are you all right, Ned?" He hurried back to her. "You have a peculiar look about you. Were you hurt?"

When she didn't immediately answer, he grasped her chin in his hand and raised her face. Their gazes met and sparked, then simmered with an emotion so unsettling Ivy turned her face away rather than yield to the temptation to press her lips to his.

"Ned?"

"I'm fine, sir. I think." She gave her head a shake—as much to clear it from the effects of the electricity as from the beguiling energy of Lord Harrow's touch. She ran both hands through her hair, still standing slightly on end. "I've never felt anything like that."

"No, I shouldn't think so."

He didn't—couldn't—understand that she referred to her feelings toward him, not his generator. The intensity of his regard had pierced clean through Ned Ivers's outer shell, leaving her shaken, confused, and entirely female.

She tugged at her waistcoat to straighten it and regarded the now silent, motionless device. "How did you stop the power so quickly?"

"The tarpaulins are coated with India rubber, an insulator. Your gloves are lined with thin cork coated with the same substance."

She glanced down at the gloves still in her hand. "Thank goodness for precautions." A perplexing realization turned her to face him again. "In truth, sir, I didn't win your challenge. I never envisioned any of this. Not so much as a speck of what you've achieved here."

"No, but you captured the spirit of exploration well enough. The others, in their fervor to impress me with all they knew, forgot to acknowledge the many things they had yet to learn. They showed arrogance where humility was required."

Had Ivy been humble? *Desperate* more aptly described her attempt to meet his challenge. She started to reply, but the tinkling of a bell cut her short.

Lord Harrow swore softly and strode to the door. He didn't exit, however. All week Ivy had wondered about the tube that traveled up the staircase wall, came up through the floor and ended at a little square box mounted beside the door. Beside it hung the bell that had chimed. Lord Harrow opened the box and leaned his mouth close.

"Yes?"

"Visitors, sir," came the slightly muffled though quite intelligible voice of Mrs. Walsh.

"Tell whoever it is I'm not at home."

"It is Messrs. Quincy and Rivers, sir."

"Hang it," he murmured into the air. He spoke into the box again. "I'll be down presently."

Slamming the little box closed, he swore again and re-

trieved his coat. As he shrugged into it, Ivy said, "I'd wondered what that was. It's an ingenious arrangement."

He laughed. "I've just subjected you to perhaps the
strongest field of electricity yet created by man, and you
find my speaking tubes ingenious?"

"I only meant..." A notion struck her. "Why aren't
there more such conveniences to be found throughout the
house?"

"Like devices that toast your bread or polish your
shoes?" He scowled. "My dear boy, I am a man of science,
not a tinkerer. The speaking tubes are a necessity. My staff
was spending so much time walking up and down the tower
steps that they could get little else done."

He swept his arm in a half circle that encompassed the
fallen gadgets and other disturbances caused by the surge.
"I don't like leaving my laboratory in such a state. Ned,
would you mind tidying up?"

Ivy experienced a surge of her own, a flurry of nerves.
Did Lord Harrow truly mean to leave her alone with his
equipment? "Of course not, sir."

Fishing into his coat pocket, he tossed her his set of keys.
"Here, lock up when you've finished."

The keys jangled in her palm. As he disappeared through
the doorway, she wondered. Did she dare see if one of them
fit the armoire?

"Will that new assistant of yours be joining your guests for
tea, my lord?"

"He will, Mrs. Walsh." Simon adjusted his neckcloth
as he descended to the main hall. "He should be down in
about ten minutes. When he comes, send him out to the
terrace."

Hands folded at her waist, the housekeeper stepped
into his path. "I've had my eye on that young man. There is
something not quite right about him."

"Really? I find him to be a top-notch assistant."

The woman neither backed away nor backed down.

One eye squinted tighter than the other, a sure sign of her agitation.

Simon blew out a breath. "Speak your mind, Mrs. Walsh."

"It doesn't do to take strangers into one's home, my lord. Do you know the first thing about his background?"

"I know enough to satisfy my curiosity." An untrue statement if ever he uttered one.

The more time he spent around his assistant, the more he hungered to know everything about her. Her pale, dazed look just now had filled him with an aching urge to hold her and kiss the color back into her lovely cheeks. He'd wanted to open his mouth and suck in her lips, her tongue, the deliciously soft curve of her chin. Now that she'd stopped smearing her skin with what he suspected was coal dust, she was a creamy, tempting little blossom, and it took all of his willpower to resist her.

Ah, but she was no wilting flower. The speed with which she'd rallied her courage proved that. Where had she acquired such a bold spirit? Did she hail from that rare family who encouraged education and ambition in their daughters?

Or were they even now pulling out their hair and agonizing over where their headstrong girl had gone? Funny how he worried about such things only when he and "Ned" were apart. When they were together, Simon thought only about . . . Well, about how good it felt to be near her.

A decidedly dangerous way to feel.

"Another thing, my lord . . ." Mrs. Walsh hadn't finished haranguing him, but Simon had quite finished listening.

He stepped around her. "My guests are waiting for me where?"

She sighed. "The library."

"Thank you. Send the refreshments out to the terrace."

As Simon stepped into the library, Errol Quincy, don and head of the university's chemistry department, placed the quartz geode he'd been studying back on an end table. With one finger he shoved a pair of oversized spectacles, so dense as to seem nearly opaque, higher on his nose. A man of diminutive stature whose bald head barely reached Simon's shoulder, Errol possessed one of the sharpest minds and most generous hearts Simon had ever encountered.

His daughter, Aurelia, had inherited all three traits, as well as his kindly eyes if not his nearsightedness.

The elderly gentleman retrieved his walking stick from where it leaned against the side of the settee, and shuffled cautiously toward Simon, renewing Simon's recent concerns about his father-in-law's health. "I say, my boy, we heard the most peculiar rumbling as we came up the drive. Earth tremors, or was it your doing, son?"

Simon's own father had never addressed him as *son*. That Errol continued to do so more than a year after his daughter's death remained a source of both pride and solace. Simon had always valued this unpretentious but brilliant man's esteem; he always would.

"Of course it was him." Ben Rivers slid the book he'd been holding back onto its shelf. He joined the other two men and clapped Simon's shoulder. "Tell us, have you managed to frighten off that new assistant of yours yet?"

Simon flashed a rueful grin as he shook hands with both men. "Yes and no. Unless there is a storm approaching, that was most assuredly my rumbling you heard. As for my assistant, she's made of tougher stuff than that."

"Pardon?" Errol and Ben exchanged a look, and with a start Simon realized his mistake.

"A jest, gentlemen. The upperclassmen of St. John's always address the younger students as ladies."

"Ah, yes." For a fleeting instant Ben stood straighter. Then the old injury curved his spine and dragged at his shoulders. "The lad is working out for you?"

"He's exceeding all expectations."

"Splendid." Errol leaned on his walking stick, his fingers trembling slightly as they tightened around its brass handle. "Are you ready to discuss results?"

Frustration tapped at Simon's pulse points. Though an achievement in itself, his generator represented a means to an end. Perhaps he'd never succeed in re-creating the "accident" that had spun his research in new, unheard of directions. *Was* he tilting at windmills, as less adventurous colleagues liked to imply?

"My generator is thus far fulfilling expectations. But beyond that . . ." He held up open palms.

He led his guests out to the terrace, offering Errol an arm to help the frail gentleman down the steps. Errol had always possessed far more intellectual strength than physical, but he seemed to have become slower, weaker, and shakier since his daughter's death—or was it Simon's imagination?

Probably not, but Simon knew his perceptions of this man were colored by guilt as much as anything else. Guilt for not having protected Aurelia as he should have done, for being away the day she died instead of at home, where he might have prevented the horrible accident. . . .

Not once had Errol pointed a finger in blame, and that made Simon's burden heavier, for he felt he didn't deserve the kindness Errol unfailingly showed him.

They took seats around a wrought iron table, overlooking the deepening autumn hues of Aurelia's gardens. Simon held Errol's chair as the man gripped the edge of the table with a heavily veined hand and stiffly lowered himself onto the seat.

A small russet hawk swooped over their heads and settled in an elm tree at the base of the gardens. A cool breeze carried the mingling scents of freshly raked grass and warm bread from the ovens. Simon sat facing the two men. "Alistair has assured me that all is set for the consortium in two weeks' time."

He spoke of Alistair Granville, a longtime friend and second cousin of the de Burghs. Though no longer a fellow at Cambridge or actively engaged in scientific development himself, Alistair continued to be a major supporter of innovative research. When Simon's father had ridiculed his son's ambitions as too plebeian for the heir of a noble family, it had been Alistair who had encouraged Simon and supplanted Simon de Burgh Sr. in the role of mentor.

This year, Alistair had offered up his home, Windgate Priory, as one of several around the country where this year's contenders for the Copley Medal would gather to compete for the coveted award.

"Yes, Alistair paid me a surprise visit at my office last week," Ben said. "It appears the Royal Society has confirmed that two of its representatives will be at Windgate Priory to judge the demonstrations and report back to the society with their recommendations for the medal." Hunching over the table, Ben ran a hand over his hair. "To be frank, I'm uneasy about the entire affair."

"If it makes you feel any better, I heard that the society came away less than impressed from a consortium in Yorkshire a week ago. That should help narrow the field."

"It isn't the competition that worries me." Ben worked his fingers into the knot of his neckcloth. "That I might inadvertently blow up Alistair's elegant ballroom is my fear."

Wry humor twinkled in Errol's faded gray eyes. "Explosions are Simon's area of expertise."

Mrs. Walsh stepped out onto the terrace and placed a tray of refreshments on the table. "Shall I remain to serve, sir?"

"No, I'll see to it." As the housekeeper reached the threshold, Simon called out, "Mrs. Walsh, has Mr. Ivers come down from the laboratory yet?"

Her nose wrinkled. "I have seen no trace of him, my lord."

She stepped back inside, and Simon lifted the teapot. "Ben, if it's a dependable power source you need for your demonstration at Windgate, I'll do my best to provide one. I've come a long way with my generator, especially since the arrival of my assistant. He has proved surprisingly helpful with my calculations." He chuckled. "The whelp even had the audacity to catch me in an error."

He passed round the teacups, taking care to help Errol lower his safely to the tabletop. But when Errol sat brood-

ing into the rising steam, worry for the man nudged Simon
once again. After exchanging a sympathetic look with Ben,
Simon leaned over and placed his hand on Errol's delicate,
too-thin wrist.

"What is it, old friend?"

"Colin," the elderly man succinctly replied. "Or the lack
of him." He glanced up, meeting Simon's gaze with a stark
if silent plea. *I am old,* that look said, *old and infirm, and I
have suffered too many losses in my lifetime.* Aloud he said,
"I asked Colin to join us today, but he declined. He didn't
say that he wouldn't be welcome here, but I could see that
he thought it. Simon, how much longer?"

Simon shot a desperate glance at Ben, hoping for . . .
What? Perhaps confirmation that he still had every right to
be angry with his sister's clandestine lover, that he wasn't
being overly stubborn or unreasonable. Ben's reply came
in his utter lack of one as he pretended keen interest in
spooning sugar into his tea.

In truth, at times even Simon yearned to forget that
awful day, to put behind him Gwendolyn's tears, the sight
of her valise on the rumpled bedclothes, and Colin's deafening, guilty silence. . . .

He longed to have his friend back . . . have him *here,*
sharing afternoon refreshments and making plans. Many
times he considered simply forgiving, but then he'd remember that as a brother he could not always do what he
wished or what seemed easy. Being Gwendolyn's guardian
meant being honor-bound to do what was right.

With a sigh, Errol reached inside his coat and brought
out a silver flask that fit neatly in his palm. "Brandy?"

The mood immediately lightened. Ben eagerly set down
his spoon. The three exchanged grins and took turns mixing
a splash of spirits into their tea.

Errol capped the bottle and returned it to his breast
pocket. Mischief danced across his aging features. "I say,
Benjamin, what could be keeping this elusive assistant of
Simon's? You don't suppose Simon has frightened the poor
fellow from the premises or—"

"Or inadvertently zapped the lad with electricity and doesn't wish anyone to know!" Ben finished for him.

Simon nearly upset his tea. Earlier, he had feared precisely what Ben described. Realizing his beguiling assistant had been stunned but not injured by the energy flow had rendered Simon nearly giddy with relief.

He regarded the others through narrowed eyes. "Very funny, my friends, but you'll meet Mr. Ivers soon enough, and you shall find him in the best of health. I merely left him above to tidy up after our morning's work."

He aimed a glance skyward, to where his laboratory windows peered out over the rooftops of the main portion of the house. She was taking an inordinate amount of time with her task, and he felt a twinge of unease. Perhaps she *had* suffered ill effects from the current. Perhaps he should race back up and check. . . .

With a tug on his fob he pulled his watch from his waistcoat pocket, consulted the time, and frowned. "Didn't think our power surge caused that much chaos. What *could* be keeping him?"

The key turned. The lock clicked. Her hand wrapped tight around the latch, Ivy froze.

Behind her, the laboratory had been set to rights, and all the equipment tidied and covered. She had fulfilled her duties to Lord Harrow; now it was time to perform her duty to Victoria. She supposed she should have reversed the order of her priorities, for surely the queen's orders superseded Simon de Burgh's.

But even now, with no excuses left to detain her, she hesitated, wishing to prolong the moment of discovery as long as possible, hoping with all her heart that she found no incriminating evidence against Lord Harrow. What if she did? It was her inability to answer that simple question that prevented her from pressing the latch and opening the door. And yet . . .

Royal or no, I am foremost a woman in the eyes of my subjects, and an impropriety like this . . .

Victoria's own words set Ivy's hand in motion. These past days had taught her many hard lessons about what it was to be a woman in a man's world, with the barriers and sacrifices, and the constant battles that must be fought simply to maintain one's rightful place. For her young friend who needed her, then, as much as for queen and country, Ivy opened the armoire's doors.

As with her first view of Lord Harrow's laboratory, the contents did not at first register coherently in her mind. A stack of black shapes filled the back wall of the cupboard, metallic octagons that stood nearly as tall and wide as Ivy herself. Reaching in, she traced the ridges that traveled rather like the lines of a maze from the outer rim to a bowl-like center lined in tin.

Baffled, she counted the octagons—six in all. A gleam in the corner of the armoire caught her attention, and she discovered a tied bundle of poles and brackets, perhaps, she deduced, for fashioning some kind of stand.

A scraping sound behind her sent her whirling. Her breath lodging in her throat, she viewed the room through saucer-wide eyes. The door had not opened and nothing seemed to have moved. The scraping came again, making her jump and drawing her gaze to the floor.

A few feet away, an iron rod, which she must have missed when cleaning up, rolled toward her with a jerky motion as if pushed by an invisible finger. It moved twice more as she watched.

Stooping, she picked it up, only to have it fly from her palm into the armoire to adhere with a loud clatter to the first of the disks. She had to use all the strength in her fingers to dislodge it, and even then the attraction between the contents of the armoire and the rod fought against her efforts.

"Magnets," she murmured aloud. But these were no ordinary magnets, neither in size nor strength. Still, she could not see a need to lock them away, as if there could be some danger if anyone found them. What danger could there be in a magnet?

Gazing over her shoulder at the sheet-shrouded generator, she remembered what Lord Harrow had told her about his quest to find, through electromagnetism, a power source that would replace steam and the chemically charged voltaic cells. According to Michael Faraday's dynamo theory, a magnet set into motion produced an electrical field that, when made to interact with conductive coils, produced a continuous current.

But such large magnets . . . What could Lord Harrow be planning to power with his generator? And if, as he had indicated to her, he had not yet met with the success he craved, could he be seeking a more powerful source of magnetism, perhaps . . . from a hunk of meteorite stolen from the queen?

A knot formed in her stomach. Had she missed any potential hiding places? But Lord Harrow hadn't denied her access to any of the cupboards or cabinets, and she had seen inside them all. Only this armoire had been locked. She looked back inside, and suddenly saw the one thing that, in her amazement over the huge magnets, she had missed.

A pine box only slightly larger than a workman's tool chest lay in the back corner, half hidden behind the bundle of poles. Crouching, Ivy first moved the poles out of the way. Then she clamped a hand on either side of the cask and dragged it closer. When the hinged lid refused to open, she tried Lord Harrow's keys again. On the fourth try, the lock gave. She raised the lid and peered inside.

Like a slingshot, her heart slammed against her ribs, then catapulted into her throat. The lid slipped through her fingers and banged shut. A yelp escaped her, but as a true scream pushed against her lips, she forcefully swallowed it back.

Her hands, she discovered, lay balled in trembling fists against her thighs. She forced them to uncurl, to reach again for the box. As her fingertips made contact with the dull, yellowed wood, she clamped her teeth over her bottom lip.

*He's keeping her body somewhere in that manor of his.
They say he hopes one day to . . . resurrect her.*

She had not glimpsed a body inside that box, but . . . she
glared down at the closed lid as if her gaze could penetrate
solid matter. Had she seen correctly, or had her imagination played a beastly trick on her?

There was only one way to find out. Her shaking fingers
once more raised the lid.

Chapter 8

"Ah, I believe that's Mr. Ivers coming to join us." Using a hand to shade his eyes from the sun, Simon made out Ned's slim figure moving through the shadows in the library. "Gentlemen, you may judge for yourselves that no harm has befallen the lad at my hands."

But as his fellow scientists turned to peer through the doorway, Ned's feet tangled in an invisible web. She stumbled, caught herself, hovered on a precarious brink, and toppled like a felled tree to land with a thump on the Persian rug.

In an instant Simon was on his feet. When he reached her, Ned was already sitting up, blinking and looking dazedly about. She had fallen in an open area, thankfully missing the edge of the desk and the marble sofa table. Simon sank to one knee beside her, resisting the urge to wrap her in his arms.

"Are you quite all right?" For the sake of their audience, he smoothed away an anxious frown and produced a carefree grin. "Must be those dastardly boots again, eh?"

As she blinked him into focus, a look of shock pried her eyes wide. She dug her heels into the woven pile of the carpet and shimmied a good foot or two backward. Then she froze, staring back at him as if he pointed a gun to her heart.

"What on earth is the matter? Did you hit your head?"

Her breath came in gasps. Compressing her lips, she visibly fought for control. "M-Mrs. Walsh insisted you wished to see me."

"Insisted . . . ?" Simon stood and reached down to help her up. "I'd merely like you to meet two of my colleagues. They've been entertaining rather harebrained doubts about your chances of surviving your apprenticeship here."

Ned made no move to push to her feet, with or without his help.

Simon leaned over her. Dispensing with caution, he caught her chin in his palm and held it, even when her nervous flinch communicated her distress at his touch. The reaction yanked at his heartstrings more than he liked to acknowledge, but he filed his dismay and the reasons for it away for later. Turning her face from side to side, he examined the pallor of her skin. He noted that her pupils eclipsed the slightly lighter irises around them.

"I'm summoning a doctor from town," he said in a tone intended to brook no debate. "Obviously the electrical current has had an adverse effect on you."

"That isn't necessary." She had forgotten to use her false tenor, and her true tone rang out, light and musical, like the higher notes of a clarinet. Her eyebrows knit, and when she spoke again, her voice plunged an octave. "As you said, it's the boots. The fall left me bemused, but I am all right now."

As if to prove her claim, she pulled her chin from his grasp but at the same time gripped his wrist and maneuvered her feet beneath her. Once on her feet, she released him and tugged her coat into place.

Simon assessed her appearance. Clothing could be righted, but would Ben and Errol see past the superficial male trappings to Ned's adorable features and sweet mouth, and in a burst of understanding realize the truth?

She flinched again as Simon reached to straighten the knot of her neckcloth and flatten her lapels. Her short curls stood a bit on end. He smoothed them with his palm, an act that produced a stab of affection that quickly burgeoned into much, much more. He couldn't stop from wondering if her lips would taste as rich as honey, as satisfying as fine red wine. His eyes assured him they would; his mouth hungered to sample them.

His hands closed over her shoulders, the desire to kiss her raging through him like the charged winds of an electrical storm. He bestowed a manly shake instead and let her go. "Are you ready to meet two of my fellow Galileans?"

"Galileans, sir?" A spark of genuine interest ignited beneath her guardedness.

"Come, and we'll explain."

She relaxed considerably as she took a seat outside on the terrace, even smiling at an anecdote from Errol, an observation from Ben. They in turn seemed to accept her as young Mr. Ivers in the same easy manner as had her dons and fellow students at Cambridge. They saw her as their expectations dictated, and if they found the "lad" a touch too skinny or a bit on the effeminate side, this was by no means unusual enough to raise the suspicions of either man.

As soon as they left, Ned became as skittish as a baby rabbit. She retired to her bedchamber on the pretext of catching up on her studies. Simon waited for her in the garden before supper, but she failed to join him for their evening stroll.

"A headache, sir," was her clipped explanation when she entered the dining room an hour later. "I trust you understand."

"You must have hit your head when you fell. Let me know if the pain becomes worse."

"Yes, sir."

Silence.

What little she ate, she ate quickly, their conversation reduced to his intermittent comments and her terse replies. At an utter loss to explain this abrupt change in her behavior, Simon fell to reviewing his every action and word spoken in his beguiling assistant's presence.

Had he insulted her, offended her in any way? To be sure, there had been numerous occasions when he'd have liked nothing more than to have his way with her, affront her maidenly honor in the most shameless terms imaginable. But no ... there had been nothing, no lapse on his part.

Yet.

The clock in the gallery stuck midnight, the chimes echoing in the corridor outside Ivy's room. Her bed untouched, she sat fully awake in an upholstered chair set beneath her window, the only light that of the single candle on the side table. Ragged clouds tore across the sky, obliterating the stars and shredding the moon. Her arms cradled the one item she had risked taking from home, secreted inside the padded lining of one of her trunks.

Years ago, Laurel had made the little doll out of old stockings, stuffing the body and limbs with cotton, sewing on buttons for eyes and yarn for hair, and fashioning a dress from a patchwork of fabric scraps. Miss Matilda had grown shabby with time, and stained from countless kisses and tears. But Ivy loved her.

She hugged her now tight to her breast and thought of home, picturing each of her sisters, and even dearest, departed Uncle Edward and the vague, faceless memories of her parents, because that was what she did when she was frightened.

The clock's last notes dissipated. The house fell silent, as hushed as a thief moving through the shadows, or a contagion lurking in a mudflat. It was a silence that made Ivy afraid to move or even breathe, or consider what she had seen in Lord Harrow's laboratory. Even Miss Matilda could not banish those images.

Propping the doll carefully against the arm of the chair, Ivy fled the room for the airy relief of the balcony. A cold wind, laden with the scents of September leaves, whipped her short curls into tangles. Its bracing slap tingled against her cheeks and tugged the edges of her dressing gown. Her *man's* dressing gown, with her equally masculine nightshirt beneath.

She had thought coming here in disguise would both free her and shield her from all risk to her person, but she discovered that her masquerade only stripped her of her most powerful defense: herself.

The Ivy who had survived a fire, overcome her parents' deaths, and, more recently, established a degree of independence in her own home and with her own London business simply didn't exist in Cambridge. Ned Ivers could not seek help from Ivy Sutherland or draw upon any of her life's experiences. Ned, the student and apprentice, was alone, and he had not the slightest inkling of how to proceed.

She wished to be Ivy again, to feel Ivy's strength moving through her, bolstering her. She wished to regain her feminine power, her confidence of knowing who she was and all she was capable of achieving.

She wished to be a woman again.

Throwing off Ned's dressing gown, she went to the balcony's edge and leaned out over the rail. The breeze swept beneath her nightshirt, lifting the hem to her knees. Goose bumps swathed her legs, but she didn't care, didn't try to pull the gown lower. There was no one to see her, no movement on the darkened garden paths but for the blowing foliage.

The same madcap wind whipped the clouds aside and freed the moon, a luminous disk as bright as Lord Harrow's magnets were black. Ivy raised her face as if the silver rays could warm her and bring a summer glow to her cheeks, as if it could surround her with a protective force that no evil could penetrate.

She raised her arms to the moon, then lowered them and smoothed her hands down her torso. Her breasts, bound by day to appear nonexistent, luxuriated in their lack of restraint. How liberating to free them, to feel the cool air against them. A thought crept into her mind, one that shocked her . . . and sent her gaze skimming over the house. All the windows but hers were dark. It was late; no one would be up. No one would see.

Quickly she untied the lacings of her nightshirt and drew the linen garment down past her shoulders to her waist. The night ran its chilling caress over her breasts, plucking at her nipples until they stood erect. Shivering only slightly, she offered a shaky smile to the radiant moon and felt the essence of her female self reawakening inside her.

A shift in the wind brought a surge of unexpected warmth. It wrapped around her, reached inside her. Suddenly it wasn't the wind tantalizing her skin, her womanly parts. It was Lord Harrow, or her imagined ideal of him—his strong arms, his large hands, his moist lips trailing down her breasts to tease her nipples. The notion sent hot shivers raining through her, tremors edged in yearning and fear, a forbidden desire as raw as any molten element produced in his laboratory.

What she had seen today all but proved that he was dangerous, deranged. Yet she longed for him with an ache that tightened her breasts and tugged at the lowest regions of her belly. In that instant, if he had stepped out onto the balcony behind her, Ivy would have thrown caution to the wild thrust of the winds and gladly offered herself to him.

Lucky for her he did not step out of the shadows. But as she pulled her nightshirt into place, scooped up her dressing gown, and hurried back inside, his image followed in her mind's eye, and his pale gaze held her trapped as she hugged Miss Matilda and tried in vain to fall to sleep.

Simon half knelt on the embrasure of the laboratory's southward window, his fingers pressing against the diamond panes, the rest of him rendered immobile by the scene taking place far below. Ned had stolen outside moments ago and now shed her dressing gown, letting it fall to the stones at her feet.

In the moonlight, her nightshirt glowed like mist as she drifted to the rail. The wind plastered the garment to her body, displaying curves Simon had only imagined until now. Helpless to resist the sight, he stared as she raised her face to the moon, her lovely curls tossing, the arch of her neck and spine revealing enticing, tormenting secrets about the shape and size of her breasts.

A tug at her nightshirt propelled him closer to the glass.

What was she doing? Suddenly she turned and looked up. Through the dark distance their gazes met; she looked right at him. Damning his indiscretion, Simon drew back.

The right thing would have been to walk away, but her next actions suggested that perhaps she hadn't seen him after all. When he thought about it, how could she have? With the moon so bright, he hadn't bothered to light a candle. The laboratory lay in shadow while soft candle glow from inside her room bathed the balcony . . . and Ned's slender, linen-clad form.

Except . . . Dear God. His breath hitched. She had slipped her arms from the sleeves and shoved the nightshirt to her waist. Simon's throat closed around an acute throbbing while flame rippled from his heart to his loins.

His body reacted even before his mind formed the question: if he held her naked in his arms, would he find her as soft and smooth as she looked right now, gilded and perfect in the moonlight?

He would likely never know. Pulling away from the window, he knelt against the embrasure. She loathed him. Or feared him. He didn't know which. But after today he knew of a certainty that she held him in low regard. He should be glad, relieved. To lust for her physically was one thing. But to love again . . .

Losing Aurelia had ripped him apart. He'd gone half mad, truly earning the nickname whispered by the students when they thought he couldn't hear.

No. *God, no.* It was far too soon to lose his heart to another.

He had one choice, then, one way to stop the madness from overtaking him as it had when Aurelia died. Reaching a decision, he braved a final glance out the window, seeking one more memory of the audacious girl named Ned, only to see that he was too late. She had retrieved her dressing gown and returned to her room, the only evidence that she had been there at all the lingering ache beneath his breastbone.

After a sleepless night, he rose and breakfasted early.

When he'd finished his coffee and grown tired of pushing his eggs around on his plate, he asked Mrs. Walsh to send Ned out to the gardens the moment he came downstairs.

"He's a strange one, that Mr. Ivers," the woman muttered beneath her breath as if not intending Simon to overhear but quite satisfied that he did.

He trudged the garden paths half blindly, bombarded with the many reminders of Aurelia's lasting influence on Harrowood. *This* arbor she had designed, and *this* statue she had purchased during their honeymoon in Paris, and *this* and *this* and *this* had all been introduced to the estate by her hands, her orders. For a brief, precious time, she had turned a gloomy relic into a cheerful haven.

This morning, through a softly veiling mist, he saw the signs of neglect, of Harrowood declining back into joylessness. It wasn't for lack of funds, but lack of spirit. He simply hadn't found the heart to love the place as she had, now that she was no longer part of it.

And yet, as he beheld the autumn blooms and the streaming jets of the fountain, he realized something vital had changed. He had begun to see Harrowood from a new perspective, one that grabbed him in a choke hold of regret.

Ned may not have contributed to the gardens or rearranged the house, but in a few short days she had left her indelible mark here. She would soon leave, but Simon entertained no doubts that he would continue to see her lovely face, framed in those unruly curls of hers, everywhere he turned. Around every corner, in every room and corridor, but most especially in his laboratory, her image would continue to haunt him. Her funny, clumsy falls, her determined, defiant little expressions, her unbridled enthusiasm with each new discovery . . .

Ah, how would he return to his equipment and experiments alone? What joy would he find there without her?

Reaching out, he stroked the dusky crimson blossom of a Dark Lady rose, one of Aurelia's favorites. Ned liked roses, too. She had mentioned that her uncle had cultivated a rose garden. Stepping closer, he attempted to pluck the flower from where the stem branched from the main stalk. A sharp pain pricked his thumb, and a drop of blood spattered to the ground.

At the same moment, a scream ripped through the morning's muffled quiet. Simon spun about in the direction from which it had come. A second scream sent him running toward the house.

Her heart pounding, Ivy made her way down the wide, curving garden steps. Why had Lord Harrow sent for her?

Had he discovered evidence of her incursion into his locked armoire? Was she about to be tossed out of Harrowood on her ear? Since discovering the shocking contents of that innocent-looking cask, she had more than once contemplated the wisdom of removing herself as far away from Harrowood as possible. But then she might never locate Lady Gwendolyn or recover Victoria's stone. No, she must stay, must complete her mission.

Yet in truth, her fear of Lord Harrow's grisly experiments posed far less of a dilemma than fear of her growing feelings for him, a man with perhaps a tenuous hold on his sanity. Today, then, assuming he did not throw her out, she must gain command of those fears—and feelings—and behave with a modicum of normalcy.

Or he surely would send her packing.

At the bottom of the steps, she continued down the sloping lawn to the half wall that marked the entrance to the upper tea garden. As she came through the arbor and around the box hedge, a hunched figure rounded on her, a pair of long, lethal shears aimed in her direction.

Ivy stumbled backward. The figure shuffled closer, emerging from the shadow of the hedges. Daylight tumbled across his distorted features: bulging eyes, misshapen cheeks, and a grotesque slash of a mouth. As he raised his weapon, his body listed at a precarious angle, his left shoulder a raised and twisted knot.

Ivy fell back into the hedge. Could this creature be the

result of Lord Harrow's experiments? Even as common sense rejected the possibility, the creature moved closer. Ivy cried out and thrashed to break free of the foliage.

The branches trapped her fast. The shears swung. Bracing for the slice of the blades through her flesh, she let out a scream that echoed through the gardens and against the house. A pair of iron bands closed around her arms and yanked her from the hedge.

"Ned! Ned! Calm down." Lord Harrow spun her in his arms and gripped her shoulders. "There's nothing wrong. Nothing to fear."

"But . . ." She raised a shaking hand to point behind her. Did he not see the creature? "That . . . man."

"Cecil. My head groundskeeper and master gardener, who has just returned from a visit with his family." Lord Harrow's lips hardened in anger. He gave her shoulders a shake, a rebuke that filled her with instant shame. "I believe you owe him an apology."

He physically turned her to face the servant. The tips of the shears were stuck in the dirt now, and the man leaned his misshapen body with a hand propped on the handles.

Her cheeks flaming, Ivy struggled to find her voice. "I am so terribly sorry. I hadn't realized you were there and . . . those shears are rather frightful. . . ."

"He was trimming the hedge," Lord Harrow ground out behind her.

"Never mind, young sir." Disturbing though his appearance was, Cecil's voice proved as soothing as a Sunday hymn. "Mine's a countenance even a mother'd be hardpressed to love, though mine did her best. No harm done."

His forbearance brought tears to Ivy's eyes; she hastened to blink them away. "Thank you. I'm so sorry. A wretched misunderstanding. I promise from now on we shall be friends."

"Very good, sir." A conspiratorial gleam lit Cecil's protruding eyes. "And we'll both be remembering that beneath every surface lies a world to be discovered." With a wink, he looked past her to Lord Harrow. "I'll be tending to the bulbs now, my lord. Must get them out and stored before the first frost."

"Yes, thank you, Cecil."

Ivy watched the man waddle off, her nape tingling with a sense that he had seen clear through her disguise to the truth. Yet he hadn't given her away. Had she found an unlikely ally? She turned back to Lord Harrow. "I'm very sorry—"

"Do you realize your ridiculous behavior might have lost me the most brilliant gardener in perhaps all of East Anglia? He is no monster, Ned."

"I realize that, sir."

"Do you? Cecil is no lowly servant, either. He hails from gentry, but he chooses to occupy this position because society will offer him no other place."

He bore down on her as he spoke, his forceful stride sending her back several steps. "He accepted my apology. What more can I do?"

"You might explain what happened yesterday to turn my gifted assistant into a blithering simpleton capable of passing judgment on my own wife's cousin based solely on appearances."

Stiffening, Ivy gasped. "Your wife . . ."

"Yes, Cecil is a distant cousin of the Quincys. But that is beside the point."

"Does he know . . . ?" she whispered. Her next words spilled out in a torrent. "Does he know what you've done to her? What you've done *with* her?"

Lord Harrow's features darkened ominously. "What the devil are you talking about? Have you been listening to rumors? Are you that much of a blasted fool?"

Fear and revulsion lashed through her; she shook her head in denial. "I didn't need to. I've seen the evidence. Dear God in heaven—"

Lord Harrow pounced, seizing the front of her coat in his fist. "Are you speaking of the armoire? Did you open it?"

"I did. . . . I did and I saw." Trying to pull from his grasp, Ivy cried out.

Lord Harrow raised his voice to be heard. "You little fool, you don't know what you saw. I'd have shown you myself when I thought you were ready."

Ivy tugged in vain against his hold. "You promised my conscience would not be compromised."

"And it has not been, not by me. But you . . . Yesterday I trusted you with my keys, with full access to my life's work. And you could not wait to betray that trust. Why, Ned?" His voice dropped to a ragged whisper. "Damn you, *why*?"

Ivy cried out again as Lord Harrow's grip on her coat tightened. Suddenly he gave a yank that brought her colliding with his chest. The garden blurred. His arms went around her and his mouth descended on hers, sending shock waves of astonishment blasting through her. But contrary to his palpable anger and the steely force running through his limbs, his lips were warm and soft, and took hers with a gentle insistence that fired her blood and turned her knees to melted wax.

His arms held her in place while his lips nuzzled hers open and his tongue swept her mouth. A multitude of sensations flooded her at once. The faint richness of coffee, the sharpness of the starch in his shirt, the abrasion of the morning stubble across his chin . . . the solid demand of his body against her own.

Heaven help her, she relished all of it, his taste, his scent, the feel of him. Caught in a surging storm, Ivy hung on and let herself be kissed, losing herself in swirling heat and the aching desire that had been mounting inside her since she first set eyes on the man.

And then, as quickly as the kiss had begun, Lord Harrow's mouth hardened and he broke away. Straightening, he towered above her and took her chin in his hand. She looked dazedly up at him, at the emotions storming in his eyes. Then the full shock of what had happened struck her as if with a physical blow.

Lord Harrow released her. Her trembling hand went to

her lips, her tousled hair, back to her lips. They were hot to the touch, moist, and swollen. She shut her eyes. "You know."

"Of course I know." She opened her eyes to see a vein pulsing against his temple, a muscle throbbing angrily in his cheek. Then his features softened in a way that discomfited her more than his ire. A brush of his fingertips along the line of her jaw sparked her skin. "I realized it almost from the first. Since that day when I met you here in the garden, I knew."

"But . . . why didn't you say anything?"

His hands convulsed into fists, then relaxed. "I thought you deserved a chance to prove yourself. To have the opportunity denied you because of your sex. And because . . ." Nostrils flaring, he gazed out over the gardens, his profile stony against the misty foliage. "Because you have talent. Vision." He turned back to her, his eyes fierce. "Come with me."

At a brisk pace he led her into the house, up the curving tower stairs. He walked so quickly Ivy had to trot to keep up. By the time they reached the laboratory, she was rendered breathless.

Her trepidation about his intentions made her dizzy. The lingering heat of his kiss left her giddy and baffled, hungering for more, and fearful of what might happen if he reached for her again. More than once, she considered turning back, retreating to her bedchamber, and packing her belongings.

But he had been correct. She *had* betrayed his trust. The truth of it tore at her, rending her loyalties in two. Victoria . . . Lord Harrow. She saw no means of being faithful to both. Did she *wish* to keep faith with both?

She crossed the threshold and stopped, her anxiety rising as Lord Harrow headed straight for the armoire, then pivoted. "Come here, Ned."

She shook her head.

His pale eyes traveled over her. Then he retraced his steps, clamped a hand around her wrist, and forced her to walk or be dragged. In front of the armoire, he plunged his free hand into his coat pocket and pulled out his keys.

"Please, this isn't necessary," she insisted. "What you do is none of my business. I should never have opened these doors. . . ."

"Hush. I know why you snooped. It's because you are like me. Your curiosity is insatiable, and your patience severely limited."

She wanted to protest that he was wrong, that her curiosity had been more than sated and if she didn't witness another marvel of science for the rest of her life, it would be too soon. Fear kept her lips clamped as, with one hand, Lord Harrow unlocked the doors and threw them wide. His other fist still firm around her wrist, he sank to his knees and drew her down beside him.

His determined gaze met hers. "If I release you, will you stay put?"

Gruesome images ran rampant through her mind. She hesitated, and then gave her pledge with a shaking nod.

With a doubtful expression he opened his fingers. Then he reached inside to drag the dreaded box to the front of the armoire. In another moment he'd unlocked and raised the lid. Ivy shut her eyes.

Chapter 9

"Open your eyes." When Ned trembled at the curt order, Simon made an effort to smooth the anger from his voice. "Please open your eyes, Ned. You won't understand until you see the truth of what lies in this box."

Her features were pinched, her breathing labored. Her eyelashes fluttered open. As if gathering her courage to look upon the devil himself, she angled a fearful gaze at the box.

"Now, then." Simon reached inside and lifted the first item. The liquid inside the jar sloshed; the contents undulated.

Ivy's hand went to her throat. Her color drained; she looked close to being ill. Necessity pushed Simon on.

"Do you know what this is?"

Her answer could barely be heard. "A heart. *Her* heart." Horror blossomed on her face, turning fear to disgust. "How could you?"

"I was asked to. Begged to." Her glaring disbelief fueled his frustration. "You *have* been listening to rumors. Do you believe I'd truly carve open my deceased wife?" He didn't wait for an answer. "Not long before she died, a colleague of mine, Nelson Evans, passed away, a victim of his own failing heart. This heart. In his final years, he had devoted his experimentation to discovering a means of regenerating a dying heart, and of restarting one that has stopped.

On his deathbed, he begged me to continue his research, and to that end, he bequeathed me his own heart."

"Oh!" The transformation in Ned's expression was akin to the clearing away of thunderheads. She peered into the jar, at the heart with its attached skein of wires and electrodes. "And have you found a means of restarting it?"

He sighed and shook his head. "I am afraid we are still a long way away from such a miracle. But I am convinced that electricity is the key. Luigi Galvani proved with his frog experiments that electrical impulses in the nervous system power the body's muscles. Well, the heart is a muscle, too, and in theory an electrical current should stimulate a beat."

"Your generator?" She twisted around. With a glance over his shoulder, Simon regarded his invention, draped in sheets.

"No, that one is much too powerful. Originally, I did experiment with different-sized generators in the hopes of ascertaining the correct voltage needed to achieve Nelson's dream. But this particular generator is intended for another purpose entirely. Something I stumbled upon accidentally."

Her eager look invited further explanation.

"Not yet, my Ned. We've still other matters to attend to." He gestured at the box, at what lay inside. "Go on. Touch it. Or do you believe the second item to have been harvested from my wife as well?"

Trepidation tumbled back across her features. "I'd prefer not to lay a finger on *that*."

"Not lay your finger on my *artificial* fingers?"

"Artificial?"

"A wax and rubber amalgam bonded to linen and stretched over a skeletal structure composed of wires, rods, and ball-and-socket hinges. *Et voilà*, one has a hand. Remarkably lifelike, no?" He held it out to her. "Go on. Hold it."

Cradling the appendage in the crook of her arm, she used her forefinger to swing the artificial fingers up and down. "Remarkable does not begin to describe it. I never dreamed it could be anything but real. I wondered how you kept it so perfectly preserved."

He said nothing as she examined the web of wiring and electrodes that entered through the wrist and wound around the metallic skeleton of each finger.

"Does it work?" Excitement bubbled in her voice.

"Depends on your definition of *work*. I devised this purely as a model to help me understand how the nervous system conveys electrical impulses from the brain to the rest of the body, to be interpreted in terms of voluntary movement."

She glanced up at him, eyes fever bright. "You are a genius."

He smiled. "No. What I am is willing to toss aside conventional thought in the pursuit of *what if*. At the time I constructed this hand, I was also desperate."

"I don't understand."

He put the hand, along with Nelson's heart, back inside the box. Then he stood and helped Ned up. "Do you wish to know the truth about my wife?"

She placed her hand in his and kept it there all the way down the spiral stairs to the first-floor gallery. Together they walked past several generations of de Burghs, all staring down at them from their canvas domains. Simon marveled at his actions while the reasons for them continued to elude him. Why speak of Aurelia? Why open himself up to the pain?

He knew only that he desperately wanted Ned to understand about his past. About *him*, the Mad Marquess of Harrow. Once that was done, it would be Ned's turn to reveal some truths.

In the corner of the gallery just beyond the door of his own suite, he stopped. As breathtaking as ever, Aurelia smiled down at him, loving, patient, ever tolerant of his foibles. "This is her. My wife. Aurelia."

The unfamiliar act of speaking her name aloud produced a pain in his chest.

Her lips compressed, Ned studied the portrait. "She was . . ."

"Buxom, yes."

"I was going to say beautiful."

"Yes. She was beautiful. Can you see what else?"

Ned took another step closer. "I detect a keen intelligence in her eyes."

"Yes, if anyone was brilliant, she certainly was. But that isn't what I meant. Do you see the chair she is sitting in?"

Ned shifted her gaze to the wood and brocade seat back framing Aurelia's shoulders. She gave a slight shrug.

"If you look closely, you can just make out the shadow of a handle on the right side." He pointed. "Just there."

"Oh . . . a wheelchair?"

His throat tight, Simon nodded. "A disease of the nervous system had slowly robbed her muscles of strength. It began before we were married."

Ned turned to him, her eyes grown large with comprehension, and with sympathy, too. Those Simon could accept. He released a breath of relief when no trace of pity hovered in Ned's expression.

"How . . . ?"

"How did she die?"

Ned nodded.

"An accident. Aurelia spent much of her time in the conservatory, among her plants. There is a door there leading down to a cellar, where the seeds and fertilizers were kept. One day, the servant assisting her left the door open. Aurelia happened to back up too far, and her chair went over the threshold. She fell twenty steps to a stone floor."

"Oh! I'm so sorry." Ned's hand came down featherlight on his coat sleeve. His first instinct was to shake it off, but he didn't. He suffered her touch, then found comfort in it, then felt the pain inside him ease, if only a fraction. "What happened to the servant? Did you . . ."

"Sack her? No. I found a place for her on another estate." He recalled how difficult that decision had been, how he'd had to dig deep inside himself for the strength not to lash out and punish the brokenhearted girl. "It was what Aurelia would have wanted."

Placing his hand over Ned's, he drew her to a nearby window that faced the lawns beyond the west wing of the house. Beneath the wide stretch of a maple gilded by the autumn chill, a stone wall encircled a small plot of graves. "She is down there, with my ancestors. More recent de Burghs have been buried at Holy Trinity in the city, but I wanted her here, where she would be close."

"Why don't you tell people this?" she asked softly.

"You mean lend dignity to the rumors of the Mad Marquess by acknowledging them?" He shook his head. Warm sunlight poured through the windowpanes, heating the alcove in which they stood. "The people who matter know the truth."

The implications of that statement zinged through him. Ned knew the truth. By Simon's own logic, that meant that she mattered. He could not deny that he had feelings for her, intense ones. But he could deny, *did* deny, welcoming those feelings. He could and *would* deny allowing those feelings the opportunity to tear his life apart all over again.

He had his work. He had his memories. That would suffice.

Her hand still rested on his arm, and her fingers tightened around his sleeve. As if she had read his thoughts, she asked in a whisper, "Now what?"

The question traveled to his core to interweave with the loss and sorrow that had made him the man he had become. He brought her hand to his lips and kissed it, letting it linger there before he lowered it to her side and released it. "Now, my Ned, you must leave Harrowood forever."

His words filled Ivy with more dread than that brought on by his preserved heart or artificial hand. She could think of only one response to that horror.

She dug in her bootheels. "No."

"Ned, you must listen to reason."

"Stop calling me Ned. My name is Ivy." Panic rose up. She was about to fail in her mission for Victoria, but more than that, infinitely more, she couldn't bear losing all she had achieved this past week working at Lord Harrow's side.

She couldn't bear losing *him.* "You cannot simply throw me out."

His features implacable, Simon gazed at some point beyond her shoulder. "I am not throwing you out. I'll arrange transportation for you to go anywhere you wish. Even back to Cambridge if you like."

"I wish to stay here."

"You cannot."

"Why not? What has changed?" An invisible fist clenched her heart. "Am I not still the same person you believed in? Have I lost my talent? My vision?"

"You don't understand. You were Ned then—"

"I wasn't. You *knew* I wasn't, yet you were willing to pretend."

"That is correct. As long as we were both pretending and keeping that barrier between us, you could stay. But we aren't pretending anymore, Ned. Ivy." He ran his fingers through his hair. "Have you any idea what your presence here could mean for both our futures?"

"I am willing to risk it."

"I am not. Not for you, not for myself, either."

"Please . . . I can't give this up. Have you any notion what this past week has meant to me?"

He sighed, a sound full of regret. "I believe I do. It is the very reason I allowed you to remain."

"Then what difference does the truth make?" Desperation nearly made her reach for him. Only pride—pride acquired through the past week's accomplishments— prevented her from clutching his arm and begging to stay. "If we could pretend before, why not now?"

"Because everything changed when we kissed." Turning his back to her, he leaned his hands on the windowsill. "Everything."

He was right, for the first touch of his lips had awakened

something new and vital inside her, a need that even now made her body ache to feel him, hold him. But she refused to accept that the dawning of one kind of passion must trigger the death of another, the passion of her ambitions. If that was what it meant to be female, then she would remain Ned forever.

"I swear to you, it will not happen again."

His laughter cut in its harshness. Shoving away from the window, he rounded on her, caught her in his arms, and crushed her to his chest. "It will, Ned. By God, it will."

He took her mouth with greed, and without mercy proved her a liar. As their lips meshed and their tongues entwined, she found herself wishing the kiss would never end, that it would happen again . . . and again. Within the fire and spark of that kiss, she silently cursed the desire that could be neither ignored nor prevented. She cursed herself for falling prey to it. She cursed *him* for simultaneously making her dreams come true and dashing them, and for being the kind of man, the *only* kind, who could ever claim her heart.

This time it was she who ended the kiss, breaking away with a feral whimper. In the same instant, footsteps thudded up the main staircase. Ivy blinked back tears and straightened her coat. His features taut, Lord Harrow strode past her and met Mrs. Walsh at the top of the stairs.

"Your solicitor is here, my lord. It seems he needs your signature on some legal documents."

"Thank you. Tell him I'll be down straightaway." When the woman had gone, Simon returned to Ivy, waiting near the window. "Forgive me, Ned. It cannot be helped. You must be ready to leave on the morrow."

"My name is Ivy," she murmured to his retreating back. Lower, she added, "And I've no intention of leaving, not just yet."

That evening, Lord Harrow went into town with his solicitor. Ivy didn't learn this from him, for he left without a word. As the dusk shadows lengthened, she wandered to the gardens out of habit, knowing full well there would be no evening stroll to discuss the day's events. Even so, she gathered the peace of the gardens around her like a fortifying shield as she considered how to proceed.

With her time here growing short, the two greatest dilemmas facing her were the prospect of failing to gain even the smallest clue about Lady Gwendolyn's whereabouts, and whether she should take Lord Harrow into her confidence.

Doing so seemed a betrayal of Victoria, who had insisted that *no one* must know about the gift from her cousin. Ivy had made her pledge. Did she have the right to reinterpret her promise, or qualify it with even the most minor modifications? Victoria had said no one, and surely that meant not a single living being on the planet. Ivy wouldn't simply be disappointing her friend; she would be committing treason against her queen.

Yet not confiding in Lord Harrow about his sister's actions seemed a betrayal to him, and treason against Ivy's own heart. Perching on the marble edge of the fountain and propping up a booted foot, she stared up at the angel as if her answers might flow from the glittering streams of water.

"I saw you walking out, Master Ned, and thought you should know that Lord Harrow can't be meeting you this evening."

As Cecil's distorted figure approached, Ivy found nothing shocking in his appearance. In fact, her suspicion that he had guessed her secret but didn't hold it against her made it easy to summon a smile for the man.

He removed his cap with a respectful nod that convinced Ivy he knew the truth of her gender. "He's abroad on business and shan't be back till late."

"Thank you, Cecil, but I wasn't expecting him. Not this time," she added sadly. She couldn't help concluding that Lord Harrow's business might just as easily have been handled from home, but that he had left Harrowood to avoid her. Still, news of his prolonged absence tonight offered an unexpected opportunity.

"It's good he's taken on an assistant. No one should be alone as much as the master is." The groundskeeper tipped his head again and started to walk away.

"I'm afraid I won't be here much longer," Ivy said. "Lord Harrow isn't very pleased with me anymore."

Cecil paused. "Oh, he's pleased, young sir. Too pleased, and therein lies the problem." Setting his cap back on his head, he gave a two-fingered salute.

A lump formed in Ivy's throat as she watched him go. Dear Cecil. Would he treat her so kindly if he knew what she was about to do? She set aside her guilt for a later time and hopped down off the fountain.

"Welcome home, my lord." The footman who had opened the door helped Simon off with his cloak. He draped the garment over an arm and held out his hands to receive Simon's gloves and top hat.

"Thank you, Daniel. That will be all tonight."

"Very good, my lord."

Wearily Simon started up the staircase. He had considered not returning home tonight and staying in town instead, with perhaps Ben or Errol. In fact, he had considered not returning at all until Ned had left.

Because he feared that if he saw her again, he might never let her go.

But staying away had seemed cowardly, not to mention callous. It might have been easy to simply blame her for her deception and believe she got what she deserved. But the truth was he didn't blame her. Had there been some law preventing him from pursuing his life's passion, he would have sought any means of circumventing it.

If he could only have remained blind to the truth, or gone on pretending. If only he hadn't kissed her.

Gripping the banister, he paused to laugh at the folly of all three notions. How could any man gaze upon those pert features and not see her beauty or her beguiling sensuality? As for pretending, he had ordered her to the gardens this morning intending to gently dismiss her from his service, not grope her, kiss her, and drive himself half insane with the press of her body against his and the image of her naked, moonlit breasts fresh in his mind.

What had happened merely proved they could not work together, could not remain in close quarters without falling prey to temptation. But if nothing else, he owed her a debt of gratitude for this past week. Her zeal was infectious, and for the first time in years he'd felt young and alive and—Galileo's teeth—idealistic. And he owed her a final acknowledgment of her talents. She must never for an instant believe she had disappointed him as an assistant.

Or as a woman.

The unbidden thought startled him and threw off his stride as he made his way along the gallery to his rooms. Sentiments like that wouldn't do, not if he was going to bid her good-bye in the morning. Taking the burning candle from the sconce beside his door, he held it out in front of him to light his way.

He needn't have bothered.

Candle glow from beyond his sitting room brought him to an immediate halt. Silently he eased the door closed behind him and blew out his candle. A few feet away, the hearth gaped dark and empty. The one in his bedchamber would as well, for he never ordered his fires lit at night until mid-November at the earliest.

There was no reason for a servant to be in his rooms at such an hour. All but Daniel and Mrs. Walsh would have been abed long ago. Equally unlikely was the prospect of an intruder having gained entrance to the house. That left . . .

He strode through to the bedchamber and followed the candle's flickering beacon into his dressing room. "Ned. What in Lucifer's name are you doing?"

In waistcoat and shirtsleeves, her hands buried in the open drawer that held his silk handkerchiefs, she froze. For several seconds they regarded each other in silence, she

pop-eyed and scarlet, he pulsing with anger and sheer be-
fuddlement. The candle went on glimmering, oblivious to
the growing storm.

He dragged a breath in through his teeth and tried not to
focus on her trembling lips, or remember their sweet taste.
This was the second time today he'd caught her snooping,
and while the first might have been excused as scientific
curiosity, this time was nothing short of a shameless violation of his privacy.

A scowl fixed in place, he crossed the room, seized her
wrist, and yanked her arm high. "Lose track of time, did
you, Ned? Didn't expect me home so soon?"

Her gaze darted to the little clock he kept beside his
shaving stand. Her brow puckered. She stared mutely back
up at him.

"First the armoire, now my private rooms." His temple
throbbed as an unsettling thought occurred to him, one
with the power to wring the joy from the past week. Still
in possession of her delicate wrist, he dragged her closer
to the light to better see her face. "Did you seek the apprenticeship in order to steal my secrets and duplicate my
work?"

"No! Goodness, no." Her head shook convulsively from
side to side. "I'd never steal from you."

The denial ignited his fury. "Who sent you?" he shouted.
"Good God, was it Colin Ashworth?"

Despite Colin's past transgressions, Simon couldn't
quite believe the charge even as he uttered it. Shrinking in
evident fear, Ned backed away the full length of her arm, as
far as she could go while he continued to possess her wrist.
"It wasn't Lord Drayton, or any member of your Galileo
Club."

The significance of her reply wasn't lost on him. "Then
someone *did* send you. You had best reveal his name, before I have you tossed in the local jail."

She remained mute, obviously regretting her disclosure
and unwilling to repeat her mistake. But where he expected tears, he was surprised to witness defiance in the set

of her lips, rebellion in the arch of her eyebrows. "Shouting, threats, brute force . . . Is this how you typically treat women?"

She couldn't have landed a more sobering blow than if she'd physically struck him with her fist. He immediately released her and backed away. "No. Blazing hell, no. I'm no blackguard, but you, young lady, are a thief, or—"

"I am no such thing, either." She pushed her sleeve back to massage her wrist, and despite his being the victim here, he experienced a wave of chagrin at the welt his grip had left on her skin. His discomfiture increased when she pursed her lips, looking very much like a schoolmarm chastising an unruly student. "Has it not occurred to you that a woman who risks donning trousers must have an urgent reason for doing so? Have you never considered that reason?"

"I thought I understood. By God, I risked my own reputation along with yours because I believed I understood the passion that brought you here." His anger surged again. She thought to turn this around on him, but the only crime he'd committed was indulging her whim.

No, that wasn't all. He was guilty of not wanting her to leave, guilty of falling prey to his own weakness when it came to this woman. It was that weakness that sent him to her now, that prompted him to take her by the shoulders and pull her closer. Their gazes met, their lips nearly so. As her breath feathered across his cheek, his indignation cooled and his desire heated by several degrees.

"For science, Ned." His arms went around her, anchoring her in place. "That is why I believed you took such a risk. For love of science."

"I do love science. That part of me is real." Shadows of remorse darkened her eyes. "I have loved every moment spent at your . . . in your laboratory."

As he had loved every moment of having her there—of having her *here*, against him, where he could smell the scent of her hair, where her warmth permeated his clothing and kindled his lust. "Then why this betrayal?"

"Because . . ."

Trembling, she fell silent, and Simon found himself holding his breath. Would she trust him? Until that moment he hadn't realized how important it was to him that she did. Just as she had done, he turned the question around onto himself. Had he, this past week, given her ample reason to place her trust in him?

He found himself hoping to God he had.

Her trembling suddenly ceased, and the fear smoothed from her brow. "If I have betrayed you, it was not by choice but because my loyalties were first pledged to another. I was sent here to find your sister and recover a valuable item she stole when she fled London."

At mention of Gwendolyn, dismay sank like a lodestone in Simon's gut. He set Ned at arm's length. "Galileo's teeth. What the devil has that girl done now?"

The tip of Ned's tongue slid across her bottom lip, leaving a tempting sheen. "I cannot tell you, Lord Harrow, unless you swear upon your honor, on your very *life*, that you will divulge the truth to no one."

Chapter 10

"You rummaged through my private things, yet it is I who must swear?"

Ivy expected scornful laughter to follow; indeed, Lord Harrow tilted back his head as if in preparation of that very response. But he only peered at her with a hooded expression that sent a shiver down her length.

Then he thoroughly surprised her. "All right, I swear. Provided you tell me something believable. Who sent you, and what is it you claim my sister stole?"

"Something valuable and quite secret that belongs to—"

His fingers fell gently across her lips. "Wait. Come with me."

Taking the candle, he led her back to his sitting room. She took a seat on the settee; he sat in the wing chair opposite, the empty hearth stretching between them. "Tell me your name."

"I told you that first day. Don't you remember?" She couldn't keep the wry chuckle from her voice. "It's Ivy. Ivy Sutherland."

"And I take it your father is not an undersecretary for the chancellor of the exchequer."

She looked down at her hands. "I have no father. Nor a mother, either. Both were lost to a house fire long ago."

He regarded her in silence, the candlelight casting his eyes and mouth in wavering shadow, so that she couldn't read his expression. Very quietly, he said, "I'm sorry. Truly. Loss is something I understand well."

The velvet rumble of his voice conveyed an empathy that made her heart contract. The grief that never truly faded pushed tears into her eyes, tears for her mother and father, and for the lovely woman who had conceived such beauty in Harrowood's gardens, though she herself could never walk its paths.

Blinking, unable to speak, she nodded.

"You mentioned sisters. Aren't they wondering where you are?"

She swallowed. "Laurel, the oldest, is presently abroad, in France. The other two are home in London, and they are well aware that I am in Cambridge." Her hand went to her hair. "In fact, they helped me prepare."

"And your connection to Gwendolyn?" His voice became stern, demanding.

Ivy chose her words carefully. "I have never met your sister. It is her mistress with whom I am acquainted."

Fresh anger iced his facial muscles. "That . . . is . . . impossible."

"I assure you it is quite possible. My sisters and I have been confidantes of the queen since we were small children, in the days when no one could have guessed the obscure little princess would ever wear the crown."

"Explain." As stiff as steel, his mouth barely moved. "And be quick about it, before I lose my patience."

"Our fathers, and my uncle Edward as well, served in the wars together," she said. "Our parents remained close friends afterward. Even after their deaths, Victoria's mother continued to bring the princess to visit us at my uncle's estate. Until she became heir apparent, that is."

Yearning, sharp and raw, came over her as she recalled those untroubled times and how abruptly they had ended. "We did not see Victoria again until about six months ago. She needed us then, just as she needs me now. You see, we are her secret servants."

"Secret . . ." Lord Harrow's jaw squared. "What kind of claptrap is this? I've every mind to——"

"You swore. You can't go back on your word now."

His eyes blazed across the dim shadows. "You are in no position—"

Ivy surged to her feet. "I am indeed, Lord Harrow. And that position is backed by the queen's authority. Yes, I came here under false pretenses. Yes, I poked through your belongings behind your back."

Hands fisted at her hips, she shook away the curl that fell into her eye. "I did so at first under orders from the queen. But I did so also because I believe in your innocence, and I wished not only to prove that you do *not* have Victoria's stone, but to clear you of all complicity in the matter. Now, if you find you cannot return my faith with a little trust, then please do summon the local magistrate."

With that, she closed her mouth and compressed her lips.

The silence stretched into an eternal, excruciating moment during which her bravado drained away by the bucketful and her knees all but knocked together. *Would* he summon the magistrate? Oh, she had no wish to spend the next several nights in a cold jail cell, until word could be sent to her sisters and the queen.

Why didn't he say something? Just when she could bear it no longer, he folded his arms across his chest. "What's this about a stone?"

Ivy collapsed back onto the settee. "I didn't mean to mention that quite yet."

"Too late. Talk."

Ivy muttered two quick prayers, one that she wasn't making an irretrievable error in judgment, and two, that Victoria would forgive her for this breach in her promise. But with Lady Gwendolyn's failure to turn up at Harrowood, matters had become a great deal more complicated than Victoria had anticipated.

Beginning with the night the queen had knocked at the

door of the Knightsbridge Readers' Emporium, Ivy told him everything. The stone, where it originated, what its discovery could mean to the queen. She considered leaving out the tale of Victoria and Albert's illicit engagement, but how else to make him understand the urgency of recovering the stone?

When she concluded, he sat frowning and shaking his head. "I knew she was impetuous, but I can't believe Gwendolyn would steal from the queen. The *queen*, for heaven's sake."

"You truly had no idea at all?" Ivy raised a skeptical, though also sympathetic, eyebrow. "No one would blame you for trying to protect her."

"Someone shall have to protect her from *me* when I get my hands on her."

Ivy believed the denial inherent in his words. She also believed his sister would come to no harm at his hands, that her disappearance concerned him far more than her actions angered him.

"So the queen believes my sister stole this stone as a peace offering to me?"

"Given the circumstances, it does seem a likely possibility. Perhaps she is waiting for an opportune moment to approach you."

"Or perhaps she lost her nerve and changed her mind altogether. Damn it, Ned, you should not have waited so long to tell me the truth. Gwendolyn's been missing more than a week now. God only knows how much more trouble she's gotten herself into."

Ivy dropped her gaze to the floor. "You are right, and I'm sorry. But please understand that I had to be certain of you before I revealed anything. Do you have any idea where your sister might be hiding?"

His mouth tightened as if at an unsavory flavor, and he swore under his breath. "I believe I may. At least, I believe I know who might be able to enlighten us. It could be that she never meant to give the stone to me at all."

Heaving himself out of the chair, he went to the liquor

cart beside the hearth and pulled the stopper from a decanter. When he returned, he handed a snifter to Ivy. He took a second one and settled back into his wing chair.

She sniffed the contents. The fumes scorched her nose, but she took a sip anyway. Though the liquid seared like fire on her tongue, she welcomed the smooth warmth that spread through her body.

"I must admit that I wouldn't mind experimenting with this stone." He swirled his brandy and stared at the dancing candle flame. "The possibilities . . ."

"If we recover it before any damage is done, Victoria might allow you to do so."

"She really believes the incident could damage her position?"

"She is convinced of it." Ivy shrugged a shoulder. "But perhaps that is something a man cannot understand."

"I understand many things, Ned . . . Ivy. Sorry." He ran a hand over his chin. "I understand that your remaining here will jeopardize your reputation and my credibility. Which is something neither of us can afford."

"There is no danger if no one discovers the truth. I've done exceptionally well so far."

"Have you?" His voice took on a distinct note of challenge. He got up from the chair and came to sit beside her on the settee. "You didn't have me fooled for very long. All I had to do was look at you." He trailed his fingertips across her cheek. "Truly look."

At his touch, a quivery thread twined with the brandy's heat to tug at her breasts, her womb. Instinct urged her to pull away; desire held her where she was. "They say people see what they wish to see."

"Then perhaps I should close my eyes." As he did so, he leaned over and pressed his lips to hers, a gentle kiss that tasted of potent spirits and sweet demands. Her senses glided into a slow spin, and she closed her own eyes and let the kiss possess her until her mouth opened and her tongue boldly sought out his.

She spiraled in heat and longing and the delicious contrast between his firm body and softly commanding mouth. Then he eased away and cupped her face in his palm, compelling her to open her eyes. When she did, she met with stormy desire, drowning in waves of regret.

"You see, my Ned? We cannot pretend this won't happen again. We cannot both be here."

"Oh, but . . ." Yes, yes, she did see. To deny that this passion growing between them blotted out logic would have been a lie.

She hadn't come to Harrowood seeking passion, certainly not love, but in a few short days she had found both. Found it in his stern looks and his brilliant mind and his acceptance of her abilities, despite her being a woman.

She wanted neither love nor a husband, not even him. What she wanted was the freedom to pursue the interests she held dear. In this man, she had found, finally, a partner who shared her dreams and ambitions in ways no one, not even her sisters, could ever comprehend. To a woman, especially one of such obscure and humble origins as hers, that was as close to a miracle as could be imagined.

Yes, Victoria needed her to remain here and see her mission through. But for Ivy herself, it was simply too soon to relinquish that miracle. There were so many reasons for her to stay, and only one forcing her to leave—the fact of her womanhood.

Tears of frustration pushed against her throat, but she steeled herself to deliver an argument he could not refute. She wouldn't bother explaining what her time at Harrowood had meant to her; she believed he understood that well enough, but that he judged the risks to far outweigh the benefits. So be it. Would he feel similarly inclined when it came to his sister?

With a quick clearing of her throat, she launched into the only battle she had a chance of winning. "You need me," she said evenly, "to help you find your sister, and to intervene on her behalf with Victoria. Only I can do that, and I will, as long as we find the stone intact and no one has learned of its origins."

She perceived her victory in the subtle narrowing of his eyes and the slight bob of his Adam's apple. "You'll do that for her?" he asked.

"I owe you that much."

He held her gaze and nodded, though whether in a wordless pledge to allow her to stay in exchange for her help, Ivy couldn't be certain. "Tomorrow, then, we'll follow the one lead I believe I have concerning Gwendolyn's whereabouts."

She would have liked to have had more from him, a real pledge that until they found his sister, he wouldn't send her away. But if she pushed him, would he banish her from the house that very night? Her fate uncertain, she came to her feet, only to sway on slightly wobbly legs.

Unused to spirits stronger than wine, she was tipsy from the brandy. She placed the glass on the mantel and made her way toward the door, mindful not to trip over Lord Harrow's long legs as she passed him. "I'll return to my room now." Some demon that would not be subdued prompted her to ask, "Must I begin packing, or not?"

She was almost to the door when his answer reached her. "Do neither."

His sultry tone sent a shiver through her and brought her to a halt. As she turned back to him, he stood and held out his hand.

"Stay, Ned. Stay here tonight."

"Here?" She glanced about the room as if suddenly shocked to find herself there. "With you?"

"I am not suggesting any compromise of your conscience."

Her mouth curved in a cynical pout; Simon laughed softly.

"Go if you don't trust me. I merely thought . . ." What? He had been trying to resist her ever since he first recognized the sway of her hips for what it was. He had failed wretchedly, and now found himself not only falling in love against his wishes and his better judgment but also lusting for an agent of the queen.

Treason? All the more reason for her to go. Except . . .

Going to her, he combed his fingers through her curls, liking the way they stood on end between his fingers before springing back into place. He liked, too, that even the shadows couldn't conceal the high color that stained her cheeks, turning them nearly as rosy as her lips. Cupping his hand round the back of her head, he drew her to him and kissed her, long and luxuriously.

They both emerged bemused and breathless.

Her bosom rose and fell sharply. "You thought *that*, did you?"

"Yes. But *only* that. I swear."

She said nothing, but the emotion melting in her dark eyes gave him all the permission he needed to swing her up into his arms. The act stabbed at his loins yet brought a grin to his face. "Have you any idea how odd it is to lift a woman and not feel the weight of trailing skirts?"

Her arms encircled his neck, and she met his smile with one of her own. "I'm afraid I wouldn't know."

"No, of course you wouldn't. All I want tonight, Ned, is to hold you." His voice became husky. Silently, then, he completed the thought. *To reach across the mattress and feel warmth again. To not be alone.*

No, God help him, that wasn't all he wanted, nowhere close. He might have taken any number of women into his bed in the months since Aurelia died, and any one of them would have served the superficial purpose of heating the mattress.

But this woman, Ned . . . Ivy . . . He didn't care what he called her, but she alone seemed able to make him feel whole, healed. It had been so long since he felt that way, and it was too compelling a prospect to resist now.

For tonight, then, and only tonight. Tomorrow he would come to his senses and remember that one could not find completion in another human being. That was a fairy tale, an illusion that crumbled too easily beneath the vagaries of happenstance. Disease. Fire. A door inadvertently left open . . .

"Ah, Ned," he whispered, and held her tighter.

"My name is *Ivy*," she murmured against his neck.

Lord Harrow. Ivy dreamed of having his arms around her, of seeking the flame of his embrace willingly and eagerly; permitting it, as she knew she should not. *Needing* it, as she knew she must not.

His warm, broad hands ran her length from shoulder to thigh, tracing her shape beneath her clothing. However wrongly, she pressed herself more fully into his palms and exhaled her desire against his linen-clad chest. Gently he tugged her shirttails free, and she allowed the glide of his fingertips, her breath catching with delight with each hot shiver that rippled across her skin.

When he reached the bindings that flattened her breasts beneath her shirt, he hesitated, and she thought he would tug the ends free and unwind the strips. Instead he explored her breasts through the silk, discovering the hardening peaks of her nipples through the slippery barrier. His restraint made his touch all the more sweet and squeezed tears into her eyes.

Like a burning wind, over and over he spoke her name against her neck, then across her belly until it quivered. Not her true name but the one by which only he called her, like a secret code that freed her dreams and unlocked the yearnings of her heart. She yearned now as she wrapped herself around him, as she gave herself over to the pleasure of his hands and solid limbs and the wall of his heated, pulsing torso. With a hushed urgency that blended with the murmur of the winds riding over the house, he bade her to trust him and then breathed a question against her sensitized flesh.

Do you wish it, Ned? Shall I, Ned?

Her answers were *Yes*, and *Yes*, and *Please*, and then a wordless cry she could not contain.

A cry that echoed palpably in her ears. Her eyes flew open and the startling details of a room that was not hers filled her view . . . and a shocking realization lashed

through her that those strong arms and seeking hands were
not imagined, but firm and solid and still upon her, and the
heights of pleasure to which he'd taken her had been no
dream but provocative, torrid reality.

For Simon, the night became an excruciating test of both
his fortitude and his honor, as he held Ned—*Ivy*—in his
arms and gritted his teeth against the throb of an erection
that could be allowed no release.

Each time he gained control over his rampaging lust, she
would move in her sleep and unwittingly wiggle her sweet
little bottom against his thighs, or she'd roll and sigh a caress across his cheek, one that bore the breathless syllables
of his name.

No, not his name, his title. More than once, he'd have
sworn she whispered an impassioned *Lord Harrow* and *sir*.
Eventually his resistance had crumbled and he'd gathered
her to him, claiming as much of her as he dared without
claiming *all*.

It hadn't helped that they'd slept in their clothes, each of
them having removed only boots, waistcoat, and neckcloth.
With that last he had helped her, standing temptingly close
as he worked the knot free, his fingertips grazing her chin
and throat, and she staring up into his face with those large,
almond eyes full of questions and doubts that mirrored his
own. The only difference was that beneath her uncertain-
ties a light of trust blazed, a trust in which he himself dared
put no faith.

Because even through their clothing, the heat of her
body inflamed him, until he could not stop envisioning her
naked breasts in a silver wash of moonlight. Until he ached
to have those small, perfect orbs in his hands, the dusky
nipples between his lips.

Why had he asked her to stay? Even as he had made
the mad suggestion, he had predicted with stunning clarity
the torment her presence in his bed would cause him. Had
he wished to make himself suffer? Oh, suffer he did. With
each whimper his wandering fingertips had coaxed from

her lips, he suffered by not sharing in her ecstasy, by being left only to ponder what wonders her touch might have wrought on him.

Yet not once did he consider unwrapping his arms from around her and moving to the leather chaise at the foot of the bed. The thought of leaving her had been more torturous than nuzzling against her squirming form and filling his lungs with the scent of her lust. A perverse sort of challenge? If they could get through the night without his ravishing her, then they could get through anything, including continuing her charade until they located his sister.

Ah, but he *had* ravished her ... or very nearly. As near as he dared without treading into the territory of permanence. Because nothing—*nothing*—in this life could ever be trusted to be permanent.

The touch of dawn against the windows brought him as much relief as it did dismay. Relief because she would leave him now, hasten back to her own room. The servants must not find her here or what would they think? What tales would they spread about their master and his assistant?

Dismay, too, because along with the morning's pallid chill came the reaffirmation of all he knew to be true and cruel about life, about his own existence, destined for precious little happiness. It simply wasn't in his stars.

With his sweet assistant he might perhaps find temporary respite for his grief, but as soothing a salve as she might be, she could not heal his battered soul. Loss would always be there, lurking in the back of his mind, a pitiless reminder of what he had endured, and what he could endure again if he dropped his guard.

Drawing in her fragrance one last time, he slowly exhaled and released her, then smoothed his fingers across her cheek. "Ivy?"

She stirred and blinked. Her eyes fluttered open. At first she didn't move, but lay gazing up at the ceiling, then the posts at the foot of the bed. With a gasp she bolted upright. "Where—?"

"You're in my room." He sat up beside her. "I didn't mean to startle you, but I thought it best to wake you now."

She glanced down at herself, then over at him. Her hand went to her shirt, still tied at the neckline but loose at the waist. With apprehension claiming her features, she peered beneath the bedclothes and released a breath of relief. Her trousers were still very much fastened. Simon hadn't needed to bare her there to send her body soaring.

He couldn't help a low chuckle. "Don't worry. We didn't. Just as I promised we wouldn't."

"Was it a dream?" Her voice was so soft he felt the question burrow inside his chest, rather than heard it with his ears.

Lying seemed the wise choice, but he knew he couldn't, not to her. "No," he said, and waited for her rebuke.

Instead, her hand closed around his sleeve. "I am glad it wasn't."

For half a heartbeat every ounce of control he'd mastered over his emotions slipped from his grasp. All his bloody effort of self-preservation, gone in a split second of weakness for this wisp of a girl, this marvel of a woman, who was able to strip his defenses with a press of her fingers.

And she witnessed it all in the fleeting but unpreventable contortion of his features. A tear formed in her eye; her hand went to his cheek. "Oh, Simon . . . why?"

His insides clenched—with joy and despondency both—as she spoke his given name for the first time. "I'm sorry," he said inadequately. "I suppose I'd hoped to prove we could be together without . . . driving each other insane. Sadly, I was wrong."

She pulled closer, her lips near enough to warm his own. "No. Why did you grant my pleasure but not take your own?"

He groped at the air, then let his hand fall with a slap against his knee. "Because nothing right could have come of it. Because I could not now be looking you in the eye."

"Is that all?" She studied him as though stripping him naked and analyzing every inch of bare skin, until he felt the urge to squirm, even as she had squirmed beneath his touch. "There is something else, something holding you back, preventing you from . . ."

Don't. He only thought the warning, but it must have shown on his face for she immediately fell silent.

"Whatever it is," she continued more quietly, "you've proved yourself correct, haven't you? We may continue as we were without worry of impropriety. We have passed the test."

"Have we?" Somehow he managed not to vent the uproarious, cynical laughter pushing against his throat. And because he didn't have the heart or the courage to wipe the trust from her countenance, he nodded.

Resting her elbows on her knees, she plowed her hands through her hair, peeked up at him, and gave him a crooked smile. "What a tousled pair we are, as if so deep in our cups last night we mutually passed out. We'd best have a care or the dean of students will gate us both."

Her jest reminded him of a much more pertinent matter. "It isn't being gated that worries me. Servants talk and rumors spread like wildfire in an academic community. It's time to get you back to your own chamber."

"Good heavens, you're right." She scrambled to untangle herself from the bedclothes. "Mrs. Walsh already abhors me." Finding one of her boots, she shoved a foot inside.

"We've nothing to fear from Mrs. Walsh, Ned. Nothing that happens in this house would ever be spread abroad by her lips. But lesser servants come and go, and their loyalty is far less certain."

He found her silk waistcoat over the arm of the easy chair. Bringing it to her, he bade her turn around and helped her on with it. Then he turned her again and began doing up the buttons. "Mrs. Walsh doesn't abhor you, by the way. She is confused. She suspects something amiss, but can't put her finger on what. It's her perplexity she abhors."

"All the more reason to avoid her this morning until I've made my bed appear slept in." She reached for her coat.

"If we do encounter anyone, we'll simply behave as if

we've been up all night working on calculations. It wouldn't be the first time."

Her cheeks were still flushed from sleep, her eyes heavy-lidded, her lips moist and red. A languid air hung about her, telling a tale that would be difficult to deny.

"Come," he said. "We'd best get you to your room."

"You're coming with me? Shouldn't I simply hasten to my chamber as quickly and quietly as possible?"

He had to agree that that would look more natural to any of the servants who might already have ventured abovestairs. But simply opening his door and bidding Ned a quick good-bye would have been tawdry and slapdash on his part; only a cad sent a young lady, albeit one dressed in trousers and a waistcoat, off alone to face the possibility of having to explain herself along the way. The Mad Marquess of Harrow might be many things, but a cad was not one of them.

"I'll see you to your door. With any luck, no one has been in yet. What time does Ellsworth usually bring your hot water and shaving soap?"

She peered at the bedside clock. "Not quite this early. Did you know he keeps offering to shave me himself?"

This produced a grin Simon tried unsuccessfully to hide. "As a matter of fact, it was I who suggested he do so."

He could not deny that he thoroughly deserved the *whop* of Ned's coat hitting the side of his head.

Chapter 11

Later that morning, in a well-appointed drawing room on St. Andrews Street at the center of Cambridge, Ivy found herself in the middle of a standoff, one she half expected to erupt into violence at any moment. She darted a wary glance from Simon—as she had come to think of him since waking in his bed—to the stately town home's owner.

Anger and evasiveness flashed in Lord Drayton's hooded gaze. The fourth member of the Galileo Club, Colin Ashworth, Earl of Drayton, presented as unscholarly a figure as Simon himself: youthful and dashing and filled with the same electrifying energy she sensed in Simon. Now the two men, one as dark-haired as the other was blond, faced each other like two negative charges about to collide with a volatile hydrogen molecule. Ivy braced for a blistering exchange.

"I asked you a straightforward question." Simon's voice plunged to a threatening rumble. "If you had an ounce of honor in you, you'd stop hedging and answer me."

"The answer is not nearly as simple as you would have it." His chin protruding, Simon's fellow scientist presented a wall of stubborn resistance.

Simon's anger propelled him forward. Ivy flinched, expecting an impact, but he abruptly halted a yard or so away from Lord Drayton. "You had best *make* it simple. Has my sister been to see you, or not?"

Lord Drayton's nostrils flared. As the tension mounted, Ivy conducted a hasty survey of the room for an object she might use to separate the two should they come to blows. A sofa cushion? A candlestick? An andiron? Could she even hope to defuse their palpable enmity?

"She is frightened of you, Simon," the earl said. "And who can blame her?"

"Frightened of me, her own brother?" The bark in his words and the ruddy color that flooded his face made Ivy a little bit afraid of him herself.

Her heart pattered against the confining silk strips around her breasts, making her feel slightly faint. Stepping between the men, she gestured to the armchairs and settee grouped near the bay window overlooking the garden. Gardens were peaceful and soothing; the view might help. "Perhaps we should all have a seat and calm down."

Lord Drayton swung in her direction as if just becoming aware of her presence. "Just who the blazes are you?"

She deepened her voice a notch. "Lord Harrow's assistant."

"And what business is this of yours?"

"Leave him alone, Colin," Simon's warned. "This is about Gwendolyn. I came here on an educated assumption. Your prevarication is turning that guess into a conviction. When did you see her?"

Lord Drayton all but spat his reply. "All right, yes. Gwen was here. Briefly. Almost two weeks ago."

"Two weeks? And you chose to say nothing? Did it not occur to you that her sudden appearance in Cambridge meant she was in trouble, and that she needed my help? Whatever else she may or may not have done, abandoning her position in the queen's household is no small matter."

"She begged me not to tell you. She said she feared what you might do if you learned she'd left Buckingham Palace without the queen's permission."

"And so you simply let her go on her way?" Simon's hands swung upward, curling into fists. "A young girl, all on her own."

"I made her promise she'd return to London immediately."

Simon flicked a silent question in Ivy's direction. She replied with an infinitesimal shake of her head. If his sister had returned to London, Ivy would have known about it by now. Victoria would have sent a special messenger racing across the sixty miles that separated London from Cambridge; a single rider could have made the journey in two days.

Simon scowled at the other man. "Either you're a fool to have trusted her with that promise, or you're lying and Gwendolyn is still here, hiding somewhere in this house."

Lord Drayton held out his arms. "Search if you like. Quiz my servants. But I assure you, she is quite gone." His posture eased. "See here, your assistant is right. We should sit down and discuss the matter calmly."

With a show of reluctance, Simon dragged himself to an armchair. Ivy followed, taking a seat on the settee. Lord Drayton completed the triangle in another of the richly upholstered chairs. His hands gripped the padded arms.

"Gwen came to me seeking advice—"

"And is that all she got from you?"

Lord Drayton's jaw turned to steel. Ivy tried to catch Simon's eye, to communicate that his sarcasm wouldn't accomplish anything useful. When he failed to cooperate, she resorted to clearing her throat. Loudly. They needed to find Lady Gwendolyn, and if Lord Drayton could lead them to her, it would do them little good to antagonize him.

Simon's mouth pulled in irritation. "What kind of advice did she want?"

"Mostly how she might appeal to your better nature without worsening matters."

"And she thought *you* could assist her with that?"

"Lord Harrow . . . " Ivy murmured a cautionary singsong. Her impatience grew in direct proportion to the anger that so obviously prevented him being objective. So be it. He might berate her later, but her obligation to Victoria demanded that she not sit silently by. "Lord Drayton," she said, "did Lady Gwendolyn tell you why she left the palace?"

"She said she was homesick," he replied tersely, eyeing her with just enough disdain to convey his annoyance at being questioned by an underling. His attention shifted back to Simon. "And that she wished to reconcile with you."

"Nothing else?" Simon's caustic retort sent frustration shooting through Ivy. She burned to ask far more pointed questions than his accusatory ones.

Lord Drayton held out his hands. "Isn't that enough?"

Ivy decided to take a chance, just to gauge the earl's reaction. "Did she perhaps mention having in her possession a particular item from the palace?"

His nostrils flared and his chin protruded. "Are you accusing Lady Gwendolyn of stealing?"

"He is accusing Gwendolyn of nothing," Simon replied before Ivy could.

Another silent battle electrified the air between the men. Obviously, their mutual resentment centered on Lady Gwendolyn herself, and Ivy's imagination took flight with possibilities.

Had Lord Drayton ruined her? Victoria hadn't mentioned that, but she might not have known the full story of why Simon had disowned his sister.

Lord Drayton was the first to break the seething hostility by flicking his gaze down at his boots. "Actually, she did ask for money to cover her traveling expenses."

Those last two words, perhaps keys to Gwendolyn's whereabouts, once more splintered Ivy's restraint. "Traveling expenses to get her where?"

Lord Drayton scowled but replied, "As I said, to London. Or so I believed."

"Did you give her the money she requested?" Ivy pressed, the difficulty of obtaining answers making her want to yank on her own curls.

The man narrowed his scrutiny on her in a way that made her want to shrink back against the cushions. "What are you, some sort of detective?"

From under his brows, Simon flashed her a warning. She chose to ignore it.

"Hardly, my lord," she said to the earl with surprising steadiness. "I am merely doing as Lord Harrow hired me to do. Assisting him by offering a second point of view."

"Humph." Lord Drayton's irritation didn't fade. "I find your questions impertinent and none of your business, young man."

"But the answers are very much my business." Simon leaned forward. "Did you give Gwendolyn any money?"

Lord Drayton sighed. "Thirty pounds."

"Damned generous of you," Simon murmured drily. "And did she give you anything in return? Or promise you something in exchange for your assistance?"

"Such as what?" Lord Drayton's handsome features twisted to a dangerous scowl. "If you're suggesting that Gwen came here to—"

Simon's chin came up. "I don't suppose she offered to help you win the Copley Medal?"

"How the blazes could Gwen do that? And why the hell would you conclude that I'd require or accept such help?"

"Because as you said, the work you're presently engaged in isn't flashy enough to attract the Royal Society's notice."

"How dare you? My work may lack a certain dazzle, but it is every bit as vital as whatever is producing those sparks you so enjoy shooting from your tower lair—perhaps more so. If my focus on finding a way to protect England's harvests from pestilence and infestation means I'll never win a Copley Medal, then I say to the devil with the Royal Society." Though indignant, Lord Drayton kept his anger in check; his quiet admonition bore a dignity that convinced Ivy he spoke the truth.

Yet Simon seemed to have heard none of the man's sincerity, for he latched on to one phrase only. "How dare I? That you of all people should pose such a question to me . . ."

Lord Drayton shoved to his feet. "That is enough. Hang it, Simon, this is precisely why Gwen got cold feet when she tried to come home. You don't listen, and you don't forgive. You haven't an ounce of empathy in you."

"Oh, now, that isn't fair. He—" Ivy pressed a fist to her mouth.

She had planned to keep a cool head through this interview. This was not her battle, yet Lord Drayton's charge incited her outrage. Ivy had experienced nothing *but* empathy from Simon. Unlike every other man she had ever encountered, he alone comprehended what it meant for women to be banned from the classroom, the laboratory, and every other place where they could challenge their intellects. He not only understood; he applauded her talents, and Ivy could not sit by and hear him so unfairly insulted. Except . . .

Both men were staring at her, Simon in censure and Lord Drayton in perplexity. Then they went back to ignoring her.

"I can't very well forgive my sister if she persists in hiding from me." Simon put emphasis on the word *sister*, as if to imply that he would readily forgive Gwendolyn's offenses, but not Lord Drayton's.

"That is between you and Gwen." Lord Drayton's lips whitened with bitterness.

Simon came to his feet and adjusted his coat with a tug. "If you did know where my sister is now, would you tell me?"

Lord Drayton again glanced down at his boots, and when he looked back up from beneath a fringe of blond hair, his ire had been replaced with a calmer, more conciliatory emotion. "I know you love her, and that you're concerned about her. If I knew where she'd gone, yes, I'd tell you. And if I could have prevented her from going anywhere but London or home, I would have. Upon my honor, she had me convinced she'd do the right thing."

For a moment Ivy thought Simon would contest that assertion. But the tension drained from his posture and he nodded. Then he strode to the doorway, issuing a command over his shoulder in a single, terse syllable. "Ned."

Ivy jumped up from the settee and trotted to keep up with him. Retrieving his cloak and top hat, he made his way down to the hall and out to St. Andrews Street. Bright leaves rustled along the thoroughfare; the brilliant sunlight offered little warmth.

They had ridden into town, a sedate ride befitting the well-bred gentlemen they appeared to be, and had stabled their horses on Market Street. As Simon headed north along St. Andrews on foot, Ivy fell in beside him. Many aspects of the past quarter hour had left her puzzled, but one question in particular nagged her.

"That encounter was painfully personal," she said. "Why did you allow me to witness it?"

Simon spared her a sidelong glance. "The queen's authority grants you the right to gather your evidence firsthand."

"Yes, but that interview involved a good deal more than fact-finding. You and Lord Drayton were practically at each other's throats."

He said nothing as they passed the gates of Christ's College. From beneath the Beaufort coat of arms, Lady Margaret's statue seemed to follow their progress with a moue of disapproval. To their left, the bells of St. Andrew the Great rang out the half hour, a note simultaneously echoed from the university's numerous colleges across the city. A few steps past the church, Simon turned west onto Market Street.

Ivy tugged the brim of her own top hat lower against the wind. "I suppose we'll attend the ten o'clock."

"The ten o'clock what?"

"Service. It *is* Sunday, you realize."

"Is it?" Simon picked up the pace, forcing Ivy to hasten to keep up and nearly sending her tripping over her feet again. "I have another stop to make. If you wish, you may attend the service at St. Mary's, or turn around and go back to St. Andrew's."

"You won't come?"

He halted and turned so abruptly she nearly ran into

him. "I have not attended church in more than a year. A year and a half, to be exact."

"Oh." She didn't need any further explanation. "If your next stop is about your sister, then I had better accompany you."

"As you like." He resumed walking. "Only this time do a better job of holding your tongue."

"I have a right to ask necessary questions."

"At the price of giving yourself away? Do you realize what would happen should anyone discover the truth of who, or shall I say what, you are?"

"Of course I do. Simon . . . I do wish you'd slow down." When he didn't, she sprinted to resume her place at his side. "Why does Lord Drayton infuriate you?"

"Back to your confounded questions, eh?"

"I cannot help but be curious. What did he do to you?"

"He exists."

"That isn't an answer. If I am to recover the queen's property and settle matters between her and your sister, I must understand the dynamics of the situation."

"The dynamics, eh?" His sarcasm stole a portion of her confidence.

She slowed, and to his back said, "Well, yes . . ."

She would have said more, but he stopped suddenly and whirled again. The sunlight slanting through the buildings flashed full on his face, carving a renewed surge of anger into harsh relief. "Very well, then. Here are your dynamics. Last winter, Colin Ashworth convinced my sister to join him at a roadside inn about ten miles outside the city. I don't know what lies he told her, perhaps that he'd marry her. All I know is that he took advantage of her young, romantic heart. Fortunately I arrived in time to prevent him from taking advantage of more than that and ruining her completely."

Disgust sounded in his voice. "Not that Gwendolyn thanked me, mind you. On the contrary, she was so blindly smitten that she cursed me for interfering and swore she'd never obey me again. With few other options, I arranged for her to join the queen's household." He laughed without mirth. "I believed that to be the one place where she wouldn't get into any further trouble."

Ivy stepped closer and placed a hand on his coat sleeve. "You lost your sister *and* your friend that day."

The angry darkening of his skin made her snatch her hand away. Fury flashed in his eyes, powerful enough to frighten her. Then it was gone, leaving him with a lost, haunted look that gripped her heart. He bent his head and nodded. "I hold few expectations of ever getting either back."

"You don't know that. There is always hope."

His head snapped up, his features this time edged in ice. "You asked why I brought you to Colin's. The queen's authority is only half the reason. I needed you there to prevent me from tearing into his throat with my bare hands."

He pivoted and continued on at a brisk stride.

Simon and Ned went next to visit Errol Quincy in his suite of rooms above the bookbinder's shop on Rose Crescent. Upon his daughter's death, Errol had deemed the house they had shared west of the city to be filled with too many memories, of both Aurelia and his deceased wife, Emily. After selling the place, he had taken up residence in town in a small but comfortable flat where he lived among his books and small experiments and where he hosted frequent symposia in his parlor.

Errol offered them tea but could offer no insights as to Gwendolyn's whereabouts or her recent antics. Simon hadn't thought the visit would yield any new information, but there had always been the off chance that Gwen had taken the elderly man into her confidence and persuaded him to silence. Simon said as much as he and Ivy returned to Market Street to retrieve their horses.

Simon paid the groom and walked both animals out into the yard himself. "Not that Errol would keep silent out of ill intentions, but my sister is like a second daughter to him. He'd do anything for her, including keep a secret."

"In Lord Drayton's defense," Ivy said, "I don't believe he kept silent out of ill intentions, either."

"And on what evidence do you base your conclusion?" Simon checked the horses' girths, tightening that of Ned's mount, Butterfly, a notch. "You don't know the man as I do."

"Which means my opinions about him aren't colored by hostility."

Simon bit back a retort, kicking at a stone in the road so forcefully the horses lurched. He gestured for Ned to mount, linking his hands together to offer her a knee up.

She lingered where she was. "What about the fourth member of your club?"

"Ben?" Simon shook his head as he unclasped his hands and straightened. "He and Gwendolyn have always been cordial, but little more than that. She wouldn't have gone to him."

"Perhaps she's staying with a friend?" Ned patted the mare's nose.

Simon mentally ran through the list of his sister's most trusted friends, many of whom were now married. "I'll send out inquiries in this afternoon's post."

"You're frightened, aren't you, about what might have happened to her?"

"Of course I'm concerned. But my dear little sister thrives on dramatics. If she hadn't been born a marquess's daughter, she might have had a successful career on the stage. But that doesn't stop a voice in my gut from warning of danger. She is only eighteen, and not nearly as sophisticated as she likes to pretend. It may be best to call in the authorities."

"No!" Ned blinked and said more calmly, "The queen requires our discretion. Besides, think of the scandal surrounding your sister if word of her theft ever got out."

She had a valid point. This could destroy Gwendolyn's reputation as thoroughly as her tryst with Colin might have done.

"Don't worry," Ned said. "We'll find her, and the stone. I promise."

He was about to question Ned's confidence when a hail rang out.

"Ivers! Ivers . . . that you, old boy?"

From the corner of Market and Trinity streets, a wavy-haired youth came running toward them. He wore no cloak or hat, but a blue and gold scarf around his neck trailed its fringed ends on the breeze behind him. Simon found him vaguely familiar.

Leaving Butterfly's side, Ned took several steps in the young man's direction. "Jasper Lowbry."

She sounded inordinately pleased. As Lowbry got closer, Simon recognized him from the St. John's residence hall where he had first found Ned following the challenge. Upon reaching them, a broadly grinning Lowbry snatched up Ned's extended hand, gave it a vigorous shake, and abruptly hauled her against him for an enthusiastic back-slapping. So enthusiastic, in fact, that as Ned's top hat tumbled to the cobblestones, Simon sprang forward to separate them and prevent her from being injured.

At the last second he remembered how such intervention would appear and stopped himself from making a glaring blunder. Still, his indignation mounted at the overblown physicality of the greeting. Must Lowbry insist on shoving Ned about so insolently? Simon willed the high-spirited student to release Ned—*release her this instant*.

He cleared his throat, and much to his relief, Lowbry stepped back. His gaze lit on Simon; his eyebrows went up. "Lord Harrow, sir, do forgive me. I . . . er . . . It's just splendid to see old Ivers again."

Simon bent to pick up Ned's fallen hat. "It's only been a week."

His grin stretching, Lowbry's attention shifted back to Ned. "Ah, but we've missed you at St. John's."

He reached out a fisted hand as if to deliver a playful punch to Ned's ribs. Instinct sent Simon's arm out to deflect the blow, leaving Lowbry looking disconcerted and Ned shuffling her feet.

Lowbry immediately brightened. "So, tell me. How goes it? Ascot and Yates will want to know if you've learned to drink brandy yet."

Simon shoved Ned's hat back on her head and patted it into place. "He does all right."

With an irritated gesture, Ned adjusted the brim. "Lord Harrow doesn't allow me much time for brandy. How are your studies coming along?"

"Well enough, but I'm sure not nearly as exciting as what you've been cooking up. Don't suppose you could give a hint?" Lowbry's hearty laughter echoed along the street. A man and a woman crossing to the south side turned to look.

"Hardly." Simon pulled his watch from his waistcoat pocket and ignored Ned's exasperated frown.

"Oh. Nearly forgot." Lowbry reached into his own breast pocket. "As you asked, I've been collecting your post for you, not that there's been any. Until the day before yesterday, that is. Here. I've been carrying this around with me everywhere I go with the intention of sending it along to Harrowood. Just hadn't gotten around to it yet. Sorry."

He held out a rumpled letter, the direction on the front slightly smudged. Over Ned's shoulder Simon tried to see where it had originated. *London* was all he could make out. A message from home, or from the queen?

Ned must have wondered the same, for her hand shook a little as she turned the missive over in her hand. The seal bore an unidentifiable indent in the shape of a rose.

"I'm meeting some of our mates at the Eagle Pub on Bene't," Mr. Lowbry said brightly. "Don't suppose you've time to come along?"

Simon shook his head and set a hand on Ned's shoulder. "We must be going."

Ned's half nod of agreement revealed a trace of regret. "Much obliged for the letter, Lowbry."

"You'll come visit one of these days, won't you?"

Ned cast a doubtful look at Simon. "I'll try. Thanks again." She waved the letter in a farewell gesture.

As they walked back to the horses, she tore open the seal and squinted in the sunlight to peruse the contents. "Oh." She sounded disappointed. "I'd hoped my sisters had forwarded a letter from Victoria."

Simon, too, had hoped the queen had written to report that Gwendolyn had returned to the palace and that all was well. "It isn't, then?"

"No, it's from Holly. It contains news from our eldest sister, Laurel. I'll read it later." She folded the letter and slipped it inside her coat. "Still, it was fortunate running into Jasper Lowbry. A capital fellow."

Simon shrugged. Feeling unaccountably sullen, he laced his fingers to once again offer her a boost up into the saddle.

She didn't move to accept his assistance. "You were rather ill-mannered with him."

"He took rather impertinent license with your person."

Her face tilted. "That's how they are at St. John's. Friendly and boisterous. You should know. Weren't you once a St. John's man?"

"That was a long time ago. We weren't nearly so infantile." Hunching against a gust of wind that whipped round the stable yard, he silently acknowledged how much more his already disagreeable mood had soured. "Galileo's teeth, I thought he'd crack one of your ribs."

"It *is* proving rather dangerous to be a man, but you needn't scowl so. Jasper did me no harm."

He might have protested that his scowling had little if anything to do with Jasper Lowbry. Gwendolyn was missing, so far without a trace, but if not for Colin's infernal, misguided meddling, she might at this very moment have been safe at home.

But Simon said nothing because, Colin and Gwendolyn aside, Ned had spoken true. He hadn't at all liked seeing the young, good-looking Mr. Lowbry taking such liberties with her, nor did he relish her cheerful reciprocation. Had St. John's men become so exuberant in their camaraderie,

or did Jasper Lowbry perceive in Ned Ivers certain qualities his other mates lacked?

Simon's pulse points throbbed. For a third time he
joined his hands together. "Would you rather ride or walk
back to Harrowood?"

She pursed her lips and set her bent knee into his palms.
He lifted her up, then swung up into his own saddle and
clucked the horses to a walk.

"Are you angry with me?"

He replied with a curt, "No."

He was angry with himself, with his very nature. He had
never been capable of doing anything halfway. His interest
in the natural philosophies meant, not becoming the patron
of a promising scientist, but rushing headlong into the laboratory himself and never fully emerging. When it came to
marriage, he hadn't chosen an attractive social equal with
whom to beget heirs, but a woman outside his social realm
who had shared his dreams and whose intellectual curiosity
had matched—and sometimes exceeded—his own.

Galileo's teeth, he had loved Aurelia. And God help
him, it was happening all over again, with this woman.

"Lord Harrow . . . Simon?"

He rode on, refusing to answer, unable to even look
at her, this female with the audacity to steal his heart and
leave him so . . . damned naked. Up Trinity Street to St.
John's, he led her in steely silence, then along Thompson's
Lane and beyond, to where the fens sprawled on either side
of Histon Road, stretching north out of the city.

The breeze here smelled of bog and grasses and peat,
of lonely wilderness and untamable forces. Gripped by a
sudden sense of futility, and by a twisting tangle of desperation and frustration, Simon snapped the reins above his
gelding's mane. Newton's powerful flanks bunched for an
instant, and then the Thoroughbred thrust forward into a
canter.

He knew Butterfly would follow. For all the mare's
gentle disposition, she was no idler. Simon angled a glance
over his shoulder at Ned's startled expression. Was she

frightened? Panicked? Should he stop? *Could* he, when every bone in his body craved breakneck speed, a bracing wind in his face, and the pounding thunder of hooves to drown out his unbidden and unwanted thoughts?

Ned's sweet face was set and determined, her chin up, her gaze arrow sharp on the horizon. Good God, did anything frighten her? Was there anything she couldn't gather the courage to face? Galileo's teeth, how he wished he could borrow some of her pluck.

With a shout he increased their pace. The stone wall bordering the road tempted him to arc Newton over it, but he judged the jump too dangerous to risk. Not with Ned.

He waited until they reached an open cattle crossing to cut over the empty, endless fields. Then he gave Newton his head, and with Ned and Butterfly hard at his shoulder, the landscape blurred to streaks of russet and brown and gold.

Ivy had never felt so terrified . . . or so exhilarated. Part of her wanted to beg Simon to slow their pace. . . . Another part wished to shout to go even faster. The ground and sky merged into a spectacular smear of color, vibrant and alive, an open expanse of sheer, dizzying heaven that she quickly discovered she trusted. Her fear of falling melted away as Butterfly's sure footing conquered the terrain, as Simon's subtle commands and his mount's immediate obedience led them around boulders and shrubs and dangerously wet bottomlands.

Her knuckles white around the reins, her knees gripping Butterfly's flanks until they trembled, Ivy felt powerful and free and splendid—more splendid than she'd ever felt before. She wished the ride would go on forever. Yet as Harrowood's towers came into view, a different sensation filled her. One of deep disappointment, of knowing that soon they would be back among other people, and that she and Simon must resume the caution and pretense that had come to define their lives. Or at least *her* life. Since coming to Cambridge, Ivy had done little else but pretend.

Perhaps it was the elation of the ride, of wearing breeches and sitting astride her horse, that prompted a small rebellion. Swinging Butterfly off the graveled drive, she continued at a brisk trot through the towering pines.

"Where are you going?"

Ivy tossed her head and didn't look back. "Follow and find out."

In truth she hadn't the faintest idea, only that she intended circling the house and gardens until she reached the riding paths that wound through the forested acreage beyond. Simon shadowed her, and it wasn't until they reached a long-neglected Grecian folly with Ionic columns, a domed roof, and shoots of ivy clinging to the cracked walls that she realized what she sought.

She and Simon had passed by here previously during their evening rides. The folly stood beside a pond that Simon had told her had once been stocked with colorful koi fish but was now half dry and choked with mud. There was a stream with a crumbling arched bridge, marble benches blanketed in moss, and straggly flower beds long since abandoned to weeds. This garden had been too far from the house to allow his infirm wife access to it, and so had been left to ruin.

Ivy brought Butterfly to a halt and dismounted. Simon remained in his saddle. "Why are we here?"

Ivy tipped her face up to meet his gaze. "Because I believe a respite will do us both good. That ride—why did you race so across the fens?"

He swung a leg over his horse's neck and leaped nimbly to the ground. "I'm sorry about that. I—"

"I'm not seeking an apology. I thank you for that gallop. What I want is to know *why* you did it. Was it because you were angry?"

"Angry . . . Yes, I suppose I was." The fisting of his right hand told her his ire hadn't completely left him. "But I don't see how this place will—"

"It is a place that provokes no memories, or relies on any artifice," she said, realizing immediately the irony of her claim. According to Simon, this garden had been designed generations ago; of course there were memories associated with it, just not ones with any power over him. Meanwhile the notion that a Grecian folly should hold no artifice was so ludicrous that she grinned. What she had meant was that here *she* need not resort to artifice.

"Here, we might both breathe easier, speak freely, and indulge in the privilege of being *ourselves*." Leaving Butterfly to graze, Ivy picked her way along the uneven, root-strewn ground to where Simon continued to hover at his horse's side. She stopped a few feet away, holding out her hand and letting Newton nuzzle her palm. "Isn't it a relief?"

He didn't answer. Instead he took a silent step closer and reached out a hand to cup her cheek. Then she was in his arms, their lips pressed together. Had he seized her mouth, or had she reached up to him? Did it matter?

In the dewy shade of the overgrown willows and the shadow cast by the folly, Simon thought of nothing but how good she felt, how sweet she tasted.

When he finally pulled back to drag in a breath, his eyes opened to behold countless questions burning in her gaze, each one dragging him back to the reality he had been so determined to avoid. He hadn't asked for this rising, irresistible passion that emptied his brain of logic. Confound it, he had wanted an assistant, nothing more. How dare fate laugh at him this way?

"Simon . . . this isn't what I meant. Surely we mustn't . . ." But instead of a command or even an appeal, Ned's assertion emerged as a drowning capitulation to the inevitable.

He pulled her close again and devoured her mouth. He held nothing back, showed her no mercy, and sought none for himself. Caught in a mad flurry of desire, he kissed her, and was kissed, until she gripped his wrists and pulled his hands from the sides of her face.

Her bosom rose and fell, and a new fierceness lit her eyes. "Has it not occurred to you that I might have as much reason as you to wish to avoid this?"

He threw back his head on a burst of soft laughter. Sobering abruptly, he dipped his head and drew her bottom lip between his teeth. When he released it, it glistened, as red as a juicy pomegranate. "Then say *no*. One of us needs to."

She conjured a scowl that rivaled his own best efforts. "Blast you, Simon de Burgh."

"Can't say it, can you?" He gave her neckcloth a playful tug, his loins tightening at the notion of pulling the knot free, of undoing the buttons and laces that confined her body. "We have a dilemma, then, don't we?"

He seized her hand and brought her to sit on one of the benches overlooking the sad excuse for a pond. Leaning close, he blew against the curve of her ear, causing her to tremble and arch her neck in response. Simon gave her earlobe a lick, a nip. The wiggle of her body against him and a soft whimper let him know he'd discovered a thing she particularly liked, a thing that silenced her arguments and left her shivering in his arms.

And that, he discovered, was something *he* particularly liked.

But she cut their enjoyment short with a sudden shove at his chest. "Stop it. I don't appreciate being rendered helpless."

Her hand lashed out, and Simon braced for a slap. Instead of striking his cheek, however, her fingers slid into his hair and closed in a less-than-gentle grip. Having effectively anchored him in place, she leaned close and set about ravishing his mouth. The stroke of her tongue sent desire streaking blindly through him.

Above their heads, birds swooped and squawked and darted through the trees. A rustling beneath an old hawthorn hedge revealed the activities of some small creature, a squirrel or rabbit or chipmunk. Simon was struck by how entirely alone they were, so far removed from reproving eyes. His insides heated at the notion of how easily he might blanket the ground with their coats and draw her down beside him. . . .

Astonished at the madcap turn of his thoughts, he pulled up short and broke the kiss. "Ned . . ."

He didn't need to say more. With a horrified gasp she released him, her bruised lips falling open in a pout of dismay. "Oh . . . I . . . Good heavens."

"It's all right."

"No, it isn't. I don't know what came over me. . . ."

Simon's guilt reared. Gingerly he touched her shoulder, her hair. "It was my fault. Entirely mine."

"No," she repeated softly. More forcefully she said, "It was not your fault at all, so do not attempt to steal the culpability that is rightfully mine."

"I beg your pardon?"

"What I just did might be wrong and entirely out of character—which I assure you, it was—but I did it. I shall take responsibility for it."

Lust motes. That must be the problem. Like dust motes, except that these floated about inside his head and distorted his perceptions. Only that could explain why his attempt to shoulder the blame for their indiscretion seemed to have angered her.

After all, wasn't assuming the blame what men did? And didn't women typically let them?

"Ned, see here—"

"That's it exactly!" He winced at her outburst, but her fervor continued undiminished. "Since coming to Cambridge, I have been Ned. You even persist in calling me Ned. And unlike Ivy, Ned may go where he wishes, say what he wishes, *do* as he wishes. . . ."

She placed her palm against his cheek. "And, however wrong, I did wish to kiss you very much. In that instant, I suppose I forgot that I am not truly Ned."

She paused as a blush stained her cheeks. The fact that the kiss lasted rather longer than an instant ran through his mind but fortunately didn't exit from his mouth. Likewise, the idea of her losing herself in her male identity—in that of all instants—was so absurd he nearly burst out in roars of ironic laughter. Luckily he again reined in the impulse.

With a surge of affection that brought an ache to his chest, he raised her hand and kissed it, then held it against his heart. "I call you Ned because that is how I have come to think of you. Beautiful, brilliant, desirable Ned, with your big eyes and your short curls and your endless legs that fill a pair of trousers as no man's ever could. I call you Ned, and too often think of you as *my* Ned, but not for a single moment have I forgotten that you are a woman. All woman."

She said nothing, but the light that entered her eyes made him inordinately glad he'd made that confession. Butterfly's soft nickering reminded him that they must return to the house, that they dared not linger in this secluded place any longer. He brushed his lips lightly across hers for a final taste. "If we are doling out blame, I am afraid we'll each have to accept our share."

"That I can live with," she said with a smile. "It is the thought of being passive, of being kissed against my wishes, that I find degrading in a way I cannot abide. At least I can say I played an active part in my disgrace." She wrinkled her adorable nose. "Does that make sense?"

He shook his head. "Not a bit. Nothing in this past week makes a lick of sense."

"I know." She laughed. "It's been the most extraordinary week of my life."

"Mine, too, Ned. Mine, too."

Chapter 12

Having arrived back at Harrowood after her extraordinary ride with Simon only minutes ago, Ivy stole out to the iron garden table beyond the library to read the letter from her sister.

The opening paragraphs assured her that Holly and Willow both presently enjoyed good health, although Willow had suffered a bit of a cold the previous week. Of late their book emporium had seen a brisk business, a fortunate circumstance that nonetheless made Ivy cringe when she thought of either of her younger sisters attempting to balance the books. Of the Sutherland sisters, Ivy alone possessed an aptitude for numbers.

While the Eddelsons continued to see to their needs, the couple was becoming increasingly out of sorts the longer Ivy stayed away from home. Holly feared they'd soon become suspicious of Ivy's story of having gone down to Thorn Grove at their cousin's request to sort through more of Uncle Edward's belongings.

And that brought Holly to a matter that, as she put it, weighed most heavily on her mind. A letter had arrived from Laurel imploring her three sisters to stay close to home, and if they did stray beyond William Street, to please do so only in Mr. Eddelson's company.

Ivy glanced out over Harrowood's gardens. "Oh, dear."

"Oh, dear, what?"

Simon's query made her jump. "I didn't hear you come out."

"No, you were too absorbed in your letter. Not bad news, I hope?"

He strolled to the table and placed his hands on the back of a chair. With the removal of his coat and the absence of his neckcloth, he might have been hard at work in his laboratory. Except that he wasn't. Here in this very public part of the manor, where a servant might happen by, Simon's dishabille seemed uncommonly—her breath caught—intimate.

Yet it wasn't his attire, really, that sank a weight of awareness in her belly; it was the memory of their stolen kisses at the Grecian folly, and of passing last night in his bed, in his arms.

Oh, one could construe Laurel's warnings any number of ways, but Simon's broad-shouldered stance, with his sleeves pushed up to display muscled forearms and his lack of coat allowing full view of his taut waist and lean hips, had Ivy agreeing that leaving home had indeed plunged her into danger.

To his question, she gave a quick shake of her head. "No. That is . . . I'm not quite certain. Holly and Willow are fine, but Laurel has sent a rather cryptic and ominous caution from France."

Simon circled the table and sat beside her. "What danger could come all the way from France? There isn't another war brewing, is there?"

"No, nothing like that. It's all rather perplexing. She says we should stay close to home and await her return. There is a postscript from her husband advising us that the very best course would be for us to take up residence in his London town house."

"One can only imagine how they would react if they learned of your present abode."

She quirked a corner of her mouth. "They'd be aghast. But it is my choice to be here."

Just as it had been her choice to share his bed last

night, and to kiss him today. Wrong? Perhaps, though she didn't feel wicked or out of control. She felt . . . more like a traveler setting out to explore a new country. Whether that country would yield treasures or wreckage had yet to be determined, but she would not be deterred by obscure warnings from hundreds of miles away.

"Laurel has made her decisions," she said with conviction, "and I happen to know that at times she has knowingly placed herself in danger. That was her right, just as it is mine now to continue my mission for Victoria, no matter the risks."

"As it was your right to break with propriety earlier?" With his fingertips he lightly stroked the back of her hand.

His touch trailed fire across her skin and sent a shiver up her arm. "Not quite like that, no," she lied. "What I said was that it was my right to take responsibility for my actions."

She didn't quite know why speaking so blatantly about their earlier encounter made her retreat into the shelter of decorum. A remnant of her old self? Or a reaction to the regret peering out at her from behind his pale eyes, a sentiment that shook her confidence and left her suddenly confused.

She resorted to the ladylike tactic of raising her nose in the air. "Those were actions I should take pains not to repeat."

"*Will* it pain you, Ivy?"

Her heart stumbled. "You called me Ivy."

His smile continued to hold a haunting trace of remorse. "It *is* your name."

"Yes, but . . ."

At the folly, he had explained all that *Ned* had come to mean to him, every word of it a precious gift. Was that gift to be taken away so soon? Was she to be Ivy again— banned from university, from the laboratory, from the glorious new life she'd found?

As Ivy, she must give it all up, and she must leave Harrowood immediately. Yet as Ivy, as a woman, she might be free to love . . . love a man like Simon de Burgh.

"You must decide," he said softly. "Is it to be Ivy or Ned?"

Holding the letter to her bosom, she pressed to her feet and went to lean against the stone balustrade. She stared out at the gardens, at the fountain's arching streams glittering in the sunlight. "I wish it could be both."

Behind her she heard the scrape of his chair, the clipped rhythm of his footsteps over the paving stones. For one fleeting instant the heat of his hand hovered at her nape. "We both know that we cannot have things both ways. Stop appealing to thin air. Take responsibility and decide."

Sudden anger welled up inside her. How dare he speak of responsibility when he so clearly wanted her and at the same time *didn't* want her; when he allowed himself to be a prisoner of his own indecision rather than the master of his desires? A sudden urge to slap sense into him swung her around. Yet the instant she beheld his handsome face, his earnest expression, she wanted to kiss him, too.

Oh, she was no better at commanding her life than he. She wanted her freedom . . . and she wanted *him*. Society would never allow her to have both. As a wife she might, with a husband's permission, dabble in the laboratory, but there could never be any hint of such activities beyond the walls of their home. A woman scientist would be an oddity to be snickered at; her husband would be considered a fool.

She turned back to the gardens. "Let it be Ned, then."

He came to stand beside her at the rail. "As you wish."

The breeze fluttered the edges of the letter. Simon took it from her and scanned the page. "Your sister's warning concerns me. Does she give no specifics about why you should exercise caution?"

"Look toward the bottom. She alludes to a disturbing incident in Bath and promises to tell us more when she arrives home."

Simon held the letter at arm's length, and Ivy realized that without his spectacles he had trouble reading the script. "This man she warns of. Henri de Vere. Do you know him?"

"I've never heard of him before. She claims he has some connection to our family, but I don't see how. We have no French relatives that I know of." Ivy shrugged. "Laurel never mentioned a word of any of this when she came home from Bath, and if she did act a bit peculiar at times, the rest us of believed it to be the result of her sudden engagement. Honestly, if she has concerns, she should share them and stop hedging. Puzzles I enjoy. Guessing games I do not."

She tapped her fingers on the rail as she thought back on the past several months. "This does perhaps explain the Eddelsons."

"The whom?"

"The couple that lives with us and sees to our needs. My brother-in-law hired them. They are not what one would expect of a housekeeper and a man-of-all-work."

Turning toward her, Simon leaned against the rail. "How so?"

"Oh, they've been unfailingly sweet to us, but on one occasion *Mr.* Eddelson bloodied a man's nose for nearly bumping Willow into the path of a delivery wagon, and *Mrs.* Eddelson has a singular talent for knife throwing."

His eyebrows surged. "Obviously your sister has neglected to convey some pertinent information."

"Obviously."

"Are you going to let her know where you are?"

"Certainly not. She'd order me home immediately."

"I'm not altogether convinced you shouldn't go."

Ivy didn't like the look on his face. She'd seen it before, on Uncle Edward, and on Laurel's husband, Aidan. It was the universal expression of a man about to make decisions for the women in his life, neither consulting those women nor gaining their consent.

"If anything," she said quickly, "I should be safest here. No one but Holly, Willow, and the queen have any idea that I'm not in Surrey visiting our childhood home."

"Hmm. Perhaps you're right."

"I am."

"I suppose I'll have to keep an extra-close eye on you from now on."

Ivy scowled. "I am not a child."

"Indeed not." His voice softened with a pensive note that raised a now familiar flutter inside her. More briskly, he said, "Come. We've work to do."

The entire conversation had left her out of sorts. She didn't like the idea of being looked after, not in the way he meant, and she didn't like that he and Laurel expected her to always jump to obey orders.

Was she not capable of rational thought? Were her opinions of no value?

"One oughtn't to work on Sunday," she murmured.

He studied her with a perplexed frown. "Very well, I shan't force you. If you change your mind, I'll be up in the laboratory."

He left her discontented and secretly wishing he hadn't accepted her objections to working so readily. Perhaps with a little coaxing she would have changed her mind. Then presently she would be working at his side, instead of wondering how to spend the remainder of the day.

She strolled down into the gardens, but found nothing cheerful in the autumn blossoms, not when she might have been helping Simon in the next step of his experimentation. They had started his generator, but she had yet to discover what the powerful current would activate. Like Laurel, Simon insisted on being enigmatic. He trusted her well enough, she supposed, but apparently believed her incapable of absorbing more than small bits of information at a time.

"Mystery, caution, deliberation," she whispered to the rustling foliage. "Is he always like this, Aurelia? Is he ever carefree or spontaneous?"

As if in reply, an explosion from Harrowood's highest tower sent her racing to the house.

Simon had vowed not to experiment alone with his electromagnets, not after the last time when he nearly blew up his laboratory . . . and himself.

When he had suggested that he and Ned adjourn to the laboratory to work, he hadn't intended engaging in anything so volatile. Rather, he had merely planned to continue the calculations and adjustments that would render his generator's output of power steadier and more predictable.

Ever since Ned had joined him, safety had become his greatest priority. But in the time it took him to climb the tower stairs, he had dismissed his vows and cautionary measures as irrelevant.

Despite Ned's presence here, Simon remained very much alone. Aurelia was gone. His sister and his erstwhile best friend were also lost to him, not like Aurelia, but in some ways worse, for theirs was a deliberate abandonment of the heart.

As for Ned, her place in his life and in his laboratory would be short-lived enough. As soon as they discovered Gwendolyn's whereabouts and recovered the queen's property, Ned would shed her trousers and return to her sisters in London as Miss Ivy Sutherland.

Harrowood was no proper place for her, however much he understood her love of science. His experiments posed too great a risk. When he had initiated his challenge for an assistant, he had done so under the assumption that a young scholar would be willing to hazard life and limb in the pursuit of knowledge. As a younger man, he had faced the risks with a careless shrug.

But he'd been wrong—wrong to ever believe endangering another human life could be justified. Ned—no, not Ned, but beautiful, brilliant *Ivy*—believed he had built his generator to replace steam power and run machinery. His aspirations *had* once leaned in those directions, until the accident last winter had sent all his notions about matter and molecules colliding.

He crossed the laboratory and opened the armoire. Did he know what he was doing? The question elicited an audible chuckle. Of course he didn't. What scientific pioneer ever truly did? One formed hypotheses based on careful research, laid out a course of experimentation, held one's breath, and jumped.

It was time, he decided, to get on with it. And he would do so alone, risking only his own life to learn once and for all if matter could be manipulated, or if he had hallucinated the entire incident that nearly killed him last winter.

Or perhaps, as Errol had once accused, he had a strange penchant for flirting with death. If so, he was damned determined not to share that penchant with Ivy.

Reaching in, he lifted out the six electromagnets one by one, straining a little under the weight of each. Next he assembled the stands and set the apparatus into position.

Before lighting the fire that would heat the vat of water, he double-checked the configuration of his magnets. He had set up the first three close to the generator. Two faced each other, while the third sat perpendicular to them, facing away from the generator but attached by wires to the power source.

When the current began to flow, the confluence of these three magnets would create an energy stream powerful enough to thrust what he called a particle beam—matter broken down into its most basic elements—across an open space, to be collected and reassembled by the second arrangement of electromagnets some fifteen feet away. Or so he hoped.

He lit the furnace. Minutes later, the water began to bubble. He turned the wheel, opening the preliminary valve at the top of the vat. Steam shot through the copper duct. Stepping down, he went to the second valve and placed his hand on the duct to monitor the vibrations of the mounting energy. Another minute . . . several more seconds . . . three, two, one—he flipped the lever.

Current sparked through the generator's coils. The pistons began to bob. The center beam tipped from side to side, first slowly, then building in speed. The bellowslike compressor pumped and the wheel rotated, spilling the

charge onto the wires coiled about the first of the magnetic disks. It, too, began to rotate, and all three octagons
began to hum. Moments later, the sound echoed from the
magnets across the room. Waves of energy pulsated from
the apparatus until the floor and walls wavered like a heat-
baked road.

Straightening, Simon released his hold on the lever. The
currents stirred his hair and clothing like a storm-charged
breeze. His skin crawled as if with an army of ants. He took
three deep breaths meant to fortify his stamina and bolster
his courage. Holding the last of those breaths, he crossed to
the space between the magnetic disks, and stepped into the
energy stream.

Blinding light flashed. Like a closing fist, the current en-
gulfed him. The floor beneath him shifted violently and fell
away, leaving him to the mercy of the flow. Voltage ripped
through his nerves and ligaments, searching out each particle of his essence and fusing with it. Pain such as he had
known only once before in his life became the entirety of
his world.

Then his physical self gave way, dissolving, merging with
his equally intangible surroundings. The pain drained away
like a dissipating storm. All sensation ebbed.

Darkness. Silence. Nothingness. Like death.

Then another burst of light and a brutal slam to his body
let Simon know he was still very much alive. But as agony
seeped through every part of him, he wondered for how
much longer.

Reaching the gallery at the top of the main staircase, Ivy
found Mrs. Walsh surrounded by a gaggle of nervous footmen. They stood with their ears tilted toward the ceiling,
brows raised in alarm. From the tower room high above
them another thunderous bang sounded, followed by a succession of sizzling bursts.

"Why are you all standing here? Did you not hear that?
Don't you realize Lord Harrow could be hurt?"

The servants traded worried glances, uncertain shrugs. The tallest footman, Daniel, shook his head. "We're strictly forbidden from ever entering Lord Harrow's laboratory, sir."

"Are you daft? Something exploded up there." Ivy gripped the man's liveried coat sleeve. "I'm sure he didn't mean to prevent you from entering in the event he lay dying."

Mrs. Walsh's formidable bulk wedged between Ivy and the befuddled footman; she removed Ivy's hand from his arm. "Lord Harrow was most explicit in his instructions. It is not for us to interpret his orders. Besides, this is not the first time we have heard such racket from the tower. I assure you, sir, his lordship has always emerged unscathed."

Ivy backed away from them. "You're all mad. I'm going up."

No one moved to stop her. She was halfway up the spiraling stairs when a painful stitch in her side forced her to slow her pace. Nearly doubled over, she kept going, gripping the railing to tug herself along. With a final burst of energy she rushed to the top and all but collapsed against the closed door. A curious vibration shook the wood beneath her fingertips. A spark snapped her hand as she clutched the knob. Gasping, she pushed her way inside.

A waft of energy struck her physically. Gauzy billows of smoke drifted through the room, while small flames danced around the generator. Sparks crackled within the conducting coils before fizzling out. The generator's wheel turned lazily before winding to a stop. A deadly quiet blanketed the room.

Coughing from the smoke, Ivy hopped about to stamp out the flames. "Simon? Simon, where are you?"

Near the generator and several yards beyond it, the familiar black shapes of the electromagnets, along with the poles and brackets that had formed their stands, littered the floor. Then she spotted Simon. On the floor beneath the north window, he lay facedown, his arms and legs sprawled.

"Simon!" Ivy went down on her knees beside him. She clasped his shoulders, refusing to let go even when electricity prickled up her arms. As she lifted him an inch or two, his arms moved limply against the floor. With a heave she rolled him over onto his back. His face was white, his lips ashen. His hair stood wildly on end. "Simon? Oh, good Lord . . ."

She pressed her ear to his chest and perceived a faint, unsteady beat. Straightening, she held her hand in front of his nose . . . and felt nothing against her fingers.

Fearful panic pounded through her. With both hands flat to his chest she pushed, once, twice, thrice, each time with a forceful command to his heart to beat, his lungs to fill. A sudden notion prompted her to press her mouth to his. She breathed into him, hoping to coax his lungs back to life. She did that several times, then scooted on her bottom to resume pushing on his chest.

"Simon, come back." She slapped his cheeks. "Come back, damn you!"

His features contorted. The breath he attempted to drag in tangled in his throat and erupted in a fit of coughing. His hands flew to his neckcloth. Gasping, he sputtered as he attempted to wrestle the knot free.

Ivy pushed his hands away. "Let me."

Furiously she dug her fingers into the knot. At the same time, Simon gripped the edges of his waistcoat and yanked the buttons open. With little pings several bounced along the floor. His cravat came loose. Ivy slid the linen from around his collar and dropped it beside her.

Simon reached to tug his collar open. Then his arm fell across his eyes.

"Oh, God . . . better." His voice was a painful rasp. "Either . . . I'm dead . . . and you are an angel . . . or . . ." One eye flickered open. "Ned?"

"Yes. Yes, it's Ned." Flooding relief brimmed hotly from her eyes and squeezed her throat. "And you are very much alive, thank heaven."

"Where . . . am I?" He struggled to sit up, only to fall prone again.

Ivy pressed her hands to his shoulders. "Don't try to move. Not yet."

He gripped her wrist. "Tell me where I am."

"You're in your laboratory, of course." A sob accompanied her impatient reply.

"No . . . where . . . where in the lab?" Brows tightly knit, he turned his head from side to side. He wasn't making sense; the explosion had left him dazed. Wiping her eyes, Ivy pushed to her feet.

"Wait here." She hurried to the shelf where Simon kept glasses and a decanter of brandy. When she returned to him, she slipped an arm beneath his head and held the snifter to his lips. "Drink some of this. Oh, Simon, what on earth did you do to yourself?"

He sputtered, but quickly regained control. The spirits brought a flood of color to his face. Blinking, he leaned back against her. "Galileo's teeth, did it work?"

"Did *what* work?"

"Am I whole?" He ran a hand over his chest.

"Of course you're whole, but I fear you must be delirious." She held up three fingers in front of his face. "How many do you see?"

Ignoring the question, he pushed unsteadily upright. Her heart flip-flopped when he twisted round and flashed her a devastating grin. He grasped her hand. "My experiment, Ivy. It worked. It wasn't an accident this time."

"*This* time? What happened to you when it *was* an accident?"

"Trust me, you don't wish to know. Ah, Ivy . . ." His expression suddenly rueful, he squeezed her hand. "However much you wish me to continue calling you Ned, I find I cannot. Not anymore. As extraordinary an assistant as you are, you are no less a woman, and it would be wrong and highly dangerous for me to lose sight of that fact. You do understand, don't you?"

She did not, nor did she see the connection between his brush with death and his sudden insistence on recognizing her gender. And what dangers, specifically, did he mean, those of his laboratory or those of their mutual passion?

"I should have been here with you," she insisted. "But I suppose it was my fault. Had I agreed to accompany you, you might not have been hurt."

"Yes, but with you here I would not have tested the process."

In frustration she tossed her hands in the air. "If I am so extraordinary an assistant, stop treating me as though I'm a delicate flower that needs protecting."

He regarded her with no small amount of bewilderment. "Do you think I'd have subjected a male assistant to the untested dangers of my experiment?"

Her anger receded a fraction. "Wouldn't you have?"

"Of course not. Or, perhaps at one time I might have, but I've learned much this week. I'm not quite the curmudgeon I was at the outset."

"You *were* rather curmudgeonly the day you set your challenge."

"And you were splendid with your courageous hand-raising. But never mind that." His arms went suddenly around her, cutting off her breath with surprising strength. "Ivy, do you know what today means?"

"No. I still haven't the faintest inkling of what happened here." As much as she savored the heat of his embrace, she pushed him away far enough to get a good look at him. Flushed excitement had replaced his pallor.

"Help me up and I'll explain." After setting the brandy glass on the floor, he leaned a hand on her shoulder. She wrapped an arm about his waist and half hauled him to his feet. He pressed his free hand to his chest and frowned. "Still a bit erratic."

"Your heart?" With a lick of panic, she pushed his hand from his chest and placed her ear over his heart. "It's racing wildly. Simon, we need to summon a physician."

"Later." He surveyed the strewn magnets. "Quite the mess, but no permanent damage, I shouldn't think."

"What about the damage to you? You're taking this much too lightly."

His pensive expression told her he wasn't listening. He was surveying the space between the two sets of toppled equipment. "Galileo's teeth. First I was there." He pointed across the room to his generator. "And then I was here, where you found me."

"Well, I'm not surprised that the blast would have propelled you all that way, but—"

"It wasn't the blast. At least not in the manner you mean." With his arm draped around her shoulders, his trembling excitement flowed into her and raised new concerns that he was far from all right. Especially when he said, "I was conveyed, Ivy, by means of electroportation."

Chapter 13

"Electro-*what*?"

Surely Ivy had heard Simon wrong. Either that, or the explosion had left him more addled than she had feared. She cupped a hand to his cheek, then to his forehead. But for a lingering sheen of moisture, he felt normal, warm and alive. Even so, she considered hastening to the speaking tube and requesting that Mrs. Walsh summon a doctor.

"Electroportation," Simon repeated. "You understand how the telegraph works, don't you?"

"Electrical impulses travel along wires from one location to another."

"Correct. Electroportation is a term I coined for a process combining the simple technology of the telegraph with the molecular process of electrolysis, wherein solid mass is broken down into its individual particles, dispersed, transported, and reassembled. In this case, I was transported and reassembled several yards from where I started."

"Simon!" Stepping out from his one-armed embrace, she gripped his shoulders and gave him a shake. "What you are describing isn't possible. The explosion has left you confused."

"There was no explosion." He grinned. "What you heard was the force of matter being manipulated." He staggered toward his generator and ran his hands over his disheveled hair. "The coils will need to be replaced, but all the rest fared well enough. Next time—"

"What are you saying? There can be no next time. You nearly blew yourself up. Do you wish to incinerate yourself, the entire house, and everyone in it?"

His look of elation faded. "Ivy, today was no accident. It was a re-creation of a process that produced a similar phenomenon last winter. You see, I'd been toying with Faraday's theory of electrical lines of force, and the notion that the direction of currents can be manipulated to create a power field that would remain active even after cutting off the source of electricity. I decided to use lightning as that source, and with my electromagnets I attempted to—"

A cold fear shimmied down her spine. "You *are* mad. . . ."

His laughter did little to dissuade her. "It might appear so, but what happened next is extraordinary. Thinking I had at least a few minutes before the storm arrived overheard, I decided to make some adjustments to the positioning of the magnets. Lightning unexpectedly struck, and I was caught in the power surge."

"But you'd be dead. . . ."

"Yes, if I'd been struck directly, but I wasn't. As it was, in a manner of speaking, I did cease to exist, at least in the tangible world. My mind—my thoughts—remained intact, but the rest of me became one with the electrified field, transported from one end to the other, and deposited whole again. Not long after that, I began building my generator."

When her growing alarm rendered her mute, he grasped her upper arms and deposited a crushing, enthusiastic kiss on her lips. "Don't you see, Ivy? This discovery changes everything we thought we knew about solid matter. It proves that nothing truly is solid, that our world is made up of intermingling particles that can be manipulated in ways we never before imagined."

"Simon . . ." She in turn grasped his arms tight in an attempt to anchor him in reality. "You are not thinking clearly. Which is understandable under the circumstances. But believe me when I say that what you are suggesting is not possible. Solid is solid." She stomped her foot twice against the floor. "We cannot walk through walls, nor can our corporeal selves be disassembled and reassembled in other places."

"Let me prove it to you."

"No. I won't let you do that to yourself again." She released him and pulled away. "It's madness."

"Perhaps you're right. Twice in one day might be pressing my luck. Tomorrow, then. You'll see that I'm telling you the truth."

"No, Simon. I won't allow you to prove anything to me."

A decision came in a burst of clarity, while the rest of her, most especially her heart, felt disconnected and numb, perceiving only a promise of future pain. All this time she had feared being sent away for her own good. Not once had she considered that she might have to leave for *his* good, to prevent him from harming himself.

"Whether or not your theory holds merit," she said quietly, "your actions nearly resulted in your death. . . ."

Her breath seized up in her throat. Ah, the pain was not so distant after all. She struggled past it, holding up a hand when Simon seemed about to speak. "I am sorry, but I will not be a party to your self-destruction." She headed for the doorway.

"Where are you going?"

Into town first, to appeal to his colleagues and see if they might be able to talk sense into him. Then . . . she supposed she'd go home. She certainly couldn't stay here, where her very presence encouraged him to take unthinkable risks.

Without turning back to face him, she paused on the threshold. "I am going downstairs to pack my things."

Her reply met with silence, and she hurried down the steps.

Simon watched Ivy go, believing that in another moment she'd grasp the magnitude of his discovery and turn back around. He *knew* she would reappear in the doorway. He waited. Just another moment . . . she'd be back. . . .

Her descending footsteps echoed from the tower. Simon frowned.

Several more seconds ticked by, each one eating away at both his exuberance and his confidence. What he had done wrong? To be sure, he had frightened her, and perhaps he deserved her rebuke for that, but she had also turned her back on the phenomenon that had been the driving force of his existence these many months.

He had been so certain she would celebrate his success. How could she, a scientist in her own right, simply walk away? The answer hovered like the remaining steam drifting over the floorboards. She hadn't believed him.

It was a possibility he hadn't considered.

Crestfallen, he turned to examine his generator. The process had left the coils charred, the pistons pitted, the luster of the crankshaft and wheel dulled. His spirits plunged. Galileo's teeth, what if she was right, and he *had* only imagined being transported across the room?

Or . . . what if either way, it didn't matter? He'd been accused more than once in the course of his career of tilting at windmills. He had always ignored the charge, but for the first time now he pondered whether he'd been chasing a useless dream. Did it matter that he managed to transport himself fifteen feet across a room? He could far more easily have walked those fifteen feet, and with less wear on his body. How could such a process ever be practical?

Ben and Errol geared their work toward easing the burdens of everyday life. Light, heat, mechanics. Both men envisioned a world in which homes and industry ran on electrical power. Colin's research focused on the improvement of farming techniques, to alleviate hunger by making food more readily available. Through means of chemistry, he sought to improve feeds and fertilizers in order to increase yearly harvest yields and strengthen livestock.

Did Simon's discovery, glorious though it may seem, amount to little more than a hollow spectacle, a sorry attempt to play God and manipulate a world that often felt out of his control?

He went still. The nature of that last thought spoke volumes about how much influence Ivy's disapproval held over him. Damn it, her opinion shouldn't matter so much.

But for reasons he didn't stop to analyze, her opinion did matter, and it sent him at top speed down the tower stairs. He didn't slow down until he reached her bedchamber door. It stood open. Inside, the wardrobe doors swung slightly on their hinges, her clothes now piled on the bed. She had dragged a leather trunk to the center of the room; a few items of apparel lay draped over its open lid.

Simon's heart pounded, no longer a result of the electrical jolt he'd received, but from a rising, strangling panic.

"Ivy?" At first he didn't see her, and when no answer came, he strode into the room and tried again. "Ned?"

Her lean figure unfolded from the overstuffed chair beside the hearth. She looked lost and indecisive, and on the verge of tears. His heart twisted.

"Please don't leave." He darted another desperate glance at the trunk, then at the open dresser drawers. Hope surged at the sight of the clothes that still filled them. Had he arrived in time to dissuade her from going? "If you object so strongly to what I did today, I won't do it again. I'll concentrate on more practical matters, powering machinery, that sort of thing. I'll still require your assistance, Ivy. Or Ned. Whichever you prefer. Just . . ." His throat tightened. "Stay."

She opened her mouth, but her lips trembled and she pressed them shut. Emotion flooded her cheeks. She looked away and gave an adamant shake of her head.

He didn't know what that gesture meant, and a single entreaty, like a prayer, echoed through his mind. *Please.*

"I came down here with every intention of clearing out." She stared into the empty hearth, then up at him. "Of leaving Harrowood this very afternoon. How *can* I be a willing party to such reckless behavior? Your claims are pure insanity. A person would have to be mad to believe you."

Her hands fisted in her lap. "But the problem is that . . . by the time I reached the bottom of the tower, I'd begun to question my own resolve, and when I opened those dresser drawers"—she closed her eyes, then peeked at him from beneath her lashes—"I came to a conclusion that shocked me to my core."

"What conclusion, Ivy?"

She gave a tremulous sniffle. "That I believe you."

The whisper filled the room, filled his heart. Reaching behind him, he shut the door.

As quickly as if he'd electroported again, he was across the room. His arms were around her, and his lips moist with the salty taste of her tears. "I'm sorry, so sorry I frightened you."

"I'm sorry I walked out on you."

"No." He buried his cheek in her curls and held her tighter, as tightly as he could without hurting her. "Perhaps if I'd been forthcoming with you from the first, rather than hiding the truth and damned near obliterating myself . . ."

"The hand . . . and the heart," she said as their lips met in a flurry of kisses, "they were for this, so you could understand the effects of electrical currents on the body."

With a nod he admitted the truth. "It didn't start out that way. At first I only sought to learn if electricity could regenerate a failing organ or a limb. But after my accidental discovery, my focus changed."

Her hands gripped his face. Her eyes were fierce, unrelenting. "And now?"

Yes, what now? As if electricity continued to flow through him, his body buzzed, vibrated. In those moments during which he'd subjected himself to the current, his physical self had ceased to exist. He'd become streaming energy, traveling light, disembodied and incorporeal. It had been as terrifying as it had been exhilarating. There had been an instant when he had doubted whether he could break free of the energy and reenter the world.

Her face had been the first thing he'd seen upon being solid again, her touch the first thing proclaiming him once more a physical being. And now, with her in his arms, words like *science* and *experimentation* lost all meaning. The intangibles of concept and theory—the very principles that had once kept his world from falling apart—gave way to brute physicality and the taste of her skin beneath the glide of his tongue.

Was he whole, real? No, not until now, perhaps not even now. Parts of him continued to feel hollow and shaky. He needed *her* to complete the process of reassembling his physical self. He needed to feel her body's response to the demand of his harder self, needed to vent the desire flooding his body.

"Now there is only this," he said, and devoured her lips.

She both yielded and demanded, as he should have known she would. Urgency made their embraces rough and volatile. They groped and tugged and pulled at each other, grabbed at clothing, limbs, handfuls of hair. The sounds of tearing, of groaning and cursing, filled his ears as they forced themselves upon each other, outrageously and indelicately. He drew her tongue into his mouth and sucked it. She scraped her teeth across his bottom lip and drew blood.

"I feared you were dead, blast you." Fury quivered in her voice. "Dear God, when I entered that room, you looked as good as dead."

He thrust an arm behind the small of her back, so that she arched against him, her breasts outthrust beneath her shirt, straining at their silken fetters. With his free hand he tore away her neckcloth and sprang open her collar to expose her pearly throat. He set his lips there, suckling the spot where her life force pulsed. "I feared you would make good on your threat to leave. Damn it, I feared I deserved for you to go."

"You won't be rid of me that easily."

Quickly he released her, spun her about, and shoved her coat down her arms. While she faced away from him, he drew her against him and slid his hands up her shirtfront until he found her breasts beneath their bindings. With a moan she leaned her weight into him, pressing her buttocks against his hips to trap his erection within deliciously warm flesh. His mouth fell to her linen-clad shoulder, and a waft of starch drew from him a near-manic bark of laughter.

"How bloody confounding. The last time I removed a gentleman's coat, it was to prevent the inebriated wearer from entangling himself in the garment after he passed out."

"And I . . ." She spun about and tore at his waistcoat buttons. ". . . I have never removed a gentleman's outer garments, not for any reason."

That candid admission pounded through his conscience and rendered him motionless but for his thrashing pulse points. Ivy's hands stilled over his waistcoat's bottommost button. Their gazes locking, vibrant energy arced between them. Her lips were bruised and gleaming with the moisture of his kisses; his own lips tingled and smarted with the heat of hers.

Her eyes darkening, she plucked that last button free. He caught her wrist before she could make another move. Without subtlety he raked his hungry gaze over her. Then he very pointedly glanced at the bed. "Make no mistake. A man can stand firm against temptation for only so long. And then he takes what he desires."

"I understand." Her lashes shadowed her cheeks as her gaze crept slowly down his body and stopped at his groin. Slowly she extracted her hand from his fist. Her fingertips hovered, slightly trembling, almost but not quite touching him. Every muscle in his abdomen and groin clenched in an agony of anticipation created by her hesitation. He died a small death of impatience as concentration rippled her brow, as her teeth caught at her bottom lip.

Her touch came, petal soft at the apex of his breeches. A violent shudder racked him. For several torturous seconds she held her fingertips against the mad pulsing of his shaft. Then with ingenuous simplicity she cupped him in her palm.

His body thundered with the pleasure of it, with the expectation of what would happen next. His hand covered hers and pressed it more fully against his arousal. "I will insist one last time that you must be clear, Ivy, about where such explorations will lead."

"Can I not simply be clear about my willingness—no, my *longing*—to take the journey?"

Both a confession of her innocence and an assurance of her desires, her avowal scattered his last qualms into oblivion. He set his open mouth to her neck and drew the tender skin between his lips. Her own lips parted on a gasp; she shivered, her weight collapsing against him.

He swung her up into his arms and went to the bed. In moments, her waistcoat, neckcloth, and collar lay in a heap on the floor. He tugged off her boots and then his own, along with his waistcoat, collar, and cravat. All this they had done before. But that other time he had set his own needs aside and saw only to hers, and in pleasuring her he had found intense if surprising satisfaction.

Today, however, the tantalizing prospect of giving *and* taking sent his blood surging in a way that precluded his being the gentleman he had been that night.

He dragged her onto his lap. Their bodies entwining, he took her lips and her tongue with a fervor that left no mystery of what would happen next. The last vestiges of gallantry turned and fled. Simon yanked Ivy's shirt from her waistband.

Ivy froze as Simon reached for the bindings around her breasts. The sunlight streaming through her windows allowed for no modesty, no secrets. More than any other article of clothing, the bindings had shielded her from the world's judgment.

"You and I have done a great deal of pretending." His voice and his warm breath caressed her cheek. His fingertips burrowed beneath the bindings to nestle against her skin. "It is time to discover the real Ivy."

When he lifted her shirt over her head, she raised her arms to help him. Where his fingertips had been, his lips descended.

"Genuine, undisguised, unrestrained Ivy." Between each

word came a kiss, light and moist, so sweet it brought tears to her eyes. Then the kisses deepened, trailing fire across her skin. Beneath their constraints, her breasts strained, aching to be freed, to be claimed and handled none too gently.

Suddenly desperate, she struggled in vain to pull the bindings free. "Get them off me, please. I cannot abide them another moment."

Before he set to work freeing her, he stripped off his own shirt. The sight of his naked shoulders and chest banished everything else from her mind.

Oh. She stared, openmouthed, her astonished gaze tracing the rugged yet oddly graceful contours of his muscled torso. Transfixed, she marveled at how the simple act of breathing expanded those contours in the most beguiling way.

"Ivy?" At the touch of his hand to her cheek, she recovered her wits and found her voice.

"The books ... never showed scientists who looked like ... *this*. Surely Galileo did not." Reaching out, she grazed one hard pectoral muscle and delighted at how it quivered at the contact. "Good heavens."

"Wrestling and rowing."

"Pardon?"

"I haven't engaged only in science here at Cambridge."

"Oh. Goodness." She wanted to feel those muscles, each and every one of them, being pressed against her body. She began tugging again; if she could only get the blasted bindings off.

He caught her wrists. "Let me."

Layer by layer, he unwound the silk strips, each rotation rendering her lighter, freer, yet more breathless. Finally, only a single narrow layer separated her from his touch. Simon audibly, shakily filled his lungs. Ivy trembled as if from cold. Oh, but she wasn't cold; her skin burned with eagerness, with a twinge of apprehension, too. Holding the end of the final strip between his thumb and forefinger,

Simon leaned in to take her mouth in a kiss that promised a sweeping adventure she would never forget.

Against her lips he murmured, "Shall I, lovely Ivy?"

"If you don't, I certainly will."

A rumbling laugh poured out of him and traveled like an electrical wave all through her. Her nerve endings tingled; her heart clattered as, with a final flick, he unwrapped her. The cool air struck her breasts and hardened her nipples, but the unfettered greed in his gaze heated her through.

He cupped a breast in his wide, warm palm and dragged the pad of his thumb across the nipple. She shuddered at the friction; aching moisture gathered between her legs. He swore softly as he looked at her, at every exposed part of her. "By God, you are the most beautiful thing I have ever seen."

In a far corner of her mind she doubted the truth of such a claim, but every other part of her came alive at the praise. Her nipples strained for him, for the touch of his lips . . . and Simon did not disappoint as he ran his tongue over the swell of her bosom and sucked a nipple into his mouth.

But for his weight holding her down, the painful pleasure streaking through her might have sent her body bucking off the mattress. As it was, she arched up into him, stretching herself taut and heightening the sensation of his suckling lips and marauding hands.

He fumbled with the buttons of her trousers. She felt the waistband loosening, the fabric being tugged down her hips. All this he did without lessening his mouth's ministrations at her breasts. From one to the other, he paid them sensual homage in equal measure, until just a stroke of his tongue across a sensitized nipple released a clenching contraction deep in her womb.

It was as one of these contractions subsided that she realized, with a shock of awareness, that she lay fully naked beneath the weight of Simon's solid body. A whimper of unbearable longing escaped her. Hearing it, Simon lifted his head and stared down into her eyes. Did he see the storm growing inside her? Surely he must, for abruptly he sat up and wrestled off his own breeches and underclothing.

Still, he didn't immediately return to his prone position over her, but remained looming beside her, his long legs stretched out, his torso twisting at an angle that emphasized his muscles and the breadth of his shoulders. Ivy drank in the sight of him, tapering and smooth, a glorious Adonis. Nearly awestruck, she brushed the backs of her fingers across his abdomen and traced his hip.

He hissed through his teeth. "Do I please you, Ivy?"

How ludicrous a question, coming from so splendid a man. "You are a most magnificent specimen, sir."

His gaze turned feral, frightening. His face a mask of raw male fortitude, he braced a hand on either side of her and lowered his body over hers. Ivy shut her eyes and wrapped her hands around his hard upper arms. Desire drove her to thrust her pelvis against his, seeking the satisfaction her body craved, yet which she had yet to fully identify.

Simon grasped her hips and held her to him. The tip of his sex, grown rigid as steel, pressed at her opening with a determined nudge. She gasped at the stroke of his shaft across her softer folds. Simon's mouth again closed over a nipple. His tongue teased, his lips plucked. Inside her, a cord that connected her female parts stretched and twisted. Of their own accord, her thighs parted wide and her legs encircled his waist.

A strident sound filled her ears—her own voice, crying out his name.

He pulled his mouth from her breast and set it on her own. Her cries became muffled, then mingled with his deeper, ragged moans. His panting breaths filling her, he opened a tiny space between their lips. "Are you certain this is what you want? Do but say the word, and I shall pleasure you as I did before."

The promise came in a rush, as if forced out before he might change his mind. Amid tumultuous thoughts and whirling sensations, Ivy found one quiet conviction. She opened her eyes and adamantly met his gaze, a gaze filled with lust, yet shadowed with honor-clad doubt.

"You have shown me a world of which I had only dreamed," she said. "Such joy has made me greedy, Simon, and now I demand that you show me not only the world, but heaven, too."

Chapter 14

She thought he would push inside her then. She braced herself for the act. However much she wished for this culmination, her fear of the unknown persisted.

His shaft retreated, and Simon kissed his way down her body, leaving no part of her unexplored. Her breasts became full and heavy, like ripe fruit at harvesttime. Her parted thighs shuddered as he kissed and licked a trail to her knee, then switched to the other leg to begin the upward trek, closer, ever closer to that most intimate of places.

His tongue speared between her nether lips. A protest surged instinctively to her lips, but she bit it back as apprehension dissolved into shocking delight. Electrifying rapture.

He increased the pressure and the speed of his strokes. Through a lust-ridden haze she felt herself being opened, felt his finger, then two, enter her, fill her. He worked his fingers inside her until her muscles ceased their protest. A push and a sudden tearing sent a bolt of pain through her.

Pleasure returned as Simon gently stroked and fondled her. His lips had receded from between her legs, yet his hands continued to work their wonders. His tongue glided over her breasts, along her throat. He took her mouth in a deep kiss as his solid weight sank over her.

"Ivy . . ." He spoke her name again and again, each time with a hot rush of breath to scorch her cheeks.

A formidable pressure beckoned at her nether lips. Ivy felt herself stretching wide, resisting and yielding, and— *oh*—filling as Simon slid his length inside her.

The boundaries between pain and pleasure blurred, each a twisting, writhing current surging higher and higher, until Ivy's being shattered and diffused, soared and reeled, died and was reborn.

Simon entered Ivy determined to be gentle, to make her first time as special as he could. He did his best to hold back, but the tight muscles of her sex enveloped him and squeezed, drowning his intentions in pleasure. She had spoken of greed, and now he found he could no more subdue his insatiable hunger for his sweet assistant than he could have stopped exploring the miracles of science.

And this, *this* was one of those miracles, the wonder of joining, of sharing the chase for ecstasy.

Harder and more urgently than he meant to, he pumped into her. His mind turned numb, his sensations dagger sharp. Ivy's body bucked beneath him, driving him fiercely on until his passion tightened into a spinning ball of energy that clenched and seized and rushed beyond his control. With a roar he buried his cock inside her and lost himself to a violent eruption of pleasure.

For seconds afterward, or perhaps an eternity, rippling charges stimulated every part of him. Inside her, his erection pulsated as if their lovemaking was only just beginning, as if he were ready to go again. Yet at the same time he felt thoroughly, supremely sated, the warmth of her body filling him with contentment.

He slid his arms beneath her and rolled until she lay atop his chest, her legs sprawling on either side of his own. Her shaky sigh stirred his chest hairs. He grazed his fingers up and down her spine. "Ivy?"

"Shh. No words." She snuggled her cheek in the hollow between his pectoral muscles. "Not yet."

He wished only to know if she was all right. If what they had done had made her happy. The melting of her body against his supplied the answers, at least for now. They both might have dozed; he wasn't sure, but at one point he opened his eyes to see that the daylight in the room had subtly shifted to a new angle.

He nudged her gently, hoping she was awake for no other reason than that, in the sultry, musky aftermath of their lovemaking, he wanted her company. "Ivy?"

"Mm."

He brushed his lips through her hair. "What made you change your mind? About believing me, I mean."

When she didn't immediately reply, he realized the foolishness of the question. What did it matter why she believed him, as long as she did?

Then she raised her head and smiled down at him. "I believed you because it was you telling me. Because I knew Simon the man wouldn't lie to me, and Lord Harrow the scientist would make no such declaration without evidence to substantiate his claims."

The simplicity of her trust awed him. "It was that easy?"

"Easy? Good heavens. A week ago, and with anyone else, I'd have reached a far-different conclusion. I assure you, sir, my faith has been hard-won."

With a delighted laugh, he rolled again until they lay on their sides facing each other, and her lips were his for the taking. Arousal stirred anew. "You are a most extraordinary woman," he said between kisses. "You know that, don't you?"

Her face grew somber. "But am I still your assistant? Has this changed anything?"

Misgiving closed around him. More than anything, he wanted to reassure her of her place in his laboratory, but as he regarded her heart-shaped face with its large dark eyes and pretty, plump lips, a painful tug in his chest affirmed that *everything* between them had changed.

A week ago, she had been some anonymous youth who first captured his notice with an audacious wave of her hand. In young "Ned's" essay, Simon had discovered the zeal he had sought in an assistant. Galileo's teeth, he remembered the same unbridled enthusiasm in everything Aurelia did. And while yesterday and even this morning memories of his wife would have caused him pain, now he found himself able to think about her without a frame of sorrow surrounding her image.

He wondered briefly why that should be, then discerned the very reason poised beside him, waiting with visible consternation for his reply.

"*Have* things changed?" she whispered.

He released a sigh. "How could things not have changed? You are not Ned. Nor are you some brazen young female stealing her way into my laboratory under false pretenses. You are *Ivy*."

Lovely, incomparable Ivy, with the power to banish the ghosts from his past *and* bring him back from the brink of death. He fingered a tendril of hair that curled against her cheek. How could he make her understand that after the intimacy they'd shared, he could no longer put her at risk, as his experiments, no matter how carefully conducted, certainly would do?

He could not bear the sorrow of another accident, another life lost. And exactly what that sentiment said about his feelings for Ivy ... Unable and unwilling to consider those feelings, and wishing he could shed them as readily as he had shed his clothing, he shut his eyes. Ah, but the feelings persisted. They were more than skin-deep; they were already part of him, in a way he thought he'd never experience again. In exactly the same way he had been determined to avoid.

"Simon—"

He placed a finger over her lips. "No words, remember? Not while we're in each other's arms. As you also pointed out, it is Sunday. I should not have worked today. Neither is it a day for arguing."

The fight drained from her features and a reluctant, crooked smile dawned. "For today, then. Tomorrow, however, I do intend to continue working, and to argue my right to do so if I must."

"I see those boys' clothes of yours have made you brash and stubborn."

"Which is better than stark raving mad."

He laughed. "Are you implying something?"

Her eyes sparking mischief, she turned in his arms and wiggled her shapely rear against him. But just as he snaked an arm around her waist and set his mouth to the nape of her neck, she let out a whimper of dismay. Her hand disappeared beneath the coverlet.

"Are you in pain? Did I hurt you?" He rose up on his elbow to peer over her shoulder and follow her gaze beneath the bedclothes. Russet stains streaked her thighs and dotted the linen sheet beneath her.

Her embarrassment was nothing compared with the guilt those stains kindled in him. He'd known full well she was an innocent, yet he'd plundered her just the same.

There was no way to undo the act. He could only summon the strength to avoid letting it happen again. Or . . .

Another possibility shoved through his disordered thoughts. Marriage. Could there be any other outcome to this reckless afternoon of lovemaking?

The old fear of loss rearing up, he feigned a calm he didn't feel and kissed her shoulder. "Never mind, darling." He drew her back down against him and gently stroked her breasts. With kisses at her nape and shoulders, he gradually coaxed her to relax.

They lay like that for another half hour or so, until Simon remembered that they were not alone in the house, and that servants relished gossip as much as they did holidays from work.

"Stay here," he whispered, and slid out of bed. He dressed quickly, and handed Ivy her dressing gown. "Put this on."

"Shouldn't I get dressed?"

"Not yet. I'll be back." After a parting kiss, he made his way downstairs and found Mrs. Walsh.

His request made the housekeeper scowl with indignation. "A bath? In the middle of the day? For a *servant*?"

"Mr. Ivers is hardly a servant, Mrs. Walsh. He is my assistant, and he risked his life earlier to save mine."

He paused as the woman's sallow complexion darkened to crimson. "The rest of us were merely following your implicit orders never to enter your laboratory uninvited, sir."

"Yes, well, thank goodness Ned experienced no such reservations. But I fear the lad received an electrical shock as he helped me stabilize the equipment. A hot soak will help ease the muscle spasms. Oh, and the poor chap also managed to cut himself. Got him lying in bed at the moment nursing the wound. The linens will need to be changed."

"I'll see to it right away, sir."

"Indeed. Oh, and Mrs. Walsh . . ." He glanced about the dusky central hall in which they stood. "This house has grown almost dingy these past months. Please give orders for a thorough cleaning."

For a fleeting instant a mask of disbelief held the woman's stern features immobile. After all, it had been Simon's enraged bellow for peace and quiet that had brought his servants' housekeeping duties to a near halt over a year ago. Then, their bustling activity had served only to remind him that the woman who had once guided their efforts was gone . . . never to return. Surely, he admitted now, allowing dust to coat the woodwork and dim the brilliance of the chandelier's crystals was no way to honor Aurelia's memory.

Mrs. Walsh's lips twitched with uncharacteristic delight. "Yes, sir. Right away, sir."

Ivy waited beside the steaming tub, her dressing gown buttoned to her chin, until Simon's valet, Ellsworth, and his team of footmen exited single file from her room. Ellsworth paused in the doorway with one last questioning glance.

"I can manage on my own. Thank you." She raised an eyebrow to convey her impatience for the man to be gone. Once the door closed behind him, she ran and turned the key in the lock, as she always did before disrobing. She could not chance a servant walking in on her and discovering her secret.

She shed her robe and, without looking down at the stains on her thighs, eased into the sudsy water. A chafing sting persisted between her thighs. Despite the discomfort, she savored the sensation. Leaning back against the side of the tub, she tilted her head against the rim, closed her eyes, and conjured images of their lovemaking until heated threads wound through her, as steamy as the soothing water.

She drifted in sensual oblivion until a touch on her shoulder sent her bolting upright with a splash.

"It's only me." Simon leaned over to kiss her.

Her heart raced, spilling its beat into his palm, which had slid to envelop her breast. "Such a fright you gave me. How did you get in? I locked the door."

His fingertips stroked her in ways that scattered her thoughts. With his other hand, he reached into his waistcoat pocket and drew out a small ring of keys. "It pays to be the master of the house."

Ivy relaxed against the tub. "Thank you for arranging this for me."

"You're very welcome." His hand drifted upward to cradle her chin. Tipping her face, he kissed her, a slow, languid touch that turned those heated threads of moments ago to bands of fire.

"Are you quite all right?" he asked.

"I should ask you the same. Had I realized how exerting . . . what we did . . . could be, I'd never have allowed it. Not after your brush with death earlier."

"Not allow it?" He pulled back, lips quirking. "Who is master here and who the assistant?"

When her mouth sprang open to retort, he kissed her again.

"You needn't answer that, for I know the answer. Of Harrowood, and of my laboratory, I am indeed the master. But here, Ivy, and of this"—his hand ran possessively down her soap-slicked torso—"you are indisputably in authority. I will take no privileges but those you grant me."

She considered that statement and the one that preceded it, the woman and the assistant suddenly at war with each other. "You never answered my question."

He sat back on his heels, his hand leaving her breast to trail in the water. "That is because I haven't reached a decision."

"You can't mean to bar me—"

"I mean to do what is right and safe, for you and for any assistant."

A twinge of panic prompted her to blurt, "I am also here on the queen's behest. You must not forget that."

He nodded his acquiescence. "True enough. However, we both know that neither my sister nor the queen's stone are hidden in my laboratory."

She started to retort but realized he was right. Her investigation had reached a standstill and would remain stalled until some hint of Lady Gwendolyn's whereabouts surfaced.

"You were not nearly so cautious with me yesterday," she murmured, "or all the days preceding."

"That is neither accurate nor fair." He pushed to his feet. Grabbing the back of the small dressing table chair, he dragged it beside the tub and straddled it. "I never intended exposing you to undue danger."

"The queen's command aside for the moment, did you or did you not hire me to assist you with this electroportation process of yours?"

"I hired you to assist me in making the calculations and corresponding adjustments to my generating equipment. I never intended to risk you or anyone else with the actual experiment."

"Fair enough. I do not ask that you electroport me." Gripping the rim of the tub, she pulled up onto her knees so that her face came nearly level with his. "I only demand that you continue to allow me to fulfill the functions I came here to perform, both for you and the queen."

His hooded gaze drifted over her, reminding her that pulling out of the water had left her wholly exposed from the waist up. His attentions lingered on her nipples, reddened and swollen from their lovemaking and from soaking in the hot water. She shivered as though he had touched her, and his lips twitched in acknowledgment.

"Are you cold?" The backs of his fingers grazed her, and her breath rushed in with a gasp. His smile grew. "No, I'd say not cold. But you are full of demands today, aren't you?"

Her hand closed over his; she pressed it to her breast and the beat of her heart. "I don't wish to be treated as females so often are, set aside and sheltered for their own good."

At that moment, both the teasing Simon and the commanding Lord Harrow faded, and in his eyes Ivy glimpsed uncertainty and a trace of what she could identify only as fear. Then both were gone, replaced by the stern slash of his brows.

"I must think more about this. I'll give you my decision tomorrow."

She resisted the urge to splash water at him. "And until then?"

His expression turned devilish as he stood, grasped her hands, and raised her to her feet. "Until then, we must find other ways of occupying our time. Come, you've soaked that luscious body long enough."

And he hauled her, dripping wet, into his arms.

Chapter 15

On Monday following breakfast, Simon called after Ivy as she all but raced toward the tower stairs.

"Not that way."

She stopped short and turned, her face filling with disappointment and even, perhaps, a glint of reproach. "You've reached your decision, then?"

He hadn't, at least not about whether to allow her to continue assisting him. Last night he had lain awake as a far more pressing issue lobbed about his brain. Marriage. Could he walk that narrow precipice again, knowing how easily one or both of them could fall? Yet there were other risks to consider besides those to his heart.

There was *Ivy's* heart, and her well-being. If they were to marry, then he owed it to her to become the kind of husband she deserved. A woman like Ivy deserved the best, not a hollow wreck of a scientist who feared love and bore little regard for the sanctity of his own life.

Had Ivy not been on hand yesterday, he might have scraped himself up off the floor—eventually—made a few new calculations, and tried walking into the energy stream again. The Mad Marquess ... had he truly begun to earn the moniker?

Then he must change, be a better man—safer, steadier, more dependable.

"I've a meeting with the Galileo Club in town," he told

Ivy rather than answer her question. "We'll be gathering in Benjamin Rivers's office in about an hour. I'd like you to accompany me. There is a matter I wish to discuss with you and I cannot think of anywhere more private than in a moving coach."

"Then you *have* reached a decision. Judging from your somber expression, I shan't find it a welcome one." She propped a fist on her hip in a gesture both masculine and oddly sensual. Her voice fell to a whisper. "Let me remind you that my obligation to the queen has yet to be fulfilled. You cannot dismiss me—"

"Ned, please." He gestured for her to go with him out to the drive. "We will talk in the coach."

She seemed to dig in her heels. "Why don't we ride as we did yesterday? Surely we can debate our opposing views from atop our mounts."

His patience running short and his nerves becoming frayed, he mustered a stern expression. Before he could counter her argument, however, she sighed and strode past him, leading the way out to the waiting vehicle.

His gut twisting, he waited to speak until they'd turned onto the main road. Ivy sat stiffly beside him, ruminating down at her hands folded on her lap. Drawing a fortifying breath, Simon covered her hands with one of his own. "I have decided the only right thing for us to do is to marry."

She flinched, swung her face up to look at him, and frowned. Deeply. As if she hadn't understood his meaning, she didn't say a word.

"Surely, you must agree that it is necessary." Even to him, the words sounded feeble and halfhearted. He cleared his throat and tried again. "We have much in common. And . . . you seem happy here at Harrowood. . . ."

"Ouch."

She tugged her hands out from under his, and he realized his fingers had clamped around hers like a vise. "Sorry. But surely you see the sense—"

"Have you never heard a single word I've said to you?"

As far as he could recall, she hadn't said much this morning.

She made an exasperated sound in her throat. "I've no intention of marrying—neither you nor anyone. In my time here I've discovered the true nature of independence and self-discovery, and I don't intend to give that up. Ever." She slid several inches farther away from him on the carriage seat. "Besides, look at you. You're sitting there as rigid as a rail and your face looks as if it were hewn from solid stone. You don't wish to marry me. You're only offering out of obligation. I'm sorry, but even if I were to marry, I'd never settle for that."

Her sardonic half chuckle that followed this outburst leveled every argument he might have made to the contrary. Most women would have been damned pleased to have secured a proposal from a marquess, no matter the circumstances. Ah, but not *this* woman, not Ivy. *I've no intention of marrying—neither you nor anyone.* She could not have made her feelings any plainer, could not have rejected his suit any more firmly.

"It isn't as if you need to salvage my reputation," she went on. "No one will ever discover what happened between us yesterday. People believe me to be Ned Ivers, and Ned Ivers I shall remain until my task is completed."

Oh, she thought she had full control over her fate, did she? "And if you are with child?" he asked softly.

As if they'd hit a particularly hard bump in the road, she reached up to grip the hand strap hanging above the door. "There is no reason to think such a thing."

"Isn't there?" The speed with which she rejected the notion of carrying his child stole his breath . . . and plucked painfully at his heart. *Neither you nor anyone.* She left him with no doubt that those were not simply brave words but a stubborn, nonnegotiable avowal.

This was not at all how he had rehearsed his proposal of marriage, nor how he'd envisioned her response. Where were the happy tears? The kisses? The joy that should have filled both their hearts?

Feeling wretched and yet, God help him, undeniably *relieved*, he tugged at his neckcloth and met her gaze. "If you are with child, Ivy, then we must marry. Whether you wish it or no, we will have no choice."

They didn't speak again until the carriage clambered onto Trinity Lane in the center of the city. She stared out the window at the passing shops. "I'd like to get out here, please."

"Aren't you coming to my meeting with me? We're to discuss our plans for the upcoming Royal Society consortium."

"Unless you truly need me, I'd like to check in at St. John's to see if another letter has arrived from London."

Hardly likely. What she wanted was time away from him. So be it. "All right. I'll drop you there."

"I'd prefer to walk."

"Alone?"

She turned toward him and raised an eyebrow. "A man's prerogative, isn't it?"

He didn't like the idea of her making her way through the city's streets and university byways unaccompanied. It wasn't proper for a woman, but he supposed her attire would shield her from any undue attentions. When the carriage stopped, he resisted the impulse to help her down to the pavement.

She placed her top hat on her head and gave her coat a dignified tug. "What time and where shall I meet you?"

"I'll collect you at St. John's. You'll be in Second Court?"

She replied in the affirmative and set off, her flapping coattails affording him mocking views of her backside. With those images lingering in his mind's eye, he pushed his way into Ben's office a few minutes later. The others were already assembled, lounging in chairs pulled around the desk.

The requisite tray of scones and sweet cakes sat at Ben's elbow, as though he could never quite compensate for the deprivation he'd suffered as a child back in Glamorganshire. "Ah, Simon, you're just in time." He pushed the tray across the desk. "Fresh from the oven."

"I've eaten. Thank you." Simon claimed the empty chair beside Errol's and tossed his hat to the settee behind them. "Any word from or about my sister since yesterday?"

Errol shook his head, while Colin mumbled a sullen, monosyllabic denial Simon found himself believing. Ben paused in his task of pouring tea and looked up with a puzzled frown.

"What's this about Gwendolyn?"

"She's gone missing from London. Left the palace without permission and ... now no one knows where she's gone."

"Good heavens, I do hope no harm has come to her." Ben lifted the teapot again. "How did you discover her absence?"

Simon was quick with his lie. "A mutual friend at the palace wrote to warn me."

His thick spectacles flashing sunlight from the window, Errol accepted the cup of tea Ben handed him. "Have you checked with Alistair?"

"I certainly intend to and soon. I've also sent inquiries to Gwendolyn's closest friends, though instinct tells me that if she doesn't wish to be found, she'll continue to elude me."

The mention of Alistair Granville's name, however, had set his pulse racing. The consortium was to take place at Alistair's home. If Gwendolyn intended presenting the stone to Simon—or one of his colleagues—she might do so during the gathering of scientists and Royal Society representatives. Such a dramatic gesture would be in keeping with her character.

Ben hunched over his desk, fingers tented beneath his chin. "Speaking of the consortium, will your generator be ready in time?"

"More than ready." Simon shifted his chair a few inches to avoid the sun angling through the curtains. "And entirely at your disposal."

Ben's mouth dropped open. "Entirely?"

Beside him, Errol gave the floor a thump with his cane. "Exceedingly generous of you, my boy."

Colin's blond hair fell across his brow as he tilted his head pensively. "This either means your mysterious project has failed, or it has yielded results you weren't expecting, which has thrown you off-kilter."

Errol frowned over his spectacles. "What difference does it make *why* Simon is making the gesture?"

Colin's gaze never shifted from Simon. "It's merely an observation."

"A correct one." Simon shrugged as if the matter were of little consequence. "Besides, I've decided you were right about pooling resources. In one way or another, each of you has contributed to the building of my generator. Errol's formulations on the velocity and magnitude of vector forces and Ben's trials with mechanical conversion of energy both played significant roles in my progress."

Colin emitted a sardonic chuckle. "Nothing from me?"

"Actually, Colin, your theories of particle redistribution through electrolysis have proved most valuable."

"Huh." The man's eyebrows surged in surprise.

Ben poured a second cup of tea for each of them. "You do realize that your generator itself might win you a Copley Medal."

"He doesn't care about the Copley Medal." There was no mistaking the sarcasm in Colin's tone.

"I don't," Simon agreed, and pinned him with a glare. "However, if the Royal Society wishes to grant me the honor based on my generator alone, the prize money will immediately be transferred to the university's School of Natural Philosophies, Physics Department."

Crumbs shot across the desk as the scone Ben had just plucked from the tray crumbled between his fingers. "I was only jesting when I proposed you do that."

Simon smiled. "Nonetheless."

Ben and Errol let out harmonious whoops, and Errol

whacked the floor again with his cane. "If you win, we all win," he said brightly.

Colin shook his head at them and smirked. "That's assuming someone outside our group doesn't take the prize."

"Bah." Errol licked cake crumbs from his fingers.

After draining their tea, the men dispersed, Colin and Errol to the chemistry laboratory they often shared, Ben to a meeting with university trustees. Boarding his carriage, Simon directed his driver to St. John's College.

As they entered through the gates, he swore aloud as he realized he'd left his hat behind in Ben's office.

Ivy rapped her knuckles on the open door of Jasper Lowbry's suite of rooms.

His back to her, he sat at his writing table, head in his hands, face perched over the open book in front of him. As if she had woken him from a light doze, he jolted at the sound of her voice.

She removed her hat and stepped over the threshold. "Am I interrupting?"

"Ivers!" The book flapped closed and a sheaf of papers fluttered to the floor as Jasper shoved back his chair. Heedless of the mess he'd created, he trod on the spilled notes and made his way to her. "Didn't expect to see you again so soon. What brings you back? Don't tell me the Mad Marquess has sacked you?"

"No, not yet anyway." Ivy's teeth almost rattled from the force of Jasper's handshake. Yet what a gratifying relief to know that this young man's friendship came with no strings attached—no demands, obligations, guilt.

He released her and pulled back. "Something in your tone tells me you aren't entirely joking. Have you run afoul of the old bloke?"

"He's hardly old and . . . well . . ."

"Come and tell me all about it." Jasper seized her shoulder and hauled her to the settee.

There was little Ivy could divulge about yesterday's

revelations or today's events, but the notion of confiding in someone proved too tempting to resist. At home, she would have tugged Holly into the bedroom they shared and told her everything . . . or *almost* everything. Or, if she found herself in a true scrape, she would have confessed every detail, however shocking, to Laurel and yielded to her elder sister's judgment.

But she had no sisters here, only a mad scientist who by turns inspired her, exasperated her, and aroused her passions. And she had Jasper and the others of their little set, an unruly, high-spirited band who had become her unlikely brothers.

Ivy had always longed for a brother. . . .

"Something did happen yesterday—"

"Wait. Hold that thought." Jasper sprang up from the sofa. He poured two brandies and returned to the settee. "Here."

"A bit early for this, isn't it?"

"My dear Ivers, it is never too early for brandy." With a hand beneath her elbow, he coaxed the snifter to her mouth. Ivy sipped judiciously. "Good," he said. "Now, out with it. How did you incur the wrath of the Mad Marquess?"

"He isn't angry with me. He's grown fearful for my welfare and is threatening to bar me from the laboratory."

Jasper's eyes went wide. "Blasted hell. Why?"

"You just said the correct word: blast. One of his experiments . . . Oh, how do I put it? It went rather awry yesterday, and now I suppose he's afraid of blowing me to kingdom come." Not to mention his other concerns on her behalf, which had prompted him to blurt that awkward proposal when any fool could see that marrying her was the very last thing he wished to do.

She wondered . . . if he had couched his offer in different words, spoken of love and devotion and his desire to spend the rest of his days at her side, would she have relented, forsworn her notions of independence and thrown herself into his arms? Sadness swept through her, for it was a question that would never be answered.

Jasper gave a low whistle. "That must have been one devil of an experiment." After a pause, he said, "Don't suppose you can give a hint as to—"

"You know I cannot."

He nodded and swirled his brandy. "Still, no laboratory is without its dangers. We all know that, and he had to have known it, too, when he took you on. So what changed?"

It was yet one more question Ivy couldn't answer, though the twinges between her thighs persisted in reminding her that if she hadn't succumbed to her feelings for Simon, her position as his assistant might not now be jeopardized.

"Well, now more than ever, you simply must find a way to convince him to let you stay." Jasper clinked his glass against hers.

"What do you mean, now more than ever?"

His hazel eyes flashed with excitement. "I've got news. Just this morning I learned that I am to be Dean Rivers's assistant at the upcoming consortium to be held at Sir Alistair Granville's home."

"Oh, Jasper, how exciting!" Ivy's free hand closed around Jasper's arm in an altogether female gesture. She immediately released him, but not before an awkward silence fell.

After an instant, Jasper blinked and his good-natured grin returned. "So you see, Ned, you simply must be there. You've no choice but to stake your claim at the marquess's side."

His words struck an ironic chord inside her. "I'll try my best."

"Lowbry?" From outside, a call echoed against the building fronts and intruded upon the quiet room. "Lowbry? I say, you up there, old man?"

"That'll be Ascot." Jasper rose and went to lean out the window. "Cease your caterwauling, I'll be down directly." Turning back into the room, he explained, "Preston and I have a supervision to attend. Spencer Yates is meeting us there. The two of them will be at the consortium, too, though only to observe and act as notetakers for Mr. Quincy and the Earl of Drayton. Are you acquainted with them?"

"I should say so, since they are colleagues of Lord Harrow." Ivy came to her feet and retrieved her hat. "I won't make you late. Lord Harrow will be coming to collect me soon anyway."

"Remember. Stand firm. Don't let the old boy brush you off."

Ivy didn't respond, didn't say that it might already be too late.

Outside, Preston Ascot paced up and down the leaf-strewn courtyard. Spotting Ivy and Jasper exiting the building, he came to an abrupt halt. "Ivers?"

Before Ivy could respond, the young man burst out laughing and charged, his coattails flying as his pocked features bore down on her. He caught her with both arms around her middle, the force lifting her feet from the pathway. Her hat bounced off her head and dried leaves crunched as her back struck the grass. The remaining breath whooshed out of her as Ascot collapsed with the whole of his considerable weight on top of her. Stars danced before her eyes.

Jasper's laughter bounced off the building front and skipped across the quadrangle. "Preston, get off the poor lad before you crush the life out of him."

From somewhere beyond the heap Ivy and Preston Ascot had become, footsteps pounded toward them. A pair of gloved hands closed over Preston's shoulders. Ivy glimpsed black hair and the fierce glare of a familiar scowl.

"Simon, don't!" she cried out as he hauled Preston's sturdy frame off her as if he were made of straw. The youth's coarse features registered shock as he was tossed roughly to the ground onto his back. His assailant leaned close, seized a handful of his coat, and drew back a fist.

"No!" Blinking, Ivy sprang up and grabbed Simon's sleeve. "Lord Harrow, *no*! I'm quite all right, sir. It was all in fun. No harm meant. . . ."

At first it seemed he didn't hear her. His arm strained to be loose, to complete the intended blow. It was only by summoning all her strength that Ivy was able to hold on.

Then his resistance began to ebb. He looked up at her, his pale eyes filled with anxious concern, with confusion, too.

"I'm *fine*," she said. Actually, a sharp pain stabbed her lower back, but she wasn't about to mention it.

On the ground at their feet, a befuddled Preston sputtered. "It's . . . a wrestling move. . . ."

Simon released him and straightened. As Preston pushed unsteadily to a sitting position, Simon offered him a hand up, which the young man warily accepted after a brief hesitation.

Leaves swishing around his feet, Jasper made his way over to them. He slapped Preston's back. "We haven't seen this much excitement since old Ivers here left us." He handed Ivy her hat and nodded sheepishly at Simon. "Lord Harrow, sir."

Simon ruefully returned the greeting. Turning back to Preston, he ran both hands over the boy's lapels, causing Preston to flinch back a little. "My apologies, lad. I thought a fight had broken out, and Ned here being my assistant, I couldn't allow him to be injured."

"I . . . understand, milord." Frowning, Preston rubbed at his broad side. "We, er, really should be going, Lowbry, or we'll be late."

As if to affirm the claim, a window across the courtyard slid open and another familiar face peered down at them. "Lowbry and Ascot, you've got exactly thirty seconds to get your arses up here or Mr. Markham says he'll lock the door on you." Spencer Yates's spectacles flashed a sunlit warning down at them. A ribbon of smoke from a cheroot curled about his face.

"Right. Our calculus don can't abide tardiness." Jasper gave Ivy's hand a firm shake. "I hope you'll stop by again soon, Ivers, but if not, we'll see you at the consortium."

"Oh?" The curt syllable came from Simon.

"Yes," Ivy told him, "Messrs. Lowbry, Ascot, and Yates"—she pointed up at the reedy young man staring down at them and holding out his pocket watch—"will all be at Windgate Priory. Jasper will be assisting your colleague Benjamin Rivers. Just as I will be assisting you. Sir."

She waited for him to concur, but he only stood silently brooding, still peeved, no doubt, at her refusal to accept his proposal of marriage. She supposed she should have been grateful, delighted ... amenable. To what? A halfhearted offer to make her an honest woman, prompted by good intentions but not by love. He'd behaved admirably, yet beneath his protestations that they do the proper thing, his palpable relief had assured her that she had been correct in declining his offer.

Preston mumbled a final apology, and the two men set off across the quadrangle. Ivy chose a direction at random and began walking.

"Where is the carriage?"

"Outside the gates." Simon pointed in the opposite direction and she pivoted to change course. "Ned, wait."

Feeling confused and out of sorts, and wishing matters with Simon had not grown so deuced complicated, she kept going, picking up speed as she strode through the passage into First Court.

"Ned."

In front of the steps of St. John's Chapel, she stopped and spun about. "Oh, it's *Ned* again, it is?"

"Of course it's *Ned*." Darting a gaze around him, Simon lowered his voice. Students and dons, some in scholarly robes, others in day attire, strode along the paths or sat with open books on tree-shaded benches; no one seemed to be paying them any attention. "You know it must be Ned whenever we are in public," he said with hushed emphasis.

Rebellion flashed in her eyes. "What difference if I am to be sacked and sent from Harrowood?"

"I have decided no such thing."

She took off again at a brisk pace. "Then what *have* you decided, other than to vent your frustrations on innocent university students?"

"I'm sorry about that." He caught up to her and set a

hand on her shoulder. "But that lout might have broken your neck or—"

"Or what?"

His answer stuck in his throat as images of a hurt, crippled Ivy filled his mind, as he acknowledged her vulnerability beneath her man's persona. His hand fell to his side. He had interrupted simple roughhousing of the sort he had once engaged in, but it was life's sundry other calamities, and his inability to protect her from them, that rendered him nearly immobile with fear and with a sense of past failure destined to repeat itself.

Grown silent, Ivy stared up at him, *into* him, if that were possible. Whatever she saw, whatever she came to understand about him in those pensive moments, gradually softened her expression. "Never mind," she said gently. Her fingertips brushed his sleeve. "I wasn't hurt, and neither was Preston."

Minutes later, the carriage stopped outside Ben's office. "I forgot my hat earlier," Simon explained when she questioned him. "Wait here."

She slid along the seat after him. "I'm coming with you."

"I'll only be a minute."

She remained adamant. "Each chance I have to be part of this academic environment is a gift, one that must sustain me for the rest of my life."

As she spoke those last words, his chest constricted painfully. The rest of her life—spent somewhere else, without him. Shouldn't that come as a relief? When she completed her mission and left Harrowood forever, she would no longer be his concern or responsibility. He need not spend his days worrying about her happiness, her welfare . . . good God, whether she lived or died.

Yes, he should be thoroughly, ecstatically relieved to have escaped such a burden. So then why this awful ache inside him?

Ben hadn't returned from his meeting with the trustees; his office door was closed but unlocked. Inside, Simon retrieved his top hat from where he had left it on the sofa, nearly crushing the brim as his fingers fisted far too tightly around it. He relaxed his grip, but as he moved to leave, he saw that the bookcase had captured Ivy's attention. Her forefinger running along a shelf at eye level, she scanned the titles, her face alight with interest.

Simon waited for her by the door. "You do realize that I've many of these same volumes at home, and you're welcome to read any of them there."

"Perhaps, but how often am I able to examine the reading material of a dean of natural philosophies?" She continued her scrutiny. "But what's this?"

Reaching the corner where the bookshelf met the room's outer wall, she plucked something from atop the row of books. In her hand lay a folded paper. "It seems I am not the only female to venture inside these hallowed halls."

Simon moved closer. The notepaper bore a scalloped edge and an embossed monogram he couldn't quite make out. Ivy brought it to the desk and smoothed it open. A crease forming above her nose, she traced a finger over the letters. Her eyebrows arced. "Simon, these initials. They are your sister's."

Chapter 16

"Let me see that." In an instant Simon crossed the space and took the notepaper from Ivy's hands. His stomach all but dropped to the floor.

At the top of the page, an uppercase *G* linked with a swooping *B*, with a lowercase *de* poised above them. Five words had been scribbled in smeared ink across the ivory paper.

Dearest Simon,
   Forgive me. I ...

That was all. In frustration he held the unfinished letter closer, as if he could discern more, perhaps detect the imprint of a message written in disappearing ink. "This *is* Gwendolyn's. But blast it, why didn't she continue? What was she going to tell me?"

Ivy searched his face. "She must have been interrupted."

"Yes, but by whom? When I was here earlier, I asked again if anyone had heard from her. Colin and Errol repeated their denials of yesterday. Ben, on the other hand, acted thoroughly surprised to hear of her departure from London."

"Perhaps it's been here since before she went away."

"That was months ago. Someone would have noticed it before now. The charwoman ... Ben himself. It could not have lain there all this time." He held the paper out for Ivy to see. "It isn't particularly dusty. She must have been in this room quite recently."

"Could Ben Rivers have been lying?"

"No. At least . . . I hope to God not." Ivy's question sent a chill across his shoulders and triggered a decision. "It is time to call in the authorities."

"Simon, the queen—"

"Indeed, let us consider the queen. She has accused Gwendolyn of theft, a criminal act, meaning that merely finding Gwen will not resolve the issue. She is in a great deal of trouble, both to her person and her reputation. I believe the time for discretion is well past. The queen made a ridiculous demand of you with this oath of secrecy. She behaved more like a moonstruck child than a monarch—"

"That isn't fair." Ivy squared her shoulders and raised her chin. "Victoria is a lone woman surrounded by men, many of whom find fault with her solely on the basis of her being a woman. Do you know what a scandal could do to her reign? She has pledged her life to the service of this country, and in return she wishes one thing for herself: to marry her cousin Albert." She drew herself up taller still. "Your sister's actions have jeopardized that wish. I am sorry Lady Gwendolyn is missing. I will do everything in my power to help you find her. But I cannot allow you to destroy the only personal dream Victoria has left to her."

A quality in Ivy's tone led him to realize they were discussing not only the queen but Ivy herself. He understood her wishes and her frustrations, too. He supposed her aspirations were in large part what had prompted her to shrug off his proposal. But while he hadn't shaped the society they lived in and would have made changes if he could, he could not ignore the realities—not as they affected the queen, his sister, or Ivy herself.

"The queen endangered her own wishes when she went behind the backs of her advisers and ministers to conduct a secret love affair." A squeak of outrage issued from Ivy's throat, but he headed her off by continuing, "Just as my sister's brash actions have endangered her freedom and welfare."

Ivy's eyes narrowed. "I suppose you'll say that I've endangered my own welfare by venturing from home alone and taking on a man's role."

"Haven't you?" He should have added that she had endangered them both by walking into his open arms. She had lost her virginity, while he had lost the walls of safety he'd erected around himself at Aurelia's death. But those were things that couldn't be changed.

"Blast you, *Lord Harrow*." Ah, the return of sarcasm. Ivy scowled. "You fail to grasp the most vital point of all. The point of *me*." With both hands she slapped her lapels.

His forehead began to throb. "And what point would that be?"

"That endangering oneself is not always a thing to be avoided. That men are encouraged to do it every day of their lives, from when they are boys and jump their horses across streams and over rock walls."

She came closer, until they stood toe to toe, almost nose to nose, so close the fragrance of her hair and skin mingled confusingly with the manly scents of her woolen coat and starched cravat, a tantalizing blend that made following her convoluted logic that much more challenging.

"Has it not occurred to you that perhaps Gwendolyn had a damned good reason for doing as she did? That ill-advised though her actions were, they were incited by desperation and the insurmountable frustrations that go along with being female?" She had the audacity to poke his chest with two fingers, as though he personally had caused Gwendolyn's frustrations . . . and Ivy's, too.

He peered down at the textured notepaper, which he'd unconsciously crumpled in his fist. *Was* Gwendolyn's disappearance his fault? He had always tried to be a good brother, though admittedly he'd grown distant in those long months following Aurelia's death. Still, if he had known of Gwendolyn's feelings for Colin, he would not have been entirely disapproving of an attachment between them. His sister was young, and he would have insisted on a yearlong courtship at the very least before he allowed an engagement to proceed. . . .

But he'd been kept in the dark about the entire matter. Gwendolyn and his supposed best friend had sneaked about, defying every proper convention, until Gwen had been left all but ruined. After that, there could be no permitting any relationship between them. No responsible elder brother would have behaved differently, and surely Gwendolyn should have realized that he had done his best for her in placing her in the queen's household.

"Has it never occurred to you," he countered evenly, "that doing what is best for others, no matter how painful or unappreciated, is part of the frustrations a man must bear?" When her perplexed expression deepened, he added, "Perhaps, Ivy, you should think about that."

He turned to go. She caught his elbow. "What about going to the authorities? Will you defy the queen's command for—?"

At the clatter of footsteps in the corridor, he pressed his hand to her lips.

Ivy considered biting Simon's finger until she, too, heard what had prompted him to cover her mouth.

A second or two after Simon released her, Benjamin Rivers stopped short in the doorway. "Simon. And Mr. Ivers, too, I see. I thought I heard voices."

"I forgot my hat earlier. But see here, we discovered this in your bookcase." His expression darkening, Simon thrust Gwendolyn's unfinished note beneath the other man's nose. "Ben, has my sister been to see you or not?"

The man regarded the item with a frown. "I told you, I wasn't even aware that Gwen had left London."

"Then how—" Simon's voice surged. He paused, and Ivy perceived his effort to rein in his temper. He asked more quietly, "How did this come to be on your bookshelf?"

"I don't know." The dean of natural philosophies rubbed

his temple, then pushed charcoal strands of hair from his brow. "I am as mystified as you are. Perhaps she came to see me when I wasn't in. . . ."

"And tucked a note in among your books?"

"I can't explain what she might have done, or why."

"Wait one moment." Ivy turned and moved back to the shelf. "The note was just about here, tossed to the very back of the shelf. Obviously Lady Gwendolyn had wished to leave Lord Harrow a message. Perhaps she could not put into words what she felt and instead left a sign."

"A sign of what?" both men asked simultaneously.

"Of where she intended to go next."

Their vocal skepticism notwithstanding, Ivy began calling out the titles near where she had discovered the note. When none elicited a response from either man, she named the authors instead, many of whom she recognized from her studies. "Carlisle, Clausius, Faraday, Galvani, Granville, Guericke . . ."

"Wait." Simon moved beside her. "Did you say Granville? Alistair Granville?"

Ivy tipped her head sideways to read the spine. "Alistair Granville. Yes, right there." She pointed to the tome.

Simon pulled the clothbound volume from the shelf. *"Diamagnetism and the Perpendicular Forces of the Earth's Magnetic Fields,"* he read from the front cover. He flipped the book open and fanned through the first few pages.

"It wouldn't be unlike Gwen to leave cryptic clues as to her intentions." He looked up at the dean. "Could my sister have meant to hint that she would go to Windgate Priory?"

"There is one way to find out."

Simon nodded. "I was planning to visit Alistair anyway. Come, Ned, we'd best set out now if we're to make it back to Harrowood before nightfall."

Ivy waited until they climbed back into Simon's carriage before she ventured to ask, "How much does your sister understand about your work?"

Simon placed his hat on the seat between them. "I've wondered that myself. Despite her impulsive nature, Gwendolyn possesses a sharp mind."

"Do you think she grasped the significance Victoria's stone could play in your research? And I don't mean in general terms."

The carriage listed as the driver turned the vehicle about and headed the team northwest, away from town. Ivy pressed both hands to the seat to prevent herself from toppling. Simon gripped the hand strap above the door. Still, his body leaned sharply until his shoulder gave hers a solid nudge. His spicy shaving soap aroused a fluttering of awareness inside her.

"Up until a couple of weeks before she went away, I'd have said no," he replied to her question. "But after my first electroportation, it was Gwendolyn who found me. Like yesterday, I was on the floor, unconscious and far more incapacitated than I was when you found me. It took hours before my strength returned, days to fully recover."

He paused, staring out at the passing scenery. Ivy caught a fleeting glimpse of St. John's entrance gates, but what Simon had just admitted held the better part of her attention.

"You very nearly killed yourself that time . . . yet you repeated the experiment. Why?"

He didn't look at her. "Science progresses in such ways."

"No." She grasped his chin and forced him to turn toward her. "Science need not kill or maim to progress. There are safer methods—"

"At the time, I'd have defied your safer methods." His sudden vehemence made her snatch her hand away. For an instant his eyes blazed in the carriage's dusky light. Then their fervor dimmed. "Even yesterday morning, I'd have laughed at the suggestion of proceeding with caution."

"And now?"

"Now I agree with you. Now I see my folly."

His sense of finality, of capitulation, spread sudden misgivings through Ivy's heart. She did not wish Simon to risk his life by testing dangerous procedures on himself, yet neither did she wish to see him lose the daring courage that led him to astonishing innovations . . . and which made him so dear to her. She felt sad to think that in some way she had undermined his confidence.

"Not folly," she whispered, and then surprised herself by adding, "You can't mean to abandon your discovery."

His eyebrows rose. "Isn't that what you advised me to do?"

"No. Yes." She shook her head. "Perhaps yesterday I believed that to be the prudent course, but I'd received a fright. Besides, you said you wished to protect *me*, not give up entirely."

"Again, that was yesterday. This morning I reached a vastly different conclusion. Electroportation disassembles and reassembles the body's molecules. Galileo's teeth, Ivy, who knows what mutations can, and perhaps did, occur? How can such a process ever be safe, for anyone?"

"You're frightening me again. I still wish you would see a doctor."

"No need, for I emerged well enough." He slapped a hand to his chest, over his heart. "But yes, you should be frightened. So should I. I was playing with a godlike force, something no man, not even a scientist, has the right to do."

Part of her, the logical and practical side, agreed wholeheartedly. But the part of her that had defied convention, donned trousers, and experienced the electrical energy of his generator flowing through her own body cried out a protest.

"If your view has changed because of me, Simon, you must reconsider. I have no wish to change you, not anything about you. Impulsiveness is obviously a de Burgh family trait, one of many that set you head and shoulders above any other man I've ever known."

Those words sprang directly from Ivy's heart, but when Simon continued to face stiffly forward, lost in thought, she realized he hadn't heard her; she realized, too, that she didn't dare confess her feelings again.

She had given her virginity to this man and did not regret a single moment of their wondrous lovemaking. Oh, *he* was wondrous; he had been solicitous of her needs and sweeter than she ever dreamed the Mad Marquess could be. She had no regrets.

But she could not ignore what had brought them into each other's arms: the alternating shock, fear, relief, and exultation that had resulted from his electroportation process. For several dreadful moments yesterday she had believed him dead, or nearly so. He, too, upon first awakening, had doubted his hold on life.

Was it any surprise that such a tumult of emotion would lead to a physical outpouring as well? Today, however, those emotions were well under control. Even during his proposal of marriage, he had maintained an emotional distance as well as a physical one.

Then she must keep hers, too, rather than expect from him more than he was prepared to give. In truth, in the interest of preserving her newfound independence, she had no wish to attach herself to any man. If only she knew of a scientific process to prevent her heart and her aspirations from getting in each other's way.

She cleared her throat. "We were speaking of Gwendolyn, and how much she understands about your work."

Some of the rigid tension drained from his posture. "She knew my injuries were the result of erratic fluctuations in my generator's electrical current. And that my greatest challenge lay in creating a current free of those fluctuations." He met her gaze and voiced her own thoughts. "Gwendolyn might think the stone is a source of steady power, a natural battery of sorts."

"Her theft is not your fault," Ivy said, voicing what *she* believed to be Simon's thoughts. He frowned, looking as though he was about to form a denial, but his sense of guilt spoke from every taut line of his face.

His heavy sigh broke the silence. "Gwendolyn's actions *are* my fault, Ivy, in more ways than one. And I suppose my failures as a brother may well cost the queen her happiness."

*   *   *

"Whatever can you mean?"

Ivy's wide-eyed incredulity might have made Simon smile, had the situation not been one that gnawed at his honor. And if it weren't time to acknowledge what he had ignored for so long.

"The theft and her disappearance, and everything that happened last winter, are a direct result of how self-absorbed I'd become after my wife's death."

"But it's understandable that you would have become withdrawn."

Fingers raking into his hair, he shook his head. "Understandable, perhaps. But not excusable. Gwendolyn and I were always close, more so after the death of our parents. Oh, she was always impulsive, always landing herself in predicaments from which I had to extricate her. But when she most needed the indulgent brother she had always relied upon, she found instead a distant stranger who had no patience for her antics."

Ivy's hand came down lightly on his own. "Excuse me for saying so, but it sounds as though Gwendolyn has always been a teeny bit spoiled."

At this he did smile; how could he not? "A gross understatement if ever there was one. Of course she was spoiled. What younger sister isn't? But she's good-natured and kindhearted as well. And innocent. Most of all that." He blew out a breath laden with regret at how badly he'd handled the incident last winter.

The suddenness with which Ivy removed her hand prompted him to catch it and bring it to his lips. "That was not meant to draw any sort of comparison between you."

She nodded, but her gaze darted everywhere but at him. With his free hand he cupped her cheek and turned her to him. "If anything, I wish Gwen were more like you, Ivy. Brave and a bit rash, yes, but also steady and determined and . . ."

"Yes?"

And everything he could love in a woman, if he were to allow himself to love again.

Being this close to her, in the intimacy of a moving carriage, roused his body to mutiny. In the flicker of bright autumn daylight sifting through the roadside trees, he became keenly aware of everything about her: the luster of her cropped curls, the soft contour of her cheeks, the perfect angle of her pretty nose.

Resolve became lost in the magnetic draw of her lips. Simon framed her face in his hands. Right before he kissed her, he glimpsed surprise and yearning gleaming out at him in equal measure, a mingling that made her more beautiful than ever and rendered him unable to resist pressing his lips to hers.

His arms went around her, and he pulled her into his lap, the feel of her booted, trousered legs against his own still an unaccustomed sensation, and still oddly erotic. When heady desire prompted him to sweep an arm beneath her knees and gather her closer, he reveled in the ease of doing so, and the simplicity of her own movements, unencumbered by corset and skirts and petticoats.

He loved, too, the freedom of access her attire granted him to her hips, thighs, and slender legs, not to mention the delectable curve of her bottom. Through her clothing his hands traced every part of her, raising mental images of what lay beneath until his own breeches tightened around his arousal.

Ivy eased her lips away from his. "Simon . . ."

"Tell me to stop, I beseech you," he whispered. When she said nothing, he caught her chin between his teeth. He tugged at her cravat, opened her collar, and licked his way down her neck. Her shivers vibrated into him until he very nearly forgot—or deliberately disregarded—the fact that they were in a carriage and not in the privacy of his curtained bed at home.

She ran her fingers into his hair and sought his lips again. "Why do we do this?" she gasped between kisses. "Neither of us wishes permanence, not of the conventional sort. Our futures do not permit it. Mine certainly does not, and despite your honorable offer, your intentions, or lack of them, are quite clear."

His erection stilled in midthrob as if deliberating her assertion. Yet if he listened to the conclusion formed in that part of his anatomy, he and Ivy would be wedded and bedded—again—that very afternoon. But he didn't listen to his desires; he listened to his brain, and the part of his heart that had suffered despair. And he listened to Ivy herself. *Our futures do not permit it. Mine certainly does not. . . .*

He blinked in a marginally successful attempt to clear the lust from his brain. He couldn't resist kissing her again, but this time with more control and slightly less fervor, just to prove to himself that he *could* control his passion for this woman. "It seems our bodies do not wish to cooperate with our intentions."

An endearing earnestness creased her brow as she considered the idea. Then with ingenuous bluntness she said, "There does seem to be a severed connection somewhere between logic and lust."

Her use of that last word—as unexpected from a woman as her gentlemen's clothes—made his pulse thump and his arousal surge anew. "Damn it, Ivy."

He pushed her down across the seat, covered her with his body, and buried his face in her warm neck. Her arms fell above her head, and he reached up and held them there, pinned to the seat. Her back arched in response, pushing her bosom higher inside its restraints. He ran a hand beneath her waistcoat, and felt her nipples harden against his palm.

His logic in tatters, he yanked her shirttails free and shoved her shirt and waistcoat high. Through the silk strips, he closed his lips around a tightly budded nipple. In his mouth, the fabric became wet and malleable, teasing with its sudden transparency. He slid his other hand down her length until he reached the humid warmth between her legs.

As he had done that night in his bed, he massaged and

stroked her through her trousers, seeking that tiny part of a woman that, when touched just so, commanded the very essence of her being. His attentions set her moaning, writhing. Ruddy color stained her cheeks and neck.

Higher and higher he carried her on waves of passion, rocking to the rhythm of the bumpy road. Her moans and the moisture building against his palm heightened his own body's needs. Desire rapped at every pulse point and squeezed the air from his lungs. Every instinct urged him to free his erection and sink mercifully into her.

But in the next instant Ivy went rigid beneath him, and clamped her lips shut to muffle a cry. Her back arched, her eyes closed tight, and her hips came off the carriage seat to crush her sex against his shaft. Pleasure, pain, and the struggle for self-control became a barbed, twisted torture inside him, unbearable, explosive. . . . Then slightly less so, but only because of the heavy-lidded, smiling satisfaction he perceived as Ivy's panting subsided and she opened her eyes. And because of the promise that spilled from her kiss-reddened lips.

She said, "Tonight, back at Harrowood, I am going to learn how to do that to you."

Chapter 17

As the carriage continued toward the village of Madingley, Ivy drifted back to earth with a new notion to cushion her descent.

Could she continue to indulge in this passion for Simon without the promise of permanence? Dare she engage in a physical relationship without entertaining thoughts of marriage?

Hadn't she already done so?

"What, may I ask, is so funny?" Simon helped her to sit up beside him. Then he threw an arm around her and pulled her close.

Her last thought had indeed drawn something approaching a schoolgirlish giggle. Bookish, sensible Ivy Sutherland, fast on her way to official spinsterhood, had of late been behaving outrageously, but instead of feeling suitably ashamed, she felt . . .

Empowered. Fulfilled. In control of her fate.

She put her arms around him, pressed her cheek to his shoulder, and watched a field pass outside the carriage window. "It isn't so much funny as simply invigorating. I am living by a new set of rules, ones I never imagined. I like it."

Had her breeches and boots made her bold? Goodness, yes. Growing up, she had often heard the adage that loose corsets engendered loose morals. Well, she wore no corset at all now, yet she didn't believe her actions resulted from a *lack* of morals . . . merely *different* ones. Scientific properties often contradicted society's accepted values, but that didn't make them any less true or worthy. Ivy couldn't see why her breach of convention shouldn't be looked at in similar terms.

She tipped her chin to look up at him. "That promise I just made to pleasure you as you have done for me. I intend to keep it."

"No, Ivy. I don't wish you to feel obligated—"

"I don't. Don't you see? We have stumbled upon the perfect solution. We each have reasons for remaining unattached. I respect your reasons, whatever they are, and I trust you to respect mine. But as you so astutely pointed out, our bodies are refusing to cooperate with our intentions. We want each other, Simon, and neither of us can deny it."

He pressed a kiss to the top of her head. "I wouldn't attempt to."

"Then here is a way to have each now without being tied to each other for always."

"Do you truly believe it can be that easy?"

"I don't see why it shouldn't be. I don't see why we should not live our lives as we see fit, as long as we don't hurt anyone or come away with any lasting reason to regret our actions."

His fingers, trailing down her neck and across her collarbone through her coat, went still. "You speak of a child," he said very softly.

"Of course I do," she said in an equally hushed tone. "But there won't be one if you and I remain firm in our resolve and seek pleasure in these other ways you have shown me."

His expression became stern. "Are you forgetting that we have already joined our bodies?"

"No . . . but that was only one time. Surely . . ."

When he'd mentioned the likelihood earlier, she had dismissed it immediately. But she had been caught off guard by his proposal; she had been disappointed and overset and, yes, a little angry. But now the possibility of a pregnancy left her feeling momentarily sickened, filled with dread. Sliding her arms from around him, she sat up straighter, at the same time snaking an unconscious forearm across her belly.

Inside her, could their separate elements even now be fusing to form new life?

Sometimes newly married couples tried for a year or more to have a child. There had been the young parlormaid at Thorn Grove, married to the head groom for two years before she conceived. And the minister's wife didn't give birth to their first child until after their fourth anniversary, after they had all but given up.

No, the odds were against it; she needn't worry on that account.

"I am certain nothing will come of it," she concluded with a conviction that felt only slightly forced.

"Perhaps not. But my point wasn't about the possible consequences of our having made love, but that we have done so at all. That we have not been able to *resist* doing so. What makes you think we will be able to resist from now on?"

With no good answer for him, she fastened her collar and tied her neckcloth. Her notions of empowerment and worthy, if different, values had seemed sound ones, but now they blurred like the mosaic of autumn scenery outside the carriage windows.

They entered a village of whitewashed cottages clustered around a lovely stone church. "We've arrived in Madingley," Simon told her. He angled a glance out the window and pointed. "And there, in the distance, is Windgate Priory."

Beyond the flat reaches of the fenland bordering the village, the graceful proportions of a châteaulike manor house scraped the sky from within a medieval-style encircling wall.

"How lovely. Is it very old?"

"The property is. It was once a fortified Cistercian monastery under the protection of the then earls of Harrow. But inside, the house is completely modern."

Upon their approach along the treelined drive, Ivy noted that the gatehouse's defenses had been replaced with topiary shrubs and flower beds. The moat, which once would have doubled as the castle's sewer, reflected with perfect clarity the deep blues and cottony whites floating high above it.

They rumbled over a bridge that had been built to resemble a working drawbridge. Ivy couldn't prevent her laughter from bubbling forth. "This is splendid! I cannot wait to see more."

"Yes, well. Either try to curb your enthusiasm or at least express it an octave or two lower."

"Oh." She pressed her fingers to her lips.

Simon reached over to give her neckcloth a corrective tug. "I don't know how you keep managing to fool anyone."

"Perhaps they are not as perceptive as you." The carriage rolled to a stop, and a servant in chestnut and gold livery opened the door.

"Don't worry," Ivy whispered to Simon. "I shan't reach for his hand as I step down."

Inside, while they waited for the butler to announce them, Ivy experienced an ironic letdown. With its sumptuous furnishings, silk-covered walls, and gilt and marble adornments, Windgate Priory possessed an opulence that would have left many jaws hanging. But as Simon had said, the interior was thoroughly modernized; its storybook charm failed to follow the visitor beyond the heavy carvings of the front doors.

"Simon, what a splendid surprise. How good of you to visit me."

In the wide curve of the carpeted staircase, a man stood poised at the railing. Olive-skinned and handsome in a more continental than English way, he wore a morning coat of burnished brocade, an artfully knotted silk cravat, and meticulously pressed trousers. As he started down, silver glints danced in his dark hair, so that Ivy judged him to be older than Simon by perhaps a decade or more. His figure was compact and well proportioned, and he moved with the easy elegance of a dancer.

"The consortium doesn't take place for another two weeks. I didn't expect to see you so soon." The man whom Ivy assumed to be Alistair Granville extended his hand to Simon, then pulled Simon into an affectionate embrace.

However affable his manner, it led Ivy to conclude that their trip here would yield no new clues about Lady Gwendolyn's whereabouts. Surely if their host had any information about the girl, he would not appear so puzzled about the purpose of Simon's visit.

In short, they had wasted their time by coming to Windgate Priory.

After the two men exchanged greetings, Sir Alistair shifted his attention to Ivy. A subtle rearranging of his even features registered mild curiosity.

"This is my new assistant," Simon introduced her. "Ned Ivers."

"Sir." Ivy extended her hand, but Sir Alistair made no move to grasp it.

"Ah," he said, and summarily dismissed her as his regard returned to Simon. "Come. I shall order refreshments brought to the solarium."

The cut should not have irked her, yet as she followed the men through the ground-floor rooms, a tingling indignation heated her cheeks. Since arriving in Cambridge, she had enjoyed the welcome of fellow university students and even the regard of Simon's Galileo Club colleagues. Prior to her masquerade as a student, no man had ever blatantly ignored her; to do so would have been considered the most ungentlemanly of acts.

For the first time in her life she felt utterly insignificant, and she didn't like it.

"I'm afraid this isn't a social call, Alistair," Simon told his friend as they entered a sunny room filled with exotic plants and lined with floor-to-ceiling windows adorned with colorful panes of stained glass. The tile floor and decorative furnishings spoke of the same costly and meticulous attention to detail that defined the rest of the house. "Nor did I come to discuss the consortium. It's Gwendolyn. She has left London. You haven't by any chance heard from her?"

"Gwen . . . ? Why, no, I . . ." Sir Alistair frowned. He gestured for Simon to take a seat at a small round table draped in richly patterned damask. "She has been in the queen's service since last winter, no?"

Neither invited to sit nor instructed to wait elsewhere, Ivy hovered beside a wispy palm a few feet away. A pair of footmen carried in platters, pewter cups, and a pitcher of punch festooned with floating fruit.

A haggard, weary look came over Simon as he accepted the cup Alistair poured for him. "Gwendolyn departed the palace without the queen's permission. Which is why it's imperative that I find her at once."

Sir Alistair tapped a finger against his chin. "Now that I think about it, didn't I read something in the newspapers about a theft from Her Majesty's household?" Simon replied to the affirmative, and Sir Alistair exclaimed, "Surely our Gwen is not implicated?"

Ivy's stomach clenched. How close a confidant was Sir Alistair; would Simon deem him trustworthy enough to reveal the truth? Only hours ago he had professed his impatience with what he termed the queen's ridiculous demands.

Silently she willed him to disclose nothing, knowing full well that if Victoria's secret became common knowledge, it would be her, Ivy's, fault. She had sworn to keep silent, but she had broken her word quickly enough. Her heart constricted around the many reasons why, even as she realized that none of those reasons could ever satisfy the queen.

Simon's eyes glinted a reluctant reassurance at her, and she breathed an inward sigh of relief. "Come, Ned. You must be hungry."

With his foot, he pushed out a chair for her. Sir Alistair made no reaction as she sat, neither of annoyance nor of consent. Simon said to him, "The theft is another matter entirely, and one that bears no relevance to my sister's actions. I believe she vacated her position out of anger toward me."

"I see. Have you inquired with . . ." Sir Alistair paused, apparently to choose the right words. ". . . your colleagues?"

"I've checked with all the members of the Galileo Club." Simon's emphasis on *all* was not lost on Ivy. She understood the reference to the Earl of Drayton. "She had been to Cambridge briefly, spoken with Colin, and apparently attempted to see Ben, but I am assured that none of them has seen her in recent days." He reached into his pocket and took out the crumpled note. "We discovered this in Ben's office, which is why we immediately came to see you."

"I don't understand."

"It's Gwendolyn's. We found it on top of a volume of your work on Ben's bookshelf. We thought perhaps she left it as a clue that she meant to come here next."

"A clue. How very mysterious of her." Sir Alistair's lips pulled downward at the corners. "Why would she not simply have left a note? Do you think she might be toying with you . . . again?"

"Again? Then Lady Gwendolyn is prone to riddles?" Ivy supposed she should have held her tongue. Assistants should listen and do as they are told, not ask questions.

"Lady Gwendolyn is a high-spirited individual." Sir Alistair's reply surprised her. Ivy had not thought he would acknowledge her so directly, and now she was emboldened to voice another query.

"Is she also prone to recklessness?" When the tug of Sir Alistair's brows indicated she might have strayed over a boundary, she added, "Lord Harrow brought me along to gain a second perspective. An objective one."

The man nodded. "Of course. However, Lord Harrow is best suited to answer the question."

Simon swirled the ruby liquid in his cup, and Ivy noticed that he hadn't taken a sip. Was it because no one had provided her with a serving of the punch? The notion made her want to smile. "Gwendolyn has always been restless and, as you say, Alistair, high-spirited," he said. "*Reckless* behavior is rather new. I can only hope she *is* toying with me, and that no harm has come to her."

He pushed a platter of tiny sandwiches closer to Ivy.

"That is unlikely." Sir Alistair watched Ivy select a creamy concoction of seafood between slices of thin white bread. "Gwen is a resourceful young woman. And perhaps you are correct. She may yet turn up here. She knows she is always welcome."

"Yes. I do have reason to suspect that her disappearance and the consortium may be connected."

"Has your sister suddenly taken it into her head to delve into the sciences?"

Simon shook his head. "I doubt that, but if it's revenge against me for sending her away that she wants, then interfering with the consortium and with my work would be a sure way to get it."

Sir Alistair drained his punch as he pondered that statement. "Well, should I hear anything from her, or of her, I will send word to you at once."

"Thank you, Alistair. Now, if you will excuse us, we must be getting back."

The man smiled indulgently. "Your secret project?"

"No." Simon exchanged a brief glance with Ivy. "I'm done with that. I am putting my generator at Ben's disposal and must make the necessary preparations for transport."

"From what you have told me, this generator alone represents a remarkable feat of scientific engineering. I am eager to witness its potency."

Simon appeared genuinely pleased by the praise. He offered his hand to the other man, and then he and Ivy took their leave.

"You were unaccountably quiet on the ride home earlier, and in the laboratory this evening as well." From across the dining table, Simon studied Ivy's expression, hoping for some clue as to what was troubling her. She looked up at him briefly before returning her attention to pushing the braised partridge around on her plate. "Even now, you've hardly said two words. Or eaten more than two bites."

Upon returning to Harrowood, they had made further adjustments to the calculations that determined the generator's power levels. Ivy's mathematical skills were impressive, some of the finest he had ever encountered, and that included his own. For the first time since he had built the device, he felt a fair degree of confidence in being able to control the force of the energy currents. Explosions, fires, and singed hands might well be a thing of the past.

Yet his satisfaction was tempered by Ivy's decided lack of enthusiasm. It mattered to him, damn it, that such things should matter to her, and when they didn't, he was left disappointed and frustrated.

The candelabra on the table between them gilded her skin and turned her eyes infinitely darker. Her thoughts remained her own, guarded in a way they had not been since she had first confessed her secrets to him.

"Have you something on your mind?" he prodded, unable to let it go.

"No. Perhaps." She put down her fork. "It's silly. Hardly worth mentioning."

He ventured an educated guess. "Does it have something to do with our visit to Windgate?"

She shrugged.

"Alistair treated you rudely."

She let out a breath. "He made me feel ... I don't know ... inconsequential. Invisible."

"You aren't used to that, neither as Ned nor Ivy."

Staring down at her plate, she shook her head. "I told you it was silly."

"No. Nothing is silly if it leaves you out of sorts."

"I'm not out of sorts," she said too quickly to lend credence to the claim.

"No one likes to be ignored," he said gently. "And for the most part, Alistair did ignore you. But try not to think too badly of him. He's a good man, but he is a product of his class."

"And a servant, which is how he thought of me, is beneath his notice." She tilted her head. A pensive crease formed above her nose. "You aren't like that."

Simon lifted his wineglass. "I didn't choose the path of a typical nobleman. As a scientist, I've learned to respect men from many different backgrounds. Take Ben Rivers, for instance. He was born a miner's son, but was lucky enough to be apprenticed to a relative who owned an apothecary shop. Luckier still, the man recognized Ben's abilities and saw that he received an education."

"I am glad for him. And for others who have had the good fortune to rise above their origins and achieve their dreams." Her voice held an ironic note that conveyed so much more than her words, as did the impatient way she tugged at her neckcloth and raked her fingers through her curls as if to smooth her hair down over her neck.

"You fear never achieving yours," he guessed. "Is that what is making you unhappy tonight?"

"Unhappy?" She shoved her plate away. "I don't know what I am anymore."

The conversation left Simon wondering. By the time supper ended, he had formed a plan he hoped would please her enough to rouse her from her doldrums. In the course of a single afternoon, he had come to miss her exuberance, and to realize how much he depended on her energy.

Her halfhearted, chin-in-hand inquiry as to whether they would take their customary evening ride or walk in the gardens only further encouraged him to take matters in hand. When they retired instead to the drawing room fire, he sat apart from her and penned a brief missive. Then he folded the page, sealed it, and handed it to Ivy.

"Would you mind taking this note out to Cecil and waiting for his reply? There are several other matters that need my attention before bedtime."

Note in hand, she made her way outside and down the terrace steps. Simon watched her until she disappeared from view. Then he set his plan in motion.

*   *   *

At the edge of Harrowood's gardens, the groundskeeper made his home in a picturesque cottage of stucco and timbers topped by a tidy thatched roof. From inside, firelight danced against the windowpanes and tossed a cheerful glow across the cobbled pathway that led to the arched front door. Ivy knocked, and steeled herself to show no reaction to the sight that would greet her when the door opened.

She needn't have bothered, for when Cecil's misshapen face filled her view, she felt no repulsion at all; on the contrary, her mood lifted at the sight of his kindly eyes and welcoming smile.

"Mr. Ivers! To what do I owe this pleasure?" He opened the door wider.

"I've brought a message from Lord Harrow." She held out Simon's note. "He asked that I wait for your reply."

"Did he, now?" Cecil took it in his meaty hand, imparting a soiled thumbprint on the ivory paper. "Then do come in, young sir. I was just repotting some begonias, but I could use a bit of human company."

Ivy took a tentative step over the threshold. "I'm not disturbing you?"

"Good heavens, dear boy, no."

The main room, with its overstuffed chairs and shelves of books, presented an inviting and comfortable prospect. A round oak table surrounded by spindle chairs occupied one corner. On the wall opposite, the fireplace stretched wider than Ivy was tall. A pot hanging from the hearth hook released spicy curls of steam. Ivy could well imagine spending happy winter days here, curled up close to the fire with a good book.

"What a lovely home you have."

"I'm quite comfortable here." Cecil glanced over his shoulder at her as he reached to take a pair of wooden tankards from a shelf. His bushy eyebrows waggled, a gesture that made her realize she'd blundered yet again, for what young man termed another man's home lovely?

Cecil carried the two tankards to the hearth. "This is my special recipe for mulled wine." Carefully he ladled steaming crimson liquid into each vessel, and held one out to Ivy. "I grew every spice myself, either in the garden or the hothouse. Try it. It will warm you now, and help you sleep well."

Ivy blew onto the surface and took a small sip. The woodsy flavors of cloves, allspice, cinnamon, and rich port melted like velvet over her tongue, tempting her to sample a deeper draft. "It's wonderful!"

"Indeed." He flashed his lopsided and thoroughly endearing grin. "Now, make yourself comfortable and let's see what Lord Harrow has to say."

Moments later, he glanced up from the page. "It isn't so much a reply his lordship requires as a certain item. Let us finish our wine, Mr. Ivers, and see if we can comply with Lord Harrow's wishes."

Their tankards empty, Cecil lit a lantern and led Ivy down the garden path beneath a stand of pines to the entrance of the smaller of two hothouses. Along the way he chatted about this autumn blossom and that flowering hedge. A quality in his eager explanations rang with familiarity; Ivy might have been listening to Simon expound on scientific principles. Though their spheres differed, both men possessed remarkable expertise.

Cecil had been correct about the wine. Though the night air carried a sharp chill, the brew's lasting warmth kept her comfortable enough.

Inside the glass enclosure, Cecil continued to point out exotic palms, hybrid roses, tiny fruits she had never heard of, as he led her along the rows. After nearly a quarter hour of this, she began to wonder if Cecil's mind had begun to wander.

He suddenly hurried forward. "Here. This is what we are looking for."

Even before Ivy could see around the groundskeeper's stout figure, a sweet perfume surrounded her. Expecting some large, leafy blossom resembling a rose, she joined

Cecil at the wooden plant stand to discover that the enticing scent was the product of clusters of tiny star-shaped flowers clinging to the shoots of several bushy evergreen plants.

He began plucking branches, laying each in the crook of his arm.

"I've never smelled anything so lovely." Ivy inhaled deeply. "What is it?"

"Night-blooming jasmine. All the way from the West Indies." Cecil gently filled her arms with the fragrant bouquet.

"Lord Harrow wants these?"

"He wishes you to bring them back to the house. To your room, Mr. Ivers."

"My room . . . ? Cecil, what is Lord Harrow about?"

"Ah, I am only a servant, sir." A mischievous light brought youthful charm to his irregular features. "I'm sure whatever Lord Harrow's intentions are, he'll soon make them clear." He touched the back of his forefinger lightly to Ivy's cheek.

If she'd ever entertained doubts as to whether Cecil saw through her disguise, that gesture put them to rest. Of course he knew. Yet the revelation didn't make her feel vulnerable or urge her to shrink from his oddly comforting presence. In fact, knowing she needn't pretend came as a liberating relief.

"Thank you, Cecil," she whispered.

"Go on now, Mr. Ivers." Speaking her name with all the deference of a gentleman addressing a lady, he gave a wink of complicity. "It is time."

"Time for what?"

He waved a hand at her. "Go on."

Ivy cradled the aromatic jasmine in her arms as she climbed the garden slopes. In her room, a vase filled with water waited on the dresser. A roaring fire and numerous candles bathed the furnishings in a mellow glow. She slipped the flowers into the vase, and turned to discover another, far more startling surprise.

The candlelight glimmered on a sumptuous green gown

spread across her bed. Ivy ventured closer, captured by the simple elegance of the silken garment with its delicate puffed sleeves, beribboned waistline, and abundant, sweeping hem.

Beside the gown lay a pair of filmy stockings that all but floated when Ivy touched them, a set of beribboned garters, and a diaphanous chemise that smelled of the same flowers she had brought from the hothouse. A pair of embroidered slippers that matched the emerald dress were arranged neatly on the floor beside the bed, and across the footboard she discovered a cashmere shawl, deliciously soft and warm. Finally, a pair of sleek, ebony combs completed the ensemble.

From her pillow, a note scrawled in a familiar hand beckoned:

> *Dearest Ivy, if it would please you to do so, put these on and wait for me outside on your terrace. Yours, Simon.*

Heart thumping, hands shaking, she hesitated. Coming to Harrowood disguised as Ned Ivers had proved more than a masquerade, more than a mission for the queen. Being Ned Ivers, wearing breeches and immersing herself in scientific experiments, had freed her and allowed her the self-expression she'd been denied all her life.

Simon knew that. He knew it and had encouraged her in ways few men ever had. Yet tonight, it seemed, he would transform her back to her feminine self. Why? What did it mean?

Her questions remaining unanswered, she lifted the beautiful gown and held it up in front of her.

Chapter 18

Having dispensed with his collar and cravat, Simon perched in the embrasure of his laboratory's southern window. A nearly full moon splashed silver across the fens beyond the property, lending unexpected beauty to the flat landscape. But then, he had always found a wealth of hidden treasures in the bogs and bottomlands, just as he alone had discerned the breathtaking beauty hiding beneath Ivy's masculine guise.

The burden of that guise had begun to weigh on her; he knew it had. He could only imagine the daily toil of maintaining such a pretense, of constantly behaving in a manner contrary to what came naturally. In his own life, the only circumstances that came close were the days and weeks following Aurelia's death, when he had been forced to pretend that he actually still cared about living.

This was different, of course. Ivy's masquerade had brought certain benefits a woman would never have enjoyed otherwise. Still, he understood something about the strain she'd been living under as she juggled identities. And he'd realized tonight that he, too, had been struggling to keep the true Ivy in focus.

Oh, from nearly the first he'd seen her as very much a woman, and that perception never wavered. But there *had* been times when he'd very nearly forgotten that her upbringing hadn't been that of a stripling nobleman, but of a carefully sheltered gentlewoman.

She had not attended Eton or other preparatory school where she would have learned to fight, both literally and metaphorically, as she established her place in the male pecking order of the upper classes. There would have been no recent year spent traveling abroad with an older male relative, during which she'd have lost her schoolroom naïveté. She had never seen the inside of a gentlemen's club, gaming hell, or brothel, never witnessed a duel, never dabbled in seduction as though it were a sport.

He had come to see her as strong and as self-assured as any university student, but in truth she was an innocent. Or *was*, before he'd lost his head and his resolve.

Was that why he had left the gown for her? As a reminder, more to himself, that Ivy Sutherland was not the cocky youth she often appeared to be, but a sweet, genteel, very feminine young lady, who deserved his respect as much as she needed his protection? Perhaps, but the question remained, would she embrace or scorn his attempt to banish Ned Ivers, at least for a night?

His thoughts screeched to a halt. Down below, a willowy shadow fell across the terrace outside her room. His pulse sped even as his heart stood still. The outer door of the bedchamber opened and a slipper-clad foot stepped over the threshold, the slender ankle encircled by the hem of the emerald dress.

Simon pushed away from the window.

He arrived at Ivy's door winded, his heart thumping. Before turning the knob, he paused to collect himself, to rein in his madcap desires and remember that tonight was not about seduction but rather about easing the burden Ivy had shouldered for the queen.

Besides, for all he knew, the image he'd spied from his laboratory had been merely the shadow of a cloud crossing the moon, augmented by the fancies of his imagination.

But the room, he discovered, lay empty, and the balcony door stood several inches ajar. The sweet, familiar scent drifting on the air made him smile. The note he had left her lay unfolded on the bed. The gown, shawl, and underthings were nowhere to be seen.

These signs of her consent emboldened him to cross the room. Through the gap in the open door he saw her. She stood at the rail, her back to him, the green gown falling from beneath the shawl in moonlit folds. Using the combs he had left as an afterthought, she had managed to pull her hair up and back into a curling coif; and with the gilded shadows adding depth and dimension to the tendrils, the style emphasized the kissable curve of her nape and made it appear that she had never cut her hair at all.

An ache spreading through his chest, he stepped out onto the balcony.

She didn't turn, but a slight angling of her head signaled that she knew he was there. He moved behind her and slid his arms around her waist. She smelled of the jasmine he had asked Cecil to gather for her—gather without haste, to allow Simon time to prepare.

Of their own volition, his lips found their way to her nape, and he spoke against her skin. "I remembered that Gwendolyn ordered a gown last winter, but hadn't had time to take up the hem before she left for London. It might have been made for you. Are you pleased?"

With a sigh, she leaned back against him. Her skirts rustled as she smoothed her palms over the silk. "Simon." Her face tilted upward to the night sky. "What are we doing?"

It wasn't so much a question as an acknowledgment that they were indeed doing ... something. Something neither of them fully wanted, something neither had yet found the power to resist.

"You were sad tonight," he said. Despite his best intentions, he couldn't resist burrowing his nose in her soft curls.

She nodded once in concurrence.

As though drawn by magnetic attraction, he pressed another kiss to her nape, a leisurely, openmouthed nuzzle that filled his soul with her jasmine-scented warmth. "I thought perhaps you were sad because you needed reminding."

She stiffened slightly before her hands slid over his where they lay clasped across her belly. "Remind me of what?"

"Of how I see you." He placed his hands on her shoulders and gently turned her. Moonlight slanted across her face, and the full impact of her transformation struck him a stunning blow.

Everything of "Ned's" youthful awkwardness had vanished, leaving a poised young woman who filled the gown's proportions with dramatic grace. Against the rich emerald silk, her skin paled to alabaster, and above the wide scoop neckline her collarbones created a delicate path to the tender hollow at the base of her throat. Within the dainty puffed sleeves, her arms were sleek and softly rounded, and her breasts, though small, were high and full and formed luscious, tempting mounds where they pushed against her bodice.

She rendered him speechless, humbled. He drank her in, feasted on the sight of her, while his heart pounded against his chest wall. She didn't move, didn't blink as she gazed up at him, the earnest little crease between her eyebrows making her look as she did when calibrating an instrument or ciphering figures, and reminding him that in any garb she remained essentially the same.

His sweet, brilliant Ivy.

The ache inside him spread until it filled every part of him, bringing with it the knowledge that his plan was founded on an error in judgment. For it proved nothing but that he desired her, cared for her—*loved* her—in whatever guise she assumed.

"Dear God, to call you beautiful is a wretched understatement." He swallowed to ease the constriction in his throat. He didn't want to love her, and he couldn't bear *not* to love her.

That funny, studious look deepened the crease between her brows. "At first I didn't know whether to be angry or afraid. I thought perhaps you were making a statement, telling me that as a woman I should remember my place."

"No," he protested, the word guttural and emphatic.

With a twitch of a smile, she pressed her fingertips to his mouth, her touch as tender as a kiss. "I know." The lovely white column of her throat convulsed. Her dark eyes glistened with tears. "Because I know you, and if you *had* wished to make a statement, you'd simply have stated it."

"Then allow me to state this."

In a single motion he swept her up in his arms, for the first time feeling the accompaniment of trailing skirts to her slight weight. Something about those fussy, feminine layers fired his possessive instincts. He held her close and buried his face in her neck, in the swell of her bosom. Then he lifted his head and found her lips, crushed his own to them, and pressed, deeper and deeper, losing himself to the heat of her mouth.

Cradling her in his arms, he stumbled back into the room, into the flickering light of the fire and the many candles he'd set about the room. He hoped she wouldn't want him to blow them out. He wanted to see her. He wanted to show her she had nothing to hide from him—never from him.

Beside the bed, he set her feet on the floor but went on holding her, kissing her. The shawl slipped to the floor, and he stroked his hands up and down her arms. Where he expected her skin to be cold from the night air, it burned beneath his fingertips. He grasped a delicate sleeve between his thumb and forefinger and tugged, baring her shoulder and exposing more of her cleavage. Ah, such beautiful cleavage she had, not overly deep, but a soft, shadowed valley that offered a tantalizing prospect for his tongue.

He gazed down at it, then up at her to see a sweet entreaty shining in her eyes. Lowering his mouth to her, he gave that lovely vale the adoring attention it deserved, while he reached around her and untied the bow at the back of her dress. The laces loosened, but he didn't strip the gown from her shoulders and arms. He wouldn't undress her yet, for he found the teasing allure of a yawning neckline, a slowly raised hem, and the beribboned edge of a stocking as erotic as the promise of having her naked beneath him.

As he pressed kisses across her bosom, she arched her lovely neck. The moisture in her eyes spilled over, trailing reflected candlelight down her cheeks. "Oh, Simon, I *had* forgotten what it felt like. . . ."

"To be completely feminine?"

"Yes. To be a woman." Her arms tightened around his neck. She pressed her forehead to his cheek and whispered, "Or perhaps I never knew. Never understood. Not like this."

Her words overflowed with emotion, with longing and sadness, and enough regret to make him wonder how so beautiful and vital a woman could ever have felt less than wanted, how she could not have known what it was to be coveted by every man around her. Surely they had all been fools, or blind.

"There is more I must show you," he said.

Slowly raising her skirts, he grazed her knee with the backs of his fingers and skimmed the inside of her thigh, enjoying the resultant quiver of her flesh. Traveling higher along her leg, he felt her heat drawing him on. When he reached the silky curls between her thighs, he gave a stroke with a single fingertip. As slight as his touch was, Ivy shuddered.

Ah, yes, this is what he would have her know, the subtle joys to be shared between a man and woman, the trust, the releasing of inhibitions, and the surrender to mutual arousal. All along he'd been pretending both to her and to himself that he could control his desires, his heart. But the truth was, from the moment he'd recognized Ivy the woman, he'd been lost. Wholly, irretrievably lost to her beauty, her intelligence, and the purity of what he'd taken from her—her innocence.

So great a gift she had given him. For tonight, then, he would stop pretending his attraction to her stemmed from mere lust and an inability to keep his hands off her splendid body. Tonight he would show her how much she deserved, whether from him or any man. Returning his mouth to her lips, he ravished them thoroughly. As Ivy writhed in his arms, he explored the folds of her sex, already moist with desire.

Their lips fell apart as her head tipped back on a moan. Her leg slid up around his waist, opening her further, and he slid a finger inside. Her muscles, so tight and sensitive, squeezed him, an embrace of consent and pleasure. Ivy's whimpers driving him on, he eased in deeper. The tightening of her hands on his shoulders signaled her heightening arousal.

Slowly he withdrew, and she whimpered a weak protest. He returned inside her quickly enough, adding a second finger to widen her. At her cry, a sense of both power and satisfaction sped his pulse. He increased his ministrations, until her sex convulsed around him and her back arched and her lovely mouth opened on a cry of ecstasy.

He eased out of her then and moved to swing her into his arms. She half leaned on him, and with a trembling hand on his chest she stopped him. Her breasts heaved as she struggled to catch her breath. Her fingers fisted on his shirt-front. "I made you a promise earlier today."

Through the roar of his rushing blood, he tried to remember what promise had been given hours, what seemed eons, ago. They had gone to Windgate Priory to question Alistair . . . and along the way in the coach, Simon had stroked her to climax even as he had just done now. . . .

God, yes, he remembered. His recollection must have shown in his eyes and in the fiery flush of his skin, for as she searched his features, a smile dawned on her bowed lips.

She released his shirt and smoothed her hand down his body to the junction of his breeches. "It is a promise I intend to keep."

Without ceremony Ivy pushed Simon down onto the edge of the bed. Leaning over to kiss him, she reached for the buttons of his breeches.

His hand came down on hers. "You don't have to."

"Oh, but I promised."

"A promise made in passion doesn't count."

"Do you believe that passion robs a person of sincerity?" She shook her head. "I believe quite the opposite, that stripped of manners and pretense we say precisely what we mean. And *do* precisely as we most wish."

Several times now he had shown her pleasure, and only once had he taken his own. Even then, her inexperience had forced her to play the passive role as he brought them both to fulfillment. Not this time. Perhaps it was the borrowed silk dress, for even as her breeches and waistcoat had emboldened her as a scholar and a human being, the gown imbued her with a new and thrilling power.

Tonight, the scholar gave way to the seductress.

Leaning over him again, she allowed her breasts to spill over the edge of her loosened bodice as she kissed him. Then with a wicked smile she pulled away, running her hands ever so slowly from his shoulders down his torso and to his thighs as she knelt before him.

His breath rasped as she unfastened the top buttons at either side of his trouser flap. Pulling his shirttails free, she ran her fingertips across his stomach, enjoying the sudden flinch of his muscles and experiencing a tightening of her own inner muscles deep, deep in her womb as she followed the light trail of hair that plunged downward from his navel.

Her heart pattering, she undid the remaining buttons, at first keeping one hand over the woolen fabric where he grew and hardened against her palm. The strength of that most essentially male part of him filled her with awe. His member pulsed against her hand and lightly she pressed back, then more firmly.

He ran a hand through her hair, freeing it from the combs that now thudded onto the carpet. "Oh, God, Ivy."

His head was thrown back, his neck knotted, his features contorted as if with pain. She lowered the flap and his shaft sprang forward, thick and engorged, to point at her in a command for attention. She gasped at the sight, then peered back up at Simon's face. He watched her from beneath heavy lids, his mouth hard as if with pain. Without breaking eye contact, she kissed the taut skin just above the bold black hair that framed his penis. His blue eyes blazed. He made a guttural noise, and his hand tightened in her hair.

"You will have to help me," she whispered. "You must let me know if I am doing it correctly."

"Blazing hell, Ivy . . ." His voice was ragged, but filled with an intensity that heightened her courage. She touched the base of his shaft, her fingertips grazing the velvety warm skin of his scrotum. His lips peeled back to bare his teeth. "You . . . are doing it correctly."

She put her lips on him then, and a violent shudder ran his length. Feeling empowered, she closed her mouth around him.

"Ah . . . yes, like that."

Using lips and tongue she moved down his length, then back toward the tip, and paused.

"God, yes."

An instinct she never knew she possessed prompted her to tease him with flicking strokes of her tongue. She added the gentle scrape of her teeth. Simon let out a rumble, while the pressure of his hand at the back of her head guided her motions.

"Like a peppermint stick," he said on a rush of breath.

She paused, at first not understanding what he meant. Then it dawned on her, that he wanted not just the sensation of her lips and tongue but the sensation of sucking inwardly—as one did with a stick of candy. In the back of her mind she knew that later she would laugh at the irony of such an image, that something as innocent as sucking candy could be so sensual.

Now she didn't laugh, for as she gripped the base of his member and used her mouth to bring him higher and higher toward the explosive crest, an aching need grew inside her, a selfish and overwhelming desire to ride that crest with him, to share in the glittering moment of climax, and to cling tight to him during the languid fall back to earth. She yearned to have him inside her, his power and strength filling her. She needed him so much, so very much.

As the thought concluded, he released his hold on her, and with both hands grasped her shoulders and tugged to raise her up. Could he have read her mind, or had he felt her hesitation? She felt suddenly torn, furiously longing to join her body with his while at the same wanting to pleasure him as he had done for her.

But a glance at him revealed an emotion imprinted like a brand across his features, the feverish, blazing image of the same sensations running riot within her.

Her heart lurched. Was she mistaken? In the next instant he'd blinked the sentiment away, but in that brief lowering of his guard, she thought she perceived a love as deep as that which she harbored for him.

He gave another insistent tug. "Ivy, come here."

The temptation proved too much to resist, and *not* yielding to it proved too much to bear. As she rose, he gathered her onto his lap and drew her legs to either side of his waist. His hands dove beneath her hems. He caught hold of her hips and lifted her, then set her down upon his length.

She found herself ready—oh, more than ready for him—and he slid into her until she sheathed him fully. She shut her eyes to the sheer, exultant satisfaction of it, her last vision that of his determined, enraptured features, a desire fierce and plain to see, and mirroring everything she felt herself.

With his powerful hands he began to move her, each stroke up and down his length a loving caress against her soul. Completion brought tears to her eyes, cries from her lips that she muffled against his shoulder, and a shocking certainty that pierced her heart.

Sated and panting for breath, she sagged into the heat of his body and surrendered to the truth. Her smug assertion today that they could find pleasure through their bodies without intercourse was like a farmer claiming he could grow crops without the sun and rain. She had believed she could command these wild, wayward desires, but in truth they commanded her. Despite her fervent longing for independence, she was no free spirit, unfettered by the demands of another human being. Her mutinous love for this man controlled her, mind, body, and soul.

"Oh, Simon, I was wrong," she whispered. She pressed her open mouth to the curve of his neck, tasting the mingled saltiness of his perspiration and her own tears. "What I said today in the coach about controlling our passion . . . I was wrong. So very, very wrong."

His chest still heaving from exertion and the throes of the climax they had shared, he tightened his arms around her and kissed her brow. "Yes, dear heart. I know."

Chapter 19

Not long after, Simon returned to his chamber and went through the motions of retiring alone. But some ten minutes after his valet left him, he donned his robe and cracked his door open. The gallery stretched empty and silent on either side of him. He slipped out and closed the door behind him.

Ivy's door remained unlocked, as he had left it. He let himself in and stole across the room to her bed. The fire had burned down, the coals in the grate giving off a russet glow, just enough to light his way. Ivy lay on her side, her gentlemen's nightshirt tied to her chin, the gown and feminine trappings having been returned to Gwendolyn's room.

A second shadow on her pillow attracted his notice. Leaning close, he made out the shape of a little rag doll with button eyes and a tangle of yarn for hair. Ivy's hand lay wrapped around the body, her chin tucked on the doll's stuffed head.

His heart squeezed at the notion of Ivy seeking comfort from what amounted to a heap of discarded sewing scraps. That small, inconsequential doll bore witness to how young and inexperienced she still was, how alone she must feel. It spoke of how he had failed in providing whatever emotional succor she required.

She didn't move as he lifted the bedclothes and slid in beside her. He snuggled close, fitting his hips against her sweet rear and draping an arm around both her and her doll. She didn't stir, but he sensed that she was awake. He wasn't surprised when she breathed a long sigh and peered at him over her shoulder.

"Simon . . ." Her voice held a tentative caution.

"It's all right," he assured her. "We'll only go to sleep now. And in the morning, I'll be gone before you wake."

Her doubts visibly warred with a clear desire to let him stay. They were not supposed to have made love, although all along Simon had perceived the impossibility of adhering to such a vow.

Without another word she tucked her chin against the doll's head and closed her eyes. Her hair still held a faint trace of jasmine. He breathed in the scent and drifted off to sleep, his last thought an acknowledgment that where Ivy was concerned, his heart had fully betrayed him.

True to his word, Simon left her bed as the first splash of dawn stained the horizon. When next he saw her, downstairs at breakfast in the morning room, all trace of Ivy the woman had vanished, at least to those who looked no further than their expectations. In breeches, a striped waistcoat, and a warm tweed coat, she had become entirely Ned again. In turn, Simon was once more Lord Harrow, and something about that pretense, along with the formality that accompanied it, erected a disheartening barrier between them.

It was as if they could no longer laugh together, or touch in even the most innocent manner, much less steal the occasional kiss. Eye contact became strained, as if each peered across the deferential distance between master and assistant. Once, before they began their day's work in the laboratory, he tried talking to her about these changes, but she remained evasive.

"It is best this way, at least for now," she said, and went about her duties.

Best, he silently agreed, because they each had their separate tasks to complete. Ivy must fulfill her obligation to the queen. Simon must see to his rebellious sister, as well as continue his scientific endeavors. Keeping their distance was best, too, because not doing so led them round and round the same inevitable circle. They had been wrong, both of them, in ever thinking they could hold their passions tightly reined. If last night had proved anything, it was that together, they too easily lost sight of their goals, and not even the strictest reasoning seemed capable of neutralizing the volatile attraction between them.

Work became the only haven where they were safe, the laboratory the only room they might cohabit without falling into each other's arms. On Wednesday, however, Ivy stood up after breakfast and announced that she would not be available to assist him for the next several hours.

"Why not?" he demanded a shade too severely. This sudden breach in their routine had caught him completely off guard.

She waited until the footmen had finished clearing off the buffet and exited through the swinging door to the servants' hallway. "It occurred to me last night that I have been derelict in my duty," she said. "Working with you ... *being* with you," she added in a brittle whisper before continuing more firmly, "has distracted me from the reason I was sent here. Your sister is still missing, but she must be *somewhere*, and finding her note in Ben Rivers's office persuades me she is hiding close by, here in Cambridgeshire."

"And you intend to search for her?"

She nodded. "Someone has to have seen her recently. I intend to make inquiries."

"And supposing you end up chasing her off?"

"I'll take that chance. With your permission, I'll ride out on Butterfly and begin a circuit of the area."

He pushed his plate away and stood. "Of course you have my permission. You'll also have my company. I'm coming with you."

"But ..."

"You didn't think I'd let you go alone, did you?"

Her gaze dropped to the floor. "I thought it would be best if I did."

"We'll keep to public roads," he assured her, "and avoid crumbling follies."

They spent that day and the next traveling as far north as St. Ives, and as far south as Saffron Walden. They called upon the families of Gwendolyn's friends and checked the roadside inns along their route, but no one remembered seeing a woman of his sister's description. Each night when they returned home exhausted and discouraged, Simon grabbed for the post tray in hopes of finding a letter from her, some word of her at all. More and more, he accepted the notion that whatever Gwendolyn had planned would be revealed at the consortium, and that he had no choice but to wait until then.

"I was so certain we'd find some trace of her," Ivy said as she sank onto the drawing room settee that Thursday night. The strain of the day's ride showed in the shadows beneath her eyes, in the slight trembling of her hands as she untied her neckcloth.

"I wasn't at all sure we would." Simon poured them each a brandy. After handing one to Ivy, he sat in the wing chair opposite, a safe and reassuring distance away. True to his word, there had been no off-the-road sojourns, nor had they utilized the private rooms at the inns they visited. When they'd taken their meals, it had been in the public rooms in full view of the other patrons. "If my resourceful sister doesn't wish to be found, rest assured she'll find a means of evading us."

Ivy sipped the brandy, shuddering as the fiery liquid went down. She compressed her lips and studied him through narrowed eyes. "You don't always think very highly of your sister, do you?"

"On the contrary. I've come to think so highly of her that I shan't make the mistake of underestimating her ever again." Hunching deeper into the chair, he stretched out his legs and crossed one ankle over the other. "If only the world were different . . . Gwendolyn might not have chased trouble if she'd only had matters of true significance to challenge her intellect."

"As I have had these past two weeks," Ivy said softly.

He nodded. "Indeed."

On Friday they began the considerable task of dismantling and packing Simon's generator for the move to Windgate Priory. Every component needed to be carefully catalogued and each crate clearly marked and stacked in precise order, first in the laboratory, then in the two wagons waiting on the drive.

Simon did most of the physical work of disassembling the equipment. He called out each mechanism and its purpose, while Ivy kept written records, correcting him whenever he misspoke and a part might have been mislabeled.

He didn't explain that his absentmindedness was because she befuddled him, that though they had reached a silent agreement that they would not repeat their activities of the night of the green dress, he thought of little else. However much he tried to focus on coils, levers, and gears, his mind ran rampant with images of Ivy's slender arms and legs wrapped around him; Ivy on his lap, her silken skirts bunched around her waist and her breasts spilling from her bodice; Ivy with her head tipped back and her body convulsing with wave after wave of ecstasy.

"Lord Harrow?"

Realizing this wasn't the first time her voice had prodded, he looked up from the web of wiring that attached the coils to the pistons. "Yes, Ned?"

She lowered her writing tablet and gestured to the dark-haired footman towering respectfully beside her. "Daniel wishes to know if we'll require any more crates, and if so, what sizes."

Simon considered the remaining generator components, then scanned the dwindling supply of crates. He was about to reply in the negative when his gaze shifted to the armoire, and then back to Ivy.

For it *was* Ivy, and not Ned, waiting intently for his answer. A hand propped at her hip, she, too, flicked a gaze at the armoirc. He had promised he wouldn't repeat his electroporting process, but when it came to abandoning his discovery, to demonstrating only the power of his generator at Windgate Priory . . .

He simply didn't know if he could do it. Pretending he'd never electroported and hushing up his discovery would have been akin to Galileo agreeing that the world was flat and that the sun rotated around the earth. And in Ivy's look of reluctant acceptance, he saw that she already knew his answer.

To the footman she said, "We'll need at least two, perhaps three more crates, large ones, some five feet wide and equally as high."

Then she returned to making notations in her tablet, until Simon touched her elbow. "I don't know exactly what I shall do at the consortium, but it seems prudent to bring the electromagnets along."

"Of course we shall bring them. I knew all along we would."

"I'm sorry. I know I promised. . . ."

Her dark eyes snapping with anger, she slapped her quill against the paper and held it there. "I never asked you to make such a promise, nor did I ever think you could keep it. To do so would be to deny your greatest passion, and we both know you are incapable of that."

She moved away to catalogue the array of small parts arranged across the main table. Simon watched her go. Beneath his breath he murmured, "Not my greatest passion. No, my love, not nearly so."

Ivy and Simon had worked so intently that evening that ncither realized they'd missed suppertime until Mrs. Walsh's shrill admonitions spilled from the speaking tube. "Lord Harrow, how are you to keep up your strength if you don't take time to eat a decent meal? . . ."

"You go on down," he said to Ivy as the housekeeper's scolding continued to echo in the nearly empty laboratory.

"Bring something back up for me," he added when Ivy tried to coax him into joining her.

With a heavy heart, she left him. They had fallen to efficiency and politeness, with so much between them left unsaid. It was best this way, of course. She had her mission. And she had new goals in life, burning reasons to remain independent, for she had no intention anymore of simply returning to her former existence. A new plan was forming in her mind, one that she hoped, with Victoria's help, might lead to a more fulfilling future.

Yet there were moments, frequent ones, when she wished to forget her new ambition and simply let herself love him. Love him, and let the future bring what it may. At those times, she forced herself to remember that she wasn't the only one with reasons to avoid intimacy. Simon had made himself clear on that point, and if his words hadn't been enough, his actions certainly had. As much as he might want her physically, and as high as he seemed to hold her in his esteem, there was always that sudden pulling back, that look of apprehension that filled his eyes, like a wolf suddenly discovering its paw trapped in a hunter's snare.

She wanted no husband, and Simon wanted no wife. But if they weren't careful . . . Her hand pressed her belly. . . .

A blond head and broad shoulders came into view as she descended the main staircase to the ground floor. In the entrance hall, Colin Ashworth stood speaking in tense undertones with Mrs. Walsh. When the earl saw Ivy, he strode to meet her at the bottom of the steps.

"I say, Mr. Ivers. Is Lord Harrow in his laboratory?"

One look at the man's harried expression confirmed to her that something was very wrong. Could his being here have anything to do with Gwendolyn?

"Good evening, Lord Drayton. What brings you to Harrowood at such an hour?"

"Something dreadful has happened," he said curtly. "I must speak with Lord Harrow at once."

A hectic flush stained his skin, and with his head bent and shoulders bunched, he looked about to push past her should she deny his request. Over Lord Drayton's shoulder, Ivy conducted a fleeting and silent communication with Mrs. Walsh. True, no one was ever to venture into Simon's laboratory uninvited, but the urgency of the earl's manner seemed in Ivy's opinion to warrant breaking that rule. Mrs. Walsh proved to be of similar mind, for she gave a slight nod, all the encouragement Ivy needed.

"This way."

He followed fast at her heels, so close in fact that she reminded herself not to swing her hips as she climbed, but to maintain a masculine bearing. She burned to question him, but this impulse she held in check as well. If his business had anything to do with Lady Gwendolyn, she would find out soon enough.

As they neared the top of the tower stairs, the laboratory door opened. "Iv . . . ers."

Simon fell mute, his near slip in speaking her Christian name evident in the surprise etched in his countenance. A glance over her shoulder assured her that Lord Drayton hadn't noticed. He came to a sudden stop near the landing and peered up at Simon. "Don't throw me out until you hear what I've come to tell you."

Poised in the doorway above them, Simon paled. "My sister . . . Something's happened."

Ivy pointedly ignored the hand Simon extended to help her clear the last step, as had become his habit whenever they climbed the tower together. Fortunately, Lord Drayton seemed equally oblivious of this slip.

"This isn't about Gwen," Lord Drayton said. "There's been an incident on campus. A death. Perhaps . . . a murder."

The last of the color drained from Simon's face. "Dear God. Who?"

"A student. A first year named Spencer Yates."

"No!" Reaching out, Ivy pressed a hand to the wall. Her knees melted beneath her and she started to go down.

Simon caught her around the waist. "Let's go inside."

Accepting his support, Ivy let him convey her into the

laboratory and settle her on a chair. He knelt in front of her. "You knew him."

She nodded weakly. "He was one of Jasper Lowbry's mates. All of them were so kind to me, taking me under their wing when I arrived at the university." A feeble smile trembled across her lips. "They thought it of vital importance that I learn to drink brandy. Spencer . . . He was forever puffing on those beloved cheroots of his. Nasty things . . . made me cough. . . . I . . ." Her throat closed around the rest. With a glance at Lord Drayton, she attempted to blink back her tears.

Simon patted her shoulder, a message of much deeper sympathy shining in his eyes. He pushed to his feet and turned to the earl. "Tell us what happened."

"A fellow student found him dead in the main chemistry laboratory this morning. At first it was believed he somehow fell and hit his head on the edge of a table. But now the coroner says he likely died of an intentional blow."

Ivy's surroundings swam in her vision. "It can't be true."

Simon dragged two stools close to hers. Then he brought over the brandy he always kept on hand. As Lord Drayton provided further details, she held the snifter Simon pressed into her hand, but didn't drink from it.

"The authorities are questioning Errol," the earl said. "Ben is with him. That's why I came. I thought you should know."

"Surely they can't suspect Errol." Incredulity made Simon's voice sharp.

"No, I'm quite certain they do not. For one, he hasn't the strength necessary to commit murder. But it *was* his laboratory. They are questioning everyone who had access to the facility over the past few days as well."

"What about the murder weapon?" Simon asked him.

"That's the strange thing. The irregular shape of the wound points to a heavy object with a rough surface. Like a rock."

"What motive could anyone have to murder a student?"

Ivy's feigned tenor shook and cracked, for an instant revealing her natural tone.

Again, Lord Drayton seemed not to notice, his attention absorbed in relating the shocking news. "The authorities aren't willing to disclose their theories just yet. I assume they are considering all the usual possibilities. Jealousy, whether over a girl or academic standing—"

"Spencer was to attend the consortium." Ivy swallowed a sob.

Lord Drayton nodded sadly. "Yes, he was to serve as my secretary and take detailed notes on the various demonstrations."

"He was *your* assistant." Simon frowned.

Something passed between the two men, a caustic tension that had Ivy sitting up straighter, gripping her brandy snifter tighter until she forced her fingers to relax around the delicate glass. Both men sat rigidly upright, their jaws bluntly squared. Was Simon accusing Lord Drayton of the crime? For another instant, the possibility of them coming to blows crackled in the air between them.

Simon was the first to look away and ease his posture. Lord Drayton immediately followed suit, taking a drink of his brandy. He settled a sympathetic gaze on Ivy. "I didn't know Mr. Yates at all well," he said. "But he seemed a promising student, and was well liked among his peers. Quite a number have already gathered at St. John's in his memory."

"You'd like to be among them." Simon didn't pose this as a question, but as a statement. When Ivy nodded, he set down his brandy and stood. "We'll go into town immediately. Errol isn't strong. If I must, I'll push my advantage as a peer to make certain he is treated with deference, and that some overeager constable doesn't interrogate him to the brink of exhaustion."

"I'd hoped you would say that." Lord Drayton came to his feet as well. "As my father's heir, I hold only an honorary title. As a marquess in your own right, you command the sort of authority that Errol may need."

"You did the right thing in coming here." And then Simon did something utterly surprising, given his history of rancor toward Lord Drayton. He extended his hand. When the earl grasped it, Simon gave the man's hand a firm shake and said, "Thank you."

Early the next morning, Simon tapped on Ivy's door. He hadn't seen her since yesterday afternoon, for they had arrived home separately last night, and spent many hours apart. While Simon had sent his carriage to collect her following Spencer Yates's impromptu memorial gathering at St. John's, he had remained in town long afterward to support Errol through the ordeal of answering endless questions.

Colin had been correct in that no one was suggesting Errol had anything to do with the boy's death, but since Yates had died in Errol's laboratory, the magistrate felt it necessary to collect every bit of information Errol could provide about schedules, experiments, and possible student rivalries.

One detail nagged at Simon, as if a mongrel had set its teeth to his nape. The murder weapon was believed to have been a blunt instrument with a rough surface . . . as Colin had said, possibly a rock. The timing chilled his blood. Dear God, could there be a connection between Gwendolyn's disappearance with the queen's mysterious stone and Yates's death?

Ivy's door suddenly opened, cutting short his troubling thoughts. Though dressed in a black wool frock coat, a stiffly knotted cravat, and a pair of gray breeches tucked into her half Wellingtons, she appeared sleepy-eyed and sweetly tousled, her curls having rebelled against her effort to tame them and her cheeks retaining the soft flush of slumber.

Inappropriate images of the two of them rolling across her still-warm bed filled his brain. They'd both been through different versions of purgatory yesterday, and the fatigue of it showed on her features. He resisted the urge to pull her into his arms, stroke her hair, and offer what comfort he could with kisses.

Instead he leaned a shoulder against the doorframe. "How did it go at St. John's yesterday?"

She blinked, her spiky lashes shadowing her cheeks. "Awful, as you can well imagine. The students are all in shock. I've never seen Jasper so despondent." She hugged her arms around herself. "How is Mr. Quincy?"

"Also in shock. He feels partly responsible, if only because Mr. Yates had been in the laboratory at Errol's request, doing some cataloguing."

"Surely if someone had wished to . . ." She broke off, pressing her lips together and bowing her head. "Someone with ill intentions toward Spencer would have found opportunity elsewhere, if not in Mr. Quincy's laboratory."

"Indeed. But I came to tell you that I've brought Errol here as my guest. I don't wish him to be alone now."

"No, of course not."

He leaned closer to her and lowered his voice. "It means you and I must be extra careful. There can be no further indiscretions on our part."

He had intended to use no particular emphasis, but the word *indiscretions* rang out like a discordant bell.

Ivy winced. Her chin rose in the air as she backed up a step from the doorway. "I assure you, sir, I shall curb my improper tendencies as best I can."

"That is not at all what I meant and you know it." He knew his next move would constitute one of those indiscretions that could prove troublesome should anyone witness it, but the chagrin on Ivy's face sent him over the threshold in pursuit of her.

With one hand he caught her coat sleeve and with the other he swung the door closed. It shut with a resounding bang he'd have preferred not to have caused, but it couldn't be helped. With equal measures of defiance and hurt, Ivy resisted the pressure of his grasp. With the best of intentions he played the bully, pressing her to the wall beside the door and trapping her there with the weight of his body.

"Listen to me," he said urgently. Her scent filled his being, and he fought to keep his thoughts from tumbling into the oblivion of desire. "All I meant was that we must be careful not to be found out. Not to alert Errol to the fact that you are not who you claim to be. For heaven's sake, would you allow yourself to be ruined for all time?"

She turned her face away from his seeking lips. "A bit late to worry about that, no?"

"Damn it, Ivy . . ." Cupping her cheeks, he turned her to him. He meant only to reason with her, but her pursed lips proved too great a temptation.

He covered her mouth, his own mouth hard and stiff with an anger he couldn't fully define. Yes, she was being stubborn, deliberately misunderstanding his meaning. But she was also presenting him with the perfect opportunity to end this unwanted relationship or whatever it should be termed. For they *had* committed indiscretions, several times over, despite numerous vows to the contrary. Why couldn't he feel the wrongness of their actions? Why didn't he simply open the door and walk away?

Unable to answer his own questions, he went on kissing her, drowning in her scent and taste and warmth, caught up in his roiling, dogged need to have her in his arms. So intent was he on drinking her in that he couldn't quite identify the moment when she stopped fighting him, slid her arms around his neck, and began kissing him back.

Footsteps out in the hall broke them apart. Ivy's eyes were burning and wild, as turbulent as the blood rushing through Simon's veins. She tugged her coat into place, fingered her neckcloth. Simon straightened his waistcoat, smoothed a hand over his hair. The footsteps passed by her door, and they both sighed with relief.

Simon took her face gently in his hands and ran the pads of his thumbs across her lips. "God help me for wanting you as much as I do."

"And me for knowing what I want and doing just the opposite." She covered his hands with her own, held them there a moment as if to memorize the feel of them against her, then slid them from her face and released him. Her arms at her sides, she straightened her spine with a brave little toss of her curls. "I'm sorry I acted the shrew. Be assured that you have done nothing I haven't wished you to do. But you are also correct. With your friend here, we can no longer indulge our fancies. What about the consortium? Is it to proceed at Windgate Priory as planned?"

The speed with which she transformed from angry lover to efficient assistant took him aback. Part of him felt loath to let their quarrel go. He'd rather bicker with her than return to polite words and passionless manners. He'd have preferred enmity and resentment to courtesy and the damned deference that restored them to their proper social stations.

He reached for the doorknob. "There has been no change in plans for the consortium. To be sure, Yates's passing will hang heavy over the event, but the Royal Society representatives and a score of scientists are on their way to Windgate Priory even as we speak."

"Then I shall be ready to leave whenever you say the word."

He thanked her, and left the room with a lingering wretchedness that nearly choked him.

Chapter 20

At the sight of the young man coming through Alistair Granville's wide-open front doors, Ivy hurried down the remainder of the staircase and bounced to a halt in front of him. "Lowbry. I'm so glad you're here. I don't know how I'd have endured it otherwise."

"Ivers." The good-looking Jasper Lowbry dropped the valise he carried, strode forward, and caught her up in a quick bear hug. "It won't be the same without poor Yates," he said as he released her.

"Is Preston Ascot coming?" she asked.

"He should be here soon."

Jasper's mouth dropped open as he took in Windgate Priory's elaborate entry hall. Activity buzzed around them. Through the wide doorway into the equally elaborate and enormous ballroom, a steady stream of servants, scientists, and their assistants busily filed in and out.

Ivy stepped back to survey the man whom she considered, against all propriety, to be her friend—her companion in academia and now in grief as well. Behind him, two footmen in the Windgate gold-upon-chestnut livery struggled at either end of a trunk; they were attempting to carry it over the threshold without upending the heavy piece or crashing it into the doorframe.

At a loud thunk, Jasper glowered at them. "Careful with that. It contains delicate instrumentation."

The servants rolled their eyes and crossed the hall to the staircase.

"Leave the luggage to them and come with me." Ivy very nearly grasped Jasper's wrist, remembering in time that men didn't tug each other along in bursts of exuberance. Instead she gestured him to follow her into the ballroom.

Sunlight streamed through the room's towering windows, reflecting on the polished parquet floor and on the array of gadgets and equipment, large and small, ranged along the perimeters.

"Criminy . . ." Jasper twisted his head this way and that.

Even Ivy continued to marvel at the sights, though she had been here for several days now. She, Simon, and Errol had been the first to arrive, when the ballroom had been cavernous and full of echoes. Members of the consortium had arrived daily since then. Now the ballroom resembled a workshop of fantastical wonders and the manor itself an exceedingly lavish men's club, for other than cooks and maidservants, Ivy was the only woman.

Like an excited child, Jasper kept raising a hand to point. "Look at that . . . and that!"

The first item to which he referred, a steel and iron tabletop contraption consisting of various-sized wheels connected by belts and pulleys, gave off a *rat-a-tat-tat* as the man standing behind it gave the crankshaft several turns. Spools rotated, and as a vertical rod bobbed up and down, a needle poked in and out of a length of a blue woolen fabric, emblazoning it with a trail of ivory stitching.

The man who watched intently over the process had deep-set eyes and a high domed forehead framed by wild shanks of hair that curled to his shoulders. After every few turns of the crankshaft, he stopped to make adjustments.

"That is Elias Howe. He's an American," Ivy explained. "No one in his home country was willing to help fund his project, so Mr. Howe sold nearly all of his worldly possessions and traveled across the Atlantic in hopes of enjoying a more welcoming reception from his English counterparts."

His brows knitting in perplexity, Jasper studied the man and his invention. "What on earth is he doing?"

"Sewing, of course."

The young man's eyes went wide with astonishment. "A device that sews. Remarkable. I wonder...." He approached Elias Howe and extended his hand. "Jasper Lowbry, sir."

The whirring and click-clicking of the machine wound to a halt as Elias Howe accepted Jasper's handshake. "Pleasure to meet you, my boy. Your field?"

"Physics, sir. Electromagnetism, specifically. Cambridge University." Jasper gestured at Howe's sewing machine. "This is quite a work of mechanical physics you have here, sir. I can't help but wonder if you've considered how it might function if hooked up to a voltaic cell."

With an indulgent smile the older man held up a hand. "One step at a time, son. Still got to work out the bugs."

"Bugs?"

"Sure. Haven't quite figured out how to prevent the thread from tangling and breaking, and the fabric from pulling and rumpling. And then there's that bit of my thumb I'll never have back." He held up the gouged appendage and chuckled, then patted the crankshaft. "This here's just a prototype, but five or ten years from now don't be surprised to find rows of my automatic stitchers lined up in every textile factory across two continents. A suit of clothes like you're wearing won't take more than a day or two to make."

"A day or two," Jasper murmured as he and Ivy proceeded through the ballroom. "I'm not certain I like that notion. Seems a bit tawdry for a gentleman's clothing to be tossed together so hastily."

Ivy nodded her agreement and slowed as another member of the consortium caught Jasper's attention. This man's balding head kept disappearing and appearing from behind the wooden boxlike contraption he had set upon a tripod. A lens encased in a several-inch-long brass cylinder extended from one side, pointing outward into the room.

"I know what this is," Jasper said before Ivy could speak. "A camera, yes?"

The man poked his head up again and fixed his gaze on Jasper. He seemed always to frown, Ivy noted, not in anger or perplexity, but in pensiveness, as though caught up in the intricacies of some elusive puzzle.

"Are you a chemist, sir?" the man demanded.

"Er, no, a physicist," Jasper replied, "or at least I shall be once I've completed my education."

"Mr. Lowbry," Ivy interjected, "I'd like you to meet Mr. William Fox Talbot, who is, by the way, a former Cambridge student. Mr. Talbot, Mr. Jasper Lowbry, of St. John's College."

"St. John's, eh? I was a Trinity man myself." Talbot didn't extend a hand, Ivy only now realized, because both of his were covered by white cotton gloves. He held them away from his body, as if they might drip some invisible but damaging substance on his coat. "You claim to be familiar with the process of photogenic drawing, do you, my young sir?"

"I've ... er ... heard of it." Jasper seemed taken aback by the other man's curtness, but quickly recovered his poise. "Hasn't a man named Louis Daguerre developed a—"

"Bah! What does that Frenchman know, with his unwieldy copper plates?" Talbot motioned Jasper closer. "See here. I'm developing a process whereby plain paper is made chemically light-sensitive and produces something no one has thought of before."

"And what would that be, sir?" Jasper asked politely.

"A calotype," Talbot declared with a triumphant flourish. "It is the process whereby an image in negative is burned into the paper and can be used to produce copies of the original over and over again."

"Ingenious," Jasper proclaimed, to which the other man nodded vigorously and then resumed tinkering with his box.

Jasper and Ivy continued their perusal of the consortium exhibits. Not all the projects were as easily identified as Mr. Howe's and Mr. Talbot's, nor were their creators as loquacious. One bespectacled man who barely reached Ivy's shoulder claimed to have invented a device for predicting the weather, but he declined to elaborate further on his smoking jumble of pumps and gears.

They saw electrogenerators and electromagnets, though none that compared in size with Simon's. Ivy thought of his giant electromagnets, still packed in their crates, which Simon had instructed the footman to deliver up to his bedchamber upon their arrival here. Would he unpack them? Would he dare demonstrate his astounding and dangerous electroportation process?

If he had reached a decision, he hadn't shown any inclination to share it with her. Ivy told herself his reticence was due to Errol Quincy's constant presence, and to the other scientists who had arrived daily. They both knew Ivy could ill afford even the slightest mishap that might reveal her gender. But it hurt, this distance between them. She missed him dreadfully, missed his smiles, the feel of his arms, and the rumble of his voice beneath her ear.

As she and Jasper walked, she gave her head a shake to banish her melancholy. Simon's generator, with its steam-producing furnace and vat, occupied the entire back wall of the ballroom, and was by far the largest apparatus there. Side by side, she and Jasper contemplated the mysterious shapes tightly covered in black sheeting. At least, what lay beneath remained a mystery to Jasper and every other man in the room. Ivy could have diagrammed and named every component by heart.

"Tomorrow night," Jasper said with feeling.

Ivy clapped his shoulder. "Yes, my friend, tomorrow night Lord Harrow will start up his generator, and I promise you, it will be truly splendid to behold."

"And with it, Dean Rivers and I shall demonstrate *his* project, and it, too, shall be splendid to behold."

But Ivy only half heard him. For as she turned to retreat back through the room, a sight in the doorway spread frissons of panic through her.

* * *

"I have been to the Three Horseshoes three times now, and the innkeeper denies having seen any sign of her." Simon released an oath of frustration that garnered him sympathetic looks from the men seated around him in Alistair's library. They had the room to themselves, an advantage of being well acquainted with the home's owner. "Where could Gwendolyn be hiding?"

As soon as he and Ivy had returned from their latest ride into the village, Simon's friends—Alistair, Ben, Errol, and even Colin—had joined him here in a show of support. Simon hadn't hesitated before airing his disappointment in front of Colin. Only a few short days ago, he would probably not have been so open, but the death of young Spencer Yates had taught him that life was too short to hold grudges.

Besides, whatever had occurred last winter, Colin had expressed sincere remorse on countless occasions; Simon decided it was time to let go of his hostility.

Sitting in the wing chair, Errol absently twirled his walking stick between his frail hands. "Have you considered the possibility that Gwen never left London?"

Colin looked up at that but said nothing. Though he appeared to be paying close attention to everything Simon said, he'd been uncharacteristically quiet since they'd all entered the room. He sat half sprawled in his chair, long legs outstretched and crossed at the ankles, a slight frown tugging at his brow. Simon guessed the circumstances made him uncomfortable with the conversation, or perhaps he feared that voicing his opinion might result in a demand that he leave the room.

Simon returned his attention to Errol's suggestion and shook his head. "As of yesterday I've heard from both of her friends who are presently staying in town. She isn't with either of them."

"One or both could be lying about her whereabouts." With a graceful motion Alistair stretched an arm along the carved back of the settee. "You know how women are when it comes to their *bonnes amies*."

"I did consider that," Simon admitted. "But I also believe both girls would fear their monarch's retribution more than they feel compelled to protect their friend. Harboring a fugitive of the queen's household would put their own positions in serious jeopardy."

"I must agree, all the more so because this monarch happens to be a woman." Ben let out a low groan as he stood and stretched his limbs. Lately, his boyhood injury seemed to be manifesting itself. Simon had never thought of Ben as old, surely nowhere near as elderly as Errol. But while the dean of natural philosophies would soon be fifty, his body appeared a decade older.

Ben ambled to the window and glanced out, then turned back to them, the daylight silhouetting the permanent hunch left by a falling rafter some thirty-odd years ago. "There's nothing a woman fears more than another of her sex."

Colin seemed about to disagree. His gaze snapped from Ben to Simon, then sank to the floor. The hairs on Simon's nape bristled. Was Colin thinking that Gwendolyn feared nothing more than her unreasonable brother?

He shoved the thought away. It was time he stopped assuming the worst about his former best friend and started figuring out how to win back his sister's regard.

Alistair gave a light chuckle at Ben's last words. Smoothing a hand over his carefully coiffed hair, he angled a pensive look at Simon. "You put a lot of store in this assistant of yours, taking him into your confidence about Gwendolyn."

Simon didn't want anyone taking an undue interest in Ivy, so in an offhand manner he said, "Why not? The boy's got sharp eyes and a keen mind, and he's been known to perceive details I miss."

The men parted soon after, and Simon made his way down to the ground floor to find Ivy, who had returned to the ballroom earlier. Her joy in meeting the scientists and watching them prepare for the demonstrations was infectious, and Simon was glad she'd found something to distract her from thoughts of Spencer Yates's death.

He reached the bottom steps just as an impeccably dressed dark-haired fellow hauled Ivy from the ballroom and along the main corridor by her elbow. The scoundrel was no one Simon recognized, and therefore could not be a member of the consortium.

Who was he, then, and what the devil did he want with Ivy?

Jasper Lowbry hovered in the ballroom doorway, staring after Ivy and her captor in perplexity. Simon paused long enough to question the youth.

"I haven't the foggiest who that is, my lord. He simply strode up to Ned, seized his arm, and declared that they had matters to discuss. When I attempted to follow, he stilled me with a look I've only ever seen at the back entrances of gaming hells. I can't explain it, but for the briefest instant I feared for my life."

Simon burst into motion. Ivy and the stranger had turned into the dining hall, but when he entered the long room, he discovered it empty. A butler's chamber lay beyond, and a contentious clash of voices led Simon to it. Careful to silence his footsteps, he crept close to the doorway.

"You are returning to London with me at once."

"That is impossible. Victoria sent me—"

"Victoria had no right to endanger you this way."

"She needs me here, just as she needed Laurel in Bath last spring." The triumphant note in Ivy's response implied that she believed she had just won the argument.

Her adversary didn't agree. "Laurel was nearly killed in Bath. More than once. Which is why I am here. There are things we haven't told you, and it's time you knew the truth."

"Unless it has anything to do with my business for Victoria, it can wait."

"It cannot—"

"Aidan, this house is full of scientists. What harm can possibly befall me here?"

"Ah." This burst from the man's lips as something of a bark. "Let us take a moment to examine this fact. You, an unmarried, unchaperoned woman, are here alone in a house full of men. In fact, you apparently have been the houseguest of one man in particular for more than two weeks now, and have kept company with him night and day. The very moment I get my hands on him, I am going to—"

"He has no idea who or what I am," Ivy countered in an urgent whisper. "He believes me to be a university student named Ned Ivers, as does everyone else here. I swear to you, Aidan. You have no cause for argument with Lord Harrow."

So she isn't going to tell him the truth. Simon briefly pondered the significance of that and wondered whom she sought to protect, him or herself. He decided it was time to discover who this Aidan person was and what claim he had on Ivy. Backing up several steps, Simon then walked forward without attempting to muffle his tread. As he crossed the threshold, the murmured debate that had continued to rage stalled to an awkward silence.

"Ah, Ned, there you are," he said breezily. "Your friend Lowbry indicated you'd gone this way." He shifted his gaze to take in the man.

He stood about Simon's height and was of similar age and build, and, as Lowbry had intimated, possessed a direct gaze forceful enough to make a lesser man cower. This, coupled with the costly cut of his attire, suggested that he, like Simon, hailed from privilege. His speech patterns hinted at a university education, though Simon's guess would be Oxford rather than Cambridge.

The man's harshness with Ivy had Simon seething at him through narrowed eyes, but he nonetheless maintained a cordial tone. "I don't believe I've had the pleasure. You can't be a member of the consortium, or I'd know you. Are you a representative of the Royal Society, then?"

Even before Aidan denied it, Simon knew he held no such position. He'd said it only to persuade the other man that he hadn't overheard his conversation with Ivy.

"I am the Earl of Barensforth," he said with an imperious curl of his lip that made Simon rather detest him, "and I have come to collect my—"

"Brother-in-law," Ivy burst out. "Lord Barensforth is married to my sister Laurel."

Simon expected the earl to correct the claim that Ivy was his brother-in-law. When he didn't, amusement at the situation made Simon smile. "I see. How good of you to come. Are you a dabbler in the sciences, sir?"

"No, I am not, sir." Ivy shot the earl an imploring look, which he summarily ignored as he regarded Simon down the length of his patrician nose. "My *brother-in-law* here has given the family a scare by disappearing from the university without so much as a by-your-leave. It's taken me days to track him down, and I've every notion to grab the bounder by the ear and haul him home."

"A misunderstanding." Ivy waved her hands in the air. "I explained everything in a letter, which must have gone awry. But as you can plainly see, I am safe and sound, and enjoying the opportunity of a lifetime."

The earl flashed her a furious look, and Simon suppressed an urge to laugh. Argue though they might, it seemed the three of them had all silently agreed on one point: to continue the pretense of Ivy being a man.

Simon strolled farther into the room, running his hand along the beveled edge of a sideboard before turning and leaning against the mahogany piece. "I'll have you know that young Ned here has proved invaluable to me."

He shifted his gaze from a clearly livid Lord Barensforth to a thoroughly unsettled Ivy. "Ned, Dean Rivers has requested that you and Mr. Lowbry assist him presently in the ballroom. Why don't you go along while Lord Barensforth and I smooth out this little wrinkle with your family?"

Color flooded her face. She opened her mouth as if to protest, apparently thought better of it, and compressed her lips. Still, an entreaty flashed from her eyes, one filled with equal parts warning and apprehension. Simon smiled in return and gestured for her to be gone.

Warming to the game they seemed intent on playing, he

clapped Lord Barensforth's shoulder. "Come, sir. I happen to know where Sir Alistair keeps his finest brandy."

That evening, Ivy found herself once more confronted by the disapproving glower of her brother-in-law and the possibility that at any moment he would seize her and carry her bodily from Windgate Priory.

And yet . . . as far as she knew, both he and Simon were continuing to uphold her masculine charade, and quite possibly for the same basic reason. Simon knew that Aidan knew that Ivy wasn't a man, but Aidan didn't know that Simon knew, and therein lay Ivy's trump card. Aidan didn't dare drop even the slightest hint for fear of destroying her reputation. For the time being, she had him over a barrel.

The two men had spent the better part of an hour closeted away in one of Sir Alistair's private salons, drinking brandy and discussing Ivy's supposed future. Afterward, Simon had winked at her and whispered, "I believed I've convinced him that I'm enough of an absentminded idiot not to have recognized the truth in front of my face."

"He's letting me stay?"

Simon had shrugged. "He remained somewhat evasive, but if he drags you home, it won't be because he fears for your virtue at my hands."

"Then we had best not discuss our sleeping arrangements," she'd whispered back. Upon arriving at Windgate Priory, she had learned that assistants were allotted cots in their masters' dressing rooms. The discovery had raised a flutter of anticipation, until Simon had established a pattern of staying up long into the night, retiring only after she had drifted off to sleep.

In truth, Aidan had little to fear in allowing her to complete her mission.

The next time she saw her brother-in-law, she could not keep from pressing him. "You and Lord Harrow spoke at length," she said. "Are you satisfied?"

"Satisfied?" he shot back. "In what inconceivable way can you imagine that I should be satisfied?"

."Lord Harrow has no inkling of my gender."

"Good grief." He reached up and grabbed a shank of his hair as if to yank it from his head. "Lord Harrow aside, there are other, even more pertinent reasons you should be safe at home, not running wild doing God knows what."

"I am not running wild—"

"Ivy, listen to me." For the second time that day he seized her elbow. This time he propelled her down the first-floor corridor outside her bedroom to the relative seclusion of a recessed window. "Laurel and I made some disquieting discoveries while in Bath."

In the months Ivy had known him, Aidan Phillips had become like a brother to her and her sisters, unfailing in his kindness, never wavering in his good-natured generosity. Never before had she seen him look so grave. And that led her to venture a guess. "Those discoveries are what took you and Laurel to France."

"Yes. While we were in Bath, we attempted to locate the home where you and your sisters grew up."

"Peyton Manor. In the Cotswolds."

A subtle change in his expression sent a chill across her shoulders. "Ivy, it doesn't exist."

"Of course it does. I have memories . . ."

"Of a manor, yes, but not in the Cotswolds. We have come to believe not even in England."

"Then . . . in France?"

"Perhaps." He angled a quick glance along the corridor. "Are you familiar with the button Laurel wears from a chain around her neck?"

She nodded. "The one with the crown and fleur-de-lis crest."

He placed his hand on her shoulder and gave it a squeeze that did little to quell her rising misgivings. "This will shock you, but while we were in Bath, Laurel was attacked by a Frenchman."

She gasped, then reacted in anger. "Why on earth weren't we told?"

"Because Laurel and I didn't wish to alarm you, not

until we had more information. But I now believe that decision was a mistake. We all should be alarmed, or at the very least wary." He fell silent as, down the corridor, a door opened. Elias Howe, the inventor of the automatic stitcher, stepped out and locked his bedchamber door behind him. He noticed them, nodded a greeting, and headed for the main staircase.

Aidan released a breath and continued. "Although the origins are vague, this crest seems to be associated with an illegitimate line of the Valois family dating back to the sixteenth century. This line settled in the northeast of France."

Ivy remained silent as the implications sank in. "Are you suggesting that we are descendants of this line?"

"We don't yet know. There's more. In questioning the local residents, we heard tales of a bloody feud that ended in a fire that destroyed an estate and a family."

"Good Lord." She stared unseeing at the darkening sky beyond the window, aware only of the cold air that penetrated the panes. With a shiver, she asked, "Who was this family?"

"I'm afraid we couldn't accurately identify them. It happened in those awful days at the close of the wars, when France was in turmoil. Those who are living in the surrounding villages were not those who lived there then. We think the original inhabitants were either forced off their land or killed."

"To prevent the truth from getting out," she said to the frigid glass.

"We believe so, yes."

She turned to him. "This man who attacked Laurel. Can you tell me anything about him? Was he that de Vere person whom Holly mentioned in her letter?"

"No. Henri de Vere was a double agent who worked for the British during the wars and who now lives here, in England. We believe he is involved, but we don't yet know for good or ill." Aidan's wide shoulders bunched as he leaned closer to her. "Laurel never got a good look at her assailant, but the villain spoke to her, or rather shouted at her, in

French. He seemed to recognize her, or at least to confuse her with someone who apparently resembles her. He called her Simone de Valentin. Does that name mean anything to you?"

"Simone . . ." An unsettling familiarity tugged at Ivy's thoughts. She felt as though a memory sat poised on a precipice, waiting to shatter into a thousand pieces. But nothing came, only a nagging sensation she couldn't shake. "My mother's name was Cecily. My father was Roderick. I know of no one named Simone." She shivered again.

"Don't worry." Aidan put an arm across her tweed-clad shoulders. "I've got a trusted and quite discreet friend at the Foreign Office continuing to make inquiries. We will get to the bottom of this. But do you see now why you should be home?"

She surprised herself with how quickly the answer came. "No. All our lives, Uncle Edward kept us tucked away at Thorn Grove, but the moment Laurel ventured out on her own, this happened."

"Yes, my point exactly. And since I know all about the stone you are trying to recover for the queen—yes, Holly and Willow explained—you may leave the task to me."

She raised her chin to him. "You are missing *my* point. Seclusion never made us any safer. It didn't make the problem disappear. My sisters and I cannot live the rest of our lives in hiding. I will not. Laurel had a mission to accomplish for the queen. Now it is my turn. The information you have just shared with me will ensure that I proceed with the utmost caution." She held up her hand when his chest swelled and his mouth opened to retort. "But I *will* proceed, Aidan. I am of age, and I am bound by the queen's authority."

He scowled at her for a long moment. Then his mouth quirked. "Damn, but you are Laurel's sister, aren't you?"

Chapter 21

The next evening, Ivy hurried to the chambers she and Simon shared to retrieve a spool of wire needed for a demonstration to take place shortly. Benjamin Rivers was to present the project for which Simon had agreed to lend him his generator.

The spool in hand, she left the room and locked the door. When a shadow fell across her path, she expected it to be Aidan and braced for another round of warnings and admonitions. Instead, beefy fingers seized her shoulder and sent shoots of pain down her arm.

Before she could shout for help, the hand spun her about. A familiar grin and pockmarked features sent relief rollicking through her. Ivy shoved at the young man, who immediately released his grip. "Preston!" she exclaimed. "It's about time you showed up. I'd feared you'd changed your mind about coming."

The diplomat's son seemed to possess no finesse of his own, but his garrulous, oafish mannerisms nonetheless endeared him to his friends, and to Ivy. Regarding her, he let out a guffaw. "I wouldn't miss this consortium for the world, Ivers. No, I stayed behind to . . ." His grin faded. "Hell, to see to Spencer's unfinished tasks for Mr. Quincy."

"Oh. Yes, I see." Ivy clapped his shoulder with considerably less force than he had used with her. "Good of you to do that." She brightened, remembering the pact she and

Jasper had made to try to enjoy the consortium in Spencer's memory. "But now you're here, just in time to witness something truly extraordinary. Come. Lord Harrow is waiting for me in the ballroom."

Preston hesitated in following her down the hall. He appeared genuinely distressed. "You won't tell him how I just greeted you, will you?"

At the memory of Simon's reaction to Preston's playful assault in St. John's Second Court, she smiled broadly. "I think that is something Lord Harrow never needs to know."

"Are you ready to make history, my friends?" Alistair Granville stood in front of the closed ballroom doors. Although he spoke to the two men standing closest to him, his voice carried through the crowd of scientists, assistants, and Royal Society representatives crowding the entrance hall.

Simon regarded Ben, who fidgeted nervously at his side. "My generator may cause a stir, but it's this man's invention that will one day revolutionize life in our cities."

Ben darted a glance at the expectant faces surrounding them. "Nothing like setting unreasonably high expectations."

The demonstrations had begun earlier that afternoon, with a Scotsman named Kirkpatrick Macmillan delighting the assembly by whizzing past on a velocipede he had constructed in his blacksmith's shop. No longer propelled by pushing one's feet along the ground, this velocipede improved on the old design by means of cranks and drive rods attached to foot pedals.

"Ingenious," Simon had agreed with the general consensus. "Now if only someone would invent smoother roads on which to ride the thing."

"Ah, the man who achieves that," Alistair had declared heartily, "will certainly win himself a Copley Medal."

Following Macmillan's velocipede, they had been treated to other inventions that made use of human rather than electrical power, but which put the principles of mechanical physics to innovative use.

Tonight, Simon would unveil his generator for the first time, and Ben would be the first to demonstrate its potential. Alistair threw the ballroom doors wide and led the way inside, followed by Simon and Ben, and then Jasper Lowbry and Ivy. Her brother-in-law shadowed her, and even without turning around, Simon could sense the man's hostility burning at his back. In many ways Aidan Phillips reminded Simon of himself, and of his reaction upon discovering the furtive affection between Colin and Gwendolyn.

For the time being, however, the earl had agreed to let Ivy stay, but with the condition that he remain as well to keep an eye on her. If Simon had needed a reason to keep his distance from Ivy, he had certainly found one in the formidable and disapproving Earl of Barensforth. Something in the man's very bearing convinced Simon he could swiftly resort to tactics of a violent sort, should he decide the situation warranted it.

The remainder of the consortium, including the two representatives of the Royal Society who had arrived that morning, shuffled en masse into the ballroom. Colin and Errol stood together at the front of the crowd. Alistair played host by moving through the assembly and ensuring that everyone would have a proper view. A buzz of conversation filled the air, the murmurs rising in volume as Simon, Ivy, and Jasper released the cords and rolled back the black canvas that had concealed the generator from view.

At Ben's request, the room's illumination had been kept to a minimum, only a few of the sconces along the walls having been lit but not the overhead chandeliers. Dollops of candlelight reflected on the apparatus. Words of admiration and surprise rippled through the assemblage.

Yet more than once, Simon detected the word *insane* whispered along with the praise. Ignoring both positive and negative comments, he continued with the preparations. The vat had been filled and the coal furnace lit, the copper chimney angled out an open window to prevent the exhaust from filling the room. Simon stoked the flames higher. With minutes, the water began to boil.

"Mr. Ivers," he said succinctly.

She took up the cork-lined gloves stashed near the generator's conducting coils, passed a pair to Simon, and one each to Ben and Lowbry. The last pair she donned herself. Then she went to stand where the ductwork met the generator's coils and placed a hand lightly on the lever.

"Mr. Rivers," Simon announced to Ben, and to the spectators as well, "my generator is yours, sir."

While Simon stood beside the furnace waiting to release the steam, Ben and Lowbry unpacked their equipment. A table was dragged in front of the generator, and upon it young Lowbry set up several globelike structures each about the size of a man's head. The glass spheres sat on copper bases, each one wired to the next in a closed circuit.

Prior to tonight, Ivy had not been privy to the project. Now she followed Ben's and Lowbry's every move, her eyes widening at the sight of the connected globes. Without leaving her position, she leaned forward and craned her neck, no doubt attempting to make out the gossamer web of carbonized silk threads that filled the interiors of the vacuum-sealed vessels.

At Ben's signal, Simon grasped the release valve for the steam and jerked the wheel into motion. Beneath his hands he felt the burst of steam enter the duct. He lessened the pressure, then continued turning the wheel slowly, with meticulous attention to the velocity of the vapor traveling through the duct. There must be no flying sparks or wafting energy in tonight's demonstration, nothing like the power needed in his electroportation process, but rather a controlled flow of the electrical currents. His and Ivy's calculations had made that possible.

When he deemed the pressure sufficient, he signaled to Ivy with a nod. She drew a breath and, with the same care he had used, flipped the lever to its open position. Within seconds the generator's coils began to glow, and soon tiny bolts of light flickered between them. The gears began to turn, the pistons to pump, the center beam to dip and rise, the wheels to rotate. Even at this power level, a tingling sensation traveled up Simon's arms. He locked the valve in place and joined Ben and Lowbry at their demonstration table.

"All is ready," he told them.

Ben dipped a bow toward their mystified audience. His hands insulated with the cork-lined gloves, he took up the longest and thickest of the wires. He paused to gesture to the footmen ranged along the walls, one at each sconce. "May we have darkness, please?"

As Ben had arranged beforehand, the sconces were extinguished all at once. But for the incandescent glow of the generator's coils, a dramatic blackness draped the room. The drone of voices added a suspenseful note to the generator's hums, ticks, and whirs. Ben raised his gloved hands. "Gentlemen, please direct your attention to the globes on the table."

With that, he moved to the generator and hooked the wire he held to the energy output terminal. Dimly, the first of the globes began to glow. Then the carbonized threads began to sparkle and brighten. A glimmer blossomed in the second globe, and so on until all five burned so brightly they lit up that end of the ballroom as if daylight poured through the darkened windows.

The effect was startling. An uproar of excitement went up, echoing against the ballroom's lofty ceiling. The audience pressed closer to view Ben's small miracle, and Simon's instincts sprang to the alert.

Seeing the potential for a regrettable accident, he hurried around the table and attempted to hold the crowd at a safe distance. He briefly glimpsed Alistair's, Colin's, and the Earl of Barensforth's alarmed faces as they, too, attempted to restore order. In the next instant, a thunderous crack rent the air and a burst of energy shoved Simon into the crush.

Glass shattered; darkness fell. An eruption of panic ensued. Simon took elbow jabs to the ribs, shoves from behind. From near him came a sharp grunt. A man fell against his chest and they both went down, knocking into others who had the misfortune to be pressed too closely. Simon hit the floor. When he attempted to roll to his feet, he discovered his chest pinned by a considerable weight. Shouts of "Candles, please!" echoed above his head. The acrid scent of smoke burned his throat and started him coughing.

Finally, a wavering pool of light angled across the ballroom, emanating from a single sconce. Soon another and another added their glow, restoring visibility and a semblance of order. As the clamor subsided, Simon realized he could no longer hear the hum of the generator. Ivy must have rushed to close the steam valves, then tossed the insulated canvas over the apparatus to cut the power. Again Simon attempted to sit up but found himself held fast by the individual who had fallen facedown across his torso.

"Sir?" He gave a nudge but received no response. The fellow's arm slid limply, his hand hitting the floor with a thump. Simon's own hand came in contact with something wet ... warm.... "I say, sir, are you hurt?" He raised his voice to a shout. "Will someone help us, please?"

A moment later several pairs of hands lifted the unconscious man from Simon's chest and laid him gently faceup on the floor. Someone offered a bundled coat to place beneath his head. Sir Alistair crouched at his side.

Dazed and winded, Simon sat up. He craned his neck to see around Alistair's shoulder. "Who is that?" Alistair shifted, and the youthfulness of the fallen man's insensible features struck Simon a blow of surprise. Pockmarked skin stretched taut and ashen across a bull-shaped face—a face he knew.

The student who had playfully tackled Ivy that day in Second Court.

Though he was aware of Colin kneeling beside him and asking if he was all right, the wetness dripping from Simon's hand drew the whole of his attention, as did the stain spreading like a rose across his coat.

"Colin," he said quietly, his insides turning to ice, "tell Alistair to check for a pulse."

*   *   *

"It's so frightfully dreadful." Ivy winced at the inadequacy of her words to convey the horror of Preston Ascot's sudden death. She and Jasper Lowbry sat side by side halfway up the curving staircase, awaiting their turns to be questioned by the local magistrate.

Jasper sat pale and staring, his eyes large and shadowed. With a shudder, he set his elbows on his knees and propped his chin in his hands. "If only our illumination globes hadn't exploded. Then the lights wouldn't have gone out and poor Preston wouldn't have tripped and hit his head. Funny, his hitting his head that way . . ."

Remembering that Jasper and Preston had attended Eton together, she placed a hand on his shoulder. "You mustn't blame yourself. If anything . . ."

Her own sense of guilt rising up in a choke hold, she couldn't continue. She and Simon had worked for days to match the calculations Dean Rivers had given him. What had caused the power surge—*what*?

Jasper lifted his face. "First Spencer. Now Preston . . ."

"But the authorities believe someone murdered Spencer, whereas tonight's tragedy was surely an accident. Jasper, you don't think . . . ?"

"I expect we'll learn the answer to that soon enough." His expression pinched, Jasper returned his chin to his palms.

Ivy gazed through the newel posts at the closed dining hall doors. The inquiries were being conducted inside, and Simon had been detained for the better part of an hour. Poor Preston had fallen on top of Simon, so naturally the constables wished to question him about everything he remembered immediately prior to the incident.

For the umpteenth time, she uttered a silent prayer of thanks that Simon hadn't been injured.

"Pack your things. We're leaving at once."

Ivy faced back around to discover Aidan looming at the base of the staircase and staring daggers up at her.

"Now, Ned."

Beside her, Jasper raised his head and took Aidan's

measure. In a murmur clearly intended for Ivy's ears only, he asked, "Is this ill-mannered chap speaking to you?"

" 'Fraid so," she whispered back.

"Who the devil does he think he is, ordering you about?"

Aidan gripped the banister and placed one menacing foot on the bottom step. "To whom do you intend to listen, me or the insolent whelp sitting beside you?"

Jasper went rigid, a muscle dancing in his cheek. Before he could fling a caustic quip back at Aidan, Ivy pressed her hand to his coat sleeve. "Jasper, this is my brother-in-law." Louder she said, "Lord Barensforth, may I present Mr. Jasper Lowbry. He was a close friend of the deceased."

The antagonism instantly drained from both men's bearing. Aidan ascended the steps and extended his hand. "I'm sorry. Truly."

Jasper accepted his handshake with a nod.

"But my purpose remains the same. Ned, go and pack your bags. *Now*, if you please. Mr. Lowbry, you are welcome to ride back to Cambridge with us."

At that precise moment, the dining room door opened and Simon stepped out. The sight of him jabbed straight at Ivy's heart, for he looked much as he did that day she found him on the floor of his laboratory: beaten and pallid and utterly lost. That Preston Ascot's death pressed heavily upon his conscience showed in the brackets of pain surrounding his mouth, the hollow disbelief in his eyes. Ivy longed to go to him, yearned to hold him and be held by him. . . .

"There is no need for anyone to pack their bags," he said in a monotone drained of all energy.

"I disagree." Aidan rounded on Simon as if readied for battle. "I intend getting my brother-in-law away from this place as swiftly as possible."

"I am afraid that will not be possible, not just yet." Alistair Granville appeared on the threshold beside Simon. For once, Windgate Priory's owner appeared less than his elegant best, a happenstance he quickly sought to put to rights by buttoning his brocade coat and straightening his silk neckcloth. "The authorities have declared the house essentially sealed until they discover how Preston Ascot died. Until then, no one but the constables will be permitted in or out. You will all therefore remain my guests until further notice."

At this pronouncement, Aidan's demeanor changed, and as he approached Simon and Sir Alistair, it was with the shrewd look of a Home Office agent rather than with the hostility of an indignant brother-in-law. "They believe he was murdered, then?"

"The coroner judged the head wound to be indicative of a blow from a heavy object with a pitted surface," Simon told him. His eyes fell closed for a moment. "The weapon bashed in a portion of Ascot's skull and left a ragged lesion."

Ivy surged to her feet. "Isn't that how Spencer Yates was killed?"

Exhaustion dragged at Simon's broad shoulders. He nodded, his head dipping low. "It appears there is a killer among us, one with a penchant for ending the lives of promising young science students."

When the day mercifully reached its end, Simon wasted no time in retiring to his chambers. Ivy had gone up a few minutes ahead of him. Now as he strode determinedly through his guest quarters, shedding his coat, cravat, and waistcoat as he went, he found her in the adjacent dressing room, clad in her gentlemen's nightshirt and climbing into her narrow bed.

"No, Ivy. Not tonight."

"I don't understand."

He said nothing more until he'd swept her into his arms. "Here is where I need you." He pressed his face to hers. "Here is where I must have you."

Turning about, he retraced his steps into the bedroom. She didn't struggle, but stared at him with large eyes and said, "But, Simon, my brother-in-law. Should he find out . . ."

"The worst he can do is challenge me to a duel, and the

authorities have already confiscated every weapon in the house."

Her fist closed over the back of his shirt. "Don't jest. Aidan is ferociously protective—"

"So am I."

"Yes, well, what's more, he is perfectly capable of making your life a misery. He is an earl, after all, and has a great deal of influence."

"Yes, and I am a marquess. I therefore win."

He reached the bed and set her down. She started to raise another protest; he leaned low and kissed her into silence. Against her lips, he said, "None of that matters. I need you in my arms tonight. A young man—a boy, really—lies dead and I cannot help but feel at least partly responsible. I—"

Her delicate fingers slid up to press his lips and stop his words. "This could not have been foreseen. It wasn't your fault. There is a murderer—"

"And I provided him with the perfect opportunity to kill again. It was my generator that malfunctioned and threw the room into darkness. If not for that—"

"Simon! Do you realize what you just said?" Her voice trilled with agitation. "The malfunctioning generator provided the murderer with his opportunity. Do you not see the significance? The power surge was no accident or miscalculation on our part. The guilty party must have tampered with the equipment."

Simon's thoughts had raced at a frenzied pace ever since he'd sat up in the ballroom and discovered Preston Ascot's blood on his hand and coat. Now they skidded to a dizzying halt. "Can it be possible?"

She gave an emphatic nod. "You've been so guilt-ridden, you didn't stop to consider the obvious. Thank goodness I'm here to offer a fresh perspective."

"I'm not glad. Galileo's teeth, not glad at all." Sitting beside her, he pulled her into his lap and enveloped as much of her as he could within his arms.

"Dear God, Ivy, when the magistrate declared it a murder, I thought I'd go out of my mind with fear for you. *Why* did I bring you here? Why did I keep you in my employ when I knew full well I should have sent you straight home to your family? I'd give anything now to see you ride away with your brother-in-law rather than have you remain within reach of a madman."

"I am not going anywhere," she whispered into his shirt-front. "A loyal assistant does not abandon her master."

With a burst of bittersweet laughter he collapsed onto his back, bringing her down with him to cover his chest.

Her face hovered above his, her curls framing a sober expression. "An unsettling thought just entered my mind."

"Go on."

"Simon, do you suppose there could be a connection between your sister's flight from London and these murders?"

He sat back up, matching her rumpled brow with a frown of his own. He had entertained this exact thought following Spencer Yates's death—entertained it and immediately dismissed it. Or nearly so . . .

"No," he said firmly. "I do not suppose. How can you even suggest my sister had anything to do with such heinous acts?"

"I'm sorry. But it is a rather extraordinary coincidence. And consider the object believed to be the murder weapon. Has it not crossed your mind that it could be the very stone your sister took from the queen?"

"Bloody hell, Ivy . . ."

"I'm not inferring that Gwendolyn is a murderess. I am only suggesting that we must consider the possibility that her actions and these crimes are somehow related. Perhaps in the morning we should—"

Once again he kissed her to stop the words. He'd heard enough, *lived* through enough, for one day. Yes, perhaps come morning they should . . . He didn't know what. For reasons he couldn't name, the thought of tomorrow filled him with dread. In the few short hours remaining to the night, he needed simply to hold on to Ivy and know she was safe. And he needed peace, the sort of peace only she seemed capable of bringing him.

"No more words," he commanded in a whisper.

Her eyes filling with tenderness, she nodded. He stripped off her nightshirt and pulled back the bedclothes.

In the morning, Ivy slipped out of Simon's bed before he awoke. She wished to be dressed and fully occupied by the time Aidan rose, in order to avoid questions he might ask concerning where she had spent the night.

She thought it a small miracle that he hadn't already brought the subject up, but perhaps present circumstances had rendered that subject one he preferred to avoid. Though an uninvited guest, he was, as an earl, an honored one, and there had been a great fuss and a good deal of guest shifting last night in order to oblige him with a suitable room.

Without bothering to light a lamp or stoke the fire, she dressed hurriedly, shivering in the predawn chill. The corridors of Windgate Priory were deserted, the morning room empty but for the footmen preparing the buffet for the guests. A pot of hot coffee and a platter of scones and muffins waited on a sideboard. Ivy helped herself to a warm blueberry scone and poured a cup of coffee.

She wandered back upstairs, drawn by the comfort of the cushioned settee in Sir Alistair's library. On her way along the corridor earlier, she'd heard voices inside. Good. The magistrate had left a warning yesterday that no one, especially the assistants, should wander the house alone. Was the killer intent on preying upon the students, or had Yates's and Ascot's deaths been a coincidence? The constables still weren't certain, and so urged everyone to have a care.

Holding her scone between her teeth, she reached to open the library door. A sudden shout from inside startled her, and her cup slipped from her grasp. It shattered against the floor and sent up a spray of hot liquid that hit her legs like tiny flames. The scone slipped from her mouth to bounce on the edge of the carpet. From inside the room came a loud thud, a sound all too reminiscent of last night's events.

For a second she wavered between bursting inside and retreating to the morning room to seek help. A slam from inside sent her over the threshold at top speed. Then she stopped so suddenly her boots slipped on the Aubusson rug. Across the room, in front of a roaring hearth fire, Jasper Lowbry lay prone and unconscious.

Chapter 22

"Thank goodness he's alive." Ivy dropped her face into her hands, trying in vain to banish the image of Jasper Lowbry lying sprawled in the library rug, a mere few feet from where she now sat. From behind the desk, Inspector Scott, chief investigator for the Cambridge Borough Police, busily scribbled down every word she uttered, even those last.

Upon bursting into the library about an hour ago, Ivy had recognized Jasper by his wavy hair, and her heart had rocketed into her throat. She'd immediately fallen to her knees beside him and dipped her fingers into the bloodied patch at the back of his head. The source of the flow proved to be a shallow gash, and when Jasper had let out a tortured groan, relief had cascaded through her in dizzying torrents.

After he'd been revived and seen by the physician from the village, the authorities had questioned him. No, he had neither seen nor heard a thing. He'd been standing in front of the fire warming his hands when a dreadful pain had threatened to split his skull in two. The next thing he knew, he'd come to with Ned Ivers's anxious face hovering above his own.

When asked why he had been in the library alone, he said he had come here with his master, Benjamin Rivers, who had left him to retrieve a book from his room. With his head carefully bandaged and a laudanum-laced tonic having been administered, Jasper was now sleeping comfortably in his bed.

"Is there anything more you would like to add to what you've told me so far?" The inspector, a round-faced man with a mustache, whose spectacles gave him an owlish appearance, dipped his quill and eyed Ivy expectantly.

"No. As I said, I heard a shout, a thud, and then a noise like a door slamming." She turned her head to view the small door between the bookcases that led into the adjoining music room. "By the time I entered from the corridor, there was only poor Mr. Lowbry lying on the floor." She pointed at the empty space in front of the hearth. "Just there."

"And why had *you* ignored my advice and been skulking about alone, sir?" The inspector aimed his quill at her as if it were a dart he might toss. "I know you young bucks tend to believe yourselves invincible, but one would think two recent murders should have divested you of such foolish notions."

"I'd heard voices in the library earlier," she said. "Besides, I believed there were enough servants about to rule out the possibility of another crime."

"Apparently not."

Outside the library doors, a buzz of voices grew steadily in volume as the consortium members learned of this second incident. She had not yet seen Simon this morning, but his impatient demands to speak with his assistant had risen above the general din some quarter hour ago. Inspector Scott had not granted his wish, though he had been kind enough to stick his head outside long enough to assure Simon that no harm had come to the boy.

Ivy wished he were here with her, sitting beside her. The initial shock of finding Jasper had left her disoriented and overset. Her hands were shaking; her stomach was a skein of knots. How she wished she had simply remained in bed beside Simon's warm, solid body.

But no. As Inspector Scott obligingly pointed out, she had very likely interrupted an attempted murder. He believed, and Ivy agreed with him, that the crash of her coffee cup outside the library door had startled the villain into flight.

Once again, her gaze drifted to the music room door. She had gone running into that room, but only after she'd been certain that Jasper was alive. By that time the culprit had long vanished. There had been no sign of him in the corridor, either.

"If only I had acted sooner," she said with no small regret, "we might now know the identity of this deranged individual."

Inspector Scott set down his quill. "My dear boy, in that case you might just as well have ended up his next victim. In fact, you are the next logical target."

Ivy felt the blood drain from her face. "How so?"

"Think about it. Among this Galileo Club Lord Harrow told me of, three out of the four assistants have been attacked." He aimed a forefinger at her. "That leaves you."

"Oh . . . goodness . . ." An icy claw gripped her. "In all the turmoil, I hadn't considered that."

"Well, do consider it, and do not attempt to play the hero. You are not to go off on your own again. And should you remember any detail that might help us apprehend whichever consortium member is responsible for these acts, you are to come to me immediately."

"A consortium member." Ivy shook her head in disbelief. "It is hard to believe a man of science could be capable of such an act."

"Mr. Ivers, it has been my experience that deviance hails from all walks of life. No class or society on earth is immune to crime. Whether a prince or a pauper, a desperate man will resort to desperate measures."

Despite his ill-fitting coat and its collar's frayed edges, the inspector proved himself a gentleman when he slipped out of the library and forbade all but Simon to enter. "You may go on in now, my lord. That assistant of yours has certainly earned his keep today. By my soul, he saved a life."

Simon shut the door behind him and turned the key.

Then he was across the room, and Ivy found herself caught up in his arms. "I'm not letting you out of my sight again."

"I'm fine, truly."

Truly she wasn't. Trembling uncontrollably, she yielded to his greater strength, let her cheek sink to his shoulder, and gave in to her shattered nerves. A few tears slipped out, and she didn't bother trying to hide them. As Ned Ivers, who would have been raised to be brave and resilient, she'd been forced to maintain a stiff upper lip. She wondered briefly how men managed to remain so outwardly stoic, why they didn't suddenly burst from restraining their emotions.

Just as on the night she wore the lovely emerald dress, she needed these moments to be Ivy, to be her feminine self. She needed time to mourn and be afraid and seek the comfort of a masculine shoulder, and to feel a firmly beating heart beneath her ear. It helped steady her, that dependable beat, as did the gentle rumble of Simon's voice and the stroke of his fingers through her hair.

Her respite proved short. A knock sounded at the door, and when Simon unlocked it, Alistair Granville leaned his head in. "Just letting you know that no one may return to his room just yet. The inspector and his men have launched a search of the entire house in hopes of finding the murder weapon, for he has deduced that the culprit wouldn't be carrying anything so weighty on his person. Until he says otherwise, we are all to remain together in the public rooms. No one is to be left alone, for no one is above suspicion."

"Ivy, see here. You were right." Simon grasped one of the bolts that should have held the gears securely to the pistons. He gave the small attachment a spin. It should not have turned at all, much less at the slightest touch of his fingers. "It's not the only one that's loose. Someone *has* tampered with the equipment."

The slackened connections between the generator's components meant that despite all the calculations and corresponding adjustments he and Ivy had made, the current passing through the generator would not have been a controlled one.

"This is why Ben's illumination globes exploded."

Ivy reached out and fingered the loose bolt. "Who would do such a thing?"

They spoke in whispers, careful not to be overheard by the others quietly engaged in their work nearby. The consortium proceedings had come to an abrupt halt, but Inspector Scott had seen no harm in granting the scientists access to the ballroom. Allowing them to occupy their time, he had deemed, would help alleviate the panic that had begun to take hold following the attack on Jasper Lowbry. Their keeping busy would also help quell speculation about what might turn up during the search of the house.

Despite the activity, the ballroom remained as hushed as a tomb. Furtive looks angled from one man to the next as each seemed to maintain a wary distance from his neighbor. Ivy caught Simon staring pensively out over the assembly.

"It's grown downright eerie, hasn't it?" she noted. "Only yesterday, this was such a lively, vibrant place."

"No longer." He took up a wrench and began tightening the loosened bolts. "I can only hope to God that we were wrong about Gwendolyn coming here, and that she is somewhere far away, safe."

"Yes." A note to her voice caused him to look up from his task. Her lashes veiled her thoughts, and she took an overly keen interest in a wire burned by the power surge.

Simon decided not to press her, not just then, for whatever she was choosing not to share. He tightened another bolt. "One face I haven't seen in a while is your brother-in-law's. Was he given permission to leave?"

Sensing her hesitation, he regarded her again. She bent lower over the wire she had already thoroughly examined. "Yes, well . . . he is busy assisting Inspector Scott."

The implications took Simon aback. Why the devil would a public official involve a civilian in a murder investigation? "Care to explain?"

"Em . . . there's something I haven't told you about Aidan." Her pretty lips compressed. She darted a cautious glance at their closest neighbors. "When I said he could make your life a misery if he wished, it was no hollow threat. You see, Aidan works for the Home Office."

It took several beats for Simon to absorb this information. Then he set down his wrench and crossed his arms. "When this is over, you and I are going to sit down together and discuss this extraordinary family of yours."

She nodded absently, her attention suddenly diverted. "Yes, when this is over. But here is Aidan now, and Inspector Scott with him. Good Lord, why do they look so grim?"

"Lord Harrow." Inspector Scott sounded no less serious than he looked. "I am afraid I must ask you to come with me."

Ivy stepped between them. "What's happened? Have you discovered something in your search?"

Puffing through his lips as if from exertion, the inspector barely spared her a glance. "I have some questions for Lord Harrow."

"What sorts of questions?"

"It's all right, Ned." Simon rested a hand on her shoulder as he moved past her and stepped away from the equipment. "Mr. Scott, I shall answer any questions to the best of my ability."

The inspector gestured for Simon to accompany him from the ballroom, and then fell into step beside him, not a step *behind* him as should have been expected given Simon's rank. At his back, Ivy let out a protest.

"Wait—"

Her brother-in-law quickly silenced her. "Don't make a scene. The others are watching."

"But, Aidan—"

The earl's hissed rejoinder sent an ominous weight dropping to the pit of Simon's gut.

"Be quiet, Ned. There is nothing you can do."

*   *   *

With no thought other than that Simon needed her, and that whatever he faced, she wished to remain by his side, Ivy moved to follow him and the inspector. Aidan's hand clamped around her upper arm.

He swung her to face him. She tried to smooth the panic and sheer desperation from her face; tried to clear away the love she knew must be clearly written across her features.

It was too late. Aidan saw it, all of it. His face became a thunderhead about to break over her. Tightening his grip on her arm, he forced her across the ballroom. From the corners of her eyes she saw the others turn their heads to stare. No one intervened; no one questioned why this earl, who had no apparent business at the consortium, had taken such a forceful hand with one of the assistants. As Ivy passed each scientist in turn, he met her gaze only briefly before swerving his attention back to his work.

Aidan hauled her down the corridor and into the servants' domains until they reached a closed door. With one hand he flung it open and propelled her into a gardening room that led to the conservatory. The door slammed behind them, causing a collection of hand rakes and small shovels leaning in the corner to clatter to the floor.

Aidan hovered before her like a bull digging in to charge. "You lied to me."

She didn't need him to elaborate on his meaning, nor did she attempt to deny the accusation. He stepped closer; she backed away.

"Lord Harrow knows bloody well that you are a woman, and what is more, you have been in his arms."

Again, she didn't deny the assertion; how could she? As her back sank into the assortment of aprons hanging from pegs along the wall, she voiced the only coherent thought her mind could form. "They can't mean to charge him. He is innocent."

Aidan lurched to a halt. "My God . . . you've been in his bed."

It wasn't so much his anger but the bitter hurt peering

out from behind it that made her press her back tighter to the aprons. She turned her face away. "That does not make him any less innocent. Aidan, please, we must help him."

"Help him? I'll see him hang."

She swung back toward him. "You don't mean that. You wouldn't condemn an innocent man."

"Correct, I would not. But neither am I convinced that Lord Harrow is innocent." An unnatural calm settled over him, which Ivy feared more than his fury. "One of the inspector's men found what is believed to be the murder weapon. It matches the description of the stone you've been searching for, and it was among Lord Harrow's possessions. So tell me, Ivy, how do you feel about your marquess now?"

Outside his bedroom windows, the afternoon shadows grew long as Simon pondered his fate. Each time he heard noises beyond his chamber door, he braced himself for more bad news. Not that matters could get much worse. Gwendolyn was still missing, and now he was officially under house arrest, accused of murdering two young men and attempting to murder a third. Inspector Scott seemed assured of his guilt. The man had ordered the electromagnets removed from this room, along with the bulk of Simon's personal effects. Simon expected at any moment to be hauled from his rooms and transported to the village jail.

He'd be damned if he left Ivy unprotected. If only he could devise a means of escape . . .

Though he had not yet seen the murder weapon with his own eyes, the inspector had described it as a stone at least twice the size of a man's fist and rough to the touch. Those details had sent his stomach plummeting. How could it be any other but Victoria's, the one his sister had stolen?

That Gwendolyn could be involved in these hideous murders iced his soul. For now, he shoved the thought away. His sister might be brash and prone to histrionics, but she was never depraved. Never cruel.

"Ah, Gwennie . . . where are you?"

The door opened; his pulse lurched and his body tensed, ready to grasp any opportunity that might gain him his freedom. His lean-faced guard peered in at him, and then stepped aside as Ivy appeared at his shoulder. At the sight of her sweet face, every bit of Simon's readiness drained from his limbs. For the span of a heartbeat she simply stared across at him, unshed tears magnifying her eyes. Then she hurried to him.

The chamber door remained open, the constable watching. Ivy stopped abruptly a foot or two away and grasped Simon's hand in both of hers. Blinking, she gave it a masculine shake for their observer's benefit.

"I know you are innocent," she said without preamble.

"Do you, my dearest?" he whispered. The constable narrowed his eyes in an apparent attempt to read his lips, but the man remained where he was on the far side of the threshold. "I would understand if you doubted me. But upon my honor, I don't know how the stone came to be in my clothespress."

"Someone obviously put it there." A ghost of remorse flitted across her features. So she had entertained a doubt or two. He couldn't blame her. But now she squared her shoulders in a show of resolve that made his throat constrict. "I promise I shall not abandon you."

The sentiment filled his heart with equal measures of joy and fear. "Ivy, please let the authorities handle this. I won't have you running full throttle into danger."

"I have an idea that may reveal the killer. We must set a trap—"

"*We* mustn't do anything." He started to reach for her, wanting to seize her shoulders and give her a good shake. The constable's presence forbade it. Simon lowered his voice to a stiff-jawed murmur. "Damn it, I want you gone from here today. Surely Inspector Scott has given everyone permission to leave."

"He has not. Despite the evidence of the stone, I don't believe he's entirely convinced he found his man. And that is why—"

"No!" Frustration raised his voice above a whisper.

The constable cleared his throat. "I don't know what the two of you are yammering about, but I'm breaking the rules in allowing you this much time to prattle." He jerked his chin at Ivy. "Collect your things, and be on your way."

She treated him to an impatient wave and set off into the dressing room. When she returned, hastily bundled clothing spilled from her gaping valise. That earnest, studious little crease Simon loved formed above her nose. "I *will* work this out."

Her conviction had him believing her. Despite his pleas to the contrary, Ivy Sutherland would do as she damned well pleased. Cradling her bag in her arms, she started to turn away. Again Simon nearly reached for her, loath to let her go so soon. She caught the sudden movement of his hand, for she stopped and questioned him with a look.

"How is your friend?" he asked.

A smile lit her expression. "Much better. Jasper sustained little more than a flesh wound and is fussing to be up, though the doctor insists he must keep to his bed for now."

"Good advice, I'm sure. Mr. Lowbry is a lucky young man."

"Ahem." The constable's signal could not be any clearer. Still, Ivy lingered.

"Please be careful out there, my dearest Ned." Simon mouthed the endearment. She nodded, blinking away a tear that undid him. He grasped her shoulder and pulled her closer, not as a lover would, but as a master wishing to convey instructions to his protégé. "I will not remain idle much longer," he whispered.

Her eyes widened with comprehension and fear, and an imminent appeal that he do nothing rash.

It was an appeal he could not satisfy, not when she and the others here were still in danger. "Windgate Priory is as familiar to me as Harrowood," he said in a rush. "If I can break free of this room, I'll head straight for the attic. They'll never find me there."

A thousand questions burned in her eyes, but she gave a single nod. Gently Simon pushed her away, and with a last look back at him she turned into the corridor. The constable reached in to shut the door.

"Not so fast," a voice commanded. "I need to speak with both of them."

Chapter 23

I vy was ushered back into the room by Inspector Scott, followed by her brother-in-law, who shut the door on the constable's curious gaze.

In his hands, Scott held an object slightly smaller than Ben's illumination globes, swaddled in gray flannel. He set it on the bed and pulled the wrapping free. A black stone, pitted and speckled with silver, rolled onto the coverlet. "This, sir, is the murder weapon we found in this very room earlier today, and which presently stands as evidence against you."

"Dear heavens." Ivy dropped her valise onto the nearest chair and crossed to the bed. Simon moved beside her, and together they beheld the stone that had caused such turmoil, which possessed the power to disrupt the new queen's reign.

Simon found the unassuming hunk of rubble absurdly anticlimactic. Reaching out, he touched a finger to the rough surface, expecting to feel . . . something. A charge. A waft of energy. Ivy had described the stone as powerfully electromagnetic.

He felt nothing other than bits of ore and sediment. A certainty filled him and he shot a glance at Ivy. "Go ahead," he urged. "Touch it."

As he had, she pressed a fingertip to the stone, then cupped her palm over the lopsided orb. Her brow puckered as she shook her head. "This can't be it. . . ." Then, more firmly, "This most assuredly is not it."

Inspector Scott reached around her and with a nudge sent the stone for a half roll. "Not what, precisely?"

"The electromagnetic hunk of meteorite recently stolen from the queen," Barensforth explained in a bland tone. He met Ivy's indignant expression with a haughty lift of an eyebrow. "The time for secrets is over."

Scott regarded him quizzically. "Is *that* what was taken from Her Majesty's apartments? The papers said it was a jewel."

No one bothered to reply to the rhetorical question. Simon burned to ask a few questions of his own, such as what Scott and Barensforth were doing here. Had they merely come to discuss the nature of the stone, or had they discovered some new evidence that pointed to the real killer? Dared he hope?

Whatever their reasons, he drew on his reserves of patience and supposed they would reveal their purpose in their own good time. His reading spectacles sat on the nightstand; he placed them on his nose and bent over the stone to examine the surface more closely. Dull, rust-colored sediment clung congealed in its crevices. "Blood."

"Correct, Lord Harrow." With a sniff, the inspector reached into his coat pocket for his writing tablet and a whittled-down stub of a pencil. "Now, would one of you be so kind as to explain fully to me what Her Majesty's stone is, and why this object cannot be it?"

Clearly dismayed at having to divulge the queen's secrets, Ivy launched into the details she had once confided to Simon. She ended by thrusting a finger at the stone, conspicuously ugly against the satin coverlet. "That, as we can plainly discern, possesses no electromagnetic properties whatsoever. It is obviously a decoy, placed among Lord Harrow's effects in a deplorable attempt to incriminate him."

"Perhaps, Mr. Ivers, but this is most assuredly the murder weapon." Scott held his pencil aloft and studied Ivy with a shrewd expression. "Or shall I call you *miss*?"

A flush of indignation flooded her cheeks. "Aidan, how could you?"

"Lord Barensforth didn't tell me a thing," the inspector said with a chuckle in his voice. "I might not work out of a posh Scotland Yard office, but neither am I a bumbling country bumpkin. Ah, but not to worry, miss. You aren't the only individual in this house to make that mistake." He made a notation in his tablet. "I'll need the name of the lady-in-waiting who made off with the queen's property."

"She is my sister," Simon offered up, rather than burden Ivy with the guilt of throwing further suspicion upon him. He removed his spectacles and returned them to the bedside table. "Lady Gwendolyn de Burgh."

Leaning against a tall bureau, the Earl of Barensforth crossed his arms over his chest and regarded Simon from beneath the jut of his brow. "And did your sister steal this stone for your benefit, sir?"

"That is a question I cannot answer, sir."

"Cannot or will not?"

Barensforth's manner toward him had changed since the last time they'd spoken. Then, Simon had managed to convince the earl that nothing untoward had occurred during Ivy's stay at Harrowood, but this new show of disdain suggested the man had guessed at the truth. Hardly able to blame Barensforth for his hostility, Simon forcibly uncurled the fists that had formed at his sides. It would solve nothing if the two of them fell to brawling, especially since the friction between them had little to do with the murders, and everything to do with Ivy.

Marginally calmer, Simon replied, "I have not seen my sister since she first entered the queen's household. Whatever her motives, she has not shared them with me. And while we believed she would turn up here at Windgate Priory, thus far we've not glimpsed a trace of her." His attention returned to the stone. "Until now, that is, because whoever thought to use this decoy as the murder weapon either possesses or knows about the true stone."

Barensforth and Inspector Scott exchanged glances, the former filled with a message of caution and doubt, the latter with the authority of a man who would reach his own conclusions and didn't give a fig what anyone else thought.

Scott nibbled the end of his pencil, then said, "It may surprise you to learn, Lord Harrow, that I have undergone a change of heart concerning your alleged guilt. Whether or not you had opportunity or the murder weapon, neither I nor my constables nor even Lord Barensforth here can conceive of a motive for you to have committed these murders."

"And believe me," Barensforth said in a low growl, "I wanted to."

"Oh, thank goodness you are a man of sound reasoning, Inspector." Ivy sank into the wing chair beside the hearth. The strain of the morning showed in how pallid she'd become, in the sheen of sweat across her brow. "You will declare Lord Harrow innocent, then?"

"Innocent?" Her brother-in-law's upper lip curled. "Hardly."

The inspector held up a pudgy hand. "Not just yet, I'm afraid."

"But—"

"At the moment, miss, it appears as though someone set up Lord Harrow to appear the guilty party. I believe it best to convince the culprit that we are satisfied with our suspect. Lord Harrow, since you are well versed in the scientific community, perhaps you can help us determine a motive, not only for the murders, but also for why the killer would wish to frame you specifically."

"I can't think of a reason why anyone would do such a thing."

"Then I must be blunt and ask if your sister holds a grudge against you."

"She . . ." Simon trailed off. Surely their last words had

been angry ones, filled with blame and spite on Gwendolyn's part, many regrets on his. In truth, if he had blamed anyone for her behavior, it was himself. He should have been watching more closely, should have been more involved in Gwen's life.

She had resented his interference, yes, but did she hate him for it? Enough to commit murder and splatter his hands with the blood?

Chapter 24

"No, Inspector," Simon concluded. "My sister could not be responsible for murder."

"You are certain beyond all doubt, my lord?"

Simon hesitated again. Was he judging his sister with a clear eye, or with the heart of a brother who wished he'd done a better job of looking after her? He glanced over at Ivy for . . . He didn't quite know what. She had never met Gwendolyn, could in no way vouch for her character. Yet in her dark eyes and solemn nod he found the confidence to answer the inspector's question.

"Beyond all doubt," he said.

"Very well, then. Perhaps if I were to enlighten you as to the suspects we are considering thus far, you might be able to suggest a possible motive." Scott consulted his writing tablet. "Benjamin Rivers, Errol Quincy, Colin Ashworth, Jasper Lowbry—"

"Jasper!" Ivy's jaw dropped. "He was a victim."

"Or an exceedingly clever actor," Scott said with a waggle of his forefinger. "Thus far, he is the only victim to escape death. He may have staged his own attack, perhaps knowing you were on your way to the library this morning. You never did see a trace of the culprit."

"But Jasper wouldn't lie." Her last word ended abruptly. "At least I don't think he would. . . ." She gave her head an adamant shake. "Jasper would not lie, nor could he ever commit an act of violence. It simply isn't in him."

A streak of possessiveness nearly prompted Simon to question how she could be so certain of the young whelp, but on second thought he held his tongue. This was no time for petty jealousies.

"And you can think of no strife among the students," Scott asked her, "that might have led to acts of vengeance?"

Again, Ivy shook her head. "None. They are . . . were . . ." Her head went down. "An affable lot."

Scott pushed his spectacles higher on his nose. "And Mr. Lowbry would have no cause to feel jealousy toward Lord Harrow?"

"Jealousy . . . ?" Ivy trailed off as the inspector's meaning apparently sank in. Her cheeks flamed, but her jaw jutted self-righteously forward. "Jasper has no inkling of my identity. He believes me to be one of his mates."

Scott nodded and scribbled some words in his tablet. "Then that leaves us with the dons."

"Don't be absurd." With fresh dismay, Simon ran both hands through his hair. "Those men are my closest friends and colleagues. There are a score of others here. The killer could be any one of them."

"Even me." Ivy gave an ironic laugh, a sound she repeated when Simon and the other two men shot her glances of incredulity. When they continued to stare, she became downright defensive. "It isn't impossible. I had as much opportunity as anyone else here."

"Ivy, don't be ridiculous," Barensforth said. "Besides, someone of your build lacks the necessary strength." Moving behind her chair, Barensforth placed his hands on her shoulders like a sentry at the ready. "For the most part, Lord Harrow, we've ruled out everyone but your colleagues. No, hear me out," he added when Simon opened his mouth to protest. "It only makes sense that the man attempting to frame you is someone you know, with whom you interact on a regular basis. Someone who envies you or your abilities, or who has reason to resent you."

Simon's objections died unspoken. Each member of the Galileo Club could potentially fit the description of a covetous rival. Despite Colin's outward efforts toward reconciliation, he might still harbor bitter resentment over the events of last winter. Likewise, Errol—however frail he appeared—might blame Simon for his daughter's untimely death. And Ben, who hailed from poverty and deprivation, could very well begrudge Simon his wealth and social position.

But enough to commit murder and frame him for the crimes?

Ben, Errol, even Colin, who had borne the brunt of Simon's anger these many months . . .

He drew himself up and squared his shoulders. "Your theory is off the mark, way off. None of the men you have implicated can be guilty. There is no way on earth."

"If that is the case," Barensforth said almost brightly, "then once again we are back to you, Lord Harrow."

Ivy shrugged out of her brother-in-law's protective hold and pressed to her feet. "Oh, no, we are not. I have a plan."

At Ivy's declaration, Simon groaned and Aidan swore out loud. She ignored them and went to stand in front of Inspector Scott.

"I know how to catch the killer," she said, "because as you said, I am logically his next victim."

A clamor of protests drowned out her attempt to explain. For once, Aidan and Simon seemed to be in agreement.

"Whatever you're planning, Ivy, forget it," Simon concluded for both of them.

Aidan thrust a hand to his hip and nodded. "Leave this to us, Ivy."

Inspector Scott studied her with a pensive twist to his lips. "What have you got in mind?"

"Do not encourage her."

"Aidan, please." She dared not glance at Simon for fear of losing her courage. Palpable anger emanated off him, leaving her no doubt that he would never agree to her plan, that he would fight her on it every inch of the way. In truth, the risk she intended to incur terrified her. But what choice did she have? Peer or no, if convicted of the murders, he would hang, and only she had the power to save him.

"We can trap the killer," she said evenly, "by dangling the bait under his nose."

"Ivy, no." Simon was before her in an instant. He captured her hand in his own and swung her around to face him. His gaze darted briefly over her head to bounce fleetingly off the two men watching them. Then she was wrapped tight in his arms, the pressure of his lips warm in her hair. "Thank you, my darling, but no. You mustn't even think of it. Put it out of your mind this instant. I will not let you, and there's an end to it."

Refusing to be daunted, she slid her hands up between them and pushed away until she could peer into his face. "I don't see that you have a choice. Besides, this is between me and Inspector Scott."

Panic flashed behind Simon's eyes. He gripped her shoulders and set her at arm's length. "Damn it, Ivy, this is not like solving a devilish mathematical equation or recalibrating my generator. This is deadly business, and I will not allow you to risk your life for mine."

"Nor will I," Aidan said as he watched hawklike from across the room.

"Besides, there isn't to be a next victim." Simon did his best to keep a scowl in place, but behind his severity she perceived a frantic tenderness. "Whoever went to all the trouble of framing me isn't about to shift suspicion away by committing another murder."

"I believe I'd like to hear the lady out." Inspector Scott set his pencil and tablet aside and went to perch at the edge of the bed.

"Thank you, sir." She paused for a steadying breath and stepped out of Simon's hold. "The murderer will likely strike again if we announce that Lord Harrow has escaped. We could claim he overpowered you and your constable and is now on the loose."

She felt Simon's steely gaze upon her. What she had neglected to mention to the inspector was that her plan would also afford Simon the opportunity to escape his confinement in earnest and use his knowledge of the house to assist in catching the killer. She knew her trust in him would not be misplaced, but she felt rather less certain that her scheme might backfire and cause Simon to appear more guilty than ever.

"We might also suggest he had an unidentified accomplice," she hurried on before she lost her nerve, "and that no one may leave until both are apprehended. In the meantime, I'll arrange to be somewhere apparently alone, perhaps the ballroom, where you and your men could be concealed close by, ready to spring when the murderer makes his move against me."

"Scott, surely you aren't going to allow this," Aidan all but shouted.

The inspector's eyebrows arced above the rims of his spectacles. "Of course not," he replied.

"What?" Ivy pushed words past the outrage that rose to clog her throat. "It is a perfectly sound plan. Certainly no one has suggested a better one."

"No one is questioning your ingenuity," Simon said with a note of condescension that sent spots of frustration dancing before her eyes. "But I am telling you unequivocally that you shall not serve as bait to catch a murderer."

She rounded on the inspector. "Surely you must see that I am right."

Mr. Scott thumped the toe of his boot against the carpet. "Were you a man, I would agree wholeheartedly. However, matters being what they are, taking your side would pit me against two peers of the realm, and I, for one, wish to emerge from this affair with my job and my hide intact."

He stifled Ivy's protest with a firm shake of his head. "I'm sorry, miss, but I believe I have just the right man for the task. There's a young clerk at my office who aspires to become a constable. He's rather a slip of a lad, with a mop of hair much like yours. This may be his chance to prove his worth."

"You are not to budge from this room. Understood?"

Ivy mustered her most compliant demeanor and assured Aidan that until he returned for her, she would not stir from a little second-floor parlor that was usually reserved for the wives of Sir Alistair's guests. That would not happen, however, until the murderer had been apprehended, or their plan to catch him proved futile. She hotly resented being excluded from the former, while praying the latter would not be the case.

An hour ago, Simon had affected his "escape," throwing not only the guests but also Inspector Scott and the constables into an uproar. Earlier, Inspector Scott had summarily refused Simon's request to be allowed to assist in apprehending the murderer. Instead, he was to be locked in a room much like the one Ivy occupied now, where no one would inadvertently stumble upon him.

As Ivy had suspected, Simon had broken free of his guard in earnest and disappeared into the house. The constables were still searching for him and still scratching their heads. Meanwhile, the scientists, assistants, and Royal Society representatives had demanded to be allowed to vacate Windgate Priory. Their complaints had nearly won over Inspector Scott, who now entertained doubts concerning Simon's innocence. Aidan, too, wondered if they'd been deceived, not only by Simon, but by Ivy as well, though he stopped short of accusing her of being Simon's accomplice.

In a way, she *had* acted as Simon's accomplice, for she had known her plan would allow him the opportunity to escape into Windgate Priory's attics. Simon de Burgh was not the sort of man to sit idly by while trusting his fate to others. Whatever happened next, she had no doubt that he would play a significant role in the unfolding events.

Somehow, she had managed to calm Mr. Scott and persuade him to proceed with the original plan. Her replacement, a clerk named Mr. Peters, would shortly make his way down to the empty ballroom and pretend to begin the job of dismantling Simon's generator.

Hovering in the doorway, Aidan narrowed his eyes at her and issued another warning conveyed from the end of a threatening forefinger. He added a verbal admonition as well. "My better sense tells me I should lock you in."

She settled into the camelback sofa and reached for the science periodical she had brought with her. "I am not about to do anything that might jeopardize our strategy."

"You are certain you do not know where Lord Harrow is hiding?

She lowered the journal, crossed two fingers, and met his gaze. "I swear I do not."

"All right, then." Maddeningly, he lingered on. "I am trusting you."

"And your faith in me is not misplaced." She'd kept her fingers crossed, but she felt wretched for lying. When Aidan left the room and shut the door, she released a breath of relief.

After counting to ten, she sprang up from the sofa. When this was all over, she vowed, she would confess all and apologize to her brother-in-law. For now, however, she went to the door and pressed her ear to the wood, and was rewarded by the far-off thuds of his footsteps fading down the main staircase. Her heart leaping against her breast, she cracked the door open.

An empty corridor beckoned. Drawing a breath and holding it, she closed the door behind her and scampered in the opposite direction Aidan had gone. Passing several paneled doors, she hurried on until the hall runner abruptly ended and she found herself surrounded by bare white walls.

She had reached the service hallway. A few more frenzied paces and she turned a corner, arriving at a back staircase. Going down would lead her to the ground floor and the basement kitchens below that. Ivy grabbed the banister and headed up, to the attic rooms on the third floor.

To where she hoped to find Simon.

At the upper landing, she paused to gain her bearings. Along a corridor to her right stretched a runner whose dull russet weave bore the flattened trail of countless tramping feet. She went to the nearest oaken door, listened a moment, and tried the knob. The door opened upon a small room containing two narrow bedsteads, a dresser, and a washstand.

Servants' quarters, she concluded, and crossed back to the much darker hallway that sprawled away to the left of the landing. She hadn't thought to bring a candle—it was nearly midday, after all. But she soon found herself wandering a maze of narrow, musty hallways, with only the light that filtered dimly beneath the closed doors to guide her way. With each step, dust motes swirled around her feet. She took pains to tread carefully over floorboards that creaked at the slightest provocation.

Every few yards, she stopped to listen. She dared not call Simon's name, nor could she expect him to give his location away by making any telltale sounds. An even more sobering possibility sprang to mind: that he was no longer in the attic, but had already made his way down to the ballroom using one of numerous hidden passages he had whispered to her about earlier. She came to a halt as the absurdity of her actions made her ashamed. What had she been thinking, disobeying Aidan and taking the risk of being followed? She might have put their entire plan in jeopardy.

But the answer careened through her, stealing her breath. Had Simon been successfully framed for the murders, he would have been transported to the Cambridge jail, and eventually shipped off to London, where he would have stood trial and . . .

Numbing horror rushed through her like a storm tide. Pressing the heels of her hands to her eyes, she tried in vain to quell the appalling images she had managed to evade until now. Simon before a judge and jury . . . declared guilty . . . condemned . . . led to the gallows . . .

No! None of that would happen. Deep down Inspector Scott still believed in Simon's innocence, or he would not be attempting to trap the true killer. Still, she trembled and hugged herself, and wished she were hugging Simon, holding on to him for dear life.

His dear, precious life.

She had come, simply, to be with him, to share these hopeful, dreadful moments together before their plan was set into action. If their theory—*her* theory—proved false, and no crazed killer stole into the ballroom intending to dispatch young Mr. Peters, what would prevent suspicion from ricocheting back onto Simon?

She took a step . . . and froze.

In the stillness she heard nothing, only the caress of the wind beneath the eaves of the roof. She started to move—and it came again. Not the wind, but a human sigh. Ivy pricked her ears and heard the whimper that followed.

The sound drew her deeper into the attic; she turned another corner, and a moan stopped her short. The sound had slid from beneath a door, but as she regarded the dark row stretching before her, she couldn't decide which. She pressed her ear to the closest one, then moved on to the next. A murmured lament sent her diagonally across the corridor.

The echo of a creak behind her drew her up sharp. In the stillness, a footstep resounded like a gunshot. Panic sent her blindly retreating through the darkness, until a splintered floorboard caught the toe of her boot and she lurched headlong into a pair of arms.

Feeling the cry rising to Ivy's lips, Simon pressed a hand to her mouth before she roused the devil himself to action. "Shh! It's only me!"

She struggled for another instant before the fight left her and she collapsed against his chest. He held her there for a long moment, one arm around her, the other hand plunged into the curls at the back of her head. He dipped his head and raised her face, guided by the warmth of her lips. Their tongues met and he inhaled her frenzied breath, her sweetness, her brash courage.

Then he opened a few inches between them. "What the blazes are you doing here?"

"I couldn't bear to wait all alone, without seeing you . . ."

She trailed off, but her meaning echoed through him. *Without seeing you one last time.*

He should have been furious with her, putting herself in danger this way. She had almost missed him, too, for he'd been about to make his way down one of the house's ancient staircases, part of the original monastery, that led to a hidden entrance to the ballroom. Despite Inspector Scott's intentions to the contrary, Simon fully aimed to be on hand when the killer struck.

Then he'd heard a muted cry of distress, a sound that had prickled beneath his skin and sent him in search of its source. Drifting through the dim corridors, he'd begun to believe that what he'd heard had been a restless Granville ghost. Then Ivy's very solid form had collided with his.

He drew her into his arms again and ran his lips across her brow. "Heaven help me, I'm glad you're here."

She nodded against his shoulder. Then her head came up. "Right before I heard your footsteps, there was a voice, sighing and moaning."

"That wasn't you?"

She pointed down the corridor. "It came from there."

He took her hand and let her lead him to a door. Not a sound issued from the other side. "I don't hear anything."

"I was so certain. . . . Wait! There."

From inside came a faint mewling, like that of a hungry kitten. His skin prickled, and the hair at his nape bristled. He pressed his ear to the door. The sound stopped and then took up again, and he experienced a powerful tug at his heart.

He tried the knob. "Locked, damn it."

"What . . . or who . . . do you suppose is in there?"

"I don't know, but I intend to find out. Stand back."

"But—"

Her caution was drowned out by the thwack of his shoulder hitting the door. The oak shuddered on its hinges.

Simon backed up and tried again, and this time he was rewarded by a splintering of wood. On the third try the lock gave and the door swung open against his weight. He careened inside and stumbled to a halt in a space no bigger than his dressing room downstairs.

An onslaught of perceptions bombarded him: the blackened window, the airless oppression of the room, the acrid scent of aging beams and floorboards and . . . something else, stale and heavy and sickly sweet.

The dull orange light of an oil lantern seized his attention. Beside it, a disheveled cot took up the length of an entire wall. The twisted heap of coverlet and linens startled him by suddenly moving. A prone figure took shape, swathed in wrinkled, soiled folds of ivory linen.

An arm came up. . . . The hand beckoned weakly.

Simon's heart wrenched as recognition raged through him. "Gwendolyn?"

He bolted to the bed. Crouching on one knee, he reached for the hand that had fallen limply to the mattress. "Gwendolyn? Gwen?" He tapped her cheek, pale and sunken nearly beyond recognition.

Her sooty eyelashes fluttered as her head lolled back and forth against a dingy pillow. Her lips parted on a moan.

Beside the pallet, a barrel cut in half served as a table. On it were scattered a cup, a bowl of porridge that had long since cooled and congealed, and a vial that lay on its side, its cork having fallen out and rolled several inches away. A small dark pool stained the wood.

"Good Lord." Her hand on his shoulder, Ivy knelt at his side. "Your sister?"

Gwen stirred again, and Simon cupped her hollow cheeks. "Gwen? Gwennie, it's me, Simon. Good God, what happened to you?"

"I can't believe it." A treble note wavered in Ivy's voice. "Can she have been here all this time? But Sir Alistair said—"

Simon shushed her as Gwendolyn's lips formed a word. "Simon . . ."

"Yes, Gwennie, it's Simon. Open your eyes."

Her eyelids formed encrusted slits. She focused on him through a misty haze before her eyes glazed over. "Where is he . . . ?"

"Where is who, Gwennie? How did you get here?" But the answer sinking in his gut was not one he wished to hear spoken aloud.

Ivy reached for the overturned vial and held its rim beneath her nose. "Laudanum. Very strong. She must be delirious."

"I don't understand." Simon looked helplessly down at his sister. "All along I believed Colin—"

Gwendolyn cut off his words. "Will . . . marry me."

"Who, Gwennie? Who will marry you? Colin?"

Her head thrashed from side to side. A reply? Simon couldn't be sure. Her hand fought his hold with surprising strength. A shrill laugh spilled from her lips. "Not Colin. Never Colin."

Stunned, Simon sat back on his heels.

Never Colin. Then, whom had she gone to meet at that roadside inn last winter? Had it not been Simon who intercepted her before her tryst, but Colin? Was that possible? But then why hadn't Colin said so?

The only logical answer slammed through him. Colin had prevented Gwen from ruining herself, and had taken the blame to save her. He must have known only that Gwen had invited trouble into her life and he had hastened out to that inn to forestall her from making a wretched mistake. Perhaps Colin's sudden appearance had frightened off the real suitor, so that by the time Simon had arrived, his friend appeared the blackguard.

Sickened, Simon leaned over to gather his sister's wasted frame into his arms. "Ah, Gwennie, we have made some terrible mistakes, you and I. But we can make amends now. I'm going to take you home, see that you get well, and . . ."

Looking up at Ivy, he perceived in her dark eyes a tearful but steady promise of redemption and new beginnings. She nodded, and her lips curved in a tremulous smile.

"There is someone here who can smooth matters with the queen," he said to his sister. "All will be well, Gwennie, I promise."

Cradling her to his chest, he started to push to his feet.

Behind him, the threshold creaked and a voice said, "Stay where you are."

Chapter 25

Ivy's breath froze in her lungs at the sight of Alistair Granville's chilling smile and the pistol in his hand.

Gently Simon laid Lady Gwendolyn back on the cot. Then he stood and whirled to face their adversary. "Alistair," he said without a trace of surprise. "Why?"

In her confusion, Ivy blurted, "But you're supposed to be—"

"In the ballroom murdering a certain police clerk who happens to slightly resemble you?" Sir Alistair's sinister leer stretched to reveal a row of small, perfect teeth. "Sorry to disappoint you, *Mr.* Ivers."

"How did you know about our plan?" she demanded.

He flicked the pistol's barrel at Simon. "Those speaking tubes of yours are a remarkable invention. I've installed them throughout Windgate Priory, and they've proved most useful. Especially the one behind your dressing mirror."

"Bastard." Simon spat the word.

"That is hardly a civil way to address your host."

Silently Ivy begged Simon not to do anything that smacked of foolhardy courage as he set himself between her and Sir Alistair's gun. "All of this," he said, "Gwen's disappearance, the murders, even holding the consortium here, were all part of some sick plan of yours. Again I ask you why, Alistair."

"I have my reasons."

Ivy peeked out from behind Simon's shoulder. "You've had the stone all along."

"Yes, I have the queen's precious stone. Gwendolyn was most accommodating in that respect."

Fury emanated off Simon in waves that heated Ivy's skin. "You irredeemable blackguard."

Have a care, my love, Ivy prayed.

"Now, now." Sir Alistair flicked a glance down at his pistol. "In case you're considering doing anything rash, Simon, allow me to explain the miracle of technology I hold in my hand. It is called a revolver. A young American gentleman by the name of Colt had it made especially for me, in exchange for funding and help in gaining a patent for his invention here in England." The weapon reflected the lamplight as he held it up higher. "It holds several bullets at once, and each time the trigger is squeezed, a fresh shell falls into the chamber. Quite ingenious, really."

Ivy had heard of such a weapon, but she had never before seen one. Dared she hope the prototype might misfire and take off Alistair's hand?

No, she could reckon their chances on no such miracle, nor on the possibility that she and Simon might devise a way of overpowering the man. The room's dimensions allowed them too little space to maneuver. They could hardly take a step in any direction without knocking into a wall or the mattress, or walking straight into the threatening pistol.

She sensed Simon, too, assessing their options and calculating their chances of success. Finally, he held out a placating hand. "What have Gwen and I ever done to you? We were friends, you and I. Colleagues. You supported my aspirations when my father scorned them."

"Your aspirations." The quiet rage trembling in Sir Alistair's voice quashed any hopes of swaying him with reason. "Damn you, Simon de Burgh. You have been a blight on my life these many years. Everything I have ever wished for, strived for, you stole from me."

"Such as what?" At a loss to understand, Simon raised his arms from his sides, then let them fall.

"Discovery, advancement, the acclaim of our peers . . ."

"I never prevented you from achieving any of that. I assisted you until I was ready to conduct my own research. And then you left the university—"

"Forced out, made to retire." The bark of Sir Alistair's reply made Ivy jump. "They said I attempted to steal credit for John Dalton's theory of atomic structure. Trumped-up charges, nothing more. If anything, he stole my ideas."

"John Dalton's theory . . ." Simon plowed his fingers through his hair. "Yes, I remember now. You told me you and he had been collaborating. . . ." He trailed off as understanding dawned in his eyes. "You lied. You claimed you had been working on those formulations all that year, that you were preparing to publish a treatise that would revolutionize how the scientific world viewed solid matter."

"And you went to Robert Leighton with the information."

"Ben's predecessor? I mentioned it merely in passing. I assumed he knew."

"And he went straight to Dalton. Another fortnight, and those results would have been to my credit, and John Dalton the one quietly charged with plagiarism and banished from the university."

"Don't be a fool, Alistair. If that theory had been yours, you could have proved it easily enough. But you couldn't, because those results were pilfered. They were a lie."

"If not for you, it would have been Dalton's word against mine."

"You made your bed. Yet in some twisted attempt at revenge, you committed murder and *this*—" Simon gestured with a shaking fist at his restive sister, half tangled in the bedclothes.

"I lost everything," Sir Alistair shouted. On the pallet, Lady Gwendolyn flinched. When Alistair spoke again, his poise had returned. "First my reputation . . . and then . . ." He thrust a finger at the unconscious girl.

Simon staggered a step forward as if to throttle the other man. "You didn't want Gwen. You only wished to use her."

"Oh, there you are wrong. I wanted her, and I'd have whisked her to Gretna Green and married her if your idiotically valiant friend hadn't shown up and botched my plans. I had just arrived and was stabling my horse when I looked up and saw him framed in the window of Gwendolyn's room, looking as if he were having an apoplexy. Damn Colin Ashworth's hide. And damn your hide."

"None of this makes sense. You're nearly thirty years older than Gwen. Why would she interest you . . . ?" Simon trailed off, then blew out a breath. "You and your endlessly expensive tastes. You finally managed to spend yourself dry, haven't you?"

"I don't understand," Ivy said from behind him.

Simon answered without taking his gaze from Sir Alistair. "Gwen's dowry. It is considerable, and he needed it."

"And I would have had it, if not for you and your meddling mate."

"You pathetic, deceitful, miserable excuse of a man . . ."

"Simon, please," Ivy whispered. From around his shoulder, she stared into the gaping black end of the pistol aimed squarely at his chest. However loose Sir Alistair's hold on sanity might be, his grip on his weapon remained firm, his arm steady. "Please, Simon, don't provoke him."

Sir Alistair's features stayed impassive. "It might interest you to know, Simon, that marriage or no, I have made your sister mine."

"You . . . didn't . . ." Simon's shoulders heaved. He lurched forward, but before he took a full step, Ivy fisted her hands on his coattails and yanked him back with all her strength. Yet she realized quickly enough that it had been the element of surprise and not muscle power that checked his onslaught. If she couldn't succeed in talking sense into him, she would not be able to restrain him.

Releasing his coat, she slipped her arms around his waist and pressed her lips to his nape. "Don't listen to his taunts, my love. He only wishes to goad you into doing something stupid. For Gwennie's sake, don't give him the satisfaction."

His head turned a fraction toward his sister, who appeared to have sunk deep into unconsciousness again. His features contorted. To Sir Alistair he demanded, "What do you want?"

"What I have always wanted." The man's eyes narrowed, transforming him from elegant gentleman to back-alley cutthroat. "To claim my rightful place in the scientific community."

Simon made a sound of disgust in his throat. "There is no place for mongrels in any community. And that is all you are: a diseased dog with no honor."

"Simon!" Ivy stepped out from behind him and faced Sir Alistair head-on. "Tell us what you wish us to do."

"Turn around and face the wall."

Alistair's command raised a cold sweat between Simon's shoulder blades. Was the bastard simply going to stand them side by side and shoot them? Knots of desperation twisted in his gut. They were far from the public portions of the house, and at this time of day there would be no servants in their attic quarters. Who would hear the shots?

As he and Ivy moved to comply, he tried to school his features and not let her see the spiraling panic slamming his heart against his ribs and threatening to render him half mad.

"Alistair, this is between you and me." Through gritted teeth he spoke to the unpainted wall in front of him. His limbs shook, and the floor beneath his feet seemed about to buckle. "There are endless hidden chambers and catacombs in this house. Take me to any of them and do as you like with me, but leave Ivy and Gwendolyn alone."

"No, Simon, I'm not leaving you."

"Be quiet, Ivy."

"Shut up, both of you." Alistair's tread on the floorboards indicated that he had stepped farther into the room.

Struggling to contain his panting breaths, Simon attempted to gauge the size of the man's shadow against the wall. Was he close enough for Simon to swing around and knock the weapon from his hand? Or merely close enough to ensure that Alistair hit a vital organ—his own or Ivy's—if the gun discharged?

He couldn't risk it, couldn't risk *her*. Uncertainty held him immobile.

A scraping sounded as Alistair kicked something across the floor. "I kept these here in the event Gwen needed restraining. Happily for her, the laudanum did the trick. Very slowly, Miss Ivy, you may pick them up."

Ivy stooped, and when she straightened, she held two lengths of rope in her hands. Simon's gut wrenched again as he guessed that Alistair planned to incapacitate him, leaving the women entirely vulnerable.

"Now, then, my dear," Alistair said almost amiably, "you will tie Simon's hands behind his back. I shall be watching, so do not attempt to tie slipknots."

"I'm sorry," Ivy whispered as she moved behind Simon and gathered his wrists together.

"Just do as he says." Paltry advice, but he could conceive of none better. He considered spreading his wrists a fraction to give himself some sliding room, but Alistair would look for that. Instead, as Ivy bound his wrists, he fisted his hands tightly and hoped the flexed muscle would give him some minuscule room with which to work.

"Now sit on the edge of the bed," Alistair instructed him.

Compliance took every bit of self-discipline he possessed. Gwen stirred as the mattress dipped beneath his weight. *You'll see home again, Gwennie, I swear.* He didn't know how. He only knew there could be no other option.

Alistair gestured at Ivy with the revolver. "Now his ankles."

As she knelt at his feet, he caught her gaze and communicated as best he could that she continue to appease Alistair. Anything—*anything*—as long as she survived.

He raised his chin to Alistair. "How did you persuade Gwen to cooperate?"

The demon had the audacity to laugh, fueling Simon's growing penchant to engage in mindless violence. "All I had to do was assure her that I loved her."

"So she stole the stone for you. . . ."

"Oh, no, my friend. She stole the stone for you." Alistair stepped back and leaned against the doorframe. Simon wasn't foolish enough to believe the casual stance would hinder his aim. Alistair Granville was an expert shot; he could split a sapling at a hundred paces. "As impulsive as our dear Gwendolyn can be, she was overwrought with guilt at having displeased her brother last winter. She saw the stone as a peace offering."

"Just as the queen supposed." Yanking the last knot tight, Ivy pushed to her feet. Regret and fear swam in her dark eyes.

It'll be all right, Simon mouthed to her. Aloud he asked Alistair, "Why didn't she simply give it to me?"

"Because she remembered what an overbearing hot-head you are."

"That isn't true!" Ivy burst out.

Alistair ignored the interruption. "She hoped I could help smooth things over and mediate a truce between the two of you. After all, you never did learn the identity of the man with whom she'd gone to tryst. For all you knew, I was nothing more than a concerned friend and relative."

"Then why did she leave an unfinished note to me on Ben's bookshelf?" The truth suddenly struck him. "She didn't. It was you, the day you went to see Ben to discuss the consortium."

"I needed to be certain you'd attend the consortium. Gwen must have started and discarded a dozen notes to you before the laudanum, alas, rendered her unable to hold a quill."

"All this time, you've kept her drugged. . . ." He paused to take in his sister's shrunken form and gaunt features. Good God, his beautiful, youthful, vivacious sister, reduced to a shadow of her former self. The sight of her filled him with dread. "For pity's sake, Alistair, she's barely more than a child."

"On the contrary, she's quite the woman, your sister—"

Inside Simon's skull, black fury exploded. He became mobile, propelled off the pallet, his head aimed for Alistair's gut. No intention formed within the molten rage except to inflict damage any way he could.

Ivy's scream filled his ears. He felt himself falling short of his mark, going down and uselessly hitting the floor. His chin cracked against a floorboard. Pain erupted on his right side, his ribs shrieking as Alistair's boot struck again and again. Ivy's half Wellingtons flashed across his line of sight.

No, Ivy! Get back! Not worth it!

There were frantic scuffling sounds, then a body hitting the back wall with a light thud. A delicate thud. *Ivy.*

Cursing his damned, reckless stupidity, Simon turned half on his side, only to glimpse the toe of a polished black boot swinging viciously toward his head. Agony shot through him, and then he floated in nothingness.

Ivy hit the wall with bone-jarring force, her head, shoulder, and right hip taking the brunt of the blow. While part of her acknowledged the pain, the rest of her didn't care.

Simon was down and Sir Alistair . . . Sir Alistair had lost the remaining shreds of his sanity. Blinking away the spots dancing before her eyes, she pushed away from the wall and threw herself down across Simon's torso. One coherent thought drove her: *Shield him from the blows.*

Mercifully, her strategy succeeded. The monster stopped kicking, but when she lifted her head from Simon's shoulder, she saw the blood trickling from a wound above his temple. His eyes were closed, his face and lips bloodless.

"Oh, God, you've killed him. You horror of a man, you—"

Sir Alistair seized her upper arm and hauled her to her feet. "He's not dead, not yet. In truth, I have no intention of killing him. Now that your absurd plan to catch the *real killer* has failed"—his tone dripped with mockery—"Simon is once again Inspector Scott's prime suspect. There is no need for me to dispatch him. The law will prove most obliging in that regard."

"Then you'll have to kill me, for I shall tell the authorities everything."

He gave her arm a vicious twist that wrenched a cry from her lips. "Who will listen to a woman who disguises herself as a man and keeps company with other men? Not to mention that you, my dear, will be implicated as Simon's accomplice."

"My brother-in-law will listen."

"I think not. I know his type. He is an aristocrat, full of arrogance and pride. He came here to drag you home and salvage your reputation, no? But after your many deplorable offenses he is sure to disown you. He'll be only too happy to wash his hands of you."

A contradiction sprang to Ivy's tongue. No matter what she had done or ever could do, Aidan would never abandon her. He was a man of honor and compassion, two qualities of which Alistair Granville knew nothing.

She held her tongue, realizing that the fiend had just provided her with a weapon. A dubious weapon, perhaps, but the only one presently at her disposal. The only hope, perhaps, for Simon and his sister. Letting her head droop, she watched from under her lashes as he took the bait and sneered.

"You see that I am right. You are now quite alone. Believe it or not, at this juncture, my dear, I am your only friend."

Revulsion made her try to jerk her arm from his hold, but he tightened his fingers like a vise and raised his revolver until it stared like a lifeless black eye into her own. "If you cooperate, I will speak up for you. I will tell them you helped me subdue Simon. That way you may avoid the gallows."

Slowly she raised her head. "What would you have me do?"

He released her arm and gestured with the pistol at Simon. "First, rip a piece of the bedsheet and wrap his head in it. Then take the blanket from the bed and roll him onto it. You're going to drag him down the corridor." When she questioned him with a look, he calmly explained, "I cannot have him found with his sister. We'll leave him near a back stairwell."

"But I don't think I can move him—"

"You will find a way if you wish to live."

Her gaze lit on the pathetic form of Lady Gwendolyn. "And her?"

"Don't worry. I fully intend marrying her and claiming her dowry. In a few days I'll begin weaning her off the laudanum. I shall tell her she's been ill with a ravaging fever, on the verge of death. She'll never know otherwise, and I will be there to comfort her over her brother's ignominious downfall."

The simplicity of his plan and his utter lack of conscience left Ivy numb with fear and ill with loathing. "You've thought of everything, haven't you?"

"The true sign of brilliance, no?" He backed up until he stood framed in the doorway. "Now take hold of him and let us be off."

Chapter 26

"Harrow . . . Harrow, wake up."

The summons came from far away, muffled as if he were underwater. Unable to fill his lungs with air, Simon felt as though he were drowning. An insufferable pressure formed an iron band around his skull, and he felt in imminent danger of retching.

"Harrow! I need you awake. Now. There is no time for lying about."

Lying about?

A nudge at his shoulder brought on waves of nausea. He shifted and nearly cried out from the pain. Someone, apparently, had stuck a dagger in his side, another into his skull.

"Harrow! Damn it, man, listen to me. He has Ivy. I believe he's taking her down to the ballroom and I need your help."

"Ivy . . ."

"Yes. Granville has her."

Danger. Madness. Murder. Recollection came crashing through the painful haze. Simon forced his eyes open. The lamp had gone out, and he could barely discern the outlines of the Earl of Barensforth, leaning over him and gripping his shoulders. Simon remembered that Alistair had forced Ivy to bind his wrists and ankles, but apparently Barensforth had untied the ropes. He raised a hand to his throbbing temple.

"It's Alistair," he ground out between clenched teeth. "He's the ... murderer."

"Yes, yes. I've figured that out for myself. Can you sit up?"

"You figured ... How? Where is Ivy ... ?" Simon accepted the other man's help, ignoring the shooting pains as he craned his neck to look about him. "Gwen?" But his sister and the pallet had vanished. Had he only dreamed he'd found her? "My sister ... where is she?"

"Do you mean Lady Gwendolyn, who stole the queen's stone?"

"I ... only have one sister." He massaged the aching curve of his neck. A sense of urgency swam up through his confusion. He attempted to gain his feet, but halfway up, the floor buckled and the walls started spinning.

Barensforth thrust an arm across his shoulders to steady him. "Look, I understand the bastard knocked you about. But you need to concentrate. When our plan failed, I came searching for you, fully intending to apprehend you—"

"Alistair predicted as much."

"Listen. After stumbling around these dark corridors for what seemed an eternity, I heard voices. Ivy and Granville had just deposited you here. He had a pistol to her ribs—"

"A revolver."

"Damn it, man, *focus*." Still supporting Simon's weight, Barensforth half walked, half hauled him down the corridor. "The point is that I didn't dare make a move against him or he might have shot Ivy then and there. He said something about the ballroom and a way down no one else knows about. Not even his servants."

Pain and queasiness had forced Simon's chin to his chest. Now his head came up, and somehow he found the strength to smile grimly. "I know the way," he said.

The stairwell's jagged stone walls tore at the elbows of Ivy's coat as she picked her way down. Despite Sir Alistair's lantern, darkness closed around her, as cold and forbidding as a tomb. However modernized the main parts of the house might be, these narrow, spiraling steps must have been original to the ancient monastery.

Whenever she hesitated, Sir Alistair prodded with his gun at her shoulder, her spine, the nape of her neck. The weight of the box in her hands hindered her steps, while the strange energy emanating into her palms traveled up her arms until they trembled.

Though she had yet to set her eyes upon it, she had at long last found Victoria's stone. Not the decoy hunk of rock Sir Alistair had used to murder Spencer and Preston and very nearly Jasper, but the real stone Lady Gwendolyn had taken from Buckingham Palace.

Her arms were weakening, her knees shaking from the exertion of the descent. Finally they reached a cramped landing. The uneven stone flooring bit into the soles of her boots, while the granite chill penetrated her clothing and made her shiver. Sir Alistair ordered her to stand to one side while he pressed his ear to a wooden door. He never took his eyes off her, nor did he avert his gun from the level of her chest.

"The inspector locked up the ballroom again when your plan failed. There should be no one inside, but it is wise to be careful."

"What is the point of all this?" she asked wearily.

Sir Alistair straightened. "The point, my dear, is that the scientific brilliance of Sir Alistair Granville will finally be revealed to the world."

She refrained from telling him what she thought of that. He turned a latch and slid the door sideways. The ballroom opened before them. After they stepped inside and Sir Alistair had closed the door behind them, Ivy saw that from this side the portal appeared to be part of the wall, covered in silk and encased in elaborate woodwork.

An eerie sense of abandonment cloaked the equipment ranged throughout the room. From the mantel of the nearest fireplace Sir Alistair took a lucifer match, held it to his lantern, and then set about lighting the wall sconces. The brightness only intensified the unsettling hush of the room, creating a sense that the scientists had deserted their dreams. Ivy felt more alone and helpless than ever.

Sir Alistair walked to where Mr. Scott had earlier instructed the footmen to deposit Simon's giant electromagnets. The crates had been forced open, the contents thoroughly examined by the constables.

"Set them up," he told her.

She gazed in alarm at the octagonal magnets with their maze of ridges. "They're quite heavy."

"You'll manage. You do know the configuration, don't you?"

"I saw it only once, but . . . I believe I remember. . . ." Her teeth caught at her lip. If only she knew a way to configure the magnets as a weapon to use against this man. Then again, perhaps she didn't need to. "Do you know what these magnets do?"

"Lady Gwendolyn was most helpful in her description of Simon's project. What does he call it?"

"Electroportation."

"Ah, yes." He nodded. "I know he never succeeded in controlling the power levels well enough to make the process predictable and safe. As a scientist, he is innovative but limited. But with this"—he tapped the barrel of his gun against the box in her hands—"I will achieve what he never could. And the world, my dear, will watch and marvel."

She shook her head in disgust. "Once again, you are stealing another man's work. Borrowing his brilliance to compensate for what you simply do not possess."

His features contorting, he swung his gun high as if to strike her. Ivy braced for a blow that never came. When she opened her eyes, he appeared to have regained his composure. "Everything he is, he is because of me. Don't you understand? I took him under my wing and introduced him to the very principles on which he based the whole of his research. He owes me this. He owes me—"

"His life?" Oh, she knew she shouldn't goad him, but his self-delusions roused an outrage she could not contain.

Lips pinched and nostrils flaring, he gestured at the

magnets standing inside the first of the crates. "Get to work and be quick about it. We don't want to keep the consortium waiting a moment longer than is necessary."

Ivy erected the first set of three magnets on their metal stands close to the generator. She worked until her back ached, her shoulders throbbed, and her legs and arms shuddered from the overbearing weight of the equipment. Sir Alistair instructed her to set up the second three magnets across the room, near the ballroom doors—a much farther distance than in Simon's laboratory.

Could someone be electroported across such an expanse?

When all was ready, Sir Alistair retrieved the wooden box that held the queen's stone. Placing it on a demonstration table, he flipped open the lid. His chin jerked upward as if an invisible blow had struck him. He backed up a foot or two. "At my command, you are to take the stone and insert it between the generator's coils."

Ivy moved closer to the open box. The charge she had felt through the wood now flowed freely through the air, sparking little pinpricks on the exposed skin of her face and hands. When she stood over the stone, the current crawled down her back, her legs, between her breasts. She felt woozy, breathless, and braced her feet firmly on the floor as she leaned to scoop the stone into her palms.

The instant she wedged it between the coils, a waft of energy shoved her backward. Tiny bolts of lightning danced among the coils. The pistons began to thrust up and down and the center beam seesawed. A red-hot glow traveled along the connecting wires, and soon the first of the magnets began to hum.

The noise grew to a roar that filled the room. The chandeliers clinked; the paintings on the walls vibrated off their hooks and crashed to the floor; plaster crumbled in snowy drifts from the carved ceiling. Ivy ducked her head and pressed her hands to her ears, but she could not quell the awful pounding of her heart, pummeled again and again against her ribs in rhythm with the driving currents.

Simon's generator had never done *this* before.

"Sir Alistair, we must turn it off. It's too dangerous."

As if he hadn't heard her, he stood with his chin raised and his eyes half closed, his lips stretched in a grin that terrified her in its mad exuberance. The revolver had sagged in his grip, and Ivy started in his direction with an impulsive, desperate hope of dislodging it. He returned to his senses and swung the gun toward her.

"They will come now," he shouted above the din. "They will hear the uproar and come. We had better be ready for them."

He'd no sooner spoken than the ballroom doors rattled and burst inward. Ivy whirled to see Inspector Scott, his fellow constables, and the startled members of the consortium filling the doorway and packing the hallway.

"What is the meaning of this?" The inspector's demand could barely be heard, but Ivy read the query on his gaping lips.

"Gentlemen," Sir Alistair bellowed back, "for your own safety I must entreat you to venture no farther. But watch as my assistant and I astound you with a feat of science never before imagined."

With that, Sir Alistair strode to Ivy, gripped her arm, and dragged her toward the first set of electromagnets.

"This way." Simon led Lord Barensforth down the spiraling stone steps. As a boy visiting here many years ago, he'd been strictly forbidden to venture into the manor's honeycomb of medieval passages, and so of course he had. He knew every secret crevice of the old monastery, where the monks had hidden in times of war, and where they had concealed their treasures from unscrupulous barons and covetous monarchs.

If Alistair had forced Ivy into one of those crevices, it could take days to find her. But Barensforth had heard the man specifically mention the ballroom, which only made sense. If Alistair sought recompense for the perceived wrongs done him by the scientific community, where better than the place they had gathered to celebrate their collective victories?

If he'd had any doubts, the clamor rising from inside the ballroom dispelled them. At the landing, he pressed himself to the door that, from the other side, was all but invisible. The wood vibrated against his ear and his flattened palms. The sensation traveled through him until the hair on the back of his neck stood on end.

Beside him, Barensforth set a hand on the door, then snatched it away. "What in bloody hell is that?"

"My generator . . . and the power of Her Majesty's stone." He slid the door open an inch and put an eye to the gap. "Galileo's teeth!"

Inside, Ivy dug in her heels as Alistair attempted to pull her into the energy that streamed between the electromagnets. Even from where he stood, Simon perceived the intensified force of the current, a power even he had never dreamed of harnessing. Such power would kill. Of that he had no doubt.

There was no time to plan, no room for stealth. Fear and nausea roiled through him until the edges of his vision swam in a sickening haze. If Ivy so much as touched the energy stream, it might instantly tear her apart.

Thrusting caution aside, he slid the door all the way open and bolted into the room. He sensed rather than saw Barensforth fall in beside him. Engaged in their struggle, neither Alistair nor Ivy saw them coming. Alistair pressed the revolver's barrel to Ivy's side, and Simon's heart all but burst from his chest.

At the opposite end of the ballroom, Inspector Scott and several of his constables spilled through the doors but jolted to a collective halt, the men colliding with a force that threatened to topple them as a whole.

Scott must have seen the weapon, must have calculated the danger to Ivy should he and his men continue their stampede. Now they stood in a confused jumble and exchanged glances, some covering their ears with their hands, others pressing their palms over their hearts. All were experiencing the effects of the electromagnetic flow.

Simon, too, halted and swung out an arm to hinder Barensforth's progress. They had one and *only* one weapon at their disposal: surprise. And a single opportunity to use it. If Alistair was to see them, he might fire his weapon or shove Ivy into the current.

Like the calm at the eye of a storm, instinct and the logical progression of what he must do overrode Simon's rampant terror of losing Ivy. If he wished to save her, he must think and act rationally, with nothing less than scientific precision.

He motioned for Barensforth to circle behind the generator. Then he himself picked his way cautiously in front of it, having to duck beneath the sizzling wires connecting the apparatus to the magnets. The current seized control of his heartbeat and each breath he drew, forcing both into an unnatural, painful rhythm. The energy heaved at him from all directions, until remaining upright became an exhausting feat of strength. Ivy and Alistair were now only a few feet away. Simon heard her pleading attempts to reason with her captor. Alistair's laughter rose above the clamor as he continued to push her closer to the magnets.

The bastard faced Simon now and should have seen him, but he was so intent on his goal that he saw nothing but Ivy and the surging, sparking energy. Simon was no more than a foot or two from losing her, from watching her beautiful body disintegrate and scatter into a million particles of matter.

Deliberately, he stepped between her and the stream. Sir Alistair gave her a forceful shove; in the same instant, he saw Simon, and shock registered on his features. Simon opened his arms, caught Ivy, and hurled her with every shred of strength he possessed into Barensforth's waiting hands. Without hesitation the earl dragged her away, though with an arm reaching toward Simon and her face filled with agony, she resisted her brother-in-law as vigorously as she had resisted Alistair.

Hot fury flashed in Alistair's eyes before instantly cooling. His mouth pulled to a feral grin. "It doesn't matter to me who electroports."

Head down and arms outflung, Alistair charged. Simon parried with his own arms to deflect the blow, but Alistair nonetheless caught his shoulder. The force sent him stumbling backward. The roar of the current filled his ears and his skull, and a thousand needles dug into his left shoulder. The pain burgeoned, becoming like burning dagger points tearing at skin and muscle and bone. Not wounding, but destroying.

The energy spread, seared, took control of his physical self. His vision darkened and blurred. Ivy's screams faded to a muted hum. He felt himself dying, disintegrating. . . .

Only one sensation remained: that of his fingers fisted around some part of Alistair. Simon could not have said which part it was. He only knew he had purchase on the man. In a burst of effort he used the leverage to yank Alistair closer. The wafting energy enveloped them both and thrust them in a vortex that reversed their positions.

Relief flowed like cascading spring water through Simon's body the instant he no longer touched the charged stream. Pain gripped him, but the devastating effects of the current eased. His vision cleared. Caught off-balance in front of him, Alistair let out a roar, flailed his arms wide, and staggered backward. . . .

The current caught him and ripped across his back, arching his body like a bow. Simon's left arm hung limply, but he reached out with his right and tried to catch the floundering man. The air snapped, and the current lifted Alistair off his feet. An exploding burst of light thrust Simon to his knees. When he looked up, a terrified Alistair stretched out a hand. His mouth opened on a silent scream, and then he dissipated into a glittering swarm of light.

A blast shook the room, wrenching Ivy out of Aidan's arms and tossing her off her feet. As she went down, she saw Simon blown back from the force of the energy. He fell to his knees and Alistair . . . Alistair reached out and then—

He was gone. Simply . . . gone.

She smacked the floor hard, her knees and hands and elbows reverberating from the impact. Still, she didn't waste a moment but shook away her disorientation and scrambled to her feet, half crawling the first few steps until she managed to swing upright. As she hurried to Simon, she spared only the briefest glance across the room to where Sir Alistair should have reappeared within the second configuration of magnets. Nothing happened. She reached Simon and sank beside him.

"My love." Anything more she might have uttered was lost in a sob. He stirred the instant her hands closed on his shoulders. A rumbling groan escaped him, and Ivy whisked her hands away. "Aidan, a doctor. He needs a doctor immediately."

Aidan relayed the command in a shout that carried over the din of the generator. Then he came up behind her. "Ivy, we have to stop this thing before it takes the house down around us."

She shot a look up at the machinery, vibrating dangerously. The pistons were pumping so furiously they appeared about to fly off their housing. Aidan moved to the wires that connected the power source to the magnets.

"Aidan, don't!" she shouted. "They're too hot to touch." She started to rise.

Simon caught her wrist. "My shoulder . . . gone . . . ?"

She heard the question in his voice and fell back to a crouch. Her heart clogging her throat, she gingerly brought trembling fingertips down on his upper sleeve. The lines of his shoulder filled his coat, and the flesh beneath felt solid enough, but what of the muscle? "Not gone . . . but . . . can you move your arm?"

The strain of doing so robbed the last of the color from his face and broke a sweat across his brow, but he managed to drag his arm an inch or two across the floor.

"Ivy!" Aidan shouted. He stood in front of the generator, ready to spring into action at a word from her. "We can't wait much longer!"

She forced herself to focus. Under normal circumstances, cutting off the steam and tossing the insulated canvas over the equipment would bring the generator to a halt. These were not normal circumstances.

"The stone," she yelled to him. "The only way to stop the current is to dislodge the stone. But don't try touching it with your bare hands."

Aidan's gaze darted about the room. Behind him, shafts, rods, and bolts worked loose from the generator and clanked to the floor. The power didn't lessen, but became more unstable. The surging current continued to crumble plaster from the ceiling and shake the room's ornate decorations loose from the walls. Once again Ivy peered down the room, searching for signs of Alistair's imminent reappearance. Again, nothing.

Aidan sprinted to the closest hearth. He seized an elaborate brass and iron poker from its stand and raced back to the generator. Once there he wedged it beneath the stone and thrust his weight against the improvised lever.

Ivy had the fleeting thought that Victoria would not be pleased by the return of a shattered stone, but then Simon lifted his head from the floor. "Ivy, my love," he said, in a soundless whisper that resonated inside her.

Amid raining plaster and the rupturing of the generator, she gently cradled his head and shoulders in her lap. His eyes fell closed and she thought he'd fainted, but then his lips parted and a corner of his mouth tilted in something approaching a smile. "My beautiful, brilliant Ivy."

This time she heard his ragged voice with her ears and not just her heart. The generator whirred down, small parts continuing to clatter as the energy dispersed and each component slowed to a stop. She tried to speak but couldn't push the words past the constriction in her throat. His image blurred behind tears.

"Neckcloth," he murmured with a gasp. Quickly she untied the knot and slipped the starched linen from around his neck. She smoothed the hair from his brow and used her sleeve to blot the perspiration on his forehead. His right hand closed over hers and weakly he whispered, "Help me sit up."

"You shouldn't."

He replied with an emphatic squeeze. Heedful of his injured shoulder, she slipped an arm behind his back and helped lift him off the ground. She winced at his grunts of pain and wished he'd lie back down, but she knew better than to insist. When he finally sat upright, he gave his head a hard shake, blinked several times, and dragged in a rasping breath.

Then, his left arm hanging limp at his side, he thrust his good arm around her and crushed his lips to hers.

Chapter 27

"Careful, now. Move her gently to the bed."

Ivy issued orders to the footmen who had improvised a stretcher and were presently carrying Lady Gwendolyn into Simon's bedchamber. Still weakened by the effects of the electromagnetic current, Simon shuffled alongside them, holding his sister's hand and watching intently over her as if to gauge by the set of her features whether she was experiencing any discomfort.

It was difficult to tell what Lady Gwendolyn might be feeling through the effects of the laudanum. Simon's pain was much more apparent, visible in every involuntary grimace, indrawn breath, and clenching of his teeth. It was a wonder he was up and walking at all, and so Ivy became his voice and did everything she could to spare him undue exertion.

In all the confusion in the ballroom, no one had seemed to notice their impetuous kiss, but now that everyone had calmed down, it became necessary to maintain a respectable, manly distance between them. She ached to hold him, to sit with him at his sister's bedside and stroke his hair, kiss his forehead, and whisper that everything would be all right.

Instead she stood sentrylike at the foot of the bed and watched as he drew the covers up over Lady Gwendolyn.

"Gwennie, I'm so sorry . . . for everything."

Ivy's startled surprise mirrored Simon's when the girl opened her eyes. "He . . . hurt me," she said with a raw simplicity that stabbed at Ivy's heart.

"I know, Gwennie." Simon leaned over her and kissed her brow. "But he'll never hurt you again."

Her hand came up, her fingers groping weakly at Simon's coat sleeve. "I thought . . . he loved me."

Simon questioned Ivy with a despondent glance, one she answered with a slight shake of her head. He nodded his comprehension and patted his sister's cheek. "He did love you," he lied. "It's just that . . . Alistair wasn't himself. He'd become ill . . . in his mind, Gwennie. His view of the world became distorted. Twisted. I'm sure he didn't understand how terribly he'd wronged you. . . ."

Ivy saw the distaste in the downward tug of Simon's lips, in the dangerous narrowing of his eyes. If the generator hadn't killed Sir Alistair, Ivy feared Simon would have. She rejoiced that such a decision had been taken out of his hands.

The physician from the village arrived and examined both Simon and Gwendolyn. For the latter, he prescribed rest, a diet rich in cream and eggs, and, much to Simon's dismay, more laudanum, but in diminishing quantities each day until her body no longer craved the drug.

The man fretted much more over Simon's condition, *tsk*ing over the state of his shoulder and pronouncing his pulse and heart rate "of concern." He again prescribed rest, adding that Simon should seek an environment free of distressing influences. Simon smirked at the suggestion and thanked the man.

Afterward, Gwendolyn slept while Simon kept watch over her and Ivy watched over him from the wing chair near the hearth. She herself dozed on and off, rising occasionally to coax Simon to drink some tea and eat some of the bread and cold meat brought up from the kitchen. His sister awoke shortly before midnight. A bit of color restored to her cheeks, she appeared more lucid than they had yet seen her.

Propped against the pillows, she ate a few bites and sipped cool water. When Simon tried to persuade her to lie back down and sleep, she refused with surprising vigor and with a mulishness Ivy found touchingly familiar.

"I've lost enough time in slumber," Gwendolyn declared in a voice still hoarse from disuse. Then her stubborn frown faded and remorse peeked from behind pale blue eyes much like Simon's own. "I took it for you, you know. The stone, I mean. I thought it would help you in your research."

"I know."

"But then I realized how foolish that was. Good heavens, I stole from the queen!"

"Don't worry." He smiled gratefully at Ivy. "I happen to know someone who is a rather good friend of Her Majesty and is willing to intervene."

"Really?" Before he could elaborate, Gwendolyn shook the thought away. "I went to Alistair believing he could help. You didn't know the truth about last winter, and you and he were still such close friends. I tried to write to you, but Alistair said he would arrange a meeting between us, and that he would make everything all right. I foolishly believed we could all begin anew, with Alistair openly declaring for me, and you being glad about it and forgiving me, and . . ." She dissolved into sobs, and her brave face fell away to reveal the distraught and frightened young girl she was.

"He was always so charming," she said as the tears fell. "So solicitous of my needs. He was handsome and clever and so much more sophisticated than the men my own age. He made me feel . . . elegant and special. Oh, Simon, can you ever forgive me?"

"Gwennie, don't be silly. Of course I forgive you." He slipped his good arm around her, pressed his cheek to her hair, and held her while she cried. Ivy saw a tear or two glistening in his eye, and her throat clogged with sorrow and joy and relief. Soon afterward, Gwendolyn drifted off to sleep, her even breathing signifying what was probably the first tranquil slumber she had experienced since she'd fled Buckingham Palace.

Simon continued to watch her, his head bent, his back bowed, his shoulders hunched. Exhaustion dragged at his limbs and his features. Even his clothing hung limp and crumpled from his frame.

Ivy pushed out of her chair. "And now you must rest as well," she told him. He started to shake his head, so she fisted her hands at her waist and mustered her sternest expression. "No arguments. Sleep in my bed." She gestured toward the dressing room.

"Where will you sleep?"

"Don't worry about me."

"Ivy . . ." He stood up and reached out a hand to her.

Ivy took it and raised it to her cheek, letting the warmth of his palm imbue her skin. They had both almost died tonight. That they hadn't constituted nothing short of a miracle, one she dared not question or analyze too deeply. They were alive, and for now, that was enough.

She shook her head at the longing that entered his eyes. "Sleep," she said. "I'll see you in the morning."

Simon awakened the next morning unable to decide if the pain in his shoulder had lessened, or if he had simply grown used to it, like a constant but irritating companion.

Gwennie lay deep in slumber, and he gave silent thanks for that. Much of yesterday remained a blur, and even her pleas for forgiveness were cloaked in a haze of pain and lingering shock. Had Alistair raped her, as he had so callously implied? Simon wasn't sure, but he damned well wasn't going to press the matter until she had fully recovered. He knew he had months and perhaps years of tender work ahead of him, to see her restored to her former spirited and, yes, often exasperating self. It would be a labor of love to which he was more than willing to dedicate the better part of his time.

He opened the chamber door to discover his fellow Galileans gathered outside.

"Is she all right?" Errol whispered.

"Are *you* all right?" Ben added. "Your shoulder . . ."

"Good God, son, the things Alistair did." Errol pressed a frail hand to Simon's good shoulder and gave a tremulous squeeze, imparting a silent promise of support to help him through the horror of his friend and mentor's betrayal.

Were those tears in dear old Errol's eyes? A tremor in Ben's smile? And Colin . . .

He stood slightly apart, leaning against the wall opposite the chamber door. Simon stepped away from the other two men and offered Colin his hand. "I'm sorry, Colin. I . . . I don't know what to say. I believed the worst and . . . damn, but I was wrong. Horribly wrong. Don't know how I could have—"

"No. You were right to be furious with me." Colin gripped Simon's hand and shook it once, twice, hard and firm. "I let you believe the worst."

He went on to explain that he had run into Gwen outside the bank in town early that winter morning. It was odd enough, her being abroad so early, but she'd also seemed skittish and in a great hurry, and when Colin had inquired if anything was wrong, her nervous laughter and hasty excuses had raised his suspicions.

At the time he'd been chagrined to find himself skulking in shadows and trailing her, but when she'd boarded a northbound coach, he'd wagered that his instincts hadn't played him false. Again he'd set out after her, this time on horseback, stopping at two inns before finding the right one. He'd had to bribe the innkeeper to gain access to her room, and upon bursting in, he'd found her alone and in a state of fevered agitation, a condition that instantly gave way to crushing dismay when she realized her plans would not reach fruition.

"She refused to tell me whom she'd gone there to meet," Colin concluded. "So I took the blame when you arrived because, the disaster having been averted, I thought it better you should direct your outrage toward me than toward your own sister. Now I realize it was the worst thing I could have done. I hope you'll forgive me."

Much more needed to be said, but Simon felt assured their friendship would mend, eventually.

But first . . . Ivy. He wanted to thank her for everything she had done for Gwennie yesterday, and for him. One sensation from last night he recalled with true clarity was the warmth of Ivy's small hands enveloping his own, and the soft caress of her voice. He didn't know when she had slipped back into his room to be with him, or how long she'd sat at his bedside. He knew only that each time he'd emerged from an exhausted, dreamless slumber, she had been there.

But now that he was fully awake, he couldn't seem to find her anywhere. He'd looked in the library, the ballroom, the morning room. With a rising sense of panic, he doubled back and skidded into the dining hall doorway.

A single person occupied the room; Barensforth regarded him quizzically from his seat at the head of Alistair's long, satinwood dining table. "Good God, Harrow, Frankenstein's monster has nothing on you."

Simon had to admit, the earl's assessment was nothing if not scathingly honest. But he took comfort from Barensforth's presence, for he realized it meant that Ivy was still here as well, somewhere. In the central hall behind him, a steady stream of scientists, assistants, and footmen raised a nonstop scuffle as they carried equipment and luggage out of Windgate Priory to the carriages lining the drive.

"Thank you, Barensforth." He showed the man a sardonic half grin, then wished he hadn't when the gesture renewed the infernal throbbing of the bruise left by Alistair's boot on the side of his head. He reached up and fingered the tender spot. "Nothing like a compliment to lift a chap's spirits."

Dizziness made him sway. He leaned against the lintel—on his good shoulder—for support.

"Don't mention it. Come and sit before you fall down." In waistcoat and shirtsleeves, the earl sipped from the snifter he held. An open decanter sat on the table before him. One look at the liquor's velvety hue assured Simon that Barensforth had chosen the very best of Alistair's stores. But then, Alistair would no longer be needing his brandy, finest or otherwise. Nor anything else, for that matter.

Yes, *matter*. Alistair's was. . . . Simon pushed off the doorframe and, with some degree of difficulty, shuffled into the room. He couldn't exactly say what form Alistair's physical matter had taken. The energy stream had ripped clear through him and torn him apart.

Simon didn't believe energy could be obliterated. Transformed, transported, rearranged, yes. So where did that leave the man he had known all of his life, who at times had been—or seemed—like a second father to him? Had he become part of this very house, his essence blended with the spirits of the monks who first dredged the stones from the earth to transform them into a sanctified fortress?

He would never know.

Using his good hand, he pulled out the chair nearest to the head of the table and sank into it. Without a word the earl abruptly stood and walked down the length of the room to the adjoining butler's chamber. When he returned, he set a second snifter down in front of Simon and splashed a generous measure of brandy into it. "You look like you could use it," he said as he resumed his seat.

Gratefully Simon tipped back half the contents. Then he relaxed and took a smaller sip. "Have the others accepted our story?" he asked once the liquor had sent its bracing fire through his veins.

He alluded to the explanation he, Errol, Ben, and Colin had hastened to devise yesterday to deflect curiosity away from the truth—a truth he simply was not ready to share with the scientific world. Electroportation had proved too dangerous to risk allowing another scientist to take up where he had left off with his experiments.

Barensforth nodded. "Everyone believes that your electromagnets were designed for the purpose of transferring electrical currents from one location to another without the use of wires."

"Good. And Alistair's death?"

"They believe the current incinerated him." Barensforth shuddered and drank some of his brandy.

"That isn't far from the truth. Or perhaps it is the truth. Victoria's stone amplified beyond calculation the power of an already volatile process. We're lucky no one else died." Simon raised his glass in a salute. "Thank you, Barensforth. I'm grateful for everything you did."

Barensforth chuckled wryly. "I only did it because I didn't trust you. That's what sent me up to the attic. I figured you were plotting your escape, and that Ivy might be foolish enough to help you." He tugged at his neckcloth. "Women in love can be . . . intractable."

Women in love . . . Did she love him? His chest tightened around the notion. After yesterday, how could he ever doubt it, or deny that he returned her feelings? Galileo's teeth, yes—he loved her. Loved her from his deepest core outward, with the essence of his most vital elements, and with every particle that made him a man, made him who he was. He loved her so much more than he'd ever believed he could love again.

A slight queasiness came over him. The future would have been so much easier if he didn't love her. Oh, he had every intention of doing the right thing, what decency dictated. Ivy had declined his offer once, but surely she realized now that after their weeks together, and most especially their nights, they must marry, and as soon as possible. What he didn't know, what utterly eluded him and sent his world sliding out from beneath him, was what he would do if he was ever faced with the pain of losing her.

That ill sensation persisted. He had almost lost her yesterday; they had very nearly lost each other. She had stood so bravely and faithfully by him through everything, had fought Alistair with such stubborn courage. Physically, Ivy was everything Aurelia hadn't been—tall and lithe and agile and strong. But in their heart of hearts, the two women were cut from the same sturdy, magnificent cloth.

No wonder Simon couldn't help loving Ivy, despite all his determination not to. He might as well admit that from that very first day, when she had defied him by raising her hand to ask a forbidden question, he had been ensnared. He might not have suspected her gender then, but his heart had seen the truth.

A truth that left him terrified.

"How's the shoulder?" Barensforth asked softly. Simon realized the earl had been watching him, closely, perhaps closely enough to guess at the train of his thoughts.

He tried to school his features to reveal no further clues into the state of his heart. With his good shoulder, he shrugged. "Hurts like the devil. The physician determined that there's been a good deal of muscle damage." He shook his head and voiced what he had yet to fully accept. "It'll likely never be the same."

Even as he spoke, he couldn't quite believe it. Somehow, there had to be a way to regenerate the nerves. As soon as he arrived home, he would review his notes on the artificial hand; now he would have real flesh and blood on which to experiment.

"And Ivy?" Barensforth pinned Simon with a glare as prickly as a surging current. "She'll never be the same, either, will she? I mean, as she was before she . . . met you."

Simon heard the emphasis the man placed on the word *met*, and comprehended all it meant, all he had taken from Ivy. "No need for euphemisms, Barensforth. I assure you I'll—"

The earl had been about to pour more brandy into his snifter; instead he banged the decanter down, sending up a spray that dotted the tabletop. "If not for euphemisms, my lord, I might find it necessary to break your neck."

Despite Simon's superior rank and slightly superior height and build, he found himself taken aback and not entirely undaunted. As the earl glowered at him, Simon sat up straighter, stiffer, sending sharp pains into his shoulder. He could only concede that Barensforth had every right to be incensed—every right, even, to do as he threatened.

With a measure of relief he watched the tension drain from the earl's posture. Barensforth once more lifted the decanter. "You'll make an honest woman of her?"

"At the earliest possible date."

"Is that so?" The defiant query and the sudden halting of footsteps in the doorway made Simon twist around without thinking, sending a fresh wave of agony through his shoulder.

Worse than that, though, was the sight of Ivy standing with her hands on her hips, her chin in the air, and a scowl on her face.

"Sorry about that, old chap. I say, Ivers, what's wrong?"

When Ivy stopped short, Jasper, walking directly behind her, bumped her spine and stepped on the heel of her boot. Now he moved beside her and glanced back and forth between her and the two men in the dining hall presently planning the course of her life.

She cleared her throat and turned to her friend. "Jasper, would you excuse us, please?"

His hand started toward the bandage still wrapped around his head. Then he gave a nod of compliance and strode off. Ivy stepped over the threshold and closed the double doors behind her.

"Simon, it is wonderful to see you up and about. Truly. But how *dare* you?"

"How dare I what?"

Simon and Aidan had both pulled back as if she'd poked them with an electrified wire. Their expressions turned equally mystified, as if she must have taken leave of her senses.

And perhaps she had. Not taken leave, exactly, but consciously cast off every so-called bit of *sense* that dictated that ladies did not attend university, did not pursue intellectual matters, did not aspire to goals other than marriage and children, did not have adventures, did not fend for themselves. . . .

She could go on and on naming all the things ladies must not and did not do, yet which she had done these past weeks, and successfully, too. Yet for all her pains, *this* was the result: lack of acknowledgment, lack of respect, lack of *consultation*.

"How dare you two think you can plan out my life without so much as a by-your-leave?"

Aidan gave a maddening, condescending shrug. "Ivy, there is nothing to ask, nothing to discuss. You have been compromised. Marriage is the only solution."

"And I am fully willing—"

"Willing?" Her gaze snapped to Simon. "How magnanimous of you, sir. However, your services in that department are not required. It so happens I've a plan of my own."

"What plan?" Aidan's dubious chuckle made her clench her fists at her sides.

She steeled herself to remain calm and give them no reason to call her erratic or hysterical or any other adjective men used when women voiced opinions of their own. "Have you forgotten my connection to the queen? I have recovered her stone, a bit chipped but thankfully not shattered despite your violent efforts to dislodge it from the generator's coils."

"I couldn't think of any other way," Aidan murmured.

"Be that as it may. Her Majesty will no doubt be grateful, and she will wish to reward me as she rewarded all of us after Laurel returned from Bath."

She noticed that as she spoke, Simon's frown deepened. But he said nothing, merely sat there with a look of pain that renewed her worry over the state of his shoulder. The physician had clucked his tongue over the damage, making Ivy fearful that Simon might never regain the full function of his left arm.

Oh, she would much rather be comforting him, fussing over him, telling him how brave he had been, how splendid.

That was what had brought her here in the first place, after she had caught sight of him from outside the open front door.

But hearing the men discuss her in such an objective manner, as if she were not a human being but some difficult calculation that required immediate solving, heated her blood to boiling. No matter what had occurred these past weeks, she would not marry for convenience' sake because . . .

Because she loved him too, too much, and couldn't bear becoming his wife for any other reason. Convenience, honor, obligation—each notion lodged like a cold stone in the pit of her stomach. No, she had rather die an old maid and remember her days with Simon as the most fulfilling and passionate of her life than marry him for propriety's sake and watch those glorious memories fade within a loveless marriage.

For surely if he could say such things as *I am willing*—as one was willing to sweep a floor or travel in the rain when one must—then he simply could not feel for her what she felt for him.

She blinked again, this time not to clear away her anger but to hold her tears in check. Her eyes burned and her throat ached. But she pushed out the necessary words. "I will appeal to the queen to request a place for me at a university, perhaps King's College in London. Oh, I've no illusions that I'll be accepted as an official student, or that I will be afforded a degree. I should be satisfied to attend classes and have use of the library, perhaps occasionally even a laboratory. And I shall continue to sell books at the Emporium with my sisters. It may seem a paltry plan, but it is my plan and what I wish to do."

"Ivy . . ." A plea to be reasonable clung to Simon's murmur. He exchanged a glance with Aidan, the two of them sitting there like coconspirators against her army of one. Her defenses fast threatened to dissolve into a pool of tears.

She didn't wish to be reasonable. She wished only to be loved. If she couldn't have that . . .

"I will not expect either of you to understand. You were

both raised on certain codes and expectations, but if my experiences have taught me anything, it is that great things happen only when one is brave enough to step beyond what is established and accepted. Now, if you will both excuse me, I will take up Jasper on his offer to ride back to Cambridge with him."

She was already out the door when Simon's exclamation of "The hell you will" reached her ears.

She didn't hesitate, but strode, almost ran, into the bustling activity that filled the hallway and spilled out the front door. She let the tide carry her down the steps and onto the drive. Countless carriages lined the way; it seemed as if every vehicle from the village of Madingley had been commissioned to convey the consortium members away.

Near one particularly battered curricle, she spotted Jasper's head of wavy hair encircled by the conspicuous bandage. He saw her and gestured her over. Without further encouragement and without glancing back at the house to see if Simon had followed her, she sprinted across the gravel driveway.

"You're coming back to Cambridge with me, then," Jasper said as she reached him.

Before she could reply, a voice from behind her roared, "Like hell she is."

"*She . . . ?* What the . . . ? Lord Harrow? Ned?" Jasper's baffled gaze darted back and forth between Ivy and Simon. He ducked his head and lowered his voice. "What *does* he mean?"

His confusion was the last thing filling Ivy's vision as Simon linked his good arm through hers and half dragged her, half walked her off the drive and onto the lawn. They walked and walked, Ivy occasionally glancing over her shoulder at a clearly startled Jasper. The young man took a few steps, then stopped, then started and stopped again, vacillating between remaining where he was and taking off after them. When Ivy finally turned to see where Simon was bringing her, she found herself near Windgate Priory's encircling moat with its mock battlements and landscaped gatehouse.

Simon pulled her inside a stone gazebo ringed with ever-green hedges and draped with vines. From within the fringe of autumn-bare branches, Jasper, the carriages, and the departing scientists seemed far away, their clamor muted by the stirring breezes and the chatter of birds.

Simon released her, and alarm shot through her. His pallor had whitened, and his eyes were fever bright. A fine sweat beaded his brow, and as he clutched his left arm to anchor it to his body, pain pinched his features even tighter than before.

"You shouldn't be out here," she said. "We should go back to the house."

"Not until we've spoken."

"Your shoulder—"

"Can blasted well wait, damn it. This cannot."

She flinched at his language. He started to reach for her, to grasp her with both hands, but with a groan he shut his eyes and said, "Ivy, forgive me. When I said I was willing, I didn't mean it."

The ground seemed to drop out from beneath her feet. She went to the circular stone bench and collapsed onto it. "Then you aren't willing?"

"No. Yes. What I mean is . . ." He hung his head, swore, and said, "I didn't mean it the way it sounded. I don't have to tell you it's been a devil of a couple of days, and then there was your brother-in-law staring murderously at me and speaking of breaking my neck."

"Did he? He can put up a ferocious front, but he'd never harm a fly."

"One wonders. But the point is, his being there made me . . . well, not say things as I might have wished." He stood crookedly before her, his right shoulder hunched, the other clearly weakened and hurting. He looked . . . troubled and contrite and so dear she suddenly wished to rush to him and entreat him to stop upsetting himself, not to overexert.

At the same time he looked like a man driven, bound and determined to speak the words that were obviously sizzling on his tongue. The blue fire blazing in his eyes made her tremble even as it tied an intricate knot of longing and apprehension and most of all hope deep, deep in her belly.

"Then," she said, "what *would* you have said?"

"I . . . Oh, hang it." He blew out a breath. "I probably still would have said all the wrong things. It took you walking out of that room to knock the truth free. Because when you left, Ivy, I realized I was about to lose you as completely as a person *can* lose someone—the one person they love above all others."

"You love me?"

He pinned her with a deadly sharp dagger of a stare. "Of course I love you. Don't you see? That has been the problem all along. Loving you, and knowing the sort of pain that could bring."

"Because I could die, like your wife," Ivy whispered.

"Yes. Oh, God, yes. I never wished to go through that again. But Ivy . . ." He broke off and staggered to her. Holding his left arm as still as he could, he grimaced and sank to his knees before her. "When you said you were returning to London, and that my services as a husband weren't necessary, I died inside." He emitted a bark of bitter laughter. "Don't you see? The joke was entirely on me, because despite my stubborn intentions, it was already too late to worry about one day experiencing the pain of losing you. When you stomped out of the room, agony struck like a barbed lance and gave a twist. It's still twisting. The pain in my shoulder is nothing in comparison."

"I do not stomp," she said indignantly. Ever so lightly, she brushed her fingertips across his injured shoulder.

"Oh, my dear, you stomp. You most certainly do stomp in those half Wellingtons of yours."

He released his left arm and set his right hand over both of hers where they lay in her lap. "Ivy . . . Ned . . . my love. Don't leave me. I need you, in my laboratory, in my bed, and in my life. You're already in my heart. Nothing can ever change that. Why, do you realize that because of you, I've made a startling discovery about hearts, about how to re-generate one that has stopped beating?"

She drew a quivering breath. "And what is that discovery?"

"It doesn't take electricity to make it beat. It takes love. Here . . ." He thumped his chest and then quickly returned his hand to cover hers. "Take a listen. Tell me it isn't kicking up a fine tempo."

She couldn't help a tearful laugh, then quickly bit the insides of her cheeks and frowned. "But there is so much against us. The things I want—"

"You can have, with me. Where better? You wish to attend classes? I can arrange it. You wish to explore the sciences? My laboratory is yours. And I swear to you, any results you achieve will be published under your name. Not mine, Ivy. Yours."

Oh. It was all too, too perfect to be true, and she almost feared to believe him. He was offering the very world she had always imagined and yearned for and never believed could be hers. Her pulse leaped, her blood surged, her entire body ached for that world . . . and for *him*. But . . .

Pulling one hand out from under his to wipe away a tear on her coat sleeve, she raised her eyebrows. "They will all ridicule you, you know. The scientific community, society, everyone. The truth about Ned Ivers has become too well-known to remain a secret any longer. I am compromised, and there are people who will never let us forget it."

"Then we will forget them." With visible effort, he pushed up onto the bench beside her. "I am the Mad Marquess of Harrow. Do you think I give a fig what people think?"

His voice fell to a tempting caress of a murmur. "Ivy, be my marchioness. Marry me, and we'll be mad together. At least once a week we'll set the laboratory floor on fire and shoot sparks out the roof. We'll explode all manner of substances and frighten the villagers for miles around. And whenever the servants threaten to quit, we'll send Cecil to reassure them." Smiling devilishly, he raised her hand and kissed the tips of her fingers. "We'll make tired old hearts beat again. Think of it, Ivy. . . ."

The prospect made her own heart clamor with joy. Was it all just a dream? She pressed her fingernails into her palm to make certain it wasn't. "I'm thinking. . . ."

"And . . . ?"

"Ned? Ned, is everything all right? I became worried when you didn't return and—"

Ivy started at the jarring sound of Jasper Lowbry's query, but it was too late to break the magnetism drawing her lips to Simon's. Their mouths met as the youth's bootheels struck the slate floor of the gazebo.

"Great leaping electrodes, what the blazes is going on here?" Jasper, frozen into a column of stunned consternation, turned several shades of red in rapid succession. "I don't under—underst-st—"

"Jasper." Ivy disengaged herself from Simon and hastened to her friend. She touched his forearm and, for the first time since meeting him, tilted her head and smiled her full smile, without attempting to mask her femininity. "Jasper, look at me. *Really* look. What do you see?" She added a coquettish wink.

His jaw dropped. "You mean . . . *no*. Good heavens. You're a . . . a . . . ?"

"I am, Jasper. I'm frightfully sorry to have deceived you, but you see—"

"Yes, yes, I believe I do see. God, but it's obvious, isn't it, if one only looks closely enough." Studying her face, he gave a nod of comprehension that sent a lock of wavy brown hair falling over the bandage and onto his brow. "I suppose you had no choice, did you? You're bloody brilliant, but they still wouldn't have let you into the university."

"That's right," she said sadly, but also with great relief. She had developed a genuine fondness for this young man, and their camaraderie meant the world to her. "So I lied. I truly hope it won't affect our friendship."

"No, I, er . . ." He squinted slightly as he continued to peer down at her. "So, if it isn't Ned . . ."

"Ivy. Ivy Sutherland."

"But not for much longer." Simon stood and joined them. He slipped an arm around her waist and, despite Jasper's presence, pulled her to his side. "It's soon to be Ivy de Burgh. At least . . ." He turned her to face him. "I believe that was what you were about to say before your friend showed up."

She smiled up at him, and in the lines of his dear, handsome features, she glimpsed a glorious map of the rest of her life. "Indeed I was. I am." She laughed. "What I mean is, I will. Marry you, that is."

He joined in her laughter and crushed her to him in a one-armed embrace that lacked for nothing, not warmth or strength or the promise that dreams were meant to come true. "I love you, my beautiful, brilliant Ned."

"I love you, Lord Harrow, and I always will." Mindful of his injured shoulder, she tightened her arms around his neck. "Together we form a compound that can never be separated."

"Ah. Right. I'll, er, just be off now." Stumbling backward, Jasper retreated through the gazebo's archway.

Simon lifted his lips from Ivy's and called to him, "Young man. The future Lady Harrow and I will be needing an assistant. Are you available for the job?"

Jasper replied with an eager smile and a vigorous nod. Then he ran back across the lawns toward the waiting carriages. As he went, he let out a resounding whoop that echoed into the trees and sent a flock of crows scattering across the sky.

Epilogue

London, 1839

"Thank you, Mrs. Eddelson, that will be all for now. You and Mr. Eddelson may retire for the rest of the evening."

Holly Sutherland accepted the plump housekeeper's thanks and finished stowing away the last of the supper plates. Then she poured the brewed tea from the kettle into the porcelain teapot, and hefted the rather weighty tray of refreshments up the stairs to the little parlor that overlooked quiet William Street, in the Knightsbridge area of London.

She had barely crossed the threshold before her newest brother-in-law, Simon, jumped up from the overstuffed chair beside the settee and reached to relieve her of her burden.

"Here, let me do that," he insisted, and swung around to deposit the tray onto the low, oval sofa table. Holly secretly chewed her lip until he'd accomplished the task and the room's new Persian rug had survived unscathed.

Several months ago, that would not have been the case. Simon still suffered the effects of the injuries he had incurred last autumn while fighting off a fellow scientist who truly had gone mad. But after a rigorous course of exercise and what he termed *electromuscular therapy*, his once damaged shoulder had regained nearly all its former strength and now sat only slightly lower than the other—so slight that only those familiar with his mishap would have noticed the difference.

Ivy called it his badge of courage, gotten in his efforts to save her life. Holly called it a deplorable brush with death, one she dearly hoped would never be repeated, neither for him nor for her other brother-in-law, Aidan, who had helped Simon vanquish the villain. The queen had been delighted by the return of her stone, said nothing about its being slightly the worse from wear, and happily resumed her correspondence with her cousin. None of them, not Simon, Aidan, Laurel, or Ivy, had ever fully explained to Victoria the dangers they had faced on her behalf.

Ah, but all were safe, and all were here tonight.

"You sit, Holly, and I'll pour." Simon's sister, Lady Gwendolyn, was seated in the corner with a book about dog breeds open on her lap. Another of mad Sir Alistair's victims, poor Gwendolyn always had a lost, enervated look about her, as if she were just awakening to discover herself in unfamiliar surroundings. Physically, she had recovered from her ordeal of nearly two weeks spent in the wasting grip of laudanum. Her spirit had suffered a blow that time had yet to heal, but Holly and her sisters loved her, and Simon maintained that she seemed happiest when she was among them.

Gwennie set her book aside and with a shy smile lifted the teapot. Simon passed round the cups and saucers, while Aidan handed out the napkins and removed the cover from the platter of desserts. Stepping around Willow, who was perched on a stool near the hearth, Holly resumed her place on the settee between Laurel and Ivy.

Holly couldn't help noting how strange it was that their growing family continually gathered above the Knightsbridge Readers' Emporium. None of them lived here full-time anymore, and with two sisters married—and married so remarkably well—one would have thought they would sell their modest bookstore.

She and Willow divided their time between Ivy's and Laurel's London town homes, and while a Mr. Randall now managed the Emporium, all four sisters continued to have a hand in running the business. It seemed they could not bring themselves to part with the place that had been their home since Uncle Edward had passed away.

Ivy insisted the Emporium represented independence and self-sufficiency, which were denied most women and had certainly been missing from the sisters' lives until a couple of years ago. Willow contended that here they all felt snug and safe from bewildering threats that came from as far away as France. But as Holly gazed at the contented faces of her sisters and new brothers, she knew that neither of those reasons quite explained their attachment to this cramped little town house.

The plain truth was that for all of them, the Emporium had become a place where adventures began . . . and ended in dreams coming true.

"Oh, dear, how inconvenient. I'm afraid I can no longer bend in the middle." The others laughed good-naturedly as Laurel attempted, unsuccessfully, to lean forward and pluck a biscuit from the tray. The poor thing bounced several times with her hand outstretched, but to no avail.

Only too happy to oblige her eldest sister—and the tiny niece or nephew presently on the way—Holly retrieved the platter for Laurel. With her free hand she gave her sister's growing belly a fond pat.

"It won't be long now, dearest, and then you'll be as bendable as ever."

At Aidan's cheerfully delivered but shockingly suggestive comment, Holly issued him a glare of admonishment that no one took seriously—not even herself. With a dignified sniff she offered the platter to Ivy, sitting at her other side.

Ivy turned her face away. "Only tea for me tonight. Of all the things to develop an aversion to while increasing. Eels and asparagus I can fully understand, but cakes and clotted cream? There is no justice."

"Never fear, Ivy-divy," Willow said brightly as she bit into a raspberry truffle. "You'll be right as rain in no time. Laurel says the worst is over in the early months. Isn't that true, Laurel?"

Before Laurel could reply, the sudden jangling of the outside bell made them all jump. Laurel frowned. "Whoever could it be at this hour?"

"I'll go see." Aidan started to rise.

"No, I'll go." Holly set down her teacup and sidestepped out from between Ivy's skirts and the table. "I'm sure it's Mr. Biglow from the bakery. I lent him a book this morning, and in exchange he promised to bring by some of his wonderful scones after he closed up tonight."

"Oh, splendid," Ivy murmured. "More treats to turn my stomach."

Downstairs, Holly moved aside the window curtain and peeked out. She was surprised to see, not Mr. Biglow's cart at the curbside, but a black-lacquered brougham of costly design and lacking an identifying crest. Likewise, the darkhaired young man waiting on the foot pavement wore plain green livery that might have hailed from the household of any number of wealthy London denizens.

At least, that was what Holly's neighbors would think. She knew better. Her heart clattering with excitement, she unlocked the door and threw it wide.

"May I help you?" She craned her neck to see past her visitor. The interior of the coach appeared empty. Was its passenger pressed to the squabs in an attempt to hide from prying eyes? Holly could hardly curb her eagerness as the young footman stooped to get a better look at her in the glow of the streetlamp.

"Miss Holly Sutherland?" His uneven tenor revealed him to be no more than eighteen or nineteen years of age.

"I am she." Her own voice trilled the tiniest bit.

"This is for you, miss." He placed a leather-bound book in her hands.

"Oh?" The title revealed the tome to be a chronicle of the Royal Ascot from the time of its inception to the year before last. "The flat races? I don't understand. Who sent this? I thought—" But she couldn't very well blurt out what she thought, because it appeared she had thought wrong. Her shoulders sagged beneath vast disappointment.

Her visitor leaned closer and whispered, "Look inside, miss."

She flipped the book open, and a folded note fluttered out. Before it hit the ground, the young man caught it and handed it to her. Holly broke the seal, her elation returning as she read the hastily penned lines.

> *Dearest Holly,*
>   *I need you—and only you. You must come to me at Windsor at once! Tell no one, except your sisters, of course. But please, make no delay!*
>
> *Yours,*
V

Unable to wipe the grin from her face, Holly refolded the letter, placed it back between the pages, and hugged the book to her chest. It seemed the Knightsbridge Readers' Emporium was about to work its magic once again.

Read on for an excerpt from

Recklessly Yours

featuring Holly's story, next in
Her Majesty's Secret Servants
by Allison Chase,
available from Signet Eclipse
in December 2011.

Windsor, England, 1839

Never had Colin Ashworth despaired so entirely at the prospect of a cloudless day. Instinctively, he would have preferred the cover of a starless night, or the onslaught of a blustery storm to chase everyone indoors and banish inquisitive eyes from the stable yard, across which he presently picked a cautious path.

It was dodgy business, coming to Windsor's mews today. A dozen or so of Her Majesty's Thoroughbreds were to be exercised in the Great Park, and he intended to make sure that a particular horse was brought out with them. Should the head groom recognize him, or one of the trainers, or even the towheaded boy half stumbling, some dozen yards away, beneath the weight of a bucket of water ... Colin shuddered to think of the consequences. His titles, estates, even his freedom—everything!—stripped away in an instant. His family would be humiliated, ruined, his friends and peers appalled. Worse still, there would be no means or hope of halting the small, localized disaster he sought to circumvent with his actions today. He hadn't given the nudge that sent the dominoes tumbling, but it had been left to him to prevent the lives of countless individuals from falling into a scattered, unrecognizable heap.

So much depended on his success in the next few minutes; he must, therefore, have a care. And yet he reminded himself that caution would not do. He must appear bold and assured, as though he belonged here—which, in many respects, he did. He'd walked these cobbles that paved the walkways of the stables countless times, always welcomed, always shown the deference due his station, and never, never for a moment questioned. But he had never before come here in such a manner that no one would think to tip his cap to him—in such a way that, in a place as bustling as Her Majesty's mews, no one would ever remember his being here.

It was a circumstance that, in its own peculiar way, lent him exactly the cover of night he desired.

Holly Sutherland knew the exact instant the brougham turned off the dirt road onto a cobbled drive: a jolt, infinitely more jarring than the countless others she'd experienced throughout the night, clacked her teeth together with a frightful noise that woke her from the fitful doze into which she'd slipped some miles ago.

Another jarring bump sent her little top hat sliding over her brow, and the book she'd cradled in her lap these many miles tumbled from her knees and thwacked to the floorboards. She bent over to retrieve the volume at the same moment the coach lurched to a stop. If Roger, the obliging footman who had spent the journey riding on the rear footboard, hadn't opened the door at that precise instant and reached in to clasp her arm, she would have collided face-first with the rear-facing seat opposite her.

"You qui' all right, miss?" he inquired in an accent that struggled not to reveal its Cockney origins. A towering youth with a head of wavy dark hair, he had the even, almost-handsome features typical of many young footmen. He released Holly and moved a deferential step backward.

"I'm ... ah ... fine, thank you, yes." With the book clutched in one gloved hand, she straightened and endeavored to recover her dignity, an effort that fell short as she accepted Roger's offered assistance, stepped down from the carriage, and attempted to take in the unfamiliar surroundings from beneath the skewed brim of her chapeau.

Chagrinned, she angled the hat into place and blinked in confusion at what the coach lights revealed. She had never been to Windsor Castle before, but she had seen its image often enough in books. The grim two-story edifice sprawling to either side of her was most decidedly not Windsor Castle. Facing her were some half dozen double doors that opened onto a cobbled forecourt, while above them dingy windows edged in beveled stone struggled to reflect the first gray glimmers of dawn.

A tiny seed of misgiving took root as many of the assumptions she'd formed in the preceding hours seemed to have been proved incorrect. "Are we . . . er . . . here?"

"We are, miss. And if you wouldn't mind terribly, I must ask you to lower your veil before we proceed any farther. Just a precaution."

However politely couched, this was no casual request but a necessary command. How well she knew that it wouldn't do for her to be recognized. The smart little hat, designed to resemble a man's miniature stovepipe, bore the addition of a netted veil that floated down her back, with a shorter layer that could be pulled down in front. The arrangement matched the black wool riding habit she had been requested to wear as well.

She reached up and dragged the somber netting over her face. She supposed the effect was exceedingly mysterious. Roger studied her a moment, gave a quirk of his lips that might have been an encouraging smile, and nodded his approval. "If you please, miss, follow me."

As he led her down the length of the building, she took in more of her surroundings, including a perimeter wall breached by a pair of rickety wooden gates sorely in need of fresh paint, which were now being pushed closed by two liveried guards. Just before the gates met, she spied a rutted road that ambled up a low ascent before disappearing into the dimness of a rolling heath edged by chilly silver mist. As Holly's gaze rose above the enclosing walls, silhouettes took shape against the steely sky: towers and turrets and imposing ramparts. Poised high above the rest like a monarch on her dais, Windsor Castle's round tower stood bravely tall over the surrounding curtain walls.

The sight sent Holly's blood racing through her veins. Was Victoria waiting for her inside those majestic walls? Oh, but then what was she doing in this gloomy place, where she could least imagine a queen ever setting foot?

"Miss?" Roger's polite query roused her with a start. She tore her gaze from the distant castle and lifted her hems clear of the paving stones.

He led her between a pair of buildings that were similar in their austere granite design, and then down a damp, crooked little passage not yet penetrated by the dawn. The walls seemed to close in on her, and with a twinge of panic, she wondered if this could be a prison. Perhaps an inmate had escaped, and it would be Holly's task to track him down. Good heavens, perhaps the villain was some deranged brute who had threatened Victoria; there had been several threats against her in the two years since she had ascended to the throne: some veiled, others quite blatant. . . .

But as they proceeded through the passage and a rectangle of dim light appeared up ahead, the scents of hay, manure, and sweat—both horse and human—permeated the stagnant air and elicited a sneeze Holly could not stifle despite her efforts.

"G' bless you, miss."

"Thank you. This is a stable," she added with no small amount of surprise.

"The Windsor mews, miss."

Gritting her teeth, she raised a hand to her nose to smother another such eruption. A stable, however lacking in charm, was certainly preferable to a prison. She had not ventured inside one in a very long while. Since her sisters' marriages, she had once more gained access to horses and had gratefully resumed riding, but the animals were always

saddled by grooms and brought out to her in the fore-
courts of her brothers-in-law's stables. And what stables,
with graceful proportions and elegant lines that rivaled the
manor houses themselves. This place, these mews, seemed
small and mean in comparison.

Perhaps, however, this explained the riding attire she'd
been requested to wear. Could she and Victoria be about to
embark on a journey on horseback?

She and Roger emerged into a dusky stable yard lined
with stalls, their sleepy occupants shuffling their feet and
snorting soft greetings as Holly walked by. A horse stuck his
head over the gate, and she stretched out her hand to give
his velvety nose a pat. The animal rewarded her with a nod
and a whicker that brought on an onslaught of memories—
those of happy days spent among Thorn Grove's horses,
learning all she could from the grooms. The recollection
reminded her that *horse* was a good and honest smell, associated with some of the most cherished moments of her life.

Roger continued on, his lengthy stride prompting Holly
to speed her pace to keep up with him. She began to hear
voices now, and the sounds of stable hands beginning their
morning tasks. Roger turned several more corners, until it
seemed, to Holly, they had entered a tiny, twisting medieval village. They entered a second yard, where a team of
workers, scarcely more than adolescents, carried buckets,
brushes, and rakes, snaking armfuls of tack, saddles, and a
host of other equipment. A couple of them tapped their hat
brims to Holly, while others acknowledged her with nothing more than a timid flick of their gazes.

Roger opened a heavy wooden door and ushered her
inside. A narrow passage drifted off to her right. Roger
walked straight ahead, opened another door and gestured.
"In here, miss."

She was surprised to step into a cozy room furnished
with a faded but comfortable looking settee, a small oaken
table and chairs, and a brazier set beside an unassuming
brick fireplace. The effect was one of a slightly shabby retreat, perhaps the furniture having been deemed too worn

to remain any longer in a drawing room but good enough to host a party of aristocratic riders. Then again, such a room in Holly's childhood home of Thorn Grove, the modest country estate owned by her now-deceased uncle Edward, would have been considered perfectly adequate as an everyday ladies' parlor.

"Her Majesty's private viewing salon, miss," Roger explained. He pointed to a curtained window behind her. "If you look out, you'll see the enclosure where the royal horses are put through their paces."

She moved to the window and glanced out the wavy panes at a paddock enclosed by high walls that sagged here and appeared to be crumbling there. A thick layer of sawdust had been strewn on the ground in a futile attempt to soak up the mud from the recent rains. Having recovered sufficiently from her bemusement, she experienced the beginnings of indignation on Victoria's behalf. Her queen—her friend—deserved better than this. She turned back toward the room. "Forgive me for saying so, but these stables are in deplorable condition. Not at all befitting a queen."

"Indeed not, miss." Roger struck a lucifer and lit an oil lamp. "There are to be new stables built later in the year."

"Well, thank goodness for that."

"Do make yourself comfortable, if you please, miss."

A cheery fire, laid earlier by some unknown hand, flickered from the grate in the hearth. Roger set about lighting the brazier while Holly settled on the settee and glanced about the room with a mounting curiosity she knew better than to voice. As in the coach, she set her book firmly on her lap, the gold embossed lettering staring up at her to announce the title: *A Chronicle of the Royal Ascot, from 1711 to 1847.*

Puzzling. But even more puzzling had been the secret message tucked inside. Both the tome and the note had been delivered only hours ago by Roger himself to the Knightsbridge Readers' Emporium, the London book shop owned jointly by Holly and her sisters. She'd barely had time to comprehend the note's meaning—that, like her sisters Laurel and Ivy before her, she was being called to the service of her country—before she had found herself whisked without further explanation out of the city and across the moonlit countryside.

Within moments, Roger handed her a steaming mug of tea. He walked away and opened a cupboard, and returned to place a covered platter on the sofa table in front of her.

"Scones, miss, fresh from the castle ovens. You shouldn't have long to wait now." With that, he bowed his way out of the room.

Wait for what? she yearned to call after him. But such a question would yield her nothing. Fellows such as Roger were trained to follow directions and follow them well, neither asking nor answering questions that were none of his concern. A smidgeon of perplexity forced a sigh to her lips, quickly followed by a yawn. And no wonder, as she had traveled through the night.

Holding her veil aside, she drank some tea and continued a halfhearted perusal of the room. She strained her ears, hearing only the hush of the immediate silence punctuated by the muffled, far-off drone of the grooms and stable hands. She nibbled an almond-flecked scone and tapped her fingers on the cover of the book. Then, in a surge of impatience, she flipped open the cover to reread the urgent summons that had brought her so summarily to Windsor:

Dearest Holly,
    I need you—and only you. You must come to me at Windsor at once! Tell no one, except your sisters, of course. But please, make no delay!

                                        Yours,
                                        V

At the approaching clatter of footsteps, she flinched and snapped the book shut. In the same instant, the undoubtedly feminine stride struck her as entirely familiar. She set the book aside and came to her feet as a petite figure swathed in forest green wool swept through the doorway.

"My dearest Holly, you are here! At long last you have arrived!"

ALLISON CHASE

Most Eagerly Yours

Her Majesty's Secret Servants

*First in a spectacular new series
of historical romance*

Raised on their uncle's country estate, the four
orphaned Sutherland sisters formed a close friendship
with the young Princess Victoria. Shortly before her
coronation as queen, Victoria asks the sisters to serve
her in matters requiring the utmost discretion.

They are to become her secret servants. The first to
serve is Laurel—who poses as a widow to uncover a
traitor, and discovers instead an irresistible rogue
conducting his own undercover investigation.

**Available wherever books are sold or at
penguin.com**

ALLISON CHASE

DARK OBSESSION

A Novel of Blackheath Moor

They wed in haste—Nora Thorngoode, to save her ruined reputation, and Grayson Lowell, to rescue his estate from foreclosure for unpaid debts. Each resents the necessity to exchange vows that will bind them for all time, and yet from the first, passion flames between them—quickly engulfing them in a sensual obsession.

But soon the lover that Nora married becomes a dark stranger to her, a man torn apart by guilt over his brother's recent, mysterious death—and driven half-mad by ghostly specters who demand that Grayson expose the truth. Has Nora married a murderer whose wicked deeds blacken everything around them? Or, together, in the secret passageways of Blackheath Grange and along Cornwall's remote coastline, can Grayson and Nora discover what really happened that terrible night—and in setting free the troubled ghosts, free themselves as well?

Available wherever books are sold or at penguin.com

ALLISON CHASE

DARK TEMPTATION

A Novel of Blackheath Moor

Exiled to Cornwall, Sophie St. Clair knows that
something is wrong in the village of Penhollow.
Mysterious lights, phantom ships—are smugglers once
again plying their illegal trade? Or have the ghosts of
long-dead pirates returned?

The answers will lead her to both danger and desire, as
the tortured Chad Rutherford, Earl of Wycliffe, returns to
his family estate near Blackheath Moor. Will the
spirits of darkness hold them both forever—or can
Chad and Sophie vanquish the evil and claim their
future together?

"A master at touching your heart."
—Jennifer St. Giles, award-winning author of
Silken Shadows (on *Dark Obsession*)

Available wherever books are sold or at
penguin.com